Into the Sound

". . . one wild ride."

—*Kirkus Reviews*

"[In] this spellbinding psychological thriller from Reinard (*Sweet Water*) . . . Reinard keeps the suspense high through to the surprise ending. Readers will have trouble putting this one down."

—*Publishers Weekly*

"*Into the Sound* is an atmospheric, character-driven thriller about how far a woman will go to save her sister. With propulsive, evocative prose, Reinard delves into family secrets and lies—and the reliability of memory. It doesn't get much better than this!"

—Melissa Colasanti, author of *Call Me Elizabeth Lark*

"A missing sister, a bad marriage, a woman broken and trapped—*Into the Sound* will have readers under its spell from the first word until the final, shocking pages. The tension is explosive as past and present collide in this intense, fast-paced, and twisty thriller; and Reinard's in-depth understanding of the ways in which childhood trauma follows into adulthood adds a deep and unforgettable layer to one woman's hunt for her sister and the long-buried secrets of their difficult upbringing."

—Danielle Girard, *USA Today* and #1 Amazon bestselling author of *Far Gone*

"In *Into the Sound*, Cara Reinard crafts a world of secrets that will leave you breathless as you scour the pages for answers."

—Dea Poirier, Amazon bestselling author

"I'm always a sucker for a sister book and *Into the Sound* delivers in spades. The pace is electric, and the twists are completely unpredictable, but underneath the high-tension story is a fraught, but very real and complicated bond forged in childhood trauma. Reinard includes a tangle with the mob, and a delve into the psychology of false memories, all without letting up the pace. Harlan Coben fans will love *Into the Sound*, especially if they're looking for a female protagonist and some deeper meaning. Highly recommended!"

—Kate Moretti, *New York Times* bestselling author of *The Vanishing Year* and *Girls of Brackenhill*

Sweet Water

"An unsparing account of 'rich people problems' that goes on forever, like all the best nightmares."

—*Kirkus Reviews*

"[A] nail-biting psychological thriller . . . Reinard knows how to keep readers turning the pages."

—*Publishers Weekly*

"*Sweet Water* is electrically suspenseful, impossible to put down until the last gut punch of a killer ending."

—Luanne Rice, *New York Times* bestselling author

"A remarkable tale of family loyalties and lies set in a fresh new world. Fans of *Defending Jacob*—both the book and the television show—will relish this sinister story of the lengths two parents will go to in order to protect their child."

—J.T. Ellison, *New York Times* bestselling author

"Reinard's domestic thriller *Sweet Water*, a story about betrayal, murder, and dark family secrets, held me riveted as one woman's search for the truth threatens everyone she loves."
—T.R. Ragan, *New York Times* and Amazon Charts bestselling author
of the Sawyer Brooks series

"Hypnotic and absorbing, a compulsive page-turner to the very end."
—Minka Kent, *Wall Street Journal* bestselling author

THE
DEN

ALSO BY CARA REINARD

Into the Sound

Sweet Water

Last Doll Standing

Pretty Dolls and Hand Grenades

THE
DEN

CARA
REINARD

THOMAS & MERCER

Text copyright © 2022 by Cara Reinard
All rights reserved.

Published by Thomas & Mercer, Seattle

www.apub.com

Amazon, the Amazon logo, and Thomas & Mercer are trademarks of Amazon.com, Inc., or its affiliates.

ISBN-13: 9781542039765 (paperback)
ISBN-13: 9781542039758 (digital)

Cover design by Laywan Kwan

Cover image: © Arina_Bogachyova / Getty Images;
© Bildhuset / Klara G / plainpicture; © Fly Of Swallow Studio / Shutterstock

Printed in the United States of America

Mom, this one's for you

If you deal with a fox, think of his tricks.

—*Jean de La Fontaine*

PROLOGUE

Pain wraps its ugly hands around her voice box. She can barely make a sound.

"*Stop,*" she tries. The word won't come.

She's being yanked along a wooded path like an unloved rag doll. The tiny stones in the packed earth embed in her wounds. The protected ferns along the trail, once good for riding horses, graze her broken body. The property leading away from the house is flanked in green and silver, shimmering in the night sky. She's lost in the veil of trees—the memory of hoofbeats.

Lost . . . she has to stay awake. Alive.

The moon is a bouncing white orb. She can barely see it.

Her eye, the one that isn't swollen shut, catches sight of a rickety wooden bridge.

There won't be anyone there this time of night to save her.

She's dropped along the creek bed, wet dew seeping into her scalp. It muddies the water with hints of red. It drips down her face and into her mouth.

She imagines the sun creeping through the trees.

By the time morning falls over the Allegheny Valley . . . she will be dead.

CHAPTER 1

The Party—Four Days Earlier

As the guests floated through the double doors and spread across the foyer with its freshly waxed floors, lacquered with a lemon-scented polish, they smiled graciously while plucking bacon-wrapped scallops and crab, cucumber, and mango lettuce wraps from the servers' platters. Everyone was handed a flute of sparkling champagne whether they cared for one or not. They were purportedly at the house to honor one of the owners, despite the disease that had ravaged her mind. The guest of honor was left to sit feebly in the corner, propped up in an uncomfortable armchair so she could greet the influx of people as they walked by. She was dressed to the nines in an off-white Chanel suit. It draped off her arms and legs like crepe paper from a crookedly hung piñata.

There was chatter about *how quickly she progressed* and *what a poor dear, but she's led a good life.*

It was almost more than Lucinda could handle. Mother's lifelong caretaker, Marian, wasn't beside her. *Odd.* Lucinda wasn't complaining, though. One less person she had to dodge.

She snatched two flutes off the tray as she counted the couples walking through the door. How much was her father raking in on donations from this ridiculous party? Surely it wouldn't all end up funding the memory-loss charity he'd set up in Mother's name.

She should just ask Christian, prodigal son, heir to the Fox Wealth Management throne.

Lucinda had avoided both her brothers tonight. She hadn't been able to locate her sister, though.

Valerie would try to get Lucinda to stay longer than tomorrow. She did need to find her, but not badly enough to extend her visit.

"Let's go shopping on Walnut Street, just you and me and Isla. Your niece barely knows you." Valerie had tried that shtick last time, as if it were a draw to go shopping in Shadyside of all places, the very name of the private school Lucinda had been booted out of—*ahh . . . memories.*

Mr. Brennan, her eleventh-grade chemistry teacher, had been ten years older. Sure, she'd come on to him and gotten herself kicked out, but he should've been arrested. Father had settled with the school out of court instead because he hadn't wanted their name dragged through the mud. His only words to Lucinda in regard to the situation were *"All the money in the world, and you still don't know how to act."*

Not that she had a dime to spend now. It was the real reason she couldn't let Valerie sucker her into staying. Lucinda didn't want to tell her family she was barely making it at the moment. Her plane ticket had left a severe deficit in her wallet. Not to mention the pesky creditors who wouldn't leave her alone.

Bubbles, light and ethereal, tickled her throat as she downed her second glass of champagne.

"You know, there's more in the back," the waitress said.

Lucinda had the crystal flute pressed firmly to her painted lips. It made an embarrassing popping sound when she pulled it away. So wound up, she'd been sucking on the glass, bracing her mouth against the sweet liquid as she gulped it down.

She placed the empty glasses down on a buffet table and wiped her mouth with her wrist, glancing to her left. An angel holding a tray stared back with inky brown-black eyes lined darker around the edges, a little smoky on the sides; full glossy lips; black curly hair pulled back in a bun.

Is she checking me out?

Lucinda cleared her throat. "Right. I detest these parties," she admitted. "None of these people are here for my mother, the guest of honor, anyway." She immediately had the urge to take this girl's hair tie out . . . unravel the bun . . . pull on it.

Let's get messy.

"No, they're just here for the party. I hate working them too. Listening to their empty conversations." The waitress rolled her eyes. "I've catered events here before, and I've seen your picture. You don't usually attend. You look so sad in the family portraits. Is that why? All the empty people?"

"*Yes.*" Lucinda loved this girl's candor. *Empty people*, they certainly were. It was like the waitress knew her somehow, had studied her from afar. "What's your name?"

"Asia, like the continent. Spelled A-J-A." She touched Lucinda's wrist, and Lucinda's internal response was . . . big as a continent. Aja's soft fingers sent a zing all the way to the toes of her four-inch pumps. "No lipstick on your wrist?" Aja commented. "How did it not rub off when you wiped your mouth? It's still on your lips too," she said, awestruck.

Lucinda grinned. Under different circumstances, she might have been creeped out at this stranger's watchfulness, but she was just wondering if Aja had seen her go to the second level of the house, where she wasn't supposed to be. "It's color-stay."

"You'll have to tell me which brand. I'm studying to be an aesthetician," Aja said proudly.

Lucinda's heart accelerated at this beautiful girl, and all these noisy people buzzing around in the background like flies she'd like to swat away so she could better hear her. "It's just CoverGirl," Lucinda admitted, regretful to reveal she'd had to go cheap since she'd moved away.

"Really? I'm amazed your drugstore brand holds up and that red complements your light coloring. Blondes don't often carry it as well . . ."

As she pretended to listen, Lucinda spotted Christian and his perfect wife, an ex–tennis pro named Glenda—like the good witch she was not—hobnobbing with all the guests who were likely also clients. Jeremy, her other brother, was predictably in their gaggle, hanging on Christian's coattails.

Lucinda still couldn't locate Valerie, but she could smell her Goody Two-shoes wafting around the party like cheap cologne at the prom. She was lingering somewhere, probably clinging to other guests she knew who were also there without a plus-one.

". . . and you know, some people might say ruby lipstick with a short, black leather dress is over-the-top. You pull it off well. Class act."

"Thank you." Lucinda continued to scan the crowd. She was eager for this night to end.

Her sister was likely hurting from her recent divorce, but Lucinda wanted to get home as soon as possible. She had a huge opportunity pending regarding her work. She'd invite Valerie to spend the weekend after she secured the funding for her project. She'd even hook her up with front-row tickets.

"I'd better get back to it. There's a presentation soon. People will want drinks beforehand." Aja pointed to their right toward the black curtain and small stage in the ballroom. Guests were often impressed by the sky-high ceilings in the room, which had housed all their indoor family celebrations.

Wait . . . no. "My father always overstaffs. Don't overexert yourself."

But maybe overexert yourself somewhere else with me.

"You're trouble." She giggled.

You have no idea. Lucinda smiled. "Don't be silly. The hard work is already done. Everyone is here. The guests will find someone else to serve them a drink."

Aja shot her a playful smirk. "Why don't you ever tell your parents how much you hate attending these parties? Give them ideas for things they could do better?"

Lucinda lifted her eyebrows in amusement at this naive, bold sprite. "As if they'd listen. How old are you anyway, Aja?" *Please be of legal age.*

"Twenty," she said.

Perfect.

Lucinda darted her gaze all over the ballroom, paranoid.

She wanted in and out of this place quicker than a time-slotted audition on Broadway.

Christian glanced her way, but she could count on him to ignore her. Lucinda didn't really exist to any of these people. They all thought she was some colossal fuckup who'd run off to New York after being ousted from their little society in Fox Chapel, at one time ranked the second-wealthiest zip code in Pennsylvania. Father and Christian managed such a large book of business, they'd once referred to Fox Wealth Management as the State Mint. Laughable.

Well, Lucinda had big things cooking too.

She heard musical instruments warming up—a string quartet. Lucinda placed her hand over her mouth, stifling her rising stomach acid.

Her father couldn't have.

She turned to Aja, who was pivoting toward the crowd, trying to walk away from her. "Did you see musicians come in with violins?" Lucinda asked. She took a sharp breath. She knew she shouldn't have come home this time.

"Yes, why?"

This should've been the year she'd told her father no. He gave her an out on all family holidays if she attended the charity ball for their mother, the one fake showing of family togetherness for all to see. But this year, she'd come with a purpose.

"He's dishonoring my mother by letting them play that." Lucinda definitely heard a violin. How could her father be so insensitive?

Aja twisted entirely in Lucinda's direction, her work obligations falling by the wayside, her dark eyes fixed on Lucinda. "Why? What is it? Tell me."

"It's nothing, really." Lucinda waved her hand, dismissing the subject.

Aja offered her a sympathetic glance. "I know you're more sensitive than they are. I read your poetry. On the bridges."

"You did?" Lucinda asked. No one had mentioned her award-winning collection in ages.

"It's fascinating. Hypnotic. There were a few copies in the family library. I took one. Hope you don't mind."

"No, not at all," Lucinda said.

"You dedicated it to 'my love,' just offering his initials, but you must've cared for him very much. Are you still together?"

My teacher, actually. But I can't have her thinking just because I had boyfriends, I can't have girlfriends too. She could check my socials to find that out.

"Oh no. He's history. People change, you know?" Lucinda tucked a loose curl behind Aja's ear.

Aja smiled. "Right. But it seems maybe your father hasn't. Tell me what he's done to upset you."

How could this girl *see* her like this? And why could Lucinda talk to her like they'd known each other for years? That feeling—the meeting of minds transcended through the eyes—it didn't happen that often. It was the way Aja listened to her every word, *from your lips to my heart.*

This girl is special. She read my words. She gets me.

Lucinda wanted to tell Aja everything. But of course she couldn't. "Okay, uh . . . before Mother totally lost her senses, Father had tickets for the two of them to go to the opera, Mother's favorite place in the whole world. But she'd gotten sick before they were supposed to leave and couldn't remember where they were going. She snapped at the help for trying to dress her in her good pearls."

Aja nodded, taking it all in.

"So Father went without her. Didn't want to waste the orchestra seats. He didn't ask any of us to go in her place. None of us really appreciated the opera anyway. Or him. He and Mother rarely went out. It was for their anniversary."

"That's terrible he left her home sick on their anniversary."

Lucinda was shaking her head—no—the sour taste climbing in her throat again. "That's not it. Mother came to. She'd go in and out like that for years before she started to really lose it. She remembered it was her anniversary after all. Our youngest brother, Jeremy, drove her down to meet Father, and Mother arrived at the opera house just in time for the overture."

"The overture?"

"The beginning." Lucinda's voice was hurried, desperate for Aja to understand what she was trying to say. Her father didn't deserve her loyalty.

"I thought you didn't know opera."

"I grew up here. I know some! Let me get this out."

"Okay," Aja said.

Lucinda could hear the introductory music, a warm-up of Giacomo Puccini's "Nessun Dorma." The violinists were just practicing, but she'd know that song anywhere from all the days Mother had played it. Luciano Pavarotti sang it best.

Aja nodded. *Go on.*

"When Mother arrived, she walked up to the private balcony at the Pittsburgh Opera and saw Father sitting alone."

Some of the waitstaff were headed their way. Aja grabbed Lucinda's arm and pulled her toward a partition, near the rear of the black curtain, in a tiny nook where they weren't visible to the crowd.

Lucinda could now see the musicians rehearsing from the corner of her eye. It was hazy backstage. Dark enough for Lucinda to unleash the rest of her story.

Aja whispered, "And?"

And . . . if there weren't a tray between them, Lucinda would be close enough to kiss her.

"And Mother walked over, and Father's head was pushed back, his eyes closed as if he was enjoying the music. It wasn't the music he was enjoying, you see." Aja was soaking it in, ingesting her pain, just as she'd likely done when she'd read Lucinda's poetry. It was more than she could say for most of her family. Mother had appreciated Lucinda's talents, but couldn't grasp much of anything right now. If she recognized the music, it could devastate her all over again.

"Why wasn't he enjoying the music?" Aja asked.

"Because he'd picked up another date instead of Mother, and the other woman was there, too, in the private balcony . . . pleasuring Father."

"Oh . . ." Aja would've dropped her tray with the single flute left on it if Lucinda hadn't swooped it up and sucked it down in one swig.

"Jeremy had escorted Mother to make sure she found him. She turned right around, walked out, and Jeremy drove her home. By the time they returned, she'd forgotten what she'd seen. Jeremy hadn't."

Aja leaned her tray against the thick wooden beam that held up the vaulted ceiling like many of the Austro-Germanic-style mansions in the area, straight out of a Hans Christian Andersen story, a cross between Craftsman-style and Tudor.

But this was far from a fairy tale. "They never went to the opera again, and we weren't allowed to play it in the house after that night."

"I'm sorry," Aja whispered.

The agony that reflected in Aja's eyes enveloped her, as if Aja felt everything locked inside her—the torment. All the family secrets Lucinda had been forced to keep and then run away from. Her siblings had been content to live with them. Lucinda wasn't. Not anymore. Like Aja had said, *"I know you're more sensitive than they are."* Lucinda moved closer. She couldn't get close enough, their lips within kissing range.

No one was breathing. Aja closed her eyes.

Lucinda's ruby-red lips gripped Aja's, and Aja hungrily devoured her kisses—as if she were trying to take the color off.

The musicians were onstage now, and Lucinda and Aja slipped farther into the fold of the black curtain, behind the musicians, to a corner where no one could see them.

And the violists strummed, and Aja's fingers found their way to the hem of Lucinda's dress.

Onstage, there was some talk about how they were playing tonight to honor Simone Fox, but no one was really honoring her. It was cruel to prop her up in the corner and then leave her to sit there all alone.

An operatic lyric tenor who didn't compare to Pavarotti tried to sing.

His Italian lyrics flowed, the story, *Nessun Dorma*—"Let no one sleep."

And Aja moaned as Lucinda unbuttoned her white blouse.

Aja positioned Lucinda on top of a speaker and found Lucinda beneath her black leather dress that she'd admired so much. Lucinda knew Aja just wanted to make her feel better, to climb inside her—fill the void left behind by all the *empty* people.

They moved to the rhythm of the singer's increasing crescendo—soft at first and then louder and heavier.

Louder and heavier.

Aja's kisses were heavier still.

When the song was done playing, the curtain pulled back, and all Lucinda could feel was the warmth of a different light shining down on her. The cascade of astonished voices crashed in her ears.

She peered up, over the hump of Aja's body still hovering above hers. Hundreds of eyes stared straight back at them. Lucinda had been invisible, nonexistent—but now she was seen. Horrified, she pulled down her dress.

The musicians scooted around them, exiting quickly. There was a spotlight right on their half-naked bodies, but all Lucinda could hear among the shock as she pushed Aja away was her sister. "Lucy, how could you?"

She'd finally found Valerie.

As Lucinda's father strode to the front of the stage, something stopped him. His shiny black shoes became glued to the floor, his face contorted into a lopsided scowl. He couldn't seem to say anything or move forward. He only clutched at his chest as if she'd broken his heart, which was foolish, because he didn't have one to begin with.

Lucinda darted from the platform, nearly plowing over a prop guy who was awkwardly waiting to retrieve the speaker she and Aja had been using. Lucinda was about to dash out the back door when she heard it.

"*Oh my God.* Mr. Fox. Call an ambulance!"

CHAPTER 2

VALERIE

Valerie rode in the ambulance with her father as they tried to resuscitate him. They allowed her to sit in the front seat, which was paralyzing, because she couldn't see or hear what was happening in the rear of the vehicle. Lights whirred, sirens blared, the EMT blurted codes that Valerie didn't understand into the dispatch radio.

The driver never spoke to her.

It wasn't his job to entertain her, she understood. She squeezed her beaded purse at the sound of the chirping siren the whole way there.

Her shoulders tightened.

What is wrong with Lucy? Their assignment for the evening had been simple—show up, smile, support Mother, and then leave and return to their lives. *Why couldn't she just do that?* Lucy had been walking a tightrope in New York, trying to make things happen for herself. Had that rope finally snapped, leaving her tangled in a mess of faulty safety nets, so lost she had to sever the only real one she had left? Lucy thought no one knew, but the collection agency had called Valerie when Lucy's phone had been temporarily turned off for nonpayment. Valerie had kept her secret. After tonight, she should tell her brothers. Lucy clearly needed help.

The cool night air blasted her in the face as they exited the ambulance, her father unconscious on a stretcher beside her. She tried to follow them as he was rushed away, but she was stopped at the entrance and slapped with paperwork, a humming fan drowning her out. *"Father."* She was the only one who knew his PCP's contact information and his current medications. They all had their place, and hers was caretaker. As her father aged, she'd had an opportunity to look after him—schedule his doctor appointments, arrange his medicines. Even though he never said it, she knew he appreciated her efforts.

Valerie had talked to him only briefly tonight, when she'd given him his pills.

She'd been a little salty with him for refusing to break one of his rules. She'd quickly asked him if they could speak later about her financial situation, but he'd only chastised her for making a bad decision marrying Karl. *I should've seen it coming.* Father had cautioned both his daughters to keep an eye on their money, always, even after they were married.

Especially after they were married.

But Valerie had wanted more out of her marriage than what her parents had—a union held together with stacks of green alone. A paper marriage.

Father's hard limit on monetarily supporting his children kicked in at age eighteen, with the exception of fully paying their way through college. He'd expected them to make their own way after that. Valerie had tried to explain that this affected her daughter, Isla, too. *Have mercy, Father.* She'd never asked for a handout before.

"Here you go." Valerie handed a receptionist the clipboard. She'd filled out what she could. Then she saw her brothers running in together.

A stream of childhood memories rushed in with them. Valerie could picture Christian and Jeremy throwing the football around in the backyard, which often resulted in them beating the living crap out of each other, and Valerie being the one to apply the Band-Aids afterward. Time had passed in an instant.

"Have the doctors been out yet?" Jeremy squinted his bloodshot eyes. Jer was the worst at dealing with stress.

"We just got here," Valerie answered. They sat down in a semicircle of chairs in the waiting room. She was happy for the comfort her brothers brought, even if they weren't the most consoling beings.

"It was obviously a heart attack," Christian said. "He was grabbing at his damn chest."

Jeremy rubbed his hands on his pants like he was trying to start a brush fire. "Well, yeah, but how bad was it? Is he going to be okay?"

"We won't know until the doctor comes out." The last thing Valerie wanted was to get in the middle of a pissing match between her brothers. Christian had to constantly remind everyone how much smarter he was than the rest of them, while Jeremy angled for a way to prove him wrong.

"Has anyone spoken to Lucy?" Jeremy asked. He wiped his nose on his sleeve.

"I called and texted, but she hasn't responded." Valerie focused on her younger brother. "Are you feeling okay, Jeremy?"

The bottoms of his pants were pooled at his ankles, his jacket a full size too big. He'd lost weight, and his shaggy dishwater-blond hair could use a cut.

"Yes, I'm fine. I'm not using again," he said defensively.

Christian cackled. "No one said you were."

"Val might as well have. Spring allergies," he claimed. "I wonder why Lucy isn't here."

"You've got to be kidding me. You wonder why *Lucy* isn't here?" Christian snarked.

"She might be embarrassed, but Dad could die," Jeremy rasped. "She should be here."

"Agreed." Valerie sighed. "I don't know what would possess her . . ." Her voice broke off because she wasn't sure which part of Lucy's backstage performance she was most upset by: the fact that she'd chosen to get half-naked with a girl she'd only just met, onstage for all of her family's friends to see, or that she'd done it during the dedication to their mother.

"People will blame Lucy," Valerie finally managed. As if her sister's name weren't blackened enough in this town.

Jeremy said, "You're being a little melodramatic, don't you think? Dad was obviously having problems with his ticker. You said he'd just been placed on new medication."

Valerie turned to her brother, surprised. "You don't think Father's episode had anything to do with Lucy's display at the party?"

Christian gesticulated, throwing his hands up, the right one getting caught in the white scarf he had draped around the collar of his tux, giving him an extra touch of douchebaggery. "Absolutely. People can be shocked or scared into a heart attack. It's where the saying comes from, 'You almost gave me a heart attack.' Father could've been fine for another decade if Lucy hadn't, if Lucy hadn't—"

Jeremy interjected. "If it hadn't been for Lucy, I'm sure one of Father's girlfriends would've revved up his heart enough to cause some damage. Maybe it's good it happened when everyone was around so we could get him help right away."

"You're disgusting." Valerie put her face in her palms.

"Sorry." Jeremy placed his hand on Valerie's shoulder and rubbed the tight muscles there. For as crass as he was, she welcomed his warmth. She looked over her shoulder at him sitting there, all scruffy with his half smile, and couldn't help but think about how he used to clown on them.

Christian remained stiff as a penguin in the corner, breathing loudly. "Please, it's not like you didn't know Dad has girlfriends. He's always had them."

"That's why Lucy did it at the dedication, I think," Jeremy said.

Valerie popped her head up. "What do you mean?"

"Dad brought in a little opera tonight for Mother. Don't you remember . . . the opera . . ." His voice rattled.

Poor Jeremy.

He'd always been the one to walk in on the family disasters—Marian's husband passing in the guesthouse where Hector and Marian had lived, Father at the opera, the chicken. No wonder he'd turned to drugs.

"Right," she said. The night at the opera had been a childhood memory that haunted her. She could still see Jeremy's adolescent face fired up with fearful anticipation for Father's return after he'd been caught with his mistress. But, upon return, Father had simply greeted them, then slammed his office door shut, as if to say, *Conversation closed.*

The golden clasp on the family picture frame that'd held them all together had been officially broken that night. Not only because they were disappointed in Father but because they were disappointed in *her* too. Mother had to have known what was going on. It was painful watching the way she'd tugged on those pearls, screaming for "Marian!" to get "the choking beads off."

"The opera . . . that sounds like a Lucy reason," Christian said, shaking his head.

Valerie suspected it'd been the public humiliation that'd gotten to Mother most.

One of Father's clients had witnessed her running down the aisle at the opera, Jeremy fretfully following her. The onlookers had also peered behind them to witness the mop of blonde hair hovering just above the opera's railing next to Father's lap.

And Mother had just walked away. The resentment festered in the months to follow, eating at Valerie's perception of her mother—the strong, respectful spine of the family. Valerie didn't understand how she could condone Father's behavior. She'd wanted her mother to confront him, but when she chose not to, it not only weakened her own place in the house but that of every woman who lived there.

"Lucy's actions couldn't have hurt Mother more than the music already had. They say music can evoke feeling in people with memory loss. The feeling that goes along with music can bring them joy—or pain—even if they can't place where they last heard it." Valerie knew this because she'd studied the subject of Alzheimer's disease in order to best help her mother. And to find a way to communicate with her. Mother had once told Valerie she'd make a wonderful mother because she was good at feeling a range of emotions without immediately acting on them. *Thoughtful* was the word she'd used in reference to Valerie.

The other three seemed satisfied putting her off to pasture at the memory center, and it was beyond disappointing. Mother had always been there for them, and Valerie wouldn't abandon her now. She still visited with her every week, usually Wednesdays after work, because Isla didn't have swim practice that day. Valerie rarely missed a week.

"It's Lucy. She doesn't think. She rides on impulse," Christian said.

"I just hope Father collapsing doesn't negatively impact Mother's health. Does she even know he was taken to the hospital? Who drove her back to the memory center?" Valerie's emotions were all over the place. She'd helped Mother get dressed tonight and had taken her to the event. She just realized that she'd left in the ambulance without making sure Mother would get back safely, and she hadn't even said goodbye. Valerie had been intent on getting him in that ambulance, being there when they examined him.

"No worries. Glenda drove her," Christian said. "She also called Isla to let her know what happened." Christian was an ass. He was an efficient ass, though. He'd pushed his emotions aside to make arrangements for Mother while Valerie crumpled like a paper bag inside the ambulance. It annoyed her a bit about Glenda. Christian had taken it a step too far by allowing his wife to alert Isla.

"Thank you. I texted Isla already," Valerie informed him. "Did Glenda say if Mother was okay?"

Both Christian and Jeremy gaped at her pityingly.

"Well, what did she say?" Valerie asked.

"Mom didn't know what was going on, Valerie," Jeremy said.

"Same as every other day." Christian sighed.

They were both wrong, because there were days Simone Fox knew her eldest daughter. And on those days, Valerie saw the glint of recognition in her eyes—recognition and love, too, if only for a moment. And to hear her occasionally say the words *dear daughter*—those were the best of days.

Valerie noticed a doctor in blue scrubs moving nimbly toward them. "Is this the family of Stefan Fox?" he asked.

"Yes." Valerie's heartbeat sped up, a drum in her ear.

The doctor's face was a blank slate. "I'm Dr. Schulman, one of the physicians working on your father. He suffered both a heart attack and a stroke, I'm afraid. We're still working on stabilizing him. We can't let you in his room just yet."

"How can both happen at the same time?" Valerie asked, although she didn't care about the answer. She was just trying to control the rising and crashing of adrenaline that had started when her father had hit the ballroom floor. He'd been on blood pressure drugs for years and had just started a cholesterol medication too. As far as anyone knew, he was in good health otherwise.

"It's not uncommon at all, actually. The same plaque that builds up in the heart vessels can build up in other areas as well, like the brain. Your father will be in the ICU for a while, and we'll know more in the coming days."

"That doesn't sound good," Jeremy said.

"He suffered a massive heart attack, and his EEG is detecting low brain activity. It's still early. We need to do a lot more testing, including an MRI once he's stable enough. You can stop at the nurses' station and provide your cell phone numbers for updates on your father. My recommendation would be to come back in the morning. You did a great job getting him here quickly."

The doctor's pager went off. "If you'll excuse me."

Valerie held up her hand. "I have more questions—"

"*Please*, go." Christian pardoned the physician, dismissing Valerie.

Wait! I'm not ready for him to go yet. Valerie watched the doctor walk away.

Jeremy rose and smoothed his hands on his pants. "It doesn't sound like there's any more we can do here."

Valerie eyed him warily. "Well, I'm staying. Isla's with her father anyway." She'd throw that in there for good measure, since neither brother had cared to ask about her divorce or inquire about how she was faring since the split.

"Really? You know Father wouldn't do the same for you, right?" Jeremy asked. At first, Valerie thought he was just trying to make himself feel better for leaving, but as she opened her mouth to argue, her eyes trailed to Christian.

"Well, don't look at me. I don't disagree. Dad would've asked Mother to *parent this*—that obnoxious phrase he'd use. Remember the mountain-biking accident?" Christian turned to Jeremy, who was already preparing to skulk away. "You nearly killed me. Fucking with my gears like that," Christian said.

Jeremy's shoulders hiked up in his oversize jacket. "We were kids."

"Shh . . . Calm down, Christian." Valerie nodded in the direction of the others in the waiting room, gawking at them.

Valerie did remember the incident they were fighting about.

The boys had been in the midst of a prank war. Eleven-year-old Jeremy had urged Christian, fifteen, to follow him to Old Squaw Trail Park because he'd found a colony of crayfish. Christian had said something smartly about bees living in colonies, not crayfish—"you moron." Valerie could practically hear the swish of their windbreaker pants as the boys pedaled away—without helmets. The gravel trail wound through heavy woods and over a rotting bridge with a stream beneath it. From what he'd told her, Christian had tried to downshift while going over the bridge, but his bike malfunctioned, and he ended up flying over the edge headfirst into a jagged boulder on the bank of the stream.

Nearby hikers had sprung into action, rescuing Christian, tending to his wound, and carrying him out of the woods to a spot where he could be transported to the hospital.

Hector, their landscaper, had retrieved the bike and informed Mother and Father the cables to the brakes had been cut. Christian received twelve stitches and had to stay in the hospital for two days. Christian still had the scar on his forehead to show for it. He hid it with a severe part and a flip of dark hair. Although, in the summertime, it sometimes reared its puffy pink head. Christian's gash had healed, but his relationship with Jeremy hadn't.

Father never came to the hospital once to see Christian while he was in there.

He'd been too busy with work, his excuse "serves him right. If those kids hadn't been messing around . . ."

It made Valerie a little sick inside to think of how her father had assigned blame to one of his children after he'd been hurt. She couldn't imagine reacting the same callous way if Isla were injured.

Christian swore at his phone.

"What is it?" Valerie asked.

"Father's lawyer," he said. "He asked how Father is, and when I texted a heart attack *and* a stroke, low brain activity, possibly unrecoverable, he said that Father's wishes were for us, all of his dependents, to come into his office immediately under these circumstances. Fox Wealth is at risk. Once his investors hear, they'll want a statement. He'll open up shop for us tomorrow."

"Why do we all need to come, though?" Jeremy asked. His voice was more a grumble, since Father had never considered Jeremy competent enough to be involved in the family business.

Christian squinted at the phone. "To discuss Father's estate and changes made to it following Mother's recent dip in health. It involves all of us."

"Estate? But that's all tied up. We don't get any of it. It goes to charities and the memory foundation. He's made that abundantly clear ever since we were old enough to open a bank account, right?" Valerie searched her siblings' confused expressions to make sure they hadn't understood differently.

"Correct. That's why I said there's been changes," Christian repeated.

"To Father's estate?" Jeremy wiped his nose on his sleeve again. Sometimes he was so boyish, Valerie wondered how he operated as a full-grown adult, but given his earlier slip, she wondered if he were drugging again, an ongoing battle that'd begun in college.

"Yes. There's been an addendum created, apparently," Christian clarified.

"Did you know about this?" Valerie asked him. Why didn't any of them know about it?

Christian glowered at her and held up his phone. "No, I did not. Just found out."

Oh boy. No one knew more about money than Christian, and if Father hadn't let Christian in on something to do with his own money, he'd be chafed. Now it seemed Christian, the golden boy, had been left in the dark.

Valerie couldn't say she felt sorry for him. Christian was so high-and-mighty, he'd never offered her a shot at working for the company. It might've been because Father hadn't deemed her suitable for financial work, but it wasn't for lack of interest. Now Christian was the one *not in the game*—and it was a little bit satisfying watching him squirm.

"Does that mean we might get some of it now?" Jeremy's lusty eyes morphed from sagging and bloodshot to alive and interested.

"I don't know. We'll all need to be present for this conversation. You need to find Lucy." Christian directed this comment at her.

"Why me?" Valerie asked. She was still floundering from her father's diagnosis.

Christian fiddled with his scarf again. "Because you're the only one who still talks to her."

She nodded, although it wasn't true. Marian still talked to her too.

CHAPTER 3

MARIAN

Marian paused to stretch her legs as she walked the path from her retirement community to the memory center.

Tiny pebbles crunched beneath her sneakers.

She'd been blessed to live in beautiful places rich with foliage, like the maples, birches, and dogwoods in full bloom all around her.

A condition of Marian's ongoing severance package from the Foxes was that she'd live near Simone at Longwood, the nicest senior community of its kind on that stretch of the Allegheny River. It was tucked up the hill from the Hulton Bridge and far enough away from the estate where Stefan still lived in Fox Chapel.

Marian had tended to Simone Fox for longer than she hadn't, and she'd been angry not to get an invitation to the party last night.

Twigs snapped beneath her feet.

She visited Simone every few days. She didn't like to drive, never had, but Simone's memory center was close enough to walk, just a half mile or so.

When she arrived, she smiled at Rosalie, the attendant at the front. It didn't seem fair that Marian lived in a place where chandeliers hung from the ceilings and plush rugs emitted the fragrance of fresh flowers, while Simone was relegated to the sterility of an upscale hospital.

"Marian, how do you do?" Rosalie asked.

"Beautiful day," Marian responded. "How's Mrs. Fox this afternoon?"

Rosalie's dimpled smile turned into a frown, and her cheek pulled up on one side. "Not so good, I'm afraid. She's verbal today but anxious. She's in the common area."

Marian nodded and made her way to see her old friend.

She sat beside Simone, who was only ten years her senior but looked much older. Marian still insisted they dye Simone's hair, because younger Simone would be aghast at going gray. The brilliant blonde color had the opposite effect, though, accentuating her ghostly pallor, drawing out her vacant stare. "Simone, it's Mari. How are you today?" Marian asked, addressing her with Simone's old nickname for her.

"Yes, dear Mari." Her eyelids flickered as they often did.

"Look at Mona and Mari, having martini hour. M&M time," the other Foxes would call it, even though Marian was the only one who'd sometimes called her Mona. Marian only had to see a martini to picture the two of them sipping cocktails on the back patio, off the glassed-in back porch, as the children played in the yard—*the good old days.*

"How're you today?" Marian tried again.

Simone looked beyond Marian, out the window, before muttering, "I've been better, dear." Simone rarely answered with anything other than "fine, dear."

"What's the matter, Simone?" Marian patted her arm, but Simone flinched when she touched her.

"Oh, I'm sorry." Marian removed her hand, remembering a moment in time when Simone had shrugged her off after Stefan had ordered a last-minute dinner party for "a very important client" and they all had to rush around to ready the lawn.

The white tents had been erected.

The food had been prepared—charcuterie boards piled with meats and cheeses, serving stations with carved beef and pork, fondue fountains.

The ice cubes had to be cracked in half.

Marian bit the inside of her cheek at the memory of Simone's particulars. How she would inspect those ice cubes to make sure they'd been clean cut to her liking with a ball-peen hammer, while Marian's toddler son, Eli, sat on the ground in his playpen pulling at the grass and everyone else ran around him in a panic. That was summertime at the Foxes', but there was no reason for Simone's distress today.

"My husband. Is he dead?" Simone asked.

"What?" Marian asked. "No, no. Why would you think that?" Marian tried to pat her arm once more.

And again, Simone flinched. "Where is he?" she asked.

"I'm sorry—I'll keep my hands to myself." Marian placed them on her lap. "Simone, did something happen at the party? Did Stefan say something to you?" Marian asked.

Simone's recall was spotty. Some days she'd retell a memory from forty years ago; other days she'd confuse Marian with Valerie. It might've been because Valerie favored Stefan and had dark hair and fair skin like Marian—or because Valerie was the only other female who visited Simone.

"Yes. They played opera." Simone's smile was lopsided, like she wanted to enjoy the memory but couldn't.

"That's nice. Was it a song you liked?" Asking Simone to name the title was just plain cruel.

"Yes. Pavarotti." Her lips tripped up as she said the name. Marian was impressed she got it all out.

"Fantastic, then." Although she didn't really think it was fantastic at all. Stefan was the one who'd soured Simone's love of the opera.

"No." Simone looked down at her hands. "Something went wrong. Lucy's done something again." She said it in the same emphatic way as when preschool Lucy had written all over the walls in Sharpie. They'd had to have their foyer repainted because of it, and Marian had been assigned the blame.

It'd been on her watch.

Years later, Simone hadn't changed her tone when Lucy had been caught with her pants down with the chemistry teacher—"Lucy's done something again." The inflection in Simone's voice stayed the same no matter how out of hand Lucy had gotten.

"Has she now?" Marian asked. If Lucy had acted up at the party, that was par for the course at a Fox gathering. Lucy still called Marian now and again when she wanted to obtain information on one of her siblings without asking them herself.

Simone's uneven smile peaked up at the corner into a half smile. Her lipstick was on straight, though, which made Marian grin. *Can't leave the house without my Violette, madam.* "She's willful. When she grows up, I think she's going to be a senator. Or an entrepreneur . . ."

"Is that right?" Marian frowned. It had been true of Lucy. Before she'd gotten expelled, she'd shown promise. She'd been a straight-A student, and when Lucy's poetry collection had gotten published, Marian thought she was finally coming into her own. And then she'd "gone and done something" again. That time with a member of the school faculty.

Simone said, "Stefan shouldn't get so mad; she's just a child . . ."

I'm losing her again.

Marian had to ask the question she'd come to address before she went away—before Simone asked if Marian had watered the gardenias in the front yard yet or had prepared snacks for the boys before their sports practices, as if it were circa 1990.

"Simone, do you remember signing legal documents? Two men came by a few—"

"Of course I do," she chirped.

Marian tried to hide her surprise. "Do you remember what they wanted?"

"Yes, they wanted me to turn over my financial rights because I've lost my wits." She said it clear as a bell, and Marian hated that it'd come down to this.

"That's not true. We're having a lovely chat right now." Simone's health had been declining noticeably the last six months, and Marian had vowed to look out for her.

"Sure, dear," Simone said.

Stefan's lawyers had assured Simone it was best to have her relinquish her financial rights to the Fox Wealth Management dynasty so she couldn't do anything wily with the business as her health worsened. Simone rarely interjected her opinions where the family business was concerned, but she had occasionally suggested that Stefan handle client accounts differently. He saw Simone's mental state as a threat.

Marian's existence—and her patio home—depended on the Foxes' continual payment for her services.

Simone had been Marian's insurance.

As long as the Foxes knew Marian was there to look after their fading wife and mother, something none of them had the heart or time to do themselves, Marian would be taken care of.

But as Simone's condition progressed, Marian had worried they'd eventually cut her off. Now she had it in writing that they couldn't, per the new agreement.

She didn't want to place the burden on her son to take care of her. All she'd ever wanted for Eli was to live the American dream; start a family with his fiancée, Giselle; ride horses. He was looking for a property now with a stable where he could have his own. He'd been given the privilege of learning to ride on the Foxes' estate like all the other children who'd lived there, one of the many reasons Marian was appreciative of Simone's graciousness.

"Those lawyers know what's best for you, Simone. They'll make sure you're taken care of in here. Don't you worry."

"But why did my husband fall to the ground last night?" Simone asked.

"Let me check in with him when I leave here, and I'll get back to you," Marian offered.

As she walked back, Marian felt something was amiss with the way Simone had been acting. Not only had she been skittish, she'd offered more in their brief conversation today than she had in months.

Marian knew why the opera had made Simone upset, and she also wondered why Stefan had chosen to play it. Marian had always received an invitation in prior years to the annual charity event to honor the woman she'd played assistant to for the better part of the last forty years.

But not this year.

Stefan had asked Marian to move out of the Fox residence the same day Simone had. He'd told her he couldn't stand to be in the house with her there when Simone wasn't. After all her years of service, that request had burned Marian more than anything else.

He must've had his reasons for trying to keep her away last night. Was his goal to push Simone over the mental brink for some reason?

He had to have known Marian would've protected Simone from the performance. Taken her away the minute that music had started playing. Or was he so far removed from his wife that he'd forgotten?

Her greatest suspicion was that he'd kept her away because Marian knew him best, all his dirty little secrets. Maybe he was afraid she'd finally spill the tea about his girlfriends. The blonde from the opera was hired. And easy to track, Marian had discovered.

That woman hadn't been the first, though.

CHAPTER 4

LUCINDA

When Lucinda awoke, she was sweating and tangled in a mess of her own hair. She could tell there was a nearby window open because she could hear street sounds—a car passing, the honking of a horn, people talking—but no air passed through the room.

"Ugh." She kicked the bedsheets off her perspiring body. A pillow partially covered her face. Her stomach swirled with intestinal hell, and her head pounded.

A voice echoed in her ear. "Good morning, gorgeous." It was like listening to a voice through a seashell.

"Mornin'," Lucinda mumbled back.

The splash of something wet and cold hit her arm as it was set down beside her. That liquid would feel lovely transported from the bedside table to her lips, but it seemed a difficult task right now. "Thank you," she croaked.

"You insisted on doing those shots last night. I told you it was a *baa-ad* idea."

She knew the voice of the giggling girl—*Aja*.

"Shots?" Lucinda couldn't remember that part. She pushed her hair off her face. Some of it had been tacked down with dried saliva. What she did remember was being exposed for the world to see, Aja hustling her out of her parents' house, but not before the show her father had put on. He'd even placed his hand over his heart as if he were auditioning for a part in a Broadway show. When she'd been nosing around upstairs, she'd seen his tickets for *Hamilton*. Lucinda wondered which one of his girlfriends he planned to take and if he'd make it there now. The old man wouldn't go down easy.

My luck, he's probably at home right now thinking of ways to punish me.

"Your phone has been beeping for hours with missed texts and calls," Aja said.

That would be my family, writing me off for good.

Lucinda could hear her cell chiming beside her head. She grabbed it. The awful feeling in the pit of her stomach churned harder and threatened its way up her throat. She threw the pillow off her face. "Bathroom?"

Aja pointed near the front of the tiny apartment. Lucinda was woozy as she sat up.

Her vision came into focus—Aja dressed in an oversize black T-shirt, sitting with half her voluptuous ass cheek on the sagging mattress, half of it off. She was wearing thick-framed glasses, and her mane of dark curls spilled over her shoulders.

Lucinda's stomach lurched again.

She placed her hand over her mouth and ran for the bathroom, slamming the door shut behind her. She collapsed on the ground in front of the toilet, retching up everything she'd consumed the evening before—except for the lies she'd told herself.

Those would stay with her.

She wiped her mouth with a tissue and hugged the carpet beside the toilet. It was damp, and she wondered if Aja's bathroom leaked or if this was just one of those musty, old units that always seemed ripe for mold. It sure smelled like it.

"You okay in there?" Aja asked.

She repositioned herself on the bathroom rug. There was makeup baked into the fibers. "I just need a minute." She was afraid she'd come away with half a face full of dried gunk.

"Just making sure you were still alive." Aja giggled again, and Lucinda was glad she could laugh about all of this. Women were more forgiving. Any man would've booted her out if she'd puked the morning after their one-night stand.

It could only be one night, because she had to get back to New York.

Lucinda cradled her phone in her hand as she lay on the threadbare rug. She glanced at the battery—15 percent. *Shit.* There were things she needed to address. Like the pending deal to finally get her play produced.

And her father.

The first one somehow still seemed more important than the other.

Lucinda summoned the courage to look at the texts to gauge how much damage she'd really done. She wouldn't listen to the voice mails, though. That would be far too taxing.

Valerie: Dad's in the ICU in the hospital. You need to get here.

Valerie: I'm staying the night even if you want to come late.

Oh crap.

Valerie: LUCY! Where the hell are you??

That was Valerie for you. She'd tell you nicely what she wanted, and if you didn't do it, she'd turn into a real bitch.

Jeremy: Hey, Dad's at Saint Margaret's. He's not doing well. Give me a ring.

Jeremy—totally laid-back. It was kind of hard not to be when he was always stoned. He didn't ride her like the others. But he probably should. She'd really done it this time.

Christian: Your father is at Saint Margaret's in ICU if you give a fuck. If you don't, please don't bother.

Christian hated her most. He'd been dying for a reason to tell her not to come back home since she was sixteen, since she had been sent to Mercersburg Academy after getting kicked out of Shadyside—also a private school her parents had paid bucketloads for. Christian feared she'd sully the family business. From the moment Father had made it clear that Christian was the only one to work there, her brother had guarded his future position like a greedy sentinel, taking every opportunity he could to point out his siblings' inadequacies so they couldn't share in the wealth.

Lucinda exhaled, and it stung her insides.

ICU didn't sound good.

It was just a little backstage kissing.

It was hard to truly accept the blame for this. She'd let him get to her for the last time in high school when he'd made it clear that she wasn't accepted in the family anymore and she never would be. It's all she'd ever wanted—a place at the table. If he was comfortable booting her out of his life after one mistake, she wouldn't rush to his side now just because he was sick, as if he hadn't made any mistakes at all.

If he doesn't care about me, why should I care about him?

Valerie: Let me know where you are in the morning, and I'll come pick you up.

Shit.

She sucked in a breath. Her cell read 14 percent. *Ugh.*

There was nothing she could do right now. It sounded as though her father had survived.

Her pending theater production weighed heavily on her mind.

Her play was important.

Her play would spur the type of conversations that made dinner parties worthwhile in New York. Her characters were voicey, and they decompartmentalized the mold for normalcy in human attraction and made space for people who didn't define themselves by their sexuality alone. She was never able to express herself freely at home, but since she'd left, she couldn't seem to stop.

Love Is Love would change the way people thought about their own relationships.

Fritz believed in her project too.

He'd produced several successful plays on and off Broadway. Lucinda had met him when they'd worked together as servers at an upscale tapas bar. In her eyes, he was the perfect person to give her a leg up. Even though it was difficult to break out a new playwright and although fewer and fewer struggling theaters were taking a financial risk on fresh talent, Lucinda's play was different, and Fritz would see that too.

This was the one.

They'd be begging her to write more after the critics got a viewing. She'd never written anything like it before.

The script had bled—*no*—poured from her fingers, as if her hands had discovered a fresh word spring, one she hadn't been able to turn off once the frantic rush of typing had started. The drafting process was as obsessive as it was cathartic, to the point she'd missed waitressing shifts, entire jobs—sacrificed a boyfriend.

Nothing was as important as *Love Is Love*. The production of the play was about more than career achievement. It was a personal statement too. Lucinda believed love wasn't conditional and that it didn't stop just because someone made an error. Love couldn't be defined by gender, an idea her family certainly hadn't adopted, so she hadn't even tried to explain it to them. Father had called Jeremy a slur word in the nineties just for growing his hair out. *Not worth it.*

Lucinda wouldn't let anyone stop her from producing her play.

Especially not her father.

Aja knocked on the door. More giggles. "Okay. Now I have to pee."

She was childish, really. All of the silly, incessant laughter. Aja was sloppy too. The kind of girl who let makeup fall on the floor and didn't bother to clean it up. She stepped on it instead, grinding it into the rug, fully aware it would never come out.

Growing up a Fox had made Lucinda particular in certain areas, and cleanliness and hygiene was one of them. She hadn't noticed any of these things last night while she was inebriated, but Lucinda would've been punished if she'd treated her home like this under Marian's rule, an anxiety she didn't care to relive right now.

Lucinda rolled onto her knees and crawled to the door, turning the knob and yanking it open.

"Oh man," Aja said.

Then again, who was Lucinda to judge? She was the one who couldn't stand up straight right now, wiping away the remnants of her own vomit as she crouched in her bra and underwear on a stranger's floor. "I'm just going to go over there." Lucinda slowly inched to the couch, where she found a new place to recover. She sank with the springs, certain she wouldn't be able to get up unassisted.

She was afraid to check her email for the acceptance to her project. She heard Aja come out of the bathroom minutes later.

"Hey, do you have an iPhone charger?" Lucinda asked. *12 percent.*

"No, sorry, I'm an Android girl."

Damn. "Okay."

Well, there was a sign right there they weren't compatible.

She knew she was doing it again. Lucinda was looking for faults in Aja so she wouldn't get attached to her. But it was only because she'd be going home soon and she didn't want anyone to get hurt. Lucinda wrote a lot about love, but she realized she still had a lot to learn.

"Androids take better pictures, ya know?" Aja said.

They all say that. "I've heard." Lucinda took a deep breath and clicked the icon for her email. Her heart did a wild thing in her chest as she saw the message she'd been waiting for from Fritz Zimmerman, subject: **Love Is Love.**

She placed her hand over her mouth and stifled a rancid belch.

This was it.

This was everything.

Her big break—the project that would set her apart.

She had actresses and actors already lined up for the parts, talented people who'd worked in the restaurant industry with her. They'd do improv after their late-night shifts, stay up well past closing hours at the bars, then continue their charade in their tiny studio apartments, drinking and smoking too much and sharing their art. Then they'd all sleep until noon and get up and do it all over again. Lucinda could barely afford her rent, but she couldn't imagine living this extraordinary life anywhere else.

It was about so much more than money for her, though. She had an important story to tell, one other people should hear. And she had a perfect vision for how to tell it.

All she needed was a foot in the door.

She clicked on the bold, unopened key to her future.

Subject: Love Is Love

Dear Lucinda,

I hope this message finds you drafting your next immersive, contemporary play. You know I think *Love Is Love* is a brilliant, relevant, current masterpiece. However, as you are aware, the funding for the studio has dwindled over the years, and I'm afraid they don't have the means to back your project with the current budget.

However, the board was moved by the script and said if you're able to crowdfund and source the $100,000 necessary, we'd be happy to reconsider. Tall order, I realize, but you'd be surprised how many people might be impassioned enough by your idea to support it.

Best of luck with your project. I'm sure you'll find a home for it.

You're an exquisite playwright,

Fritz

She sank back into the couch like the withering, dying soul that she was.

No. She could not have read that correctly. It'd taken her months to get into Fritz's pocket and convince him to pitch her play. She'd waited until he really loved it too. Not like he was just doing her a favor because they'd once served canapés together. Fritz had told her not to get her hopes up and that it was a long shot. That's why she'd been looking for Valerie at the party, to sell her sister on her idea in the event Fritz turned her down. Lucinda was hoping Valerie might invest in her play. No chance her family would help her now, though.

He wants me to try a Kickstarter? What?

No one was going to give her money. She hadn't self-produced anything. She was an unknown. It was the whole point of getting the studio support.

The disappointment didn't end with her. She'd have to tell her whole cast. They'd been just as excited as she was. There was no way she could couch surf at her friends' apartments after she'd crushed their dreams. Creating her art, writing, had been Lucinda's way to escape as a child. She hadn't fit in, and she'd wanted so badly for this play to be the thing to finally give her purpose. Lucinda's family had teased her for "wasting time" scribbling down her poems, and this was her way to prove them wrong and bring love into the world.

Sure, she could cut part of the cast and still make a show, for maybe a little less than $100,000, but any amount over zero was still more than she had.

If she cut the role of Violet she'd given to her best friend, Aster, what would her Act II be without her working on the complicated feelings of being attracted to two very different people?

Fritz knew it too. That's why he hadn't recommended that she rewrite her play for a more affordable budget. Instead, he'd suggested she fund it herself. It seemed like such an impossibility, but it was something she had to figure out. Her show was something the world needed to see. *But how?*

Lucinda was going to lie on this girl's couch and stare at the popcorn ceiling with the brown watermark stain directly above her until someone made her move. Because this was *de-vas-tating.*

She couldn't live right now.

"Do you want pancakes?" Aja asked from the kitchen.

"Sure," Lucinda said absently.

"Great, I wasn't sure if you have anywhere to be. I don't work or go to school on Sundays."

Lucinda heard Aja banging around in the kitchen, different dishes and pans, and she could only imagine lots of bottoms without matching lids in this girl's cabinets. "No, I'm good," Lucinda replied.

She should head to the hospital and visit her father, check in with her family, but her feelings of dejection were immobilizing. She wanted to know if his condition was serious, but it was hard to make anything matter when she'd just been killed herself.

Leaving this apartment at all was completely negligible. Her utter indifference to just about everything was ubiquitous and all-consuming until she could write something else, something Fritz Zimmerman thought was worthy of allocating part of his budget to.

She'd have to start from scratch. All over again.

"Hey, do you want chocolate chips in yours? I prefer them, but I can make yours without," Aja said.

"I'm okay with whatever you want to make me," Lucinda said, although she didn't really like chocolate in her pancakes. It was best to be a good houseguest, since she was going to be homeless soon.

"Goody!" Aja said.

There was a banging at the door, and at first Lucinda wondered if she was back in her seashell state because she had a pillow over her face. She took it off and heard the distinct pounding again.

"Oh shoot. Can you get that? I just poured the first batch. You know how pancakes are. You can't let them stick," Aja said.

"I only have on a bra and underwear," Lucinda said helplessly. She was draped beneath a fringed blanket that smelled like wet dog. More troubling, there'd been absolutely no evidence of a dog in that apartment.

The banging was louder. "I'm not expecting anyone," Aja said.

Maybe it's the police coming to haul me away for killing my father.

Lucinda had always feared if she returned home for too long, her family would drag her under somehow. She'd had a few warning signs lately. The silence on the phone line when she'd called her sister had more or less whispered in her ear not to come home this time. Aster had told her not to ignore what she referred to as Lucinda's "sick sixth sense." But here she was . . .

"I'll get it," Lucinda announced.

She wrapped the blanket around her like a makeshift toga and stumbled to the door. "Who is it?" Lucinda asked, because if Aja wasn't expecting anyone, she wanted to rule out the possibility of the police. She'd seen a window that led to a fire escape in the rear of the apartment. It wouldn't be completely out of character for her to run from the cops, although it might be beneath her to run from them half-naked.

"It's Valerie, Lucy. Open the door."

Valerie. What?

"Why're you here? I was going to swing by the hospital later."

"We just need to talk. We're not here to yell at you," Valerie said in her ultra-soft conniving voice.

"I'm not going to open this door if you're just going to harass me." She really couldn't deal with her sister right now. Not after the bitter pill she'd just swallowed on the couch.

"This isn't about Dad. It's about his assets. For us," Jeremy said.

Jesus. Jeremy's here too? They're here . . . about Father's money?

Curiosity piqued her interest enough to pull open the door. Flaky pieces of paint plucked away from the doorframe.

Valerie and Jeremy eyed her with alarm.

"What're you not wearing?" Jeremy asked.

Valerie said, "*Wow.* I was worried about you, you know?"

"Pancakes are ready!" Aja announced.

Jeremy scrunched his brows together. "Do you like girls now? Is that what you're into?"

Lucinda couldn't answer his question with certainty. Her stomach was growling beneath her blanket. "Assets?" she asked. "I didn't think we got any of those."

"We can't discuss it here." Valerie offered a tight-lipped smile. "You need to come with us."

Is this a trick? "Do you mind if I eat my pancakes first?" When she was younger, they'd often lie to her to get her to do their bidding. "Lucy, we all take turns mucking the stalls." This wasn't true. Valerie had just wanted her horse tended to, and she hadn't the time to care for it herself. Over the years, Lucinda had learned to question their demands.

Valerie shook her head, mouth wide open, no words.

"I made enough for everyone," Aja said.

"Well, I don't see how it could hurt." Jeremy shouldered his way through the door and stopped full-on once he took in the rattrap of an apartment. He must have believed it suitable to dine in, though, because he proceeded to walk to Aja's slim galley-kitchen countertop.

"Here ya go." She handed Jeremy a plate of hotcakes and a bottle of syrup.

"Why, thank you. Ooh, chocolate chip," Jeremy said.

Lucinda turned around and left her older sister hanging in the doorway. She could hear Valerie quietly shut the door and shuffle behind her.

"And for you." Aja set a plate of pancakes down in front of her, which Lucinda unapologetically shoveled into her mouth. She hadn't eaten in a long time. She'd gotten one bacon-wrapped scallop down before she'd guzzled six flutes of champagne at the party, and that was at eight o'clock last evening.

"Would you like some?" Aja called to Valerie over their shoulders.

Lucinda watched Valerie tiptoe around the mess on the floor—Lucinda's dress, an open bag of cheese curls, underwear that was not Lucinda's, a medicine ball. "No, I'm good. Thank you," Valerie said.

This was a disaster. Their theme of "Lucy the problem child" would continue. Blame was her real worry here. Did they think she was responsible for Father?

"How did you find me?" Lucinda asked.

Jeremy fought to finish chewing, pancakes gone. He always could house food in minutes. "I don't like using it. I only do it for court hearings, typically, but as the regional manager of TeleCom . . ." He paused. "I used the Find My Phone app and located you. I can do it with any customer. It's totally illegal, though, so please don't turn me in."

Lucinda scowled at him as her phone timely chimed—low battery.

"We sell a new portable battery you should invest in. It's saved lives for people stuck in remote places," he said.

Lucinda nodded, feigning interest. "Right. Where're we going to discuss the . . . assets?"

"We have an appointment with Piedmont in forty-five minutes across town, so you should eat quicker," Valerie said.

Corbin Piedmont was the family attorney. He used to come over and smoke cigars with her father on the outdoor patio. There'd been a rift many years ago, before her parents were married. Piedmont had gone on a single date with Mother, only to be sidelined by sneaky Stefan Fox. Lucinda had never cared for Piedmont much. He oozed toxic masculinity and was as pretentious as the vintage cars he drove.

"All I have is the dress I wore last night," Lucinda said.

"Not my problem," Valerie said. She was probably still mad at her for not texting back. She made Lucinda feel bad with the whole "I was worried about you" song and dance. Valerie was an expert guilt-tripper. It must come naturally for someone who never made mistakes.

"Piedmont will probably love it. He's divorced again," Jeremy said.

"Gross . . . stop that," Lucinda said.

Aja slammed her cast-iron pan in the sink. "Really inappropriate thing to say, considering where you're at, don't you think?" Her eyes were gleaming dark and angry, and all three of the siblings exchanged a look of surprise.

Aja had gone from happy pancake maker (with chocolate chips) to scary jealous, and Lucinda was officially ready to go now.

"Thanks for everything, Aja. I really need to get to this appointment and sort out things with my father." Lucinda left her empty plate on the counter and hurried for her dress, which she slipped on right in front of her siblings. They'd already seen all her bits last night anyway.

"Ready? Did you get your phone?" Valerie asked, always mothering. There was a near-twelve-year age difference between them, but Valerie treated Lucinda more like her daughter, Isla, who *was* twelve years old.

"Yes, let's go," Lucinda said as she hopped into her black stilettos. She felt much better after eating.

Jeremy said, "That was delicious. Thanks so much."

"Let's go, Jeremy." Valerie rushed him.

"Okay, call me later." Aja returned to her upbeat, perky self, as if she hadn't just assumed the personality of a frightening bunny boiler with a frying pan. "I know you said you'll be hanging in town while your dad is in the hospital."

Did I say that? She didn't remember saying it. "Okay, thanks for everything, got your number." Lucinda waved her phone in the air, and Valerie and Jeremy followed her out of the apartment.

CHAPTER 5

VALERIE

They climbed into Valerie's BMW. "What in the fresh hell was that, Lucy?" Valerie asked.

Lucy grabbed her wavy hair and twisted it savagely into a knot on the top of her head. She had this skill of taking a skinny strand and wrapping it around her bun and tying it off without a ponytail holder.

"I don't know. I just met the girl." Lucy seemed withdrawn, slumping in her seat, oddly quiet, if not a bit shocked by her girl fling's behavior.

"Jeez, this road." Valerie was meandering down a street on the South Side Slopes that appeared to be two-way but should've been one lane, cars parked practically hanging over a cliff, chairs in other spots to reserve parking spaces for the residents who lived there.

"So is that your thing now? Chicks?" Jeremy asked his inane question again, his obsession with the topic a little creepy.

"I don't have a *thing*. I'm not attracted to gender. I'm attracted to people," Lucy explained.

Valerie said, "If your little act was for shock value, no one cared. They felt sorry for you."

Lucy pounded the side of the door with her fist. "It's not like that."

"Dad seemed to care a bit." Jeremy peeped from the back seat. He was probably just happy someone else was disappointing Father for a change.

"Right. Christian said you gave Father a heart attack," Valerie confirmed. "At least they don't think Mother saw anything," she said in a softer voice. Valerie couldn't imagine how mortified Lucy must be.

Lucy was still going off. "You have to fit everyone into a neat little box, Jeremy."

"Neat boxes. That's what Lucy likes now." Jeremy erupted into laughter.

"Gross. You're such an asshole. Worst. Joke. Ever," Lucy seethed.

"Disgusting, Jeremy," Valerie concurred.

"You love me," he said. "And so do you, S&M walk-of-shame Barbie." He cackled again.

"Enough," Valerie begged. She caught Jeremy making a goofy face in the rearview mirror. Lucy eyed him strangely too.

"What? It's a tension breaker," he said.

Valerie and Lucy giggled. "You are good for that," Valerie said.

"That's about it. Are you *okay*, though, Jeremy? For real?" Lucy asked.

"I'm fine . . . Hey, will Christian be at this meeting? He'll deem you impassable, Lucy."

"It's his meeting," Valerie said. *Impassable* was a ridiculous word Christian had used to describe when they were unsuitable to "sit at the table" with the rest of the family. Valerie thought it was Christian's way to create a greater divide between his brother and sisters so he could cleanly and easily take over the company one day, and they all hated him for it.

"Screw off." Lucy pulled the visor down in the car and flipped on the lighted mirror. "Oh wow. I really do look like shit."

"And what's with the pink acrylic on your cheek?" Jeremy asked.

Valerie could see it too. It was like war paint—a line of pink smeared on Lucy's face, just below her nose, all the way to her chin.

"That's Aja's makeup." Lucy stuck her filthy finger in her mouth and began rubbing her skin with her saliva. "She's a cosmetologist. It was everywhere. Her products," she lamented.

"Classy," Jeremy said.

"Who uses the word *acrylic*? Is that what your interior designer girlfriend calls it? I thought you were getting engaged," Lucy said.

Valerie smiled. As much as she didn't get along with her siblings, she missed their savage banter, an eternal roast. In high school, Jeremy had listened in on a landline call where Christian was dumping his girlfriend. He'd asked Valerie to partake in the eavesdropping because he was concerned Christian was going to break this girl's heart. At the end of the call, Jeremy had piped up and asked the girl out. She was two years older than Jeremy, but she'd said yes, and Christian had been livid. Valerie had been delighted, laughing at Jeremy and scolding him simultaneously.

"I thought you were getting engaged too," Valerie said.

"I'm working on it. Daphne is worth the effort." Jeremy spoke of his newest love interest, who hailed from a prominent family in Squirrel Hill, Pittsburgh's Jewish epicenter. Jeremy couldn't have fit in. He wasn't Jewish, and he was wealthy only by name. She worried his struggles with addiction and quirky behavior might make it impossible to find a good partner, although true love could be the very thing he needed to stay clean.

"Gotta sell a lot of cell phones to buy her a suitable ring, I imagine," Lucy said.

"I'm way, way beyond the sales rep role," Jeremy stated.

"Well, excuse me," Lucy said.

"*All right*, you two." What had been enjoyable only a few minutes ago had already started to grate. Valerie's head was throbbing.

When they neared Attorney Piedmont's high-rise office in downtown Pittsburgh, Valerie entered one of the awful parking garages that reminded her why she rarely crossed the Allegheny River. Before their divorce, Karl had sometimes asked her to meet him for lunch at PPG Place. As lovely as his postmodern office building was, built entirely of matching glass, the parking situation made it almost not worth it.

"What're we discussing? Is Father not going to make it?" Lucy asked, her voice small.

Valerie drove down and down the eternal parking garage ramp to hell—and what were they, six floors underground now? She felt claustrophobic on top of her headache and annoyance with her siblings. "I was wondering when you were going to ask about him."

"I was in no condition to come to the hospital last night, okay?" Lucy said.

"No. It's not okay." Valerie made a hard left to continue her downward spiral.

Lucy remained quiet, looking out the window, playing with her fingers in her mouth again, gnawing on her nails as Valerie located a parking spot. She'd always been sympathetic to Lucy's mishaps, but she wouldn't excuse her for last evening. *Too far.*

"Christian said Dad probably had underlying health issues." Jeremy threw Lucy a bone.

"Christian doesn't know what he's talking about." Valerie pulled her car in a spot and shifted into park.

"I didn't know how bad he was last night. I'm here now," Lucy said.

Valerie's hands twitched on the steering wheel. "Apparently, there've been some legal changes to the estate made since Mom got sick. Let's go see what they are." They exited the car. "This way to the elevator." Valerie pointed to the sign shining in the distance.

Valerie could hear them whispering in front of her. Lucy asked, "Do you know how much we'll get? See, I have this play . . ." Valerie gritted her teeth. Lucy was already thinking about all the things she could buy with her inheritance before Father was even dead.

"I have no idea. At least a million dollars, I would think," Jeremy replied.

Valerie understood that the idea of receiving a lump sum was beyond enticing for her siblings who lived paycheck to paycheck, but they could at least temper their hopeful expectations, considering their father lay in a hospital bed, fighting for his life.

No one needed that payout more than Valerie.

Her credit was currently frozen, pending her husband's investigation. Karl had squandered all their money on a bad investment in a risky hedge fund and then tried to cover it up by making more terrible decisions. He'd depleted Isla's college fund in the process, which came with a steep financial penalty for early withdrawal. All of that could've been recoverable if he hadn't embezzled money from his own firm to cover his losses. The only way to protect what was left of their assets was to divorce him.

"I swear I was going to pay it back, Val."

Famous last words.

Valerie had been so enraged when he'd fessed up, she'd smashed a Philistine vase over his head before the repo men could confiscate it. Men had been there, hauling their financed things away, and Karl had been forced to confess at that point. It's the only reason he did.

She'd told Karl their marriage was over, right then and there. It wasn't so much the money as it was the lies.

Oh, the lies, Karl! All of their money.

Millions, he'd lost.

Valerie remembered how her father had excused his own lies by throwing the money he'd earned in their faces. To have the lies and lose the riches seemed a cruel embarrassment—one Valerie couldn't live with, and one she couldn't tell anyone about either.

Isla had been so angry with her for hurting Daddy, tears streaming down her face. Valerie never did properly explain why she'd hit him. They'd spared their daughter all the nasty facts, claiming "financial difficulties," until they learned more about the charges.

Karl had been so good at paying close attention to details at one time. It was one of the things that'd drawn her to him. When she'd met him post-college at an art exhibit at the Duquesne Club, as equally beautiful as it was stuffy, Karl had been so taken with the historical building, he'd left the crowd to observe the fancy sculptured edging of the interior walls. He'd touched it tentatively, as if it were a sacred artifact. Valerie had approached him to find out what was so interesting, because she'd been bored.

"Hello there, whatcha looking at?" she'd asked.

He'd peered down at her through thick, trendy glasses. "Oh, hi yourself. This building is fascinating. The Romanesque design on the inside is a surprise, fit for a king. No wonder this place was ranked number one last year for best clubs in America."

"Are you a builder?" she'd asked, intrigued.

"An architect. Seeing design work like this for the first time is remarkable. Exquisite . . . a rare find." He eyed her in her black dress as if he thought she was a rare find too.

"It is." She glanced around at the room dressed in regal golds and burgundy, taking in the length of the chalky pillars. "My first time here."

"Mine too. Women couldn't join this club for years, ya know? They used to sneak them in the side door."

"Well, lucky for me, I guess," she said sardonically. "I'm more of a modernist anyway. My future home will have lots of windows and straight lines. This isn't for me." It was her way of throwing him shade to see how he'd handle it.

He laughed. "Let me take you out, and we can talk about what our future house might look like together."

She'd blushed at his forwardness, but his passion for his craft, his ability to dig deep when he loved something, made her say yes to the date. And when he'd asked her to marry him a year later, promising to fill that house they'd jointly designed with loyalty, mutual respect, and a child, she'd said yes again.

And now he'd left Valerie and Isla in a lurch, and Valerie was the one who had to figure out how to make it better. She feared she was failing her daughter.

In any case, she was in much more dire need than the two yo-yos walking in front of her. It was as if they hadn't been affected by Father's episode at all. Jeremy and Lucy were waltzing to the elevator with an extra pep in their step like they were on their way to lottery head-quarters to redeem their Powerball tickets. And did they even know how badly their mother's health had gone downhill the last couple of months?

As they rode up the elevator, no one spoke. Valerie's nose tweaked at the smell emanating from her little sister—a combination of expired yogurt and grape Jolly Ranchers.

When the three of them entered the office, Christian and Mr. Piedmont were huddling over some paperwork, bickering about some-thing Valerie didn't quite catch. She'd only been in Piedmont's office once, and the decor hadn't changed, the photo of his prized Ford Model T still hanging on the wall behind his desk. What had changed was Mr. Piedmont himself. He'd really aged, his gray hair turning white, his jowls weighing down his rounded face.

"We're here," Lucy said, as if she were announcing a prize.

Christian glanced up quickly and then did a double take. "What in God's name happened to you?"

Valerie sighed, not wanting to answer for her sister. "Lucy?"

Lucy licked her lips, which were cracked with dried lipstick. "I was abducted by a waitress who doubles as a cosmetologist who pretended to be a laid-back party girl, until I tried to leave, in which case she transformed into a bunny-boiling psychopath. She made me chocolate chip pancakes and asked me to call her later, so it's all good."

Christian blinked a whole bunch but moved no other part of his body. He'd certainly deemed Lucy impassable at the moment. Just because Father was ill, Christian wouldn't let the standards he'd instilled slip.

"Accurate," Jeremy said.

Mr. Piedmont stared at them blankly, perhaps a little scared.

"Well, while you were having your fun, we were looking over legal documents. More important, kids, I'm reading Father's revised trust, and I don't like how it looks," Christian informed them.

Valerie hated when Christian called them "kids." She'd heard him refer to his own children with the same condescending ring.

Mr. Piedmont raised his hands. "There's no way to change it with Stefan in an altered state. Just let me inform your sisters and brother of the details as I'm instructed to by your father in this instance. And remember, we're only going over this *now* because your father's medical condition is critical, and Fox Wealth Management will expect a statement. Also, if he were to be pronounced brain-dead or otherwise incapacitated, the Den would kick into effect."

"The Den?" Valerie asked.

"Yes, it's the name for the Fox family trust," Piedmont clarified.

"Cute," Lucy said.

Piedmont shuffled from behind his desk and handed them each sealed manila envelopes.

"Sounds good to me." Jeremy set his envelope down on the desk and rubbed his hands together as if he were about to throw dice. "We should all have access to this information." That was a rib at Christian. He'd been privy to family financials they hadn't in the past.

Christian stared him down. "As if you know a thing about finances."

Lucy pulled at the leather watch on her wrist. It looked as though it'd been embossed into her skin. "That'd be great, actually. I have a flight to catch."

"Not sticking around to see Father through?" Valerie asked. *Not surprised.*

"I have to work," Lucy said.

"Why don't I disclose to your siblings what I discussed with you?" Mr. Piedmont said to Christian.

"Fine," Christian snipped.

Piedmont cleared his throat. "Simone's recent decline in health made it abundantly clear to your father that she could no longer make financial decisions, so your father chose to cut her legal rights as one of the financial grantors of the Den," Mr. Piedmont said.

Valerie gasped. The way he said it—*gah*. It sounded inhumane, cutting the mother fox from her den.

Mr. Piedmont continued. "The details are in your envelopes. Your mother was consulted when she was in the right state of mind. Stefan suspected her condition would continue to deteriorate, which it has. He didn't want you all to wait around to collect your dues if he died first, provided Simone might lose all cognitive function. There is substantial money set aside for her care. All the way until her death."

Valerie inhaled a sharp breath at the sadness of it all. "Why did Father change his mind about leaving us money?" It was something she'd been wondering since she'd learned about the trust.

Piedmont looked up from his papers. "He'd told me once that he didn't intend to raise lazy children. And that if you all knew you had an inheritance coming, you would never reach your full potential."

"Makes sense," Christian said.

"Therefore, the trust reads as is stated . . ." Mr. Piedmont rambled a bunch of legalese Valerie didn't understand, but her ears latched on to, "Give it to my children in equal shares. In the event any of my children shall predecease me, said deceased child's share shall be distributed equally among my then-living children."

"How much is it in total?" Valerie asked.

"The total amount"—Piedmont flipped through some documents—"is . . . $10,005,000."

A squeak escaped Lucy's parted lips.

Christian shot her a dirty look. "Timing of distribution?"

Mr. Piedmont cleared his throat. "All sums will be paid out no more than sixty days from the date of death and deposited into the account of the designated bank account as determined by Lathrob and Piedmont. That's me," Mr. Piedmont added, as if they might not be sure.

"Hold up. What does the part about predecease mean?" Jeremy asked.

"It means if one of us were to die before Dad, whoever is left gets to split their share," Christian clarified.

Valerie didn't like the hint of interest in Jeremy's eyes any more than she cared for his prying question about her sister's sex life.

"There's nothing in there about his grandchildren? If I die before Father does, Isla gets *nothing*?" So much had been taken from her daughter already. Valerie felt Isla had been shorted once again.

Piedmont nodded. "He put no provision in for the grandchildren."

Jeremy didn't seem to care. "If the bunny boiler gets the best of ya, it would be a dirty shame, Luce."

Valerie's expression of repugnance couldn't have matched Christian's if she'd tried. Jeremy sometimes cracked jokes to hide his true emotions. She hoped this was one of those times.

"Glad to see you're taking all of this seriously. What're you going to do with your share, Jer? Use it to buy your way into another woman's pants or shove it up your nose?" Christian asked.

Mr. Piedmont made a horrible sound in his throat. "Just one more clause."

"For your information," Jeremy said, "I'm now considered on the executive level of my company, and I've been given buy-in options for the stock program. I've worked my way up the corporate ladder, something you wouldn't know anything about, since Dad just handed you a job."

Very true, Valerie thought. Christian had been the only one Father had thought was suited for his line of work, and no one had felt that pain more than Jeremy—the other son.

Christian sucked in his cheeks, positively livid. "Stock options? In telecommunications? The least profitable of all the sectors? Wow, yes, as your financial adviser, I'd recommend you invest . . . none of it there. Moron."

"Don't be cruel. Jeremy's made great strides at work," Valerie defended.

"He sells cell phones, Val," Christian said.

Jeremy made fists with both his hands. "I am not in a sales rep role anymore!"

Silence filled the room.

Mr. Piedmont took the momentary pause as an opportunity to continue. "As I was saying . . . the proceeds from the sale of the Fox residence, at 591 Old Mill Road, shall go to the memory center and corroborating charities as outlined in the section in the documents marked *charities,* including the remaining share of the Den appropriated for the funding of the Satellite Kids foundation, serving poverty-stricken families and displaced unwed mothers, and will continue to be distributed over a span of no more than the next twenty years."

"Please let them know the financials on those," Christian griped.

Piedmont scrunched his face as if he was having a hard time reading the paper.

"Five million dollars, payable each year in an amount of no more than $250,000—"

Christian interrupted. "That's what I'm contesting. That was Mother's charity. It shouldn't be connected to our trust. Father didn't give a shit about that charity. Why is this provision tied to the Den?"

"For tax purposes, it falls under charitable donations in the trust and has been signed off on by your father and your mother, for that matter, when she agreed to cut herself out, provided all her health-care needs and those of her personal caretaker would be met."

"So Marian has been written in?" Jeremy asked. "She helped Mother when she started that charity."

"That's right. However, Ms. Vega doesn't have any part of running it anymore," Mr. Piedmont clarified.

"Ms. Marian. The biggest backstabbing bunny boiler there is. Never let us off the hook for a thing. She liked to tattle more than Valerie," Lucy said.

Valerie could hardly stifle a laugh. If Lucy had behaved better, there'd be no need to *tell on her*—but of course she'd omit that part.

"The only reason she's hung around this long was for that hoity-toity retirement home they put her up in," Christian said.

"Well . . . after how Mother treated her, how did you expect her to act? One minute her best friend, the next a hired hand," Valerie said. "Marian still tends to her, you know?"

"Why do you have to defend everyone? Some people don't deserve to be defended," Lucy said.

Valerie shot Lucy an evil glance. She should watch her tongue. Valerie was the only person in the family who'd ever stuck up for her. Valerie had told her parents about the teacher Lucy had been chatting with online only because her sister wouldn't listen to her pleas to stop. Valerie had asked her parents to go easy on Lucy and explained to them how it was a different world than when their other three children were teenagers, with all the extra lures of the internet, but they'd sent Lucy to boarding school anyway, and she had always blamed Valerie for it.

Mr. Piedmont talked right over them, clearly itching to be done with their crazy family. Valerie was too. "Contesting the provision is no use. It was drafted and signed by the presiding party, your father, before he got sick. And it will tie up the other funds if you contest it, Christian. Your siblings' funds." Mr. Piedmont said the last part in a low voice.

"Come on, Christian. You're already getting the family business," Jeremy said.

Christian shrugged, but this was also true. He was inheriting millions, none of which any of them would see, just by taking over Father's book of business. "This money isn't being distributed in a way that makes any sense. You might be comfortable leaving five million dollars on the table, but I'm sure as hell not."

"You don't have to ruin it for the rest of us just because you've got a stick up your ass about an old charity," Lucy said.

Christian turned to her. "It's five million dollars, Lucy. That should be going to us!"

"An amount equivalent to fifty percent of what we're receiving in totality is going to that charity," Valerie interjected. Christian did have a good point, but it wasn't significant enough for Valerie to raise a stink—$2.5 million was plenty fine, especially right now. "But I don't see a reason to oppose Father's wishes," she concluded.

"Well, that is kind of horseshit. I'm okay with cutting bait, though. It sounds like red tape we can't tear through," Jeremy said.

"Your logic is based on two clichés jammed together," Christian said to his brother. "What if Father wakes up?" Christian's tone didn't indicate he was exactly joyful about that prospect now that the numbers had been rolled out.

Valerie couldn't say she was either. She was in danger of losing her house. The benefits of the trust would all be for Isla, really, to preserve what they had left.

Mr. Piedmont's cheeks colored. "Then you can ask him yourself, I suppose, but the neurologist on staff said his brain function is still low, unfortunately."

"We need to get back to the hospital," Valerie said. *Brain-dead is gone* . . . She swallowed.

But sixty days is way too long. Karl could be in prison by then . . .

"If you'll just give me your bank accounts and your social security numbers, I can have all the paperwork drafted up for you to sign and your deposit information ready in the event your father passes," Mr. Piedmont said.

"I've got mine." Jeremy waved his phone. "All under my Contacts section." He smiled naughtily, like the time he'd found their Christmas presents stashed in the garden shed.

"Wow. That's smart. Who keeps their social security number in their Contacts section of their phone? It's like you're begging to have your identity stolen," Christian said.

The office printer started humming, and Jeremy flicked Christian off as he picked up the paper and handed it to Mr. Piedmont. "I connected to your air printer. Hope you don't mind. Information is all here."

Christian clapped. "Oh, lookie. Someone knows how to use Wi-Fi."

Jeremy took a threatening step toward Christian. Christian made a mocking dancing gesture that reminded Valerie of an angry orangutan, as if to say, *What're you gonna do?*

"Stop, Christian," Valerie said.

"Boys," Mr. Piedmont yelled. "I'm not your playground referee. I'm here to honor your father's legal requests. Keep it together."

They both eased up. Jeremy took a step back, and Christian stopped his silly provocations.

"Slow your roll, Christian. Jeez. You're a special brand of asshole today," Lucy said.

Lucy was speaking the truth for once, and if Christian held up the trust, Valerie swore she was going to knock his smart grin right off his smug mug the same way she'd cracked Karl.

"Mr. Piedmont, I know my social, but my banking info is in a hidden file on my phone. And my phone is dead." Lucy held it up for good measure.

"Surprised your girlfriend didn't charge it for you while you slept," Jeremy said.

"She's an Android girl," Lucy explained.

"Oh no. You don't want one of those. High-maintenance," Jeremy said.

"Agree," Lucy said.

Valerie said, "I have an iPhone charger in my car. You probably don't remember where we parked. I'll go grab it. You can have my info, too, Mr. Piedmont. I agree to the terms and don't see a reason to contest this thing. It's written the way Father wanted it."

"I don't believe that. I've worked with him for over twenty years, and I can't see this being something he'd sign off on," Christian protested.

Valerie clenched her car keys in her hands. She had the feeling that Christian's hissy fit had less to do with the money and more to do with the fact that Father hadn't told him about it.

Mr. Piedmont shrugged. "It is what it is."

"I need a smoke. I'll come down with you, Val," Jeremy said.

As they exited the office, Christian continued to argue with Piedmont, and Lucy stood in the corner and bit her fingernails.

Valerie watched Jeremy dash for the stairs as she waited for the elevator, then rode it down to the dungeon to retrieve her charger. On her way back, she noticed a line for the elevator. "Bloody hell. On a Sunday," she mumbled.

She finally took the stairs, and when she made it to the street level, she caught sight of Jeremy. He was angry-smoking while talking on the phone.

Just three years ago, Valerie had visited him at a drug rehab facility. He'd been in a real bad way back then, brought in by a friend after a weekend bender, rail-thin. Valerie had taken the sweatshirt off her back, a women's medium, and given it to him because he'd been admitted without any belongings. She'd arranged for his things later that evening and made sure his treatments were paid for, long before Karl had blown through all their money.

It'd pained her to watch him in withdrawal. He'd been kinder to her after that—appreciative. He'd wanted so much to do better, to be better. And he had. Promoted to regional manager. In love. Valerie was happy for him.

As she got closer, Valerie overheard his conversation.

"It's a good deal. The best. They don't make that cut here. I'm having it imported from Africa. No, no one died. It's just the only place you can find it."

Dammit. He was talking about drugs.

He's going to use Father's money to buy some rare, imported drugs and resell them.

He was already talking to a dealer. It felt like a personal betrayal after all she'd done to get him on the right track, but she knew the power of addiction could be stronger than love. And she did love him. She just didn't know how to reach him.

Valerie did an about-face and decided to walk around the building the other way. *Oh. My. God.* What could she say to him to get him to change his mind?

She wanted to kick Jeremy in the teeth for being jazzed about collecting their trust-fund money just so he could throw it away on a huge drug order, not to mention poison their streets. She'd assumed he'd been clean for years. And if he was clean, Valerie didn't think he had the strength to deal and not use. If she came at him too hard right now, though, she could jeopardize the opportunity to work this out reasonably. Valerie could tell him he'd lose Daphne over this. No—she'd convince him of it.

She reminded herself there was no money to be had yet.

She still had time to talk Jeremy out of it.

Her phone buzzed in her purse.

It was Christian. If he was even trying to bully her into not handing over her information to Attorney Piedmont, she was going to tell him where to go. Christian probably assumed she was making out financially in the divorce. She answered the phone. "Hello."

"We need to get to the hospital."

"Oh no. Is Father—"

"Alive, but he had a whole lot of something suspicious in his system."

"What?"

"There are cops there now. They want to speak to everyone who was at the party."

CHAPTER 6

MARIAN

The chairs in the Longwood lobby were padded with years of sadness, soaked into the patterned fabric by all the bodies who'd sat there before she had—some passing the time watching television or the birds outside, others waiting for family members who never came. Occasionally, the visitors would be the ones to sit and warm the chairs, but they never stayed long.

Marian's quarters didn't offer the kind of space to entertain many, and even though her patio home was the nicest of its kind in the retirement community, with the eat-in kitchen and outside entertaining area, she'd asked to meet the detectives in the lobby instead. It was imperative to establish boundaries and end this interrogation when she saw fit.

To hear from Eli about Stefan collapsing in front of a room full of people was troubling enough. She hadn't observed it herself, but she wanted nowhere near the people investigating it. It would look bad if she refused to speak to them, Eli advised. She should listen to her son. No one knew how to massage the law better than lawyers.

Marian sat with the cops and sipped her chamomile tea, waiting for Eli as the detectives made small talk in the elusive form of questions—none of which she gave clear answers to because these weren't straightforward people they were inquiring about.

"Tell me about your time while employed at the Foxes'. Anything odd we should know about?" the female detective asked.

"No," she answered simply. "I was merely the cleaner, the cook, and the nanny." She found herself at a loss for words to describe the exact type of humans who trapped their employees in their own skin and then asked them to be thankful for it. As New York transplants with no formal education, Marian and Hector had few employment opportunities in that town outside of the Fox residence, and the Foxes knew that. "My main priority was the children," she said.

"So they never involved you in their personal or business affairs?"

"Just anything having to do with the kids." Shame on these officers. They were trying to shake loose truths from the Foxes' arbor of lies after she'd told them she wouldn't talk about them without her son present. Especially the male detective. Marian recognized Luke from his younger days. He probably didn't think she knew who he was. The detective was most certainly the dark-haired boy who'd carried the clubs at the Fox Chapel Country Club—the one Valerie had favored and briefly dated. Marian hadn't suffered a memory lapse. That was Simone. Was he being coy or did he truly not remember Marian from the day Valerie broke up with him?

The detective flipped through a page in his notes. He had stacks of them, a disorganized mess. "Your son is a lawyer. I assume he's *your* lawyer, Ms. Vega?"

"Oh, I don't need a lawyer. He just said he should be here for this, since he grew up with the Foxes." No sense admitting to even a thread of guilt where the Foxes were concerned—not a single, silky string of fault.

Eli was making his way through the entrance now, across the room, beneath the crystal chandelier that gave off a myriad of colors. You couldn't find a better senior community around. It was Oakmont, after all, adjacent to the greens that housed the US Open more times than any other golf course, just over the hill from the most renowned bakery within one hundred miles. And it was her retirement package for working for the Foxes for as many years as she had.

Marian could feel her dry lips break away from her teeth into a smile at the sight of Eli, devastatingly good-looking in his navy-blue suit.

"I apologize for my lateness. My appointment ran over." He extended his hand.

"That's fine. Hello, I'm Detective Lucas Kapinos, and this is Detective Teresa Sharpe." All three greeted one another with handshakes as Marian leaned back and tried not to get in the way.

Detective Kapinos gripped his papers. "We've asked your mother what it was like working for the Foxes. I believe you also grew up on the property, did you not, Mr. Vega?"

Marian was annoyed that he was wasting their time asking questions he already knew the answers to. It was clear Detective Kapinos didn't recognize Marian at all. The help were often glossed over like that.

"That's correct." Eli crossed his legs as he sat on the patterned chair.

"And how would you describe your upbringing there?" Detective Kapinos asked.

Eli offered a grin. "Extraordinary, to say the least. I was the mere housekeeper's son, but I was afforded all the luxuries of the other children who grew up there. I have nothing ill to say of the Foxes." He spoke with the confident diction of a platoon leader, and it touched Marian to hear him say such things about his upbringing. Although they'd both had ill things to say about the Foxes.

"I see," Detective Sharpe said. "And that didn't cause animosity among the other workers in the house? The ones who weren't afforded such *luxuries*."

Eli replied, "I was just a child. No one gave me too much flak." Marian smirked at his comment. The other children had given him plenty of flak. Stefan too. He'd mostly addressed Eli as "Boy." "Boy, could you grab my golf clubs from the Mercedes and put them in the Rover?" Marian had commented once that "he has a name." After having four children, Stefan claimed he could no longer keep track, but Marian had found it disrespectful.

"Just normal sibling rivalry," Eli added.

If Eli pushed back to their demands, Stefan would say things like, "You like your horse lessons? Don't you think you should pay for them?" Stefan had only been trying to teach him a lesson about earning his worth like the others, but it had to have hit Eli differently because he wasn't one of them. Eli had been given gifts and then made to feel he owed something for them afterward. She'd reasoned it was better than not having them at all.

"I see," Sharpe said, unsure. "So you felt like one of the family?"

"Pretty much. I knew where I stood and never pushed boundaries, but I got a lot of things other kids in my position didn't. Blessed, all things considered."

Blessed? My goodness.

Was this what living with Foxes had turned them into—a bunch of trained liars?

"All right, then." Detective Kapinos shuffled his papers. "Ms. Vega, do you think any of the Fox children could've had intent to hurt their father?"

Eli patted her knee. "You don't have to answer that."

"No, it's all right. I will." This time, she wouldn't be stubborn. This was an easy one. "I think they all did. They all had reasons for hating him."

"All four of them?" Detective Sharpe asked in disbelief.

"That's right. They all despised him at one time or another. Who knows what resentment still lingers."

"Why do you say that?" Sharpe asked.

"It was as if Stefan made them compete for his approval, but no one ever seemed to measure up," Marian answered.

Thanksgiving came to mind. The children would have to formally present a charity they wanted Stefan to contribute to. Christian usually won the bid, but every once in a while, Stefan would throw one of the other children a nod, just to get under Christian's skin, it seemed. Or perhaps to keep him humble. Marian thought it borderline child abuse. Especially when Marian overheard some of the remarks he'd made to the losers.

"Why'd you'd pick a homeless shelter charity and expect to win, Jeremy? What do you know about that, walking around here having Ms. Marian do everything from cut your sandwiches to wipe your ass?"

"Little Lucy chooses Literacy Pittsburgh. Are you hoping I'll donate money to your pitiful career choice of writing? I've read your work. Better get used to asking for donations now."

Marian had asked Stefan if the recap was necessary.

"It will make them strong competitors in the game of life," he'd said.

Marian disagreed, just thankful Eli was never allowed to play. The Fox siblings seemed to entertain Eli's company only when they had nothing better to do. The rest of the time, he was assigned chores.

"How did he make them feel like they never measured up?" Sharpe asked.

"Pecking order. You had to understand who they were."

Kapinos stifled a frustrated sigh and rocked back in forth in his chair. But this wasn't just any old family he was asking about, and this wasn't any old town either. "How do you mean?"

Marian leaned back in her chair. "The Foxes are rumored to have descended from the heirs who settled the land, donating a good portion of it to a chapel, hence the name Fox Chapel. Three hundred acres are reserved just for the walking trails and the birds. Good heavens, the birds. The Audubon Society would have your head if you disturbed them."

"Fascinating," Kapinos said. Marian was trying to get the detective to admit he grew up near there too. Not in the borough but close enough. He wouldn't budge, though. "Tell me about pecking order."

Marian continued. "The Foxes consider themselves kings of the castle. They're rooted to the town, and you can't break up their skulk and dissect them one by one. They're all tied together whether they want to be or not."

"How so?" Kapinos asked, confused.

Marian glanced at Eli to see if he had a comment, but he was lost in his phone. Apparently, she was boring him. He'd asked her to say as few condemning things about the Foxes as possible, and she was—in her own way.

Marian grinned at Luke. "Back to the birds. Did I tell you I had chickens on the property when I lived there, Detective?"

"No, you didn't mention it." Kapinos was clearly agitated, rocking faster now. All he needed was a pair of oars.

"Yes, my employers liked farm-to-table cooking, and I enjoyed raising the chickens. Not so much killing them. My husband did that part. But the thing about chickens is that they have a pecking order, you see."

Eli's head snapped up from his phone, his lips parted. She knew he was about to ask her to stop, but the chickens were the best example she had for how the Foxes worked.

"Tell me about that," Sharpe said.

"Once that pecking order is established, strongest to weakest, it can't be disturbed. If it is, it can result in death. The stronger chicken can kill the weakest, peck it to death for stepping out of its spot in the flock's hierarchy," Marian explained.

"That's an interesting way to describe a family," Kapinos commented.

"All families have their fair share of competition," Marian said.

"Was theirs . . . different in any way?" Sharpe asked.

"Nah," she commented. *It sure was, but let them do their own research.*

The year Valerie had won the Thanksgiving charity battle, there was a high school Christmas talent show, and Valerie had signed up to play piano. All the children played. Christian hadn't told anyone he'd signed up, too, but if Marian were to guess, it had been right after Valerie had bested him at the charity competition. Valerie practiced her heart out and played "Dance of the Sugar Plum Fairy" from *The Nutcracker*. She won second place. Christian had learned what song she was playing and studied a much harder one, Liszt's "Piano Concerto No. 1." Christian took first place.

Valerie had been pecked in the artery that day. In a way, Christian had cheated by knowing what his competition was playing, but all that mattered to him was putting Valerie back in her place. Showing her who was more accomplished.

"It's hard to understand what you mean without a specific example," Sharpe said.

Eli finally spoke up. "Mom, I don't think you should say any more."

Both officers sat up straighter in their chairs. "Do you know something you want to tell us about Mr. Fox's case, Ms. Vega?" Sharpe asked. They'd already asked her that in the beginning, and she'd told them no.

Marian gave Eli a stern look, and he leaned back in his own sad, tufted chair and buried his face back in his phone. "I'm saying the Foxes were always testing that pecking order—"

"Mother, as your lawyer—"

"As my son, you need to let me explain this very simple family structure for the officers."

"Fine, then." Eli exhaled.

Marian continued. "They all wanted to be the dominant one. The leader. No one could ever trump Stefan Fox, you see. The biggest cock of all. But you know all about that, don't you, Detective?" Stefan had wanted Kapinos gone from Valerie's life. And boy, did he ever succeed. With Marian's help, of course, but Kapinos wasn't aware of that part.

Kapinos tilted his head in her direction, confused. "Why is that?"

She wouldn't fill in the blanks for him. Remind the detective how he had been eliminated from Valerie's company. Watching him now, a little jumpy, papers everywhere, Marian wasn't sorry. He wasn't right for Valerie. She settled on, "Everyone in town knew that."

"And which one do you think was the dominant one, Ms. Vega? If not Stefan, who'd be next in line?" Sharpe asked.

"That's a trick question," she said.

"How so?" Kapinos asked.

"Because not a one of the Fox siblings would let the others to the front without a fight. You should give up your hunt. They're foxes, after all, and we're all the chickens, ya see. They'll always win."

CHAPTER 7

LUCINDA

Jeremy rode with Valerie, because he and Val were already outside when Christian received the call from the hospital. Lucinda hitched a ride with Christian, because she had no better option. It was the first time she'd been alone with him since she was a kid. She'd never known how to take him. He was just like Father.

"Tell me, what've you been up to in New York?" he asked.

"Please don't act like you actually care." The small buildings and downtown streets here depressed her—Sixth Avenue, Wood Street, Smithfield Street. She missed the bright lights and busyness of home, the sidewalk performers, the vendors, even the stray whistlers on the corner who reminded her she was still alive.

Small cities are where people come to die.

Forget the suburbs—dead and buried.

"I don't. Just making small talk. I do wonder how you survive, though. Restaurant business good?" Christian asked.

At least he admitted he didn't care. "Actually, it is. Good and unending. The city never sleeps, and the people who live there never stop eating."

He chuckled. "Nice. Still writing?"

Lucinda clenched her eyes shut, willing away the email from this morning. If Fritz had said yes, she'd have been able to answer her brother in a way that might actually impress him.

So glad you asked, Christian. One of New York's most prestigious studios has decided to produce and fund my off-Broadway play. He says it's extremely progressive and what people need right now to feel connected.

"I've written a play that has garnered some serious attention in the theater district, but I'm afraid I'll have to produce it myself."

She hadn't aimed to impress Christian, but she knew he thought she'd never amount to anything, that her talent was nonexistent, just another trust-fund baby posing as an artist. When her older siblings and her father would make her feel smaller than she was for loving what she did, she'd turn inward to her writing, journaling and expressing that fury on paper. Even after she'd won a prestigious award for her poetry, Christian hadn't given her much praise. But this play wasn't merely a collection inspired by the wanderings of a sixteen-year-old girl. It was everything she'd learned as an independent woman who'd broken free from an oppressive upbringing. She had created something extraordinary this time.

Christian pulled at the collar of his Brooks Brothers shirt as if loosening an imaginary tie. "Hmm . . . actually, what that means is that no one is interested. Because if they were, they'd be funding the play."

"It's a money issue, not an interest issue," she clarified.

He scrunched his forehead, leaving a large crease. *When did he get so old?* "And I suppose that's what you want to use your share of the Den money for?"

"Yes. Please don't contest the trust. It sounds like a futile effort anyway. You know if Father had a legal document written, he likely made it ironclad. And think of the rest of us. We could *really* use this money."

He huffed. "If you wait and let me look into this other mismanaged account, you might end up with more, Lucy. Your problem is, you've never been patient."

"Some of us don't have the privilege to be patient. I'm busted if I can't get this play up and running."

Christian rolled his hazel eyes. "What's your play even about?" He sounded overly annoyed that she'd been constructive with her time.

"It's called *Love Is Love*. It's a coming-of-age story about an early-twenties girl who finds herself in love with two people, different genders, and the way the world perceives her because of it. And another girl who isn't attracted to either, to anybody, and can't figure out why." Lucinda bonded with people regardless of age or gender, and she'd been made to feel poorly for it when she was younger. She couldn't explain how the attraction happened, only that when it did, it was genuine.

"Psh. I should contest the trust just so you can't make that. Sounds like drivel. Not to mention if Father doesn't survive, he wouldn't approve of using his money for that."

"Christian, I've put everything I've got into this play." Lucinda didn't feel like hiding who she was anymore. She used to say little in the presence of her siblings, but she was no longer afraid of their judgment. Their viewpoints were tight, constrained, so Western Pennsylvanian, it suffocated her. A little understanding wouldn't hurt, though.

"Okay, well, I'm sure it has its merits, but I wouldn't blow the family pot on it. The reason I want to contest the trust is because something doesn't feel right here. I'm curious to see what the police have to say. Father didn't touch drugs. You know that. Did someone drug him?"

Lucinda braced her feet on the floor of the car, sinking deeper into Christian's leather seat. "Does he have enemies?"

Christian shook his head. "Does he have friends, you mean?"

"He has lots of friends . . ." Lucinda paused. "There are always droves of people at his events."

"Those are his clients. He'd been making riskier moves at work with people's investments, getting a little adventurous in his old age. I've questioned him on more than one transaction lately. Was someone so unsatisfied with his services that they spiked his drink?" Christian asked in a nefarious voice.

"This isn't a fucking game of Clue, Christian." Although, if it were, she hoped they didn't determine her as the one holding the poison in the parlor. "If Father doesn't come out of this, don't delay the trust fund. Please. It's pointless. You're being selfish." She was so frustrated, she could scream.

"Ha! Am I? I'm the one who's being selfish? Not you, who decided to get experimental with the waitress at a benefit to honor Mother just to get under Father's conservative skin? This is why your play won't work. You make bad decisions. You just realize your mistakes too late."

She pulled in her shoulders and sank farther into his seat. That one stung. *Which life choice is he referring to?* Lucy didn't think he was talking about the teacher incident but perhaps the aftermath. She'd heard the man's marriage had ended after their affair in a public, brutal divorce. The wife was in an accident of some sort following it, but Lucy couldn't be blamed; she was just a teenager.

She could barely look at Christian as he demeaned her, all haughty and dressed in his overpriced clothes, driving his swanky car, life all put together—just like Father. He was just as greedy too. He thought he could get a bigger payout if he questioned the trust, but Christian couldn't outfox Father. If Father had wanted the trust written a certain way, it would be impossible to change it.

She didn't have time for him to tie up the money for months in legal purgatory while he figured it out. She had a feeling Fritz's offer would expire if she didn't come up with the funds soon. He'd forget all about her—on to the next emerging playwright. He'd believed in her in a way no man had, and she didn't want to disappoint him.

"The rest of us could use a break."

"Okay, but I'm trying to get you to see that maybe your brilliant play isn't so brilliant after all. And that maybe, if you'd let me, I could help you set some of that money aside for investments instead. You might actually be able to retire one day."

"Oh, stop with the 401(k) crap. People like me don't have them. Did you know the guy who wrote *Bird Box* couch surfed for years, searching the return slots of pay phones for coins, camping out at restaurants to eat people's leftover food before he hit it big? Now he can afford any meal he wants, tons of shows under his belt. I want to be that guy."

"That's who you want to be? The girl who eats other people's leftover food?" Christian grumbled. "Movies bring in more than plays. And his premise was about people dying if they opened their eyes outside. It's unique. Yours is about some queer college kids discovering each other with a live audience. It's been done before."

Lucinda strapped her arms over her chest to assuage her wounded pride. How did he have cinematic insight into *Bird Box*? Didn't knowing everything about his own stupid job keep him busy enough? She should be flattered Christian was having a real conversation about her work. He was trying to guide her—in his own manipulative way. It still hurt to hear that her premise was tired. And the fact that he had some solid justification to back up his theories sucked even worse.

"Okay, well, I don't have to use my whole portion of the money on the play, just some of it. You can have a little to set me up a money market account or something else reasonably deadening to my soul. If you just agree not to contest the trust." She could gouge his eyes out right now. Christian was making her doubt herself and her work. If he let her out of the car and drove himself right into oncoming traffic at the moment, she didn't think she'd care. A feeling of hot air washed over her. She could practically see the steel pieces of his Mercedes wrap around his body, pulling at his ligaments as he came apart, searing him the same way he'd scalded her with his negativity and practicality. People like him were bad for her. All he did was shine a light on everything he had and everything she didn't.

"That's not top of mind. First, we need to figure out who put what in Father's system," Christian said, although Lucinda took it as a stalling tactic.

"Who would want to hurt Father?" Lucinda asked. "He's an old man now."

Christian made a crazed expression. "You still want to hurt him, don't you?"

Christian and Lucinda stood on either side of their father's still body. There were tubes sticking out of his mouth and invading the crooks of his arms. Bags of liquid hung at his side, a mask over his face. Tireless threads of red and green and blue lines blipped on an electronic screen above him.

Lucinda drew in a large breath. "Do people think I caused this?" she asked.

"We have to see what the doctor says." Christian's tone was flat, as if he didn't blame her, but he didn't *not* blame her either.

She'd wished her father dead a hundred times before.

And now, there he was, unconscious and barely breathing. It wasn't fair that she felt so much guilt for someone who'd destroyed her when she was younger. The anger and resentment combined with the sadness made for a vile mix of emotions.

Although, if he'd just stop breathing, it'd solve all her problems—just like that. The Den would go into effect, and Christian wouldn't have time to contest it. Looking at Father now, death seemed inevitable. She kind of wished he'd just hurry it along if that was to be his fate.

His long arms were limp at his sides.

Strangely, all Lucinda could think was that she couldn't remember the last time he'd hugged her with them.

"Thirty-four, thirty-five, it's hard to find the right length for his shirts," Mother would complain. She'd always tried to get everything right, while he just sort of existed to tell her when she'd messed up—when all of them had.

Lucinda guessed she'd been very young the last time he'd wrapped those arms around her, before she realized he hated her. She'd arrived into the world late in his life. Father had thought he "was done having little brats running around the house." Lucinda had overheard him say those exact words to the gardener after she'd messed up the shrubs chasing squirrels.

It's funny the things your parents say that you actually remember. She'd been maybe five or six at the time. Father's admission was an awful way to find out she wasn't really wanted.

The truth was, he'd never touched her again after the chemistry teacher had. Lucinda had shamed Father, damaged his image, negatively impacted his business—a sin in their house. He couldn't even look at her afterward. She'd been sent away to the middle of the state, dismissed.

It'd gotten her out of the house sooner, though.

I don't care if you fucking die.

Many times she'd thought it. Prayed for it. She could still feel the venom coursing through her veins from the months that'd followed the court settlement—the hate. Father hadn't wanted a formal trial, because court hearings go on public record. Lucinda had been a pariah until everything was settled. Afterward, she'd become something much worse than a pariah.

They'd made her an expat.

If she couldn't respect the rules in the house, she'd be sent away—and never really welcomed back. Is that what Valerie had wanted when she'd outed her? Valerie had claimed it was what was best for her safety, but her sister had a tricky way of moving the chess pieces to her advantage. Lucinda had wanted out of that house but on her terms.

Valerie and Jeremy rushed into the room. "Parking lot was full," Valerie said, exasperated.

Christian nodded.

Jeremy asked, "Has the doctor been in yet?"

"Not yet," Lucinda said. She continued to stare at her father, confliction gripping her from the inside out. Every time she tried to feel sorrow, anger usurped her emotion.

A man in a white coat with a stethoscope around his neck finally entered. "Hi. You must be the family of Stefan Fox?" he confirmed.

"That's right," Christian answered. "What's this about my father being drugged? The police asked us to come."

"Yes, they're in the waiting room."

"They are?" Lucinda asked. She hated cops. Even when she wasn't guilty, they always made her feel like she was. Too many close misses, she supposed.

"Yes." He eyed Lucinda suspiciously. "I'm Dr. Stephen Faraday, the cardiologist treating your father. I wouldn't say he was drugged, exactly. He may have been poisoned, though. We found an unusually high amount of mercury in his system."

Mercury? Poison in the parlor for sure.

"Mercury? Like what's in thermometers? Could it be environmental?" Christian asked. He immediately started typing things into his phone to investigate.

"It's unlikely the amount found in his system would be naturally occurring. Although, you might want to check and see if there's anything odd or leaking around the house. The reason we don't think it's environmental is because no one else got sick at the party. Well, that we've seen. If you hear of any strange illnesses from anyone who attended, please let the hospital know."

"They're mostly our clients. I'll likely hear about it if they do," Christian said.

Jeremy puffed out his cheeks, clearly annoyed. Lucinda was just shocked that no one had pointed the finger at her yet.

"Could the mercury have built up over time in the house if it *were* environmental? And that's why just Father got sick?" Valerie asked.

Lucinda scratched her head, because these were all smart questions she wouldn't have thought to ask. It didn't mean Christian was right about her play, though. Her siblings always made her feel idiotic. Everything she did or said going forward felt like a test of good judgment since Christian had proclaimed she made terrible decisions.

"Not likely. Mercury often settles in the water. That's why it can build up in seafood and shellfish."

"The bacon-wrapped scallops!" Lucinda offered. "At the party."

"I don't think a few scallops did this, Lucy," Christian said.

"Most likely not," Dr. Faraday confirmed.

"Did the mercury poisoning cause the heart attack? He did have one, right?" Jeremy asked.

"Yes, he did. And we think so. Mercury buildup in the system can affect the heart. Your father was recently placed on medication for high cholesterol. They also detected a cardiac arrhythmia that he opted not to treat. Mercury toxicity can cause a heart attack, especially in patients with cardiac issues such as these."

"I didn't cause the heart attack, then?" Lucinda asked. Everyone ignored her, including the doctor, but she wanted confirmation that she was free and clear from their suspicion.

"Let's talk about recovery. What're his chances? What does mercury do? Are there long-term side effects? Could someone have slipped him the mercury at the party?" Christian asked.

Christian did ask good questions. Although Lucinda suspected his main concern was what he would say to the investors at Fox Wealth.

"Mercury poisoning can cause neuron loss in the cerebellum and throughout the cerebral cortex, which may lead to permanent brain damage. Right now, your father's brain function is low. The other troubling part is the stroke."

Valerie said, "Oh no."

Lucinda wanted to feel bad about this diagnosis, but she was incredibly relieved, because this medical report would keep her off their radar.

She pushed down the other emotion. The one that still longed to find a spot at Father's table. She'd hoped he'd take notice of her once she had success in New York, but it didn't seem she'd have the chance to prove herself to him now.

"We have a toxicologist coming in to determine possible recovery due to the mercury poisoning. I have to admit I've never seen one in the twenty-seven years I've been in practice. To answer your other question, mercury is extremely toxic. It isn't something you can carry around in your pocket. There was a scientist who died working with it in the lab because she had an unknown tear in her hazmat suit, and some had leaked through and attached to her skin. It's that kind of substance."

"Wow." Lucinda placed her hand over her mouth. It all sounded very sci-fi.

"What're you saying? If he comes out of this, he'll be a vegetable?" Christian asked.

"We'll know more once we get the consult from toxicology. We need to run more tests as well."

"A vegetable . . . like Mom," Jeremy whispered.

"Don't you dare call her that!" Valerie backhanded him on the shoulder. Jeremy didn't flinch.

If Father was indeed a goner, it only made sense to take him off life support. If Lucinda was sure he wasn't coming back, she'd suggest it herself. But then she really would be all alone, with Mother getting sicker and Father gone. She could feel the black hole of loneliness spreading all around her. The theater and her friends were all she had left.

Fritz will forget about me in sixty days.

"Here's my card." Dr. Faraday handed it to Christian. *Of course.* "If you have any questions about your father's condition, please have me paged. We'll talk again once the toxicologist has had a chance to perform a complete workup and once we're able to do an MRI. Your father's condition is still marked as critical. In the meantime, the officers are waiting for you outside."

CHAPTER 8

VALERIE

Valerie fidgeted with her purse, the phone charger she'd grabbed for Lucy hanging out and twisting around her fingers.

"Here." She handed it to her. "I'm glad you've been proven innocent," Valerie said, even though she thought it was incredibly rude how Lucy had blurted out her internal thoughts for all to hear.

They say when a traumatic event occurs early in a person's life, they stop maturing at that age. Lucy's was sixteen. Valerie had only been trying to protect Lucy back then by alerting their parents of her promiscuity, but resentment still hung between them like a wet rag.

Lucy snagged the charger from Valerie's hands. "Thank you."

Two officers lingered in the same dreadful waiting room they'd sat in the night before, with its blurry television, plastic chairs, and scratched wooden tables. The cops weren't in uniform, but the badges they had slung around their necks made them easy to identify.

Everything was still fuzzy in Valerie's mind after hearing the prognosis of her father's condition. If the only option was for him to remain in a vegetative state, she wished he could just go quickly so she could properly grieve—collect her trust money and put her life back together. Father would hate to see himself like this, this existence *impassable*. Her emotions were in limbo until they received a definitive prognosis.

And then there was the absolute contempt she held toward Christian, who seemed to be hell-bent on none of them collecting the trust money without a complete audit.

Her rage for Karl and the vase came back in a flash. Greedy men were a sore spot for her at the moment.

If she weren't so angry with her brother, she'd ask him for a loan, but then he'd think the only reason she didn't want him to contest the Den was for her own self-interests. That would only make him dig his heels in deeper. If he found out she was bankrupt, he'd know she was desperate for the money.

And he would do the opposite of what she asked.

Valerie had to remain silent about her home situation, although she was dying to lean on somebody—a light post, anything. She'd always been the shoulder for everyone else to cry on, but now that she needed support, it was nowhere to be found.

She was about to push Christian about not contesting the trust, but then her vision zeroed in on the male cop, and her heart did a two-step. *Oh my God.* "Luke?" she bumbled.

Inhale. She blinked to make sure it was him. It'd been nearly twenty years since she'd seen him up close. He looked just the same—handsome, wavy black hair curling around his ears, olive complexion, piercing black-brown eyes. *Exhale.*

She'd spied on him and his lovely wife and kids when she'd come across them a couple of times in public—once at a Pirates game and another at Beechwood Farms. It was still hard to look at him after all that had transpired between them. Marian had made her come to her senses and realize what was best, back then. Seeing him still made her feel vulnerable, though—remembering how she'd loved him in that unguarded way that seemed possible only before adulthood. It was the only time Valerie had ended a relationship and wondered later if she'd made a mistake.

"Hey, Val, I'm sorry about your dad. I've been assigned to his case because of the mercury poisoning. I'm in the homicide division now." He held up his badge, sympathy laced in his words. His voice was as gentle as she remembered. If he still begrudged her in any way, he was good at hiding it.

"Homicide?" she said, aghast. They really thought Father had been targeted.

"Oh, great. Captain Casanova," Jeremy said. He cackled in a way that made Valerie want to kick him in the balls. Luke may have just been a summer fling, but the memories they'd made together were lasting. The two of them had gone away for the weekend to Ohiopyle, the rocky campground with the roaring river where she still couldn't believe he'd talked her into white water rafting. Every time she saw Luke, that same thrill of dropping with the rapids returned.

"Jeremy. Christian, how do you do?" Luke nodded at them.

"Fine, thanks." Christian bobbed his head in acknowledgment.

"This is Detective Sharpe," Luke said, introducing the female officer standing up straight and tall next to him. She pursed her lips at them as if she were already displeased. *Yes, Detective Sharpe, my brothers are assholes; you're correct in your initial assessment.*

"Who is this guy?" Lucy asked, pointing at Luke.

She'd been too young, only six or seven, to really remember Luke and all the events of the fateful summer Valerie had decided to slum it with the country club caddie. He'd meant more to her than that, but her family hadn't cared to take their relationship seriously, so Valerie had tried not to either, even though she'd wanted to.

"Old friend from the golf course. He used to carry Pritchard's clubs," Valerie said.

Luke made a face as though he'd been impaled by her introduction. Clearly, he'd expected more.

"Richard Pritchard? Father's golfing nemesis? That must've been a treat," Lucy said, which told Valerie the two men had still been at battle on the greens long after Valerie had graduated high school.

"Dick Prick," Jeremy added.

"Jeremy," Valerie scolded.

"I never called him that." Luke shook his head.

Detective Sharpe took out her notepad, unamused. "Okay, now that we're done with the reunion . . . we're wondering if each of you can tell us where you were during the party when your father had his episode. Did you notice anything strange? Anyone hanging around him who seemed out of place?"

"Start with Lucy. Ask her where she was." Jeremy laughed.

They all turned toward Lucy.

"I was preoccupied with the waitress behind the stage when they pulled the curtain. When Father saw me, he collapsed." Lucy shifted her body away from all the eyeballs leering at her and chewed on her fingers. They'd all suffered more than they were letting on from Father's attack, Lucy included.

Detective Sharpe stopped writing mid–pen stroke, inhaled, and then kept going. "See anything out of the ordinary in regard to your father before he fell to the ground?"

"No," Lucy said.

"When you spoke to him, did he seem out of sorts?" she asked. "Like, was he struggling in any way, health-wise?"

"I actually never spoke to him the entire night. I typically keep my distance at these events," Lucy answered.

Detective Sharpe's shrewd eyes darted up from her paper. "So you never came into contact with him at all?"

Lucy shook her head, her messy bun bouncing around. "Not once."

Sharpe seemed satisfied and addressed the rest of them. "Same questions."

Christian answered next. "Jeremy and my wife and I were near Father at the event most of the evening. I didn't see anything strange. Just his usual clients, mingling."

"That's right. I have nothing to add. It was all superficial chitchat. Nothing remarkable," Jeremy said.

"And you . . ." Detective Sharpe turned to Valerie, searching for her name.

"Valerie," Luke answered for her.

"Oh, that's right, you two know each other." Detective Sharpe's voice dripped with sarcasm. Valerie imagined a painful car ride back to the station for Luke. "Valerie, then? Anything on your end?"

"I actually didn't get a chance to talk to him either. He asked me to grab his pills right before the event started, and I did. But that's the last I spoke with him." Every time she recalled the evening, all she could remember was Father's towering body crashing to the ground, Mother staring ahead dazedly, unaware. Valerie knew she'd somehow ended up in the ambulance but couldn't remember the moments in between, only the way she'd trembled as the sirens blared.

"Which medication did you bring him?" Sharpe asked.

"Both his blood pressure and cholesterol meds. He usually takes them after dinner, but he didn't want to forget with the party."

Christian gave her a puzzling look but didn't offer a comment.

"Well, as you're aware, this case has been marked suspicious. We'll be interviewing the catering staff, the help at the house, everyone who worked the party, and possibly some of your clients, Mr. Fox." Luke directed his attention to Christian.

"Absolutely. Do what you need to do," he said.

"Lucy, I'll need the name and contact info for the waitress you were with last night, if you have it," Sharpe said.

Lucy eyed her phone charging against the wall. "As soon as I can get it to you, it's yours. Her name is Aja."

"Okay, thank you. We'll undoubtedly have more questions as the investigation moves forward. Please let us know if you hear of anything that could help the case. In the meantime, we'll be on our way. Here's my card." Luke gave one to each of them. When his hand touched Valerie's, his fingers remained grasped to hers for a beat. Did he not want to let go? They never did get a proper goodbye. It was strange being thrust back into his orbit again, and at this precise moment.

He's married, her subconscious screamed. *Hands off.*

He shot her a concerned look. "We'll see what we can find out, Val."

"Thank you." She watched him walk away, remembering the last time they'd parted. She'd asked him not to call her again, and she knew he'd listen. It had been awful, Luke on his knees, crying, tears streaming down his face. She'd climbed in the town car afterward and had Marian speed away, kicking up stones behind them.

She'd thought about that moment on more than one occasion, especially since her divorce. There were few men in her life who'd cried in front of her, but he'd been the only one who'd ever cried *for* her.

"Was he your boyfriend or something?" Lucy asked.

"Or something," Valerie replied. He wasn't allowed to be her boyfriend. He was from O'Hara, not the borough, and according to Father, he wasn't rich enough, educated enough, or white enough—Luke being Greek. His family owned a chain of restaurants that did quite well, but Stefan Fox wouldn't have his daughter running around with "the gyro maker's son. The caddie, for God's sake. He's starting out in life carrying clubs. He'll never be a 'player.'"

Ugh. She did hate Father's little jests. He thought he was so clever. Valerie wondered if Luke's former animosity for her family would impact his investigation.

"You're still gawking after him," Jeremy mused. "Why don't you run through the halls in the wretched hospital lighting, straddle-jump him, and tell him how much you still care for him like a bad episode of *ER*."

"Will you cut it out?" She cracked him on the shoulder again. He could be so damn annoying. As she did, she caught sight of his dilated pupils. *I knew it.*

"We need to have someone come into the house and test it for metals." Christian was focused on his phone, no doubt already in problem-solving mode. Valerie thought his concern was more about Father's business than Father himself. Valerie knew it was urgent that Christian get a press release out to his clients, but they didn't have all the information yet, and the delay was probably driving him crazy.

"Do you think it's environmental?" Valerie asked.

"I don't know what to think," he said, frustrated. "But I do know I'm officially contesting that trust now. Something is not right here."

Jeremy lost his smile quickly. "What if the rest of us don't agree? Don't you need all of us to contest it?"

"No, I don't. As a matter of fact, I could have it tied up for months while I get a forensic accountant to come in and dissect that miscellaneous five-million-dollar charity, dollar by dollar."

Jeremy's temper flared, and he charged Christian. "You don't care about anyone but yourself." He shoved Christian in the chest. Christian grabbed his wrists and then hit him back, swatting at his face, and then landed a solid blow on his shoulder.

"Stop this! You're acting like children." Valerie positioned herself between them. They continued to try to jab around her. "Quit it! Someone's going to call security."

There was clapping behind them, and they all turned around to find Eli Vega standing there dressed in a business suit. "Just like the old days, eh?"

"Why're you here?" Lucy asked. She was seated on a chair next to her charging phone watching her older siblings' quarrel as though it were a form of entertainment.

"My mother sent me to check on Stefan," he said, nonplussed, hands in his pockets like he'd rather be anywhere else but there.

83

"Couldn't you have just called?" Christian asked.

"Don't look so happy to see me. I did call. But I couldn't get much from the nurses' desk other than, 'he's listed in critical condition.'"

Valerie narrowed her eyes at him. The way he spoke of Father's health status made it clear he had no idea how serious it really was. "He had a heart attack and a stroke, Eli. He isn't doing well. He also has mercury poisoning that seems to have precipitated his attack."

"It wasn't my fault," Lucy clarified.

"Oh . . . yes, quite a performance, Lucy," Eli offered. "Sorry about his condition. Now, what's this about forensics? Stefan is still alive, right?" He looked quite confused.

"Yes." Christian sighed impatiently. "If Father doesn't come to, we have financial things to figure out. A forensic accountant. Not your concern."

"Oh, right." Eli bared his brilliant white teeth. They'd been crooked as a child, and Mother had insisted on paying for his braces. Eli was such an odd fixture in their lives. He'd arrived when Valerie was in high school, but Jeremy and especially Lucy had sort of grown up with him.

"How's my mother?" Valerie asked.

"I haven't visited this week, but my mother said Simone is rattled from the party," Eli answered.

"Oh no." Valerie's heart sank. She had to get over there. She'd been meaning to; there'd just been a barrage of distractions.

"We're having the house tested for mercury," Christian informed him. "Did you see anything strange last night, Eli?"

"No. It was another beautiful night at the Foxes'." He offered a tight grin.

"How's law school, Eli?" Valerie asked. She knew his upbringing with them hadn't been easy. He'd lost his father before he was born and was left having to put up with theirs. Father had treated Eli like an extension of Marian. It was confusing, because Marian was a paid member of the staff. Eli was not, but he'd received benefits in exchange for . . . his child labor? It all seemed perverse now when Valerie looked back. Her biggest offense had been handing him her coat when she'd returned home from college break. She'd thought it cute—Eli the little butler. Maybe he hadn't.

Eli stood up taller. All five feet ten of him. "I've been practicing for two years now, Val."

She waved at him. "My mistake. It's hard to keep up."

He rocked uneasily on his heels. "Still cutting my teeth but doing well. Thanks."

"You'll get there, brother," Jeremy said.

Eli's lip twitched. Valerie suspected he hadn't cared for Jeremy's facetious term of endearment.

Christian snickered. "Ask Jeremy—he'll give you all the tips for how to skyrocket to the top."

"Yes . . . ," Eli said and then whistled through his teeth. Valerie could taste the tension in the air, foul and bitter. "Well, I'm going to check in with the nurses. I can give my mother a formal report that way. She wants it to inform your mother in case she asks. That's why I'm here."

Christian sighed. *And he'd better not say a damn thing about Mother.*

"Thank you," Valerie offered. Mother was allowed to feel discomfort even if she didn't know why. And Marian was allowed to comfort her, for that matter.

"Let me know if you find anything at the house. I wish Stefan a speedy recovery," Eli said. Although Valerie thought he'd attended the charity event only out of respect for their mother, who had treated him as one of her own, and that's where his loyalty to their family ended.

"I need a smoke. Can anyone give me a ride home? Val gave me one here." Jeremy shot Valerie a pleading glance. Jeremy might murder Christian if he rode home with him. And Valerie understood why. She wanted to murder him too.

"I actually need a ride to *the* house. My overnight bag is still there," Lucy said. She tugged on the hem of her leather dress. Valerie couldn't imagine how uncomfortable she must be.

"Okay, I'll give you both a ride. Go outside and smoke, Jeremy. I'll meet you there. I need to check in with Karl and let him know that I might be late to get Isla."

"Okay." Jeremy made for the door, shouldering Christian on the way out. "I'm contesting *your* bullshit," he said. "You aren't the one in charge."

"Touch me again, Jeremy, and it will be the last time," Christian threatened. He was red-faced, and Valerie smelled a brawl, like the kind they used to get into when they were younger, jumping on each other, punching and kicking relentlessly until Father eventually came between them.

Jeremy just threw his hand up, dismissively, waving his cigarette pack in the air. Valerie never got a chance to talk to him about the drugs, although she could put that lecture on pause, since it didn't look like there'd be money to collect anytime soon.

Damn you, Christian. My daughter is going to lose everything! She'll blame me, and I'll never get her trust back.

He was really screwing everyone involved. If there was some way just to veto him or move him out of the way, that would be ideal. Could Christian really even contest the trust?

As she waited for Lucy to gather her things, Valerie texted Karl, indicating she'd be delayed, and he texted right back—no problem. It was difficult, because Karl had been a good husband until he was a bad one, and a great father.

When Isla had gone through her mermaid phase—naturally—it'd been Karl who'd carved a life-size mermaid out of wood and hung it above her bed, complete with aquatic wave border. Karl wasn't brawny, although he was handy, and great with a wet saw. But he'd messed up— big-time. And he couldn't design his way out of this one.

Karl was staying at his parents' home in Edgewood for the time being. Valerie dreaded explaining to Isla how he'd broken the law. Isla was such a sensitive girl. Ever since she'd turned into a tween, the hormones and crying jags were unimaginable.

How would she react when Valerie told her Daddy was going to prison and had drained all their money and that they might lose their house, too, because her uncle was a selfish asshole?

Karl's investigation was still pending, but she suspected they'd eventually arrest him. She just had to make sure the dreaded conversation with Isla happened before that, because Isla would never forgive her for keeping the secret about her dad. Valerie had agreed with Karl to hold off for as long as possible, but it was time.

"Ready?" Valerie asked. Lucy was scrolling mindlessly through her phone, completely washed out, like she'd seen a ghost.

"Uh-huh," Lucy said.

Valerie could see Christian around the corner on a call. "Christian, we're going." He didn't turn her way, only offering her a thumbs-up. "Something wrong?" Valerie asked Lucy.

Lucy didn't answer right away. "Do you mind if I make a quick phone call?"

"Okay, but make it snappy. I really do need to get home."

Lucy nodded and ducked around the corner. Valerie walked over to her father's room again and watched through the window as the respirator helped him breathe. It was hard, yet not as hard as it should be, which somehow made it harder. He'd been such a powerhouse of a man reduced to nothing, but who had he really been to her before that? Her love for him had been obligatory up until this point, she now realized.

For so long, Valerie's little unit of three—Karl, Isla, and herself—had been enough of a family for her. The family she'd come from was based on meeting expectations, but the Merrick household had been held together with nothing but love. Now that united front was torn apart, and she wondered where it had all gone wrong. Her marriage. Her family. Why she didn't have siblings who were loving and caring.

And when she searched for the answer, really dissected her own dysfunctions, it boiled down to one simple answer—it was because of *him*.

Mother had really tried, at least when they were kids. But Father had still somehow damaged them all, set up an example for cursed relationships, made them hate one another, vie for his love even though he had none to give. On the rare occasion when Father did demonstrate any affection, there was really only one child viewed worthy of it—Christian.

Father hadn't approved of Luke. Maybe she wouldn't have ended up with Karl if he had. She had many grievances for a man who practically lay on his deathbed. Although it seemed that someone else had even more issues with him. Enough to poison the man.

Valerie couldn't watch her father die anymore.

She let out a huff and rounded the corner to find Lucy shouting into her phone and yanking on her bun. "Can you ask him to extend it? How can they evict me? I'm only one month behind . . . okay, maybe two," she whisper-screamed. "No. No, the play didn't come through. I have a shift tonight, though. He threw out my stuff? He locked me out? *Fuck*."

Oh boy. Lucy's evicted.

"Yeah, yeah, as soon as I work my shift."

Lucy caught sight of Valerie watching her. "I've got to go," she said. "Please hold my stuff for me until I get back." She ended her call.

"You know I'd normally let you stay with me, Lucy, but I have a shitstorm at home right now." Lucy couldn't be there tonight when she dropped the Daddy's-probably-going-to-prison bomb on Isla. That was to be a private explosion.

"I don't want to stay with you," Lucy said, but she sounded unsure. "Your house has bad vibes. It's like a robot mated with Frank Lloyd Wright or something. It freaks me out."

"Thanks." Karl had designed their home, which she loved and didn't want to part with. It was inspired by Frank Lloyd Wright's architectural masterpiece Fallingwater, built in 1939 although still considered modern, with its concrete ledges, stone facade, and large glass windows. Ironically, she'd visited it for the first time with Luke while camping in the area near Ohiopyle. Wright's Fallingwater was a local treasure, a work of art built for the Kaufmann family, of the old Pittsburgh Kaufmann's department store, but Lucy still managed to trash it somehow.

Lucy trashed everything. Valerie wanted to believe her sister was just a hurt little kid inside who acted out because she felt like she didn't belong, but Valerie had bigger problems to contend with right now. She had to mother her own daughter first.

"I thought you wanted to go shopping on Walnut Street." Lucy ripped her phone charger out of the wall.

"You can stay maybe in a day or two, but I've got some serious family problems to deal with. I can't have you at my house right now."

"That's fine. I'll figure it out," Lucy said.

Valerie sighed. "Let's go." As they walked to the elevator, Valerie was overwhelmed by her younger sister's unpleasant scent. "Why don't you take advantage of the shower when we make it to the house before you find your next landing spot?"

"You're such a bitch. And I was planning on it if Marvin lets me."

"I'm trying to help you out. If you're going to persuade someone to let you stay on their couch, it might go smoother after a bath. I've heard Marv has settled down." Marvin was Father's latest butler, a stickler for Father's rules, one of which was: the children were not to use the showers in the main house.

Christian breezed by the three of them. "See you all later. In a room where legal papers will be changed and filed."

Valerie shot him a dirty look.

Christian ignored her and kept walking, right into a waiting elevator. He pushed a button and waved at them like a dick.

"Ugh. I really hate him," Lucy said. Valerie concurred.

When they reached Jeremy, he was sweaty and rubbing his nicotine-stained fingers on his pants again, a smear of black ash extending from his wrist to his elbow. He was shaking and sweating as if he'd just been lifting boxes in a warehouse.

"Hey, you all right?" She placed her hand on Jeremy's shoulder, but he brushed it off.

"Fine, just ready to get out of the hospital. You know I don't like them," he said.

Jeremy didn't care for anything that involved emotional confrontation. She wondered how he acted with Daphne, and if their relationship was healthy.

"Okay, well, let's go home, then," Valerie said. As she said the words, she could see Christian tearing out of the parking lot. *In a hurry to screw us over . . .*

They both shot her a wry smile, because even though she was dropping Jeremy off first, it'd been an eternity since Valerie had said those words and had meant the Fox residence.

CHAPTER 9

MARIAN

Eli spoke frantically as he tried to describe to Marian what he was witnessing.

"There's a lot of smoke. It looks really bad, Mother. I tried . . . I tried to pull over." He sounded breathless. Marian stumbled as she walked over and opened the window. She could hear the emergency sirens.

"Do you need me to come there?" She didn't know what else to say or do. Her son was panicking, and he rarely did.

"No. Do not leave!"

"Okay." Didn't have to twist her arm. "But, Eli. Can you see how bad it is? Is Christian going to be all right?"

Eli breathed heavily into the phone. "Mother, Christian's Mercedes was crinkled up like a tin can on the northbound side. Of 28."

"Oh no." That road was like the little autobahn of Pittsburgh, the only direct route to downtown from the east side without crossing a bridge, making it heavily traveled and one of the most hazardous roadways in the area.

"I don't know how he could've wrecked so horribly. I don't understand how it even happened," Eli said.

Marian understood.

It had happened again, just as she'd suspected it might. Stefan falling to the ground at the charity ball had just been the beginning.

The first domino clacked down, bringing the next along with it.

Stefan had finally been taken out, and the pecking order had ensued. Christian was next in line for the Fox Wealth Management throne, after all. She had a feeling there wouldn't be any Foxes left when this was all over. These "accidents" were the result of something that had been brewing in that household for a very long time. Marian had tried to tip off the police. It wasn't her fault they hadn't listened. Maybe they would after this.

"What's happening now?" Marian asked, but she didn't really want to know the answer.

"I don't think he's walking away from this one." Eli sounded distraught. "Mother, there . . . are flames." His voice stretched out in shock.

She'd assumed as much when he'd said smoke. The common phrase "where there's smoke, there's fire" came to mind, but logic was lost on her son at the moment. Poor Eli. Now Marian was really worried.

"That's awful," Marian said. "Are there ambulances? On the scene?"

"Yes, many emergency vehicles."

"Well, maybe they got him out in time. An injury or two might even make him humbler," she added, although it seemed unlikely.

"Mother. The accident was *very bad*," Eli stressed.

They'd made it all this time without a death in the family. She'd always feared Eli had suffered in the absence of Hector. She couldn't protect him from the tragedies of life forever, though, she realized. At least he hadn't witnessed his father's death. Time marched on. People died.

She didn't want to hear this sad news, though. She was attached to every single one of those children, even though she didn't like to admit it. "Airbags are amazing these days. How fast could he have been going on 28? It's a congested roadway. I've not been able to go over twenty miles an hour this time of day." Although she rarely ventured in and out of the city during rush hour. All the roads leading to downtown eventually bottlenecked into bridges and tunnels, and it happened so quickly that if you weren't in the correct lane, you'd get booted in the wrong direction, making it impossible to turn around.

"It looked like Christian's car had slammed into the back of a box truck. None of the other vehicles were in terrible shape," Eli said.

"Sounds like reckless driving, which doesn't sound like Christian at all." Christian must've been really out of sorts over Stefan. He rarely lost his cool, his father's little soldier.

"He'd probably just come from the hospital. Everyone was upset. They're investigating Stefan's heart attack and stroke. There was mercury in his system."

"Someone tried to poison the old goat?" She hid the amusement bubbling to the surface. "How does one poison someone with mercury?"

"I actually looked into prior cases at the office on our legal database and couldn't find much for that type of poisoning. I didn't have time to do more research. I planned on doing it later. They think it could've happened at the party."

"I'm glad I didn't get an invite this year." A lie, of course. She missed the hubbub, the details of prepping for a Simone Fox party— the glorious food, the chatter of the upper class. She still yearned to be in the mix. "Well, you be careful on your way home. Please keep me informed on Christian's condition. You don't have to do a house call like with Stefan. I just couldn't get much when I called the hospital." She inhaled deeply. *How can I tell Simone about this? First her husband, then her firstborn?*

"I know. That's what I told the Fox kids regarding my visit to see Stefan, but I said I was the one who'd called. All right, Mom, Giselle is waiting for me with cold dinner."

"Why're you at the office this late anyway?" she asked.

"I'm working on a medical research contract that I really need to come through."

Eli would never know how much she'd sacrificed so he could have these opportunities. "Don't work too hard. Bye, E. Love you."

"Love you too. Goodbye, Mother."

She hadn't wanted to send Eli into the Foxes' lair to investigate, but she'd seen no other option. Stefan wouldn't want her there. Still, to this day, Marian felt as though she had to hide the complicated relationship she and Eli shared with the Foxes—like a family, but not really. Marian and Eli were protective of each other. Until Giselle had entered the picture, Marian was all Eli really had. He'd been acting a little shady since they'd gotten engaged, distancing himself from Marian. She supposed it was natural.

If Simone were her old self, she'd tell Marian, *"Petit a petit, l'oiseau fait son nid"—little by little, the bird makes its nest.*

Marian had picked up some favorite French phrases from Simone, and this was one of them. She imagined Simone telling her to let Eli go so he could build his new life with his fiancée. It would be sound advice coming from Simone, a woman she considered a coparent to all the children.

Only Marian and Simone shared the intimacy that came with coaching kids through potty training, riding a bike, first heartbreaks, the messy stuff.

She and Simone were the ones in the stands when Christian had hit his first homerun, Valerie was awarded her first equestrian blue ribbon, Jeremy's team made it to States in lacrosse, Lucy was appointed the first teenage poet laureate of Pittsburgh for her *Burgeoning Bridges* anthology—an ode to the 446 bridges in Pittsburgh and the people they are named after.

Stefan had craved that same closeness with Simone but hadn't wanted to do any of the work to achieve it.

Marian had been there, though. And Eli had been there too. It had to count for something.

Stefan would return from work grumpy and agitated. "Must be nice to sun yourself in the stands all day while I'm grinding away at work. Good job, (insert child's name)." With each passing year, Marian could feel his resentment building.

Hector had cautioned her not to get too close to the Foxes. To "understand your place." And then near the end of his life, Hector had flat-out told her the relationship she shared with Simone was unhealthy. They were "friends," but Simone had no problem barking orders at Marian when it was time to get to work.

Marian defended herself, flipping through the tabloids, showing her husband that nannies of celebrities were integral to family function, especially large families. Her husband had responded by saying he'd never seen a paparazzi photo where the celebrity was pictured drinking cocktails with their nanny. And for that comment, Marian had no response. It was something she and Simone did often.

She could feel that her presence was an underlying problem in Simone and Stefan's marriage, one she tried not to make worse, only doing her job.

Stefan would sometimes talk to Marian about the children in lonely little snippets. "I noticed the school report about Jeremy and his social/emotional spectrum. What in the hell is wrong with him? Simone said she'll take care of it. What's your take?"

"I think Jeremy will be okay, but he's showing some emotional processing difficulties. It just means he has thoughts and feelings that he sometimes has a hard time expressing," Marian had said.

"Sounds like he just needs to toughen up a little. These kids had everything handed to them. It's made them soft," Stefan had said.

Marian had kept her lips pressed firmly together. Even though there was some truth to that, Jeremy had issues beyond silver-spoon syndrome.

He was prone to temper tantrums and impulsivity. Simone had wanted to take him to a counselor, but Stefan had refused. "Imagine if someone found out my kid needs a shrink?" Ironically, when the court ordered that Lucy see a child psychologist after her indiscretion with the teacher, Stefan hadn't balked. It was probably because it would look bad if he didn't comply. Marian hadn't agreed with Simone's approach of tackling Jeremy's issues herself but . . . not her child.

"Will it affect him later in life?" Stefan had asked. "Will he outgrow it?" He had been concerned about his children but didn't know how to relate to them. Perhaps his emotional processor was broken too.

"They learn to adapt, yes. Sometimes you have to identify their triggers and make accommodations." Marian had finished her task of putting away the linens.

Stefan had moved toward her. "Please keep me updated. Simone doesn't talk to me about these things."

"I will." She'd stared into his dark eyes, and there was true anguish there. He was a man who desperately wanted to bond with his family, his wife, but didn't know how. He wasn't all bad—just domestically disjointed.

He'd patted her arm. "We appreciate you, Mari."

CHAPTER 10

LUCINDA

After dropping off Jeremy, Lucinda and Valerie pulled up the long driveway leading to the Fox residence, one of the massive homes on Old Mill Road. Like many houses in the area, theirs included a guesthouse that had once been a different structure. Their guesthouse had embodied the former personality of a barn.

"You can't pay for the kind of character old manors and chateaus offer." Mother liked to compare their grounds to an exclusive French estate.

The secluded property had always appeared hulking and dismal to Lucinda. Today brought on a whole new kind of gloom.

Strangers rushed in and out of her childhood home dressed in jumpsuits and masks. Their bright white suits made the alabaster patches in between the half-timber framing of the Tudor-style home appear dingy in comparison. Not to mention the extra splotches of moss and funk that had built up in the corners—added mucus to the infection that had started in the house and had spread outside.

First, their mother, losing her mind. Next, their father with his failing heart.

Did he let the house go a bit since Mom moved out?

"What's going on?" Valerie said, throwing her car in park. Lucinda remained sitting, staring at the surreal scene. A lot had transpired in the last twenty-four hours, and she wasn't sure she wanted any more uncovered.

"Lucy, let's go! They might've found something." Valerie yanked her out of the car, then pulled her along like she used to when she was little. It irked Lucinda, but she followed Valerie anyway, because she wasn't sure what else to do.

"Should we be wearing one of those?" Lucinda pointed at a man in a hazmat suit. There was a woman on the front steps holding a plastic bag that likely contained evidence. She'd apparently been inside but wasn't wearing a rubbery suit.

"I don't think so. The police don't have them on," Valerie said, referencing the people in plainclothes and navy-blue uniforms.

Lucinda was being dragged up the front steps before she had a chance to protest. Valerie was in a hurry, her obvious concern for her father trumping her logic. Lucinda didn't have those same concerns. All she could focus on was the flashing lights and police cars. Fear and threat were strung around the house like an ugly wreath.

Lucinda planted her feet on the front porch. "Maybe I'll just wait out here."

Valerie glared at her. "I'm pretty sure that whatever is festering on your body is more toxic than what's in that house."

"Not funny. Look at their protective gear, Val. Are there poisons in there?"

Valerie shook her head. "Just a precaution, I'm sure." She grabbed Lucinda's hand again, forcing her through the front door. Lucinda was hesitant as her heels clacked on the marble floor in the foyer.

"See, the police don't have on suits." Valerie pointed to where her ex-boyfriend stood in the kitchen. Lucinda's only knowledge of her sister's love life prior to today had been her husband, Karl, a conservative dolt who'd never made eye contact when he spoke to her. Lucinda had many questions about this old flame of Valerie's, none of which her sister would answer on the car ride there. Valerie had been good at keeping secrets when she'd wanted to. Her relationship with Luke seemed like one more. *What is she hiding?*

"Go take a shower before Marv tries to stop you," Valerie said.

"Right." She did need to move quickly if she wanted to bathe.

Marv was like Father's little watchdog. He didn't hesitate to bite, his unbridled joy evident when he caught them overstepping their ridiculous occupancy boundaries. When they stayed overnight, it was in the guesthouse, but Lucinda didn't want to rely on the fact that there'd be ample supplies. Last time there'd been no towels.

She darted up the stairwell, itching to get her damn dress off. Mr. Piedmont's eyes had lingered on her barely there cleavage this morning, which made her feel dirtier than anything else. It seemed he had as much affinity for young women as he did old cars. A bit of a perv if you asked her.

As much as she'd wanted to collect on the trust money and return home, the actors in this place were not to be trusted. She reminded herself that her true family, those who supported her, were in New York. Aster had even bragged on Lucinda's writing at her own Broadway audition. With limited minutes to spare, that was ballsy. Lucinda had only heard about it from Thea, a fellow writer who frequently swapped pages with Lucinda for feedback. Creative friendships were different, welded together with dreams, passion, and grit.

As Lucinda ran the water, she thought about her father's poisoning as if it were a play. It's how her mind worked sometimes to untangle life's mysteries. Perhaps it would help her to better understand this one.

Poisoning?

It all seemed theatrical, impossibly Elizabethan, out of time. It was like she'd stumbled into the end of a *Romeo and Juliet* spin-off—mercury, instead of nightshade, attempted murder born of hatred instead of forbidden love.

Act 1
Scene 1:

The charity ball begins in honor of a sick woman who sits in the corner. The main lights are flipped on. A regal STEFAN FOX walks into the room to greet his guests, mostly clients at his financial firm.

STEFAN: Thank you for your contribution.

An inquisitive, dark-haired waitress talks to a distressed female guest in a black leather dress . . .

Lucinda stripped out of her outfit that had begun to feel like plastic casing and climbed into the shower. She hurriedly applied some salon-grade shampoo into her palm, because her father was a metrosexual and only bought the good stuff to lather his full head of dark hair. He'd lose his mind if anyone dared call him anything other than heterosexual. Father had blamed her sexual exploits on rebellion, but maybe she wouldn't have pushed back if he could've somehow managed to be a decent human, one who wasn't a homophobe, preferably.

As she massaged the shampoo through her hair, she'd decided the offensive odor Valerie had been complaining about all day was indeed vomit.

Not that Lucinda would own up to it.

Back to her script.

She rinsed out her hair and thought about the first act. The entire premise of the show, the true conflict, must always be presented in the first act. The motivation for violence in every production she'd ever worked on was the result of one of three things: love, money, or power.

There wasn't any love in the room at the charity event, that was for sure. Except maybe the brief moment she'd shared with Aja.

At seventy-two years old, Stefan Fox had already amassed all the money a man could desire, but someone else could've been aggrieved at him for how he'd handled theirs, as Christian had suggested earlier.

If this were a play, Lucinda was going with *money* for the motive. Power and money were tied together in this case. She'd used her writing life to assess her real life before, and she'd been surprisingly accurate most of the time.

After thoroughly soaping up her body, Lucinda let the water scald off the dirt. As she toweled off, she listened for pounding on the other side of the bathroom door and was elated to find that she'd gone unnoticed by Marv.

She was safe—for now.

She found the hair dryer and got to work, thinking about the speed of how everything had occurred last night. It was the nature of how emergencies happened, she supposed. Her parents were growing older, and she knew she'd most likely lose them sooner than most women her age.

Still, she wasn't ready for her mother to pass away yet. She'd meant to visit her while she was home, but it didn't look like she'd get the chance. As the baby of the family, she'd had the most one-on-one time with her mother. Lucinda missed her dearly, but what was left of her was in pieces. She'd protect Lucinda right now if the others were after her, though.

If a scapegoat were required for Father's poisoning, and the other Foxes had to pick one sibling to take down, it'd be her. It was another reason Lucinda didn't come home often, a foreboding feeling that if she stayed too long, her family would be her end—either physically or mentally. Christian had already gotten her to doubt her own play today. She'd hated him in that moment, vitriol pulsing through her veins like she'd never felt for another human.

It's what her family did to her self-worth that was most damaging. How Christian had made her question a project that she held close to her heart. She'd confided in him for the first time in years about what she was working on, and he'd just shat all over it.

Nope. She wouldn't put false imprisonment beyond a one of them.

They clearly hated her. Always the baby, she'd received the most attention, and they'd been eager to steal it back from her at every opportunity. Like when Father had made them play those stupid games. You'd think they'd let little Lucinda win once—fat chance.

Lucinda grabbed her overnight bag and slipped on her skinny jeans and her bohemian-style blouse. She put on a fresh coat of makeup and braided two of the front pieces of her hair, then pulled them away from her face. It was long, thin, and angular like her mother's. Aster often told her she was "lost in your hair."

When she walked down the stairs, Lucinda found her sister in an intense discussion with Detective Kapinos, or as Valerie playfully referred to him, "Luke." They were standing around open trash bags, and the men in weird suits and masks were meandering around like strange little astronauts. As Lucinda tried to enter the room, Luke held up his hand. "This is a crime scene investigation; neither of you should be here."

That must've been what they were squabbling about. Luke wanted her out, and Valerie was being her demanding self.

"Is it safe, though?" Lucinda held her breath. "To even be in here?" She'd partied in old warehouses that'd been previously condemned for asbestos, but for some reason, this situation bothered her more.

"You're fine to breathe the air," Luke said. "You just can't come in the kitchen."

Lucinda found this comment interesting, considering Valerie was standing in the kitchen. Right next to Luke, arms crossed at her chest. Had Valerie already toed the threshold for contamination, or was Dashing Detective Luke giving her special attention? The hazmat men were bagging boxes of smelly cardboard they'd plucked straight from the trash. Marvin likely hadn't bothered Lucinda because he'd been busy standing around the trash bags in the kitchen with a worried expression on his face.

"What is all that?" Lucinda asked. "Garbage from the party?"

Valerie exited the kitchen and grabbed her elbow. She shoved her into the dining room, and Lucy really wished she'd stop forcefully touching her. She'd have to talk to her sister about personal boundaries once they left there.

"What?" Lucinda asked. The dining room had always wigged her out. It was too dark with deep cherry-stained wainscoting from floor to ceiling and portraits of England, Germany, and France on the walls to represent their parents' heritage.

Good Lord was it stuffy. The long, dark wooden table was too lengthy, even for the six of them.

"Father was eating copious amounts of swordfish," Valerie said with the pontification of a preschool teacher who'd just found out her student had swallowed paste.

"Okay, why is that important?" Lucinda asked.

"Swordfish has a ridiculous amount of mercury."

"Oh. Father poisoned himself, then? This is good news. There's not a murderer on the loose." She smiled.

Valerie raked her hands through her hair, a layered shock of umber she never changed up. "Nothing that has happened here is good news, Lucy."

"Right," Lucinda said, although she disagreed.

"Marvin said Father had been told by the doctor to lay off red meat because of his heart and that someone at the Field Club had told him that swordfish was the steak of the sea. He'd been getting it special-ordered from Wholey's on a near-daily basis."

Lucinda shouldn't feel relieved by this information, but she was. Her father didn't do things in moderation. Nothing was out of his price range either. If he wanted fresh swordfish couriered in every day, he'd make Marvin drive to the strip district and pick it up at the best seafood market in town, then have it prepared to his liking. "It's a shame that in an effort to eat healthier, he poisoned himself instead. A bit ironic, no?" Lucinda asked.

Valerie looked at her, stunned. "You really don't care what happens to him, do you?"

"Look, I wasn't coming home to bury my father, but you don't have to pretend you're so devoted to him. Or that you don't care about that guy in the kitchen."

Valerie's cheeks tinged pink. "Old news, Lucy. You're deflecting."

"I'm not. You project the life you want everyone else to see, but it's not real. You want people to think you're upset about Father, but you're not that broken up about it. He treated you like crap just like the rest of us. He missed half of your equestrian shows. He wasn't there to see you off to prom. He was annoyed on your wedding day."

"That's not true about my wedding day. It was hot," she said between clenched teeth.

"Yet no one else complained," Lucinda said. Valerie's wedding day was so horribly humid, it'd wilted the lilies the bridesmaids were intended to hold. It was held in a church that wasn't air-conditioned. Father had almost missed walking Valerie down the aisle because he was hiding in the cool limo. When he'd finally showed, he was fanning his face and dabbing it with a handkerchief from his jacket pocket.

"*Lucy.*" She sounded exasperated. "He's still our father. You could laugh about these little blips of his instead of throwing knives. He's sick. You have to appreciate him for who he is."

"Or you don't because he's a terrible person. As is his little prodigy, Christian." She couldn't hold back the spite in her voice after her car ride with him. The more she thought about it, the madder she became.

"You're heartless." Valerie looked away. "We should get out of here, though." She seemed suddenly distracted. Lucinda thought it was just because Valerie knew she was right.

Lucinda wasn't done with this conversation. "And you pretend Luke is nothing to you, but I've never seen you look at someone like you do him. Maybe you're afraid because he's not as safe as Karl."

"Karl is not safe. That's why I divorced him," she whisper-shouted.

Interesting. "I thought he'd finally bored you to your bitter end."

Valerie's cheeks had gone from pink to angry-red. "No, things have been really not boring in my house lately. Trust me."

"Well, I'm just saying, if you still have feelings for that guy in there, maybe you should let him know." Lucinda nodded at the kitchen. *You're divorced now, sis. Get your big girl pants on and find your happiness. He's right freaking there.*

"Relationship advice from you?" Valerie strapped her arms across her chest, just like she had in the kitchen. She became defensive when people didn't agree with her or when she was trying to hide something.

"I'm not in a relationship because I don't want to be. Not because I'm afraid to be," Lucinda said.

"And I'm going through a divorce," Valerie lamented. "Not exactly dating material right now."

Luke stepped into the room with a startled expression on his face, serious. "I'm sorry to interrupt." Valerie glanced down into the V of her army-green shirtdress.

"Christian has been in a car accident. He's at Allegheny General."

Valerie glanced up in shock. Lucinda kept her gaze pointed at her feet. *A car accident? Like the one I imagined? Like the one I . . . created?* Her visions sometimes snuck up on her.

"What? *No,*" Valerie said.

"Was it bad? The accident?" Lucinda asked. No point in getting all gushy if he was just in a fender bender.

"He was speeding on 28 and slammed into the back of a truck. That's all I know," Luke said.

"Oh my God." Valerie placed her hand over her mouth.

Earlier, she'd imagined Christian twisted with metal. Could they smell her guilt? She kept her eyes fixed on her pumps, convinced they could.

"So it was his fault?" Valerie asked.

"I don't have the full police report," Luke said.

"It couldn't have been Christian's fault," Lucy said. Her oldest brother didn't engage in careless activity. Lucinda and Jeremy held the placeholders for that spot on the family roster.

"Do you want me to drive you?" Luke asked. Lucinda didn't think that was normal protocol, especially since he was investigating an attempted homicide at their home. Although maybe the empty boxes of fish had quashed his investigation.

Her mind flashed to Christian and how she hadn't believed anything could really hurt him. He'd always seemed invincible. This crash wouldn't take him down. Even though her imagined one had.

"No, that's all right. I'll drive with Lucy," Valerie said.

What a wimp.

Lucinda would've bowed out if Valerie had said yes, let the two of them catch up, allowed Luke to confront her in a way that might untie the knot that was clearly still tangled up between them. The tension made Lucinda edgy, like she was the one caught in the middle.

Upon closer inspection, Lucinda saw no ring on the dark, brooding officer's finger, and if Lucinda had to make this union happen herself, she would. It was frustrating to see two people resist each other who clearly wanted to be together. Unless there was something else keeping them apart, which was Lucinda's first inclination.

Love is love, Valerie. Stop being such a frigid bitch.

"We'll catch up when I find out more," Valerie said.

"Please let me know later how he is." Luke sounded genuinely concerned, but what Lucinda also noticed was a clear invitation for Valerie to contact him later. She was sure her sister had missed it, though.

"Okay. Let's go, Lucy." Valerie pulled on her arm for the third time that day, and just like the last two times her big sister had forced her hand, Lucinda let her.

CHAPTER 11

VALERIE

By the time Valerie walked into the lobby of Allegheny General to check on her brother, she'd had her fill of hospitals for the day. They all made her angsty, especially after the early days of her mother's disease when she'd frequently walk off, injure herself, and not remember how she'd gotten there. Valerie was the first person listed on her emergency contact form.

Lucy was lagging behind Valerie, moving too slowly. Valerie understood she just wanted to get back to New York, but with nowhere to stay when she arrived, Valerie wondered if she had a backup plan.

Deep breaths. Valerie found the hospital reception desk.

Christian would likely be his normal cranky self once they arrived, blaming the crash entirely on someone else's negligence. The accident couldn't possibly be *his* fault.

Although the fact that he'd been speeding and had somehow lost control had rubbed Valerie the wrong way. It wasn't like Christian to spiral out of control, on the road or otherwise.

"Can you tell me where to find a patient, Christian Fox?" Valerie asked the woman at the front desk. She was elderly and wearing a volunteer vest. Anytime Valerie witnessed a healthy older person still working, it saddened her. Mother could barely remember her name. "ICU. Third floor," the woman said.

"ICU?" Valerie asked.

The woman's sympathetic grin pierced right through her. "That's right. You'll have to ask the nurses' station for permission to see the patient. Immediate family only."

"Right." Valerie backed away. She already knew the instructions for the ICU. She'd just heard them earlier at Saint Margaret's when she'd gone to visit her father. Was Christian as bad off as he was? Or worse?

Valerie turned around to find her sister, completely ashen. "Come on, Lucy."

"Maybe I'll just wait down here. They might limit people in his room, and I don't want to take up unnecessary space. Glenda and the kids are probably up there. You can text me."

"No," Valerie said. "You can't keep ducking out when things get hard. That's not how to face life." Valerie was living these words. She'd made some excuses for Karl at first when Isla had asked her what'd happened. Until she discovered that the Feds could seize every red cent she'd ever earned. If she'd just let the legal system have their way with Karl, stuck her head in the sand, hoped for the best, she'd be left with nothing—just like her sister.

Lucy didn't respond to her demands, only followed Valerie reluctantly to the elevator like a sulky little duckling. Inside the elevator, Lucy closed her eyes and held on to the sides. "What's with you?" Valerie asked.

"This is all my fault," Lucy said.

Valerie turned to her, not that Lucy would notice because her eyes were shut. It was an annoying habit she'd had since she was a child, a way to disappear when she was forced to be somewhere she didn't want to be. "What do you mean?"

"I wished Christian dead earlier. In a car accident. I saw the whole thing in my head," she whispered.

"Why?" Valerie blurted out. "What in the world, Lucy—" Sometimes there were just no words for how to handle her. She was like a cruel, imaginative teenager without a filter.

"Because he told me the premise for the play that I've written, which was highly considered, was a dumpster fire, and so was I, basically. And if I used my trust money to fund it, I'd be throwing it all away. I've never worked so hard on anything in my life."

"Did you tell him you wished him dead?" Valerie asked, although she wasn't sure why it mattered. She knew the power of persuasion could be strong, but it wasn't like Lucy could will someone to die.

"No," she said quietly. "But I saw it happen. In my head."

Lucy looked like she was going to puke. "Well, that's really shitty of you, and I'm sure you're freaked out, but your imagination didn't make Christian crash, Lucy. Maybe you had a premonition of sorts, though . . . Did he make it?"

Lucy's eyes popped open. "What do you mean?"

"In your vision. Did Christian survive the accident?"

"No," Lucy whispered.

Valerie's breath caught in her throat as the elevator doors slid apart.

"Christian Fox?" Valerie asked.

The nurse frowned and looked at a chart on her desk. "There's no update in my computer. Who are you?" the nurse asked.

"His sisters," Valerie answered for them.

The nurse nodded. "Okay, his wife and kids are around the corner in the waiting room. The doctor may have been in to speak with them already."

"Thank you," Valerie said.

Lucy was lagging again.

"Let's go." Valerie was headed to the waiting room but caught sight of her niece, Emerson, bawling her eyes out and wrapped in her mother's arms. The sign on the door read FAMILY CONSULTATION.

"They're in here," Valerie said to Lucy.

Emerson was the same age as Isla. The two girls shared an oversensitive palette of emotion. They'd been best friends when they were little girls but had drifted into different friend groups in their tweens. Christian's teenage sons, Julian and Royce, were standing against the wall, staring straight ahead, as if they were waiting for their mug shots to be taken.

Valerie entered the room and placed her hand on Emerson's shoulder. "Glenda, how is he?"

Glenda was dressed in her tennis skirt and athletic gear, a strong, unwavering look on her face. She'd likely just given a lesson when she'd been called to the hospital, her long gams muscled and exposed beneath her skirt. Valerie was fairly certain that Christian was a loyal husband, because if he wasn't, Glenda might smash him to pieces.

Glenda wouldn't make eye contact. "He didn't make it, Val." The words came out in a sputter, taking Valerie by surprise.

"What?" Her vision blurred, a rush of hot and cold hitting her simultaneously. She looked past Glenda, speechless, to the boys. What'd looked like mug shots earlier were two teenage boys fighting tears, bodies stuck to the wall, grappling with their new reality.

"We just saw him this morning . . ." Valerie trailed off. Emerson cried harder, and Glenda shook her head at Valerie as if she'd said the wrong thing.

Glenda completely disregarded the fact that Lucy was in the room. Glenda's children did the same. This wasn't new. They were by-products of Christian, and he'd likely told them awful things about her.

Lucy glanced to and from the window like she wished to jump from it. She had her hand pressed against her forehead, pushing back her hair, focused on her phone, plugged into the wall again with a charger that Valerie had already decided she would never get back.

"Lucy, Christian is gone," Valerie whimpered. The words were wrong. Everything was wrong.

"I know. I'm just texting the restaurant that I won't be in tonight." She wouldn't look up, still ghost-white, her only sign of distress the way her hands shook as they typed on her phone.

"You can go on home, Lucy. You've done enough here," Glenda sniped.

Lucy looked up, her bright blue eyes fearful. "You think this is my fault?" Lucy asked. Valerie felt sorry for her after what she'd confided in the elevator.

"Every action has a reaction," Glenda said simply. She was good at getting her point across without saying much. Glenda was insinuating that Lucy had caused Father's episode, which had resulted in Christian's accident somehow. It was an awful thing to say, but it was hard for Valerie to separate the events in her head too. Tears fell involuntarily down Valerie's face. She collapsed in a chair. The unexpected news had just hit her at the knees and taken her out.

"I see," Lucy said through bared teeth. "I'm leaving. Let me know the arrangements, Val."

"Where're you going?" Valerie asked.

Lucy concentrated on her phone again. "I've got a place to stay. Don't worry about me." Valerie wouldn't press her on where, but she did feel guilty. She used to sit by Lucy's crib for hours when she was a baby. Valerie really didn't want to be alone right now. At least Isla would be there, but could she really spill the news about Karl *tonight*?

Valerie rose from her chair and walked over to her. "I can't believe he's gone."

Lucy didn't seem shocked. She had always been a little witchy when it came to her sixth sense. Mother had claimed it was part of her intuitive creative side.

And like most things to do with her sister, Valerie thought it was total bullshit.

"Me either. I gotta get out of here," Lucy said.

"Okay." Valerie wouldn't fight her, but as she watched her leave, she saw that Lucy had her calculator pulled up on her cell phone. The screen displayed a number, something close to $3.3 million.

Valerie watched her walk all the way out the door before she figured out it was Lucy's precise sliver of the trust now that Christian was dead.

Valerie had missed Karl's drop-off. Isla had been asking Valerie to leave her home alone more and more as she approached the teenager mark, but if Valerie had to guess, this wasn't one of the days she wished to flex her independence.

She hugged Isla so tightly, her glasses poked into Valerie's shoulder.

"How's Grandpa?" Isla asked.

"Oh . . ." Valerie paused because she'd just realized how much she hadn't told her daughter. It was awful not living with her on a day-to-day basis. She didn't know how Isla's day was at school the weeks she was with Karl. Valerie missed preparing her meals, the preteen drama, the giggles from the constant phone calls and texts. The noise.

Valerie didn't know a person could be this lonely until all her family had disappeared on nearly the same day. Isla would be upset about her grandfather. She didn't know about her uncle yet. It was an impossible day to tack on bad news about her father too.

"Is he okay?" she asked worriedly. "Dad said he was in the hospital, but stable as much as he could tell from his phone calls."

"Your grandfather suffered a heart attack and a stroke. He still hasn't woken up. We need him to before we can figure out the rest."

Isla bit her lip and nodded. She lacked the emotion Valerie wished existed in relation to her grandfather, and Valerie understood why.

Father hadn't shown his grandkids any more attention than he had his own children.

At least Karl had called the hospital to check on Father, just like he'd texted to look in on Valerie the last few months. He was a generally good person when he wasn't being a thief. That was the difficult part of the divorce. He really did still care about her. Both of them.

"Summer is coming. Don't forget to change the air-conditioning filter, Val."

He continued to take care of her in his Karl way. He was still the guy at that art show trying to somehow build a perfect life for her, but none of it mattered now. She hadn't known about the air conditioner, and there were a lot of things she'd have to figure out on her own, but she was prepared to do it rather than live a life of lies. She was angry with him for making this moment more difficult.

"Let's go sit on the couch and talk," Valerie said.

Valerie didn't know how to break the news about Christian to Isla. She'd barely had time to process it herself. Her insides felt scorched with disbelief, yet, like every parent, she had to push aside her own discomfort and be strong for her daughter.

Her grandfather was one thing, but Christian was another.

Glenda and Christian had made a point to spend holidays with them. Christian would make small talk with Karl and Isla when in their presence or at the country club. Isla would be driving in a few short years. What would the memory of how her uncle went down in a fiery car crash do to her?

"Mom, are we going to the hospital to see Grandpa tomorrow?" Isla asked.

"Let's see what tomorrow brings," Valerie said. It seemed like the most loaded statement in light of everything that had just transpired. "There was something else I wanted to talk to you about."

Valerie hesitated, the ugly words teetering between her teeth. Her daughter's legs hung long and spindly from the couch. Everything on her was lean except for her shoulders, which were broad and toned from swimming. A shy girl, Isla came alive in the water. She turned her head in Valerie's direction, her dark hair spilling over her shoulders, her eyes holding that inquisitive look, still a girl, not yet a teen.

How will you handle this? What will it do to you?

Valerie sucked in a giant breath, remembering something Christian used to tell her. "The best way out of a tough situation is through." "Isla, your uncle Christian was in a car accident today."

"What?" Isla seemed to take in the full effect of Valerie's runny nose and bloodshot eyes. "Mom, is he . . ." She shut her eyes behind her lenses, too smart not to understand.

"He's gone, Isla. I'm so sorry." She held her daughter, and Valerie was devastated when Isla went limp in her arms, sobbing so hard she was barely audible.

"Poor Emme." She wailed for her cousin.

"Yes, I feel terrible for them all." Valerie's voice shook.

But maybe if Christian hadn't been so greedy and angry, the terrible accident could've been avoided. They sat there for a long while, crying and staring at the blank wall. The painting that used to hang there had been confiscated by the repo people. So much had been removed from their lives in such a short period of time.

Isla nearly cried herself to sleep on Valerie's shoulder. It had been a bad year for her, and if Valerie could, she'd absorb all the heartache for her daughter.

Isla would remember these wounds long into adulthood. Valerie feared Isla might even have more emotional baggage than she did just from the past few months alone. Valerie felt her phone buzzing in her pocket. "I'm sorry, I have to get this," she whispered to Isla. *It could be about Father.*

"Hi, Val, I'm so sorry about your brother." Luke's voice still made her uncomfortable.

"Thank you. I can't believe it."

"I'm afraid this isn't just a courtesy call, though. I probably shouldn't be telling you this, but Christian's car was tampered with."

"What're you saying?" Valerie asked. She tried to hide the alarm in her voice from Isla. Valerie was trying so hard to protect her daughter from all of this—and failing.

"I'm saying someone messed around with his car, possibly at the hospital, causing it to crash."

"Oh my God. Poor Christian." Valerie couldn't imagine how scared her brother must've been, barreling onto Route 28, his car malfunctioning.

"You were all at the hospital. I'm the detective on this case. I'm going to need to talk to everyone," he said. "Sooner rather than later."

Valerie's head swam with the gravity of what this all meant. Someone had sabotaged Christian's car, just like someone had tried to kill her father. And the police were investigating.

"Let me know where you want to meet," she said.

"How about Moondog's? One hour."

"Moondog's?" It was the dumpy bar in Blawnox, the one they'd gotten into underage when they were teenagers. The memory of that place sparked lightness and happiness, and she shut it right out.

"I need somewhere dark where no one will recognize you, relatively close to Oakmont. If you have a better option, let me know."

"No, that's fine," she said. "No one will recognize me in there."

The tiny little bar on Freeport Road was much the same as Valerie had remembered. The restaurant portion, Starlite Lounge, had been featured on Food Network's *Diners, Drive-ins and Dives*. Maybe it'd gotten better, but Valerie guessed it was the "dive" part they were highlighting on the show. Everything felt dingier and darker since she'd left the hospital.

People were laughing at the bar and joking, and it didn't seem right. How was she supposed to just put one foot in front of the other and keep going as if everything was fine?

I shouldn't be here . . . talking to Luke.

But Luke would talk to her about the investigation, and it was necessary to find out what he knew. It seemed like a step forward.

As she walked by a few tables, the stale smell made her turn up her nose. She used to love to come here with Luke, back when any opportunity to do things she wasn't supposed to was a thrill. Until she'd gotten burned and then vowed to never be so careless again. Valerie had broken all the rules for Luke, because she knew her time in that town before she left for college was short.

Luke was sitting at the bar with a beer. She was having a hard enough time getting ahold of herself after leaving the hospital, and when she looked at him, it was as if she were transported back to 1998. It was dangerous. She should be concentrating on the criminal circumstances surrounding her brother's accident, not escaping to an easier time.

Her eyes had just continued to leak since she'd left. *Leak* was the best way to describe it, because you couldn't control a leak until someone fixed it. But there was no repairing this. Maybe Luke had some answers.

"Hi." She waved and sat down at the barstool.

"Hi, yourself." He gave her a quick hug, which she appreciated. The scent of his cologne was familiar, the brush of his skin too much to handle right now. "Val, I'm so sorry. I'm going to do everything I can to figure out who did this to your brother."

She sighed and realized this was going to be her conversation with people for a while. The reawakening of these monster emotions, the flash of memories—Christian fighting her to put the star on the Christmas tree when they were kids. Christian ratting her out when she'd come home plastered after the Market Square Saint Patrick's Day parade.

Christian—holding Isla in the hospital, one of the first ones to visit.

Christian—proudly offering to take the place of Father walking her down the aisle when he'd been late to the church the day of her wedding.

"Thanks." She wiped at her eyes and shook her head. "It's unreal. He was such a huge part of our family. Losing him feels like the end of us all, in a way."

Luke pulled back on his beer and just sort of watched her, sympathy oozing from his brown eyes. She'd gotten lost in those eyes for days when they were teens. Every night they were together was an adventure, even if they were just hanging out at the drive-in movie theater trying not to get caught as they undressed in the back seat.

"Shouldn't be drinking on the job," she teased, then waved for the bartender to get her a drink.

"Glass of Chardonnay, please."

"Chardonnay? What happened to my Iron City girl?"

"No, thanks," she said, her voice dry and cracking at the end. That girl was long gone, sadly.

"I'm officially off duty, but I'm continuing to work because this case is troubling. And I shouldn't be talking to you about it, Val. But if you know something about who'd want to hurt your father and brother, you should tell me now before anyone else gets hurt."

"I thought it was the mercury . . ." She trailed off.

"Why did it catch up to him at the party, though? Shortly after he'd returned from the doctor with a bad health report. And all of a sudden he starts eating this fish? Who'd told him to start this diet? They said he'd heard it at the Field Club. Who goes to the Field Club, Val?"

She rubbed the wineglass stem between her fingers. "His clients. Basically, every single man and woman who was at that party."

"And what does Christian have in common with your father?"

"They work together," she said in a low voice. "But why would they do it there?"

"Why not? Crowded events offer lots of potential suspects. Which client had it in for your brother?"

"Lucy mentioned something about Christian saying Father was making risky investments."

She thought of Karl's crimes and her father's. Why were men so greedy? Why wasn't what they had ever enough?

"What was done to Christian's car?" Valerie asked. She couldn't get the look of fear she'd imagined etched on Christian's face as he lost control on that busy roadway out of her mind. Or that of his frightened children, protective Glenda, trying to hold on to the beautiful life they'd built together.

"I shouldn't be discussing it," Luke said.

"Was it something sophisticated? That might link to one of his clients. Like a computer chip malfunction. They invest for a ton of strip district start-ups, like the robotics people."

"It wasn't actually . . ." Luke focused on his beer. He appeared conflicted, and Valerie had the strange urge to touch his shoulders and rub out the kinks.

Oddly, she could envision herself sliding behind Luke after a long day on the beat and rubbing his neck. She never had these sorts of fantasies about Karl and his corporate job.

Valerie also noticed that Luke wasn't wearing a wedding ring, just as Lucy had observed at the house. She'd blabbered about it in the car on the way to the hospital and said that Valerie needed to suck it up and have a real conversation with Luke about their old relationship so they could start a new one. Valerie couldn't think about that right now.

"Tell me, Luke," she insisted. Valerie used to be able to get him to do whatever she wanted. "What was it?" She'd like to think she still had that power over him, because she was desperate for information linking to her family's case.

"I'm only telling you because I think you can help." He gave her a long stare, as in, *This is confidential.*

"I won't say a word," she said.

"Someone cut Christian's brake lines," Luke said.

"What? No." She could feel her blood leave her upper extremities. She immediately looked away.

He grabbed her hand, and she wanted to yank it from his grasp, but she let him hold it, because she could use a steady hand.

"The brake fluid leaked out slowly. Christian still had a few taps left before he ran out completely. Just as he was merging onto 28."

Oh my God.

"Val, what is it?" His face was close to hers, a soapy scent—comforting. His cheek, with the little bit of stubble, brushed her face. There was something sexy about the fact that he didn't have facial hair when they'd dated and he did now.

Confused, she couldn't answer him, all the traumatic feelings of the day jumbling together. Something sensual still simmered between them. It wasn't right to engage in those thoughts. Not now. Because if Christian's brake lines were cut, there was only one person the police should be looking at, and it wasn't anyone on Fox Wealth's client list.

It was the same person who'd cut Christian's brake lines when they were kids—Jeremy.

He'd been at the hospital with them all. He'd disappeared to "have a smoke" after the two of them had fought. He'd been irate with Christian for insisting on contesting the trust.

Jeremy did have a motive, and it had everything to do with an investment, as Luke suspected, just not the one he was thinking of. If Christian died before Father, Jeremy would collect Christian's sliver of the Den money. His multimillion-dollar sliver.

If Jeremy was using again, he wasn't thinking straight, and he could've acted rashly. The police would think so too.

Their friends had sometimes said that Jeremy "wasn't quite right." He blurted out inappropriate things at awkward times. It was almost a nervous tic, like when he'd asked Lucy if she "liked girls now." He could be offensive.

While those things didn't outright make him a murderer, Valerie didn't think anyone would be completely surprised to find out that he was.

She needed to go. Check on Isla. All this murderous talk was making her feel protective of her own family. She shivered and coughed at the dry air in the bar, suddenly starved for oxygen.

"I've got to go, Luke. I left Isla with Karl. She needs me," Valerie lied, struggling to remain normal.

He still had his hand on hers. "You can trust me, Val. If you know something, you should tell me. I'm one of the good guys."

They met eyes again for a moment. He parted his lips. Everything that was between them when they were younger was somehow still there. The attraction. The understanding. The way he could temper her with just a glance. He pulled her closer until his knee rested in between her legs. His touch still undid her. Luke tried to get closer, but she wouldn't let him.

The first time had almost ruined her. "I've got to go, Luke. Please tell me what you find out." Valerie tore her hand away and rushed out the door.

CHAPTER 12

MARIAN

When Marian saw the detective enter the lobby of the facility, she was actually thankful for the interruption. She'd gotten herself into a conversation with Bea, short for Beatrice, a widow in the retirement community who'd talk anyone's ear off. Social interaction was what Marian had thought she'd needed to quell her nerves after her phone call with Eli, but now she regretted it.

"I don't know how you can be satisfied with the stylist at the salon here. She butchered me." Bea yanked on a piece of her unnaturally dark bob.

"You look fabulous, Bea," Marian gushed.

She was a pro at flattering rich, old women. It was one of the reasons she'd asked to be placed at Longwood. There'd been enough drama in the Fox household to last a lifetime, and all she'd wanted in her retirement years was peace and quiet and mindless chitchat with people like Bea who were too old to cause trouble but who once had.

It made for fun story time at dinner. Although Marian was careful about what she divulged of her years at the Foxes'. She didn't want to incriminate herself.

As much as she didn't miss the Foxes, she had to admit she was out of sorts without problems to tend to. Missing the charity event was beyond disappointing. Marian hadn't wanted to admit how much she looked forward to it. She just didn't know what to do with herself without her work and her people, as wretched as they were.

She hoped Eli set a wedding date soon. Then he and Giselle could marry, produce grandkids. Grandchildren would make Marian feel useful again. It might even give her enough of a reason to drive somewhere. Simone was fading, and so was her need to have Marian at her side.

As he approached, Detective Kapinos shot his hand up at her in a wave that was more like a salute. Marian wondered if he had a military background and how much of a problem he was truly going to be for her. There were certainly past crimes committed in the Fox residence. Crimes of passion, crimes born of fear, others hate—but Marian had confidence that Kapinos wouldn't dig that deep. She also wondered where his partner was. "Could I have a word, Ms. Vega?"

"Yes, of course. Excuse me, Bea."

Bea eyed the detective with curiosity. "Did you order him for my birthday? It's later this week, ya know." Bea winked.

Kapinos offered a tight-lipped smile.

"Don't mind her," Marian said as they walked away. Bea must've been really hard up. The detective wasn't even wearing a full cop uniform, only slacks, a dress shirt, and a ball cap with the Pittsburgh Police Department logo on it.

"Friend of yours?" he asked.

"Sort of. I'm forced to talk to a lot of people I don't want to, living here," she said.

They walked back to the sitting area with the couches in the alcove beside the large picture window. The birds were fluttering around in the pear tree in happy song outside as night settled in. Marian was a little irked that she was still being pulled into her employer's messes after retirement.

"I see. Is that how you felt living at the Fox residence?" he asked.

The question made her chuckle. "I was their worker. I wasn't there for the conversation. What can I do for you, Detective?"

"Thank you for talking to me without your son here," he said.

She nodded, squinting at him. He had to know she would answer only what she chose to. The trick was making sure she didn't say anything interesting enough to place her on a witness stand if the time ever came. The last thing Marian wanted to do was perjure herself if she had to appear in court.

If the detective had made a last-minute house call and had come alone, it meant he wanted to talk to her in private. And finding out dirt on the Foxes was far too interesting to turn down. Her boredom may just be the thing to get her pinched.

"It seems my caseload for your favorite family has doubled. Christian Fox careened into oncoming traffic today and unfortunately didn't make it."

Her hair stood up on end.

Didn't make it? It was true, then. Christian Fox was dead.

She fought the terror invading her body, the fear of the ripple effect that might come next. How much would the cops dig into the archives of that household now? Eli likely didn't know the news yet. It's probably why he hadn't called her to let her know. She'd instructed him not to check on Christian personally.

"Ms. Vega? I'm incredibly sorry if I'm the one to deliver the news."

"I didn't know." She'd raised Christian more carefully than the other children. The first one always got the most attention. Every little cry from Christian's nursery made Marian run. By the time Jeremy came along, both Marian and Simone had adopted the phrase, "Let him cry a bit."

"Oh no. I thought someone would've told you. The car exploded on impact. There was nothing that could've been done to save him."

"His poor children," was all Marian could mutter. "He had three."

It would destroy Emme. She'd had the worst separation anxiety of all the grandchildren. She would've climbed back inside Glenda's womb if she could've. Marian shook her head. It didn't seem right, yet right on course at the same time.

"It appears the wreck may have not been an accident," the detective revealed.

"Oh my," Marian said, pushing down the tremor rising in her chest.

"I'm here because of what you told me about pecking order. Stefan ruled the roost, and he went down first and then Christian, just as you predicted. He was the next eldest. The next in line, even though you said there wasn't a clear leader."

Marian looked outside, trying not to imagine Lucy holding the head of that mangled chicken. It was the first thought that came to mind when anyone brought up foxes and chickens.

"Ms. Vega?"

"Yes, it seems you're catching on, Detective."

"And it seems you know something you're not telling me," he said. "Who do you think is going after the Foxes?"

"I think . . ." She paused, trying to collect her thoughts. *They're likely going after each other, dear boy. Didn't you listen to me the first time?* ". . . I don't have all the information on the case, and if I don't have all the information, then I can't possibly answer your question. I haven't been around the Foxes all together for quite some time, and I wasn't at the party. But . . ."

"But?" Kapinos asked.

"If Stefan and Christian were targeted, then it most certainly has to do with money, because they held the lot of it." She squeezed her hands tightly on her lap.

The detective's thick black eyebrows shot up in interest. Marian remembered how Stefan hadn't liked Luke or his dark complexion and hair. "We're exploring that option. Which Fox sibling disliked Christian the most? In your opinion."

Marian sighed at the unfortunate answer to his question. "Well, all the children disliked Christian equally. He thought he was better than them. He bossed them around. He was Stefan's favorite. And Stefan would actually say those words out loud, 'Christian is the only one who will make anything of himself.' They all hated Christian for that reason. No matter what they did, they paled in comparison to him, predetermined successor to the family business."

"Why was he Stefan's favorite? And why wasn't the other son considered to take over the company? Or the daughters for that matter?" Kapinos asked. Marian hadn't noticed until that moment that he'd taken out his notepad. A warning lurched in her throat, and she knew that she'd already said too much.

Marian said, "Jeremy wasn't good in school, especially math. If you ask me, he had a learning disability that was never diagnosed. He was intelligent, but he struggled to pay attention. Stefan had nixed him as a candidate for financial work because of his poor grades. He couldn't have tried to work for him even if he'd wanted to."

"That's awful," he said.

"It is. Stefan wasn't great at the parenting thing. Simone was better, offering those kids every opportunity to broaden their horizons. Valerie had wanted a horse and lessons, and that summer a stable was built right on the property. Lucy wanted to paint, and an art studio was erected, just like that. Stefan never considered the girls for the family business, though, because they were . . . well . . . girls."

"So he was sexist?"

"Sure, you could say that." Marian shrugged. "Valerie tried to get in his good graces. Out of all of them, she wanted to please her father most and help keep the other children in line. She made excellent marks in school, was an expert equestrian, played piano for Stefan's guests, which he loved. But she'd never shake the pedestal her older brother had been thrust upon. There was plenty of pressure for Christian to remain up there too." If the police dug deep enough, they could find this information from anyone who'd known the Foxes. Marian just had to be mindful of details that were private. The ones that could get her in trouble. "The younger two, Jeremy and Lucy, didn't really have a fighting chance with Stefan, so they sort of gave up trying."

"We're looking closely at the client list," he said, pausing and giving her a stern look.

"I don't know anything about their business." She had no idea who the sneaky Foxes partnered with to make their fortunes.

"I see. Did any of the children express bouts of violence when they were younger? Cause undue harm?"

Marian gulped and averted her eyes at the memory of Lucy and the chicken. "Well, yes." Marian didn't know why she was admitting these things. Perhaps the mental pictures would go away if she talked about them. She was getting on in age anyway. How much longer did she really have to live with images dancing in her mind that she couldn't forget? Hector dead in the bed they shared, for one. The Foxes hadn't allowed her to move into the main house afterward even though there were enough bedrooms.

Eli might be acting too cautiously with how much they told the police. If she gave them enough, maybe they wouldn't come back for more. How to describe Christian's relationship to the others, though?

Marian still remembered the precocious child who'd taken his first steps. Christian was a sweet boy before they'd soured him by giving him too much of everything, only rewarding him when he'd achieved more. When Christian was promised the business, it'd made him fiercely protective of it. It was in his best interest to undermine the other children so they couldn't take it from him. Did Christian have any other option but to become greedy after having grown up with that kind of incentive plan? She wasn't sure. Christian had marked the beginning of it all for Marian. They'd hired her and Hector after he was born.

"Go on," the detective nudged. "You'd indicated the children showed signs of violence?"

"I may have told you the Foxes preferred farm-to-table food, and I know I mentioned the chickens." Eli would have *her* head for telling this story, but Kapinos needed to keep his eyes where they belonged—on the Fox family.

"Yes, you did."

"Well, my husband culled and cleaned the chickens. It was the one thing I didn't like to do."

"Okay, understandable."

"And after my husband died, a brain aneurysm . . ." She hurried with the explanation because the recollection still got to her. "They'd had a hard time finding a replacement. Especially for that job. After one guy had up and quit, Stefan threw a fit about wanting his hormone-free chicken. He was always on odd diets, determined to keep his thirty-four-inch waistline."

Luke appeared unenthused. "What happened next?"

"Well . . ." She paused. "Lucy would've been about eight or nine at the time, and who knew she even had the strength to crack an axe across a tree stump, let alone sever that chicken's neck."

Kapinos stopped writing. After all he'd seen as a homicide detective, Marian reckoned it was hard to surprise him with gruesome facts, but maybe she just had. "She tried to kill the chicken?" he asked.

"She did. Stefan was always angry with Lucy. She was untamed to begin with, and by the time she was born, Stefan really didn't have any patience left for children. Lucy might've been trying to please him with the chicken, an offering of sorts, but she didn't do it right."

"What do you mean?"

Marian shook her head. "You're supposed to stretch the chicken's head so you dislocate it from the spine first. It doesn't feel the pain that way. But she just whacked it best she could and only cut its neck part-way. Jeremy had found her in the culling shed and started screaming, and by the time the rest of us arrived, the bird was running around—you know the saying—like a chicken . . ."

"With its head cut off," he finished, mercifully. She nodded.

"Don't they do that, though?" the detective asked.

Marian knew Luke had no idea from personal experience. The Kapinos family lived in O'Hara township on a small scratch of land in a ranch home with a trailer on the property—no hormone-free chickens to chase around there, only dollars.

Marian knew this because she'd driven Valerie there to break up with him. Valerie'd had an academic scholarship, more than Marian could ever hope or dream for, and Marian had only wanted the best for her. "They do. However, they stop after a couple of minutes. Lucy didn't cut clean through, so the chicken flopped around for a long time spurting blood. It'd suffered. And she just stood there and watched."

"What happened?"

"I ended up killing it, taking the final swing." Her skin chilled at the memory of slaying a living, breathing thing for the first time. "Lucy was just trying to help. She said she thought it was funny, the way the chicken danced around, half-headless. Stefan's appetite had been spoiled by the whole thing, and he quickly disappeared to the country club to eat dinner there instead, by himself."

They'd all found their own quiet corner to self-soothe after that. Doors had been slammed shut. Simone's sobs echoed through the house. Marian had been ordered to make sandwiches and bring them to the children's rooms, two of whom were home on college break. It'd been summertime, and that house boiled with blood and guts and dismay. When Marian had brought Lucy her sandwich, she'd seemed the least affected, just shrugging. "I'm sorry, Mari. I didn't mean to hurt it."

"Why did you do it, then?" Marian had asked.

"Sometimes I see things before they happen. I knew that chicken was going to bleed."

"Like a vision?"

Lucy nodded slowly. Marian's skin prickled, but she did believe her.

Lucy had seemed more shaken by what she'd done than anything else, but even as a child, she had the instinct to kill. How had that instinct matured as an adult?

"Was Lucy punished?" Kapinos asked.

"I don't know. Simone wasn't sure what to do with her. Lucy had been trying to help, we thought, but as she got older, her cries for Daddy's attention became profound."

"I heard about the teacher."

"Yes." Marian frowned. "He never worked in the school system again. Stefan made sure of that. Stefan was on enough boards in town."

Marian sucked on her teeth. Was Kapinos judging her for working for these cretins for as long as she had? He'd dated one. They had to be on even footing here.

"She was just a teenager," Luke reasoned.

"Maybe yes, and she was the wrong one punished. That's the complicated part of her. She's an attention seeker, always has been. You heard what happened at the party. She used to take her clothes off in front of Eli all the time. He got so desensitized to her provocations, he'd just turn his head. Even when he was old enough to be interested. I'm sure she did things like that with the teacher. Lucy was angry enough with her father to act out until he paid attention to her, but he sent her away instead. And that made her angry."

"Angry enough to poison him?" the detective asked.

"Perhaps." Kapinos would've had to live in that house to understand how much it hurt those children to have to compete for their father's love. They had to juggle for his approval. The detectives would be fools to think one of them hadn't become tired of the dance and decided to take him out once and for all.

"And what about her brother Christian? Did she hate him as much?"

"Stefan and Christian are one and the same to Lucy, practically identical people."

"I see. And do you think Lucy Fox could've tampered with Christian's car?"

Marian let out a low laugh. "Lucy's not exactly mechanically inclined. I told you what happened with the axe. She's not efficient."

"Right." The detective inhaled sharply.

But Valerie is. She was capable of merely cleaning up the blood and walking away. She was the one who'd helped Marian clean the area by the culling shed. Marian thought it was just because she wanted the incident to be over with as soon as possible, but the effective way she did so made Marian believe it really hadn't bothered her that much.

"She might've been able to hire someone else to do it," Marian puzzled.

"Well, somebody did it. And as far as I'm concerned, anyone connected with the Foxes is in danger. I want you to watch your back."

"Sir, if they'd wanted me dead, they would've done away with me long ago." She immediately covered her mouth at her mistake.

He glared at her, surprised. "Well, that doesn't sound like a friendly work environment or a great place to raise your son."

She silently fumed at the mention of Eli. She'd stayed *for him*. The fact that the officer was calling out a mistake she was afraid she'd made a hundred times before infuriated her. "We were afforded very nice things. Things we couldn't have had elsewhere."

"But what was the price you had to pay for them? Living in fear of making a wrong step?"

"Isn't that the way most jobs work?" Marian asked.

"Sure, only most jobs don't leave you fearing for your life if you make an error."

She pulled her cardigan closer at his words. "It never got that bad."

"I'm sure." He widened his eyes at her. "I'm going to talk to Mrs. Fox next. She's here, down the road, right?"

Marian's back went rigid. He couldn't talk to Simone. If she was having an "on" day, she might say the wrong thing. She might tell

Kapinos about those papers, and Marian just had a dreadful feeling about that. Kapinos didn't need any more fresh trails to explore. Marian's goal was to keep him on the ones that led away from her and Simone. "It's late. She'll be getting ready for bed. And she's not reliable these days."

"I'll take my chances." He rose from his chair to leave.

Marian stood right in his way. "If she remembers you were the boy with Valerie, it will make her go into a fit. You don't want to upset her. There could be legal implications to badgering an ill, old woman. I'd hate to disclose that you spoke to her against my wishes. I'm her designated caretaker. Especially when I told you I'd rather you not speak to her. Not this late. And not on the same day she lost her son."

He stopped in his tracks. "What's this now?"

"You don't remember me, sir. But I remember you. Mrs. Fox didn't want to speak to you when you were seeing her daughter, and she doesn't want to speak to you now."

CHAPTER 13

LUCINDA

Aja applied a layer of foundation on Lucinda's face with a brush she claimed had bristles made from recycled pop bottles.

"Have you ever contoured?" she asked. "You have cheekbones made for accentuation."

"Thank you. And no, I haven't," Lucinda said dreamily. It was easier pretending yesterday hadn't happened than suffering through explaining it. Anything to detract from the horror of her reality—that she'd willed her brother to die.

"You could seriously be a model with these babies." Aja tapped her cheeks with a blush brush.

"Thanks." Lucinda had inherited her mother's distinct features, the apples of her cheeks high and rounded, a thin nose with a perfectly pointed tip. She didn't have to splurge on expensive cosmetics because her bone structure did half the work for her. She wouldn't tell Aja that, because right now she was letting Lucinda stay at her apartment for free. Lucinda would let her play makeup artist—and whatever else she wanted—until she could get through her brother's funeral. The vision of him crashing kept rolling through her mind like a guilt-trip freight train that never stopped. Maybe if she stood before the minister at the funeral, she could ask for absolution, although that sounded like the wrong religion. She'd never been much for it. If for any reason the police suspected her, attending his funeral would keep her off the suspect list. Skipping it would place her at the top.

"You'll love what I'm doing here. You're going to be, like, one step closer to Kylie Jenner."

"Every girl's dream." Lucinda beamed.

"I know, right?" Aja asked.

"Totally." Lucinda tried not to roll her eyes beneath the swab of the brush. "I have to visit my family today." The morning light crawled through Aja's hazy window. It was neither shielded by a privacy blind nor tinted—it was just dirty.

"That's okay. I have to go to class. And then an interview. The catering company fired me after what happened at your mom's event . . . so . . ." Aja made a *yikes* face, and Lucinda hadn't realized Aja had been identified by her company in their little charade.

"I'm really sorry you lost your job." Lucinda thought they might've gotten out of there before anyone could get a good look at them, but that'd been foolish. Everyone had seen them. And no one would forget.

Lucinda's plan was to check in with Valerie on funeral arrangements and book a plane ticket to return home immediately following the funeral. The last two days had been some of her worst. She'd ask Valerie to contact her when their father finally passed away too. With any luck, it'd be soon. She'd sleep on Aster's couch until she could collect the trust money.

Waiting around for her father to die made her ill inside, but she was more angry than sad. She'd feel differently about him if he'd been better to her, but he hadn't been. And there wasn't anything she could do to change that now. It was about survival at this point. She'd figure it out. She just had to get out of Shitsburgh and find an adequate place to hunker down until she could cope and cash in.

"I'll slay my interview. No worries," Aja said.

Lucinda strained a smile through the cake of makeup on her face. She already felt like a monster after visualizing Christian's death. It was almost like she couldn't fully realize the tragedy of it, as if it were all a twisted fantasy.

"I have no doubt," Lucinda said.

"I am a little nervous, though," Aja admitted, still hard at work on her contouring.

"Anyone would be lucky to have you," Lucinda said.

"You're too sweet," Aja gushed.

"No really, they'd be fools not to hire you," Lucinda said.

"Thanks," Aja said, so pleased she was almost purring. Lucinda had to be careful not to overencourage whatever this relationship was. "Will I see you for dinner, then, Lucy? I can pick up something from Whole Foods on my way home and cook."

"Why did you just call me Lucy? I told you my name is Lucinda." Something about this slip made her skin hot and itchy beneath all the gunk that'd just been applied to it.

Aja dusted her face with powder. "Oh, it's what your brother and sister called you. I just thought . . ."

"I don't prefer that name because it's what *they* call me. Like I'm still a little girl." Now she was the one going bunny boiler, and she didn't even care. It annoyed her. Her siblings had to ruin everything, especially how other people viewed her.

"Okay then. My mistake." Aja dabbed an extra-hard bit of blush on the apple of her cheek and then finally placed her brush down. Lucinda couldn't wait to go home, where people addressed her as a proper adult, took her ideas seriously, and didn't play dress-up with her for amusement (well, only when it was her idea).

When Lucinda arrived at Saint Margaret's hospital, Jeremy and Valerie were there. No Glenda or the kids, thank God. After a few long days, Lucinda would leave this strange planet and return only twice more—once for her father's funeral and once for her mother's and then never again. She was in full exit mode now. Christian's death was a siren call for her to flee before it was too late.

Although, when she approached Jeremy and Valerie in the waiting room, they were arguing. Nobody stopped bickering to fill her in on what was going on. She thought they'd only met there to check in on Father and discuss arrangements for Christian.

"You were angry enough to kill him the other day. You swung at him," Valerie said.

"I did not try to kill Christian, my own brother." The veins in Jeremy's face appeared as though they might erupt through his skin.

What trouble is Valerie cooking up now? She's good at assigning blame. Calling people out.

The feeling of horror from when Valerie had shown their parents her AOL Instant Messenger account came flooding back. She swore her sister found pleasure in revealing what she'd done, because it only made her look better. *Perfect Valerie.*

"Well, someone cut his brake lines, Jeremy. Worked for you before," Valerie argued.

"Christian's brake lines were cut? In his car?" Lucinda took a step away from Jeremy instinctively. She knew why Valerie was grilling him now.

"It wasn't me." Jeremy put his hands up in defense.

Lucinda and Valerie exchanged a knowing glance. How many times had Jeremy lied to them before about using drugs? Maybe a thousand. He'd stared right in their eyes like he was doing now and swore up and down that he was clean, and that same weekend he'd been taken into rehab by a friend after an overdose.

Jeremy was a practiced liar.

Most drug users Lucinda knew were. They had to lie to others so they could manage until their next hit, and they had to lie to themselves because there was no other way to live with their disease. In any case, it was believable that while high and anxious and mad as hell at Christian, he was capable of murder. And that's all that really mattered.

"Are you using again, Jeremy?" Lucinda asked. He looked like he was. His eyes were droopy along with his pants. He'd always been skinny, but he looked junkie-skinny at the moment.

"No. God, no! I'm done with that life. I told you—"

"Then why do you look like hell?" Lucinda asked, even though she had no room to talk. It was a balmy day, and she'd borrowed Aja's poplin maxi dress, which was two sizes too big and billowed around her middle, as was the style. She'd packed light for her trip. She hadn't planned on being here this long.

"I've been under stress. Daphne is pressing me for a ring. You know how the pounds fall off me when I'm under pressure," Jeremy said.

It was true, but Lucinda's pulse throbbed in her neck the same way it had when Aja had called her by the wrong name. They were the only ones who knew about Christian's bike accident. It wasn't something they'd publicized when Christian was in the hospital. There was no social media back then. Christian's brake lines had been cut twice. It had to be the same person. Lucinda was certain the cops would agree.

"Jeremy, if this was just a mistake, something done in the moment, out of anger, we get it. It doesn't need to leave this circle." Valerie drew an oblong oval with her fingers that Lucinda didn't wish to be a part of.

Jeremy's glance flitted between them like a bouncing ball. "Stop that. I would never kill my own brother over a stupid argument."

Christian had picked on Jeremy harder than usual at Piedmont's office, and there'd been witnesses. Even though Christian had always terrorized him, it made sense for Jeremy to lash out fiercely this time.

Especially if he was using.

He had been prone to doing a lot of shit that didn't make sense. Like the night he'd been arrested for getting high and trying to climb the Duquesne Incline, the cable car once used to transport people to and from Mount Washington. Back in the day, mill workers used the cable cars to get from the steep mountaintop to the riverbank on the west end of the city where the steel mills once roared. Jeremy had fallen asleep on the hillside where the cable car still ran, above the railroad tracks—which also still ran—clinging to the transport wire. He was lucky the morning operator found him before he started the car and it crushed him.

Jeremy was also lucky he hadn't been arrested, thanks to Mother's quick call to the county commissioner's wife, a woman she'd befriended at the country club eons ago.

"Might you do it for another reason?" Valerie pressed. She had her hands on the hips of her jeans, leering at him the way Marian used to when she'd tried to wheedle the truth from their lies.

Jeremy pushed his fingers through his unruly blondish hair. "What're you talking about?"

"The Den money," Valerie whispered. "You were the first person to ask Mr. Piedmont about the sibling disclaimer. You even joked with Lucinda about stealing her share."

Jeremy's eyes practically bugged out of his head. "N-no, I was only joking."

"Piedmont heard you, Jeremy," Lucinda piled on. "He could testify. If you did something to Christian's car, there's time to rectify it. Or cover it up, I should say. Tell us! That way we won't be paranoid someone else is out there." She said the last part in a threatening voice.

Valerie glanced at her sideways but didn't protest. The thing with this place and these people was that Lucinda didn't have to see them again once she left. She could squirrel away in some nondescript apartment in New York City, and they'd never find her. When Lucinda wasn't trying to get discovered in the bustling city, she was using it to hide.

Either way, she intended to board a plane in a few days and leave all the chaos behind no matter what the police thought. They had nothing on her, and she'd collect a significantly larger payout from the trust now.

Valerie could never do the same, though—walk away from the accident.

Even though Valerie had always been in competition with Christian, she would need to make everything right. Or she would need to make it appear kosher, like they were a loving family who cared for one another, Father and Christian included.

Then again, Christian hadn't crapped all over her dreams.

"I didn't do anything," Jeremy insisted. "I swear."

Lucinda pressed her lips into a thin line. They'd heard it all before. She noticed the detectives coming their way. "You guys, shh." She glanced toward Luke and Detective Sharpe.

Valerie immediately stuck out her chest, and Luke stared right at his old love. It was obnoxious, really, a near mating dance.

"Oh God, Val, you didn't tell him about the bike brakes, did you? When we were kids?" Jeremy whispered.

Valerie gritted her teeth. "No, I did not. But I spoke to him, and Christian's case is definitely being investigated as an attempted murder."

"And Dad's isn't anymore?" Jeremy asked.

"They aren't sure, still," Valerie said, and she seemed equally unsure herself.

"It was mercury. Jeremy Piven went down the same way," Lucinda declared.

"What're you talking about?" Jeremy asked. "Celebrity gossip, now?" he jabbered.

"It's true. I work in theater. Piven was supposed to do a play in New York. He had to be hospitalized after eating tuna every day. Mercury poisoning. I didn't remember until after we'd left the hospital. People were really bummed he had to pull out of the show."

They gaped at her as if she'd just made that up. It was factual information they could easily verify themselves. To her siblings, everything she said was shrouded with doubt.

"Hello there," Detective Sharpe said. "Sorry if I'm . . . interrupting something?"

"No, you're fine. We were just talking about how a movie star was hospitalized for consuming too much fish, just like Father," Lucinda said.

"As interesting as that sounds, we're here to talk to you about something serious," Detective Sharpe announced.

Luke stood behind Detective Sharpe—wuss. Lucinda's muscles tensed beneath her dress. Every moment she spent there was one minute closer to her own death. She could feel it in her bones.

She needed to get on a plane.

"The heavy metals in your father's blood were high. His tox screen also showed thallium, a metal in pesticides. Combined with the mercury, we suspect that's what caused his nervous and cardiovascular system to break down when it did and how it did."

"What does that mean?" Valerie asked.

"He had two poisons, then?" Jeremy asked.

What is happening?

"In addition to that . . . ," Luke started.

There's more? There can't be more.

"Both the gas line and the brake lines were cut in your brother's car. It took us a while to do a thorough intake. The overnight crew caught it."

"What does that mean?" Valerie asked in her ultra-gaspy voice. It'd always reminded Lucinda of a terrible soap opera actress.

"It means that whoever cut his brake lines intended for his car to blow up on impact. Which it did. We're guessing the perp expected the car to have a much larger explosion, destroying all the evidence that the car had been tampered with. That wasn't the case here," Luke said.

"Jesus," Jeremy said.

Both Lucinda and Valerie glared at him, but neither one let their eyes focus on him for too long. Jeremy may have had motive to kill Christian, but anyone who knew Jeremy would doubt he had the mental wherewithal to carry it out. Lucinda was fairly certain Jeremy hadn't passed chemistry. Lucinda had gotten straight As in chemistry. She stiffened her shoulders at the thought.

"Someone tried to murder our father *and* our brother?" Lucinda clarified.

"Are you slow?" Jeremy asked her. And he'd better bite his tongue if he didn't want her to disclose his history with brake lines. Her body still tingled with suspicion over the coincidence. She didn't really believe in them. She was sure things happened for a reason or with a purpose.

"Any leads?" Valerie asked.

"We're questioning everyone who was at the party. Mercury isn't portable, but thallium is. It's also tasteless and odorless. It blends well in food and drinks."

Valerie gasped again, and Lucinda wanted to slap her. "Why didn't we know about this before?" Lucinda asked.

"Thallium is hard to detect sometimes. There was someone in the lab at the hospital who insisted we run more tests. It showed up a tad in the blood and a ton in the urine. They hadn't initially tested his urine for metals. The lab assistant was the one who recommended it. The urine contained a toxic amount of thallium," Luke said.

Jeremy scratched his bedhead. "You suspect it was a client?"

"The only guests in attendance were clients and family," Detective Sharpe said.

Lucy said, "Right . . ." They let Sharpe's words hang in the air, because what she really meant was—it was either a client or a family member.

"I wasn't near Father all night," Lucinda said.

"I hadn't talked to him really, either, before he went down. I only fetched his meds," Valerie said. "I'd been planning on speaking with him later, though, of course," she'd added for good measure. Valerie had to make it known she was the good daughter.

"I remember you saying that," Luke said.

And then something strange happened. Everyone's eyes trailed to Jeremy, because he had been standing near Father and Christian most of the evening. Lucinda remembered seeing him mingling, making small talk, trying to fit in even though he never quite did. "Just because I actually spoke to my father at a party dedicated to my mother—" His words got lodged in his throat, and Lucinda thought he might cry.

Luke said, "No one's accusing you, Jeremy. If you'll come with us, we do want to question you in private. You spent the most time with your father before he was poisoned, and we want to talk to you about the other people who were around him. If you can remember specific names, that would be great."

Luke and Sharpe beckoned Jeremy out of the waiting room, and Lucinda watched as he reluctantly walked away, completely distressed. Lucinda wondered if he should have legal representation before he spoke to the cops. She'd even considered calling Eli, but she didn't think he practiced criminal law.

Plus, it wasn't like he was dying to do them any favors.

Lucinda hadn't been nice to Eli growing up. She'd toss her paintbrushes at him—"clean them." She'd taunt him, too, slipping off articles of clothing when she'd reached adolescence in the hopes of getting him into trouble. Marian had lost her mind over it and had demanded she be punished. Lucy had been grounded.

She'd only behaved that way because it wasn't fair.

Eli had no father to please, no battle of wits to play for acceptance. Lucinda never had a fighting chance against the others because she was a decade behind.

"Do you think he did it?" Lucinda asked Valerie.

Normally her sister was vigilant about defending Jeremy. Protecting everybody who wasn't Lucinda. Valerie had regarded Jeremy's addiction issues as "a disease," whereas she referred to Lucinda's problems as "self-created." An outpouring of support from her sister was expected.

Instead, Valerie turned to her with more decisiveness than Lucinda would have liked. "Maybe."

CHAPTER 14

VALERIE

Valerie was surprised that Jeremy hadn't come back to speak to them after the officers were through with their questioning. He must've exited down the back stairwell of the hospital to avoid them.

He must be scared they've found him out.

There was the bike accident that made this crime point directly at Jeremy, but there'd been other things too. He'd spook the horses on purpose to make them run, and it would drive Valerie out of her mind. He'd laugh as they darted across the property in fear. Valerie would have to catch them, calm them. She'd hated him for it. Much like she detested him now just thinking about it.

Valerie was still waiting to hear back from Glenda on when Christian's funeral would be. She couldn't imagine having to pick out all the details for Karl. And she didn't even like Karl at the moment.

As they left the ICU, Lucy asked, "Do you think they arrested him?"

"Jeremy would've had to confess to committing a crime first," Valerie said. Why was Lucy asking, really? Was it because she truly cared about Jeremy, or was she trying to rule somebody else out? All that talk about there still being time to cover it up made Valerie think Lucy was keeping secrets of her own. What did she know?

Lucy appeared awfully eager to make this whole thing go away, even if it made her an accomplice. While it was true Lucy hadn't gotten along with Christian, it did make Valerie wonder if Lucy was trying to pin the tail on someone else's ass to save her own.

"The cops probably didn't have any more to say to us," Valerie concluded, trying to hide the fact that it bothered her that Luke hadn't made a special trip back to tell her goodbye.

She shouldn't be surprised after the way she'd run out on him at the bar two nights ago without much of an explanation. She could still feel his fingers pressed to her flesh, trying to hold on to her as she ran away.

It was the station she'd served in his life.

Valerie reminded herself that Luke's purpose, present day, was to investigate her family. And her family was in trouble. He'd easily put his job before her.

"Jeremy looked pretty close to confessing something," Lucy pondered as she trailed behind her.

"He kept saying he was innocent, but the frantic way he'd tried to convince us of it spoke otherwise. I'm afraid we pushed him too hard about the drugs, though. Combined with the accusations of murder . . ." Valerie's throat closed around the word *murder*. "You know what, it's probably a client of theirs. Christian and Father's," she said, hoping that if Lucy knew more than she was letting on, she'd spill it.

"We did come on strong in the hospital. He buckles when people corner him. He might hate us," Lucy said.

"He should," Valerie said. Lucinda glanced at her skeptically. It was an anomalous occurrence when they actually agreed with each other.

"I mean, do you think Jeremy could cut all those lines, brake and gas, in the time it would take someone to smoke a cigarette?" Lucy asked.

"I don't know. I'm sure it's more complicated than snipping brake lines on a pedal bike. You can't just sever car lines with a pair of wire cutters. They require serious tools. I've watched the mechanics at my auto shop cut down my rotors. They use metal vises with big blades on the end. Jeremy didn't have equipment with him. He rode with me to the hospital."

Valerie watched Lucy's gears turn in her head as her eyes moved around in their sockets. "Right, and there was no way he could possibly know Christian's car would be at the hospital to plan this out ahead of time."

"In order to hire someone else to do it, you mean?" Valerie asked.

"Yes. Unless . . . unless he was the one to poison Father. Then Jeremy would know Christian would drive to the hospital to see him. And that his car would be parked there. It's just a giant lot, no cameras. It'd be easier to tamper with a car there rather than in a highly monitored parking garage," Lucy said.

Valerie bobbed her head in agreement. Lucy was right about the parking lot at Saint Margaret's. She was also thinking in a premeditated fashion. "Jeremy *was* standing next to Father much of the night at the party. But the whole poisoning plot seems too sophisticated for him. Didn't he fail biology?" Valerie questioned, fighting the tremor in her voice. She could trust no one. Her desperation to get this money was making her paranoid.

"Yes, although I believe it was actually chemistry," Lucy said sheepishly, at the mention of the class of the much-older teacher she'd been caught with.

"Right . . . well, still . . . he wasn't good at science."

"Or math," Lucy said.

"You'd need precise measurements to poison someone, right?" As Valerie asked the question, she felt sick to her stomach, not to mention exhausted at the onslaught of information they were left to muddle through. "You couldn't just go at it willy-nilly," Valerie went on.

"Father is still alive. Maybe Jeremy didn't measure right," Lucy said.

Valerie looked at her, startled. She was right. If Lucy could deduct that the person hadn't dosed Father enough to kill him, the detectives would too. The killer was a person who hadn't paid attention to detail, and the first person who Valerie could think of who fit that description was Jeremy.

"What if it was more than one person?" Valerie puzzled.

"There were a lot of people at the party. Maybe they shouldn't be looking at individuals but couples," Valerie added, trying to deflect. "Daphne couldn't make it that night because of a family wedding, but that doesn't mean Jeremy didn't conspire with someone else."

"Who would want to hurt them? Father and Christian?" Lucy asked passively. Valerie gritted her teeth because she knew Lucy had wanted to hurt them both. *Is she playing me here?*

"A client of Fox Wealth, maybe. When the cops connected the dots, the common thread between Father and Christian was the business," Valerie said.

Lucy had gone off the rails the last few years, living on couches when she couldn't afford her rent, placing all her energy in the theater, which wasn't paying her back. She needed an insane amount of money to get some play produced. Christian had mentioned it before he died. With all that stacked against her, Valerie could see a world where Lucy had committed this crime. Others would see it too.

The news correspondents would say she'd lost touch with reality, that this was her final act of mutiny against a family she felt had never fully accepted her. Too bad the truth was that Lucy had been given every opportunity in the world to succeed but had self-sabotaged every single time. Private schooling, expensive art lessons, all the things to nurture her creative appetite. Father could've told her he wouldn't pay for art school, but he hadn't. He'd paid. Afterward, it had been up to her to figure out how to make a living from her degree.

"This all seems . . . elaborate," Lucy said.

Valerie turned to her. "I don't know what a client would gain from killing them. There has to be more to it."

Lucy eyed her strangely, likely puzzled that Valerie was agreeing with her again. Maybe she and her sister were turning a corner on the same street for once. "Then they might not be done? The murderer?" Lucy panicked.

"Maybe not." Valerie hadn't had time to think about that part yet. She sucked in a deep breath, feeling woozy as the elevator dinged for the lobby floor. This time Lucy walked out first, and Valerie trailed behind.

Valerie gripped her cell phone. "I should ask Luke to order police protection for Father."

"Right." Lucy turned around to face her, breathing hard. "I think I need to go home, Val. I'm sorry. I don't think I can be here anymore. I have a bad feeling that if I stay—"

"I knew it," Valerie shouted. *Lucy is bailing.* "They'll suspect you if you leave now. And no one will ever forgive you if you miss Christian's funeral." She wasn't getting out of burying her brother.

Lucy yanked on the back of her long hair. "They ruled me out. I didn't talk to Father at the event. What more do I have to offer them?"

"They haven't ruled anything or anybody out yet, Lucy. Your actions at the party were not met with good intentions. In fact, they were met with harm." Valerie knew her words would slice right through her sister. She didn't care anymore. Valerie hated being rough on her, but Lucy never fully understood the consequences of her actions. "The fact is everyone who was at the party is a suspect."

"I have a terrible feeling something will happen to me if I stay here. I'm also going to lose my job if I don't get home," she tried.

"More psychic visions?" Valerie asked.

"Not exactly. Just a general overwhelming feeling of doom."

"If you'd behaved at the party, you might be okay to leave, but given your display . . ." Valerie shook her head. "Not to mention not showing up at the hospital the night Father had his attack . . ." Memories of riding in that ambulance all alone resurfaced, Father unconscious with an oxygen mask strapped to his face as he was being wheeled into the hospital. If Lucy had cared to show up, Valerie might give her some leeway. But she couldn't separate the pain Lucy had caused from everything that had happened next. And she sure as hell couldn't let Lucy leave her to deal with it all on her own.

Lucy tapped on her phone frantically. "Shit."

"What?"

"I can't get a flight today anyway. All flights to New York are already booked. And you're right. I need to go to that funeral," she squeaked.

Valerie locked eyes with Lucy's pretty blue ones. Even Lucy had to realize it would be unforgivable, the ultimate show of disrespect, to not attend her brother's funeral . . . or was she just afraid they'd suspect her if she didn't show?

"I'm glad you're staying. But I want you to listen to me, Lucy." Valerie grabbed on to her sister's bony shoulders. Lucy often skipped meals to buy other necessities. At thirty, she was too old to live like this.

"Okay," Lucy said.

"You cannot tell the cops about Jeremy cutting Christian's brake lines when we were younger, and you cannot tell them about the trust money."

"Why?" Lucy asked.

"They'll start digging into our family. Things we don't want anyone to know. They'll make assumptions where they shouldn't. None of us knew about this revised trust until Father got sick. They'll try to use it as motive."

"Shouldn't we give them everything? Somebody close to Father and Christian did this. And it could be *him*," she whispered.

"Who?" Valerie asked.

"Jeremy. Shouldn't they know about the bike accident?"

"No. We have to figure out who did this first. Protect Jeremy, not throw him to the larger carnivores," Valerie insisted.

Lucy looked at her, shocked. "Normally, you're strictly by the book. If I didn't know better, I'd think you were the one with the ulterior motive."

"Ha! How's that?" Valerie asked.

"You talk to Mom. She had to sign papers to change the trust. Maybe she said something to you in one of her moments of confusion. Maybe you're having money problems since the divorce." Lucy put her hands up in a *maybe* manner, and all Valerie could do was laugh at her.

If she only knew about my money problems.

It was good that she hadn't told her siblings about Karl. She'd be a suspect too.

"I knew nothing about it. Just promise me you won't say anything to them until we find out more," Valerie pleaded.

"Oh-kay." Lucy threw up a peace sign and walked away. Unbelievable. Lucy didn't trust *her*.

And how incredible, Lucy bartering with Valerie to tell the truth.

Offering the information about Christian's bike accident would only damn Jeremy. He was an easy culprit. Valerie wasn't ready to hand him over just yet.

On her drive home, Valerie phoned Luke. The flutters that erupted in her chest when her finger scrolled over his number were annoying. *Get it together.*

"Hey, I was just going to call you," he said, his voice gruff.

"Good. I was thinking we should probably get security for Father's hospital room." She remembered that she really needed to stop and see her mother soon. She wasn't even sure if Mother knew about Christian's accident yet. She should text Marian and find out. Lucy's accusations about Mother revealing the changes in the trust early had rattled Valerie.

Who else could Mother have told? Valerie had known about the trust for a while, but back then it'd seemed insignificant because both of her parents had been relatively healthy, and in the old disclaimer, the children could collect on it only after both parents had passed. Even though she'd been the only one who usually visited Mother, the others could have stopped by to see her too.

There was no sense bringing it up at the hospital after Father's incident or in Piedmont's office because changes had been made to it that Valerie hadn't been privy to. Besides, Christian would've been so pissed off he hadn't known about any of it, it would've only made him more defensive about investigating the trust.

She'd quizzed him in the hospital, reminding him that the money had been earmarked for the memory center and charities, not them, and Christian hadn't flinched. He couldn't have known about the trust. She was sure of it. Admitting she'd known about it all along would only complicate matters now.

"That's already been done," he said. "Valerie, we need to talk about Karl."

"Karl?" she asked. *No, Luke, we really don't ever need to talk about Karl.*

"Your husband?"

"Correction. Ex-husband."

"Okay. That makes a little more sense. We should still make sure your assets are safeguarded."

"What're you talking about?" She'd already taken care of that.

"Val, did you know Karl was arrested today?"

"*What?*" She swerved through a lane of traffic. Car horns beeped. Her vision blurred. She swung into a gas station parking lot on her right.

"Val, are you okay? Are you driving?"

"Yes, I'm parked now. It's fine," she said, but nothing was fine, and this had happened too fast.

"Did you know he'd been arrested?" Luke asked.

"No. I just talked to him yesterday." She breathed heavily into the phone, fighting panic.

"Shit, I should've asked you that first. I thought you had to have known. Where're you?" Luke asked.

"You don't need to come to my rescue. Christ, Luke."

"Listen, we still need to talk. $1.2 million—"

She couldn't have heard him right. "One million? No, you're mistaken. It was only $200,000."

"No, I'm not mistaken. I'm actually an officer of the law who is privy to this exact type of information."

"Motherfucker." She was gulping for air now.

Karl had lied about how much money he'd stolen. From her research, Valerie knew that the max sentence for embezzlement was ten years. However, for cases in the hundreds-of-thousands-of-dollars range, the average time served was two to three years.

Sneaky bastard. Valerie hadn't found Karl out until the day men had started removing furniture from her house. Her father would consider it a failure to be in financial ruin to the point of having her possessions revoked, and she couldn't say she disagreed.

But . . . this amount of stolen money would lengthen Karl's sentence.

It would take him away from Isla longer. It would also make any future reconciliation between Valerie and him impossible, because Karl had lied to her—again. She'd considered possible couple's counseling when he got out. If anything, to show her daughter she'd at least *tried.* Her intention hadn't actually been to reunite with Karl, but this new development eradicated that option.

When it was finally time to fess up and do what was best for his family, Karl still couldn't come clean. And Valerie sure as hell wasn't waiting a decade for him to come crawling back.

Luke's voice was more urgent this time. "I'm sorry if this is coming as a shock. There is something else I need to discuss with you. We can do it on the books or off."

"What does 'on the books' mean?"

"On the official police record," he explained.

"You're homicide. You don't have anything to do with Karl's case." She wasn't a fan of procedural law shows, but even she knew this wasn't his department.

"Right. Val, I spoke with Mr. Piedmont today. He was in attendance at your father's party. Remember, I told you I would interview all the guests?" he asked.

Damn it. What an oversight. Of course Luke would talk to Piedmont. He'd never missed a party or a chance to take home one of the waitresses in between his divorces. Lucy had just beaten him to it this year.

"I think I know what he told you." *The Den.*

"You think?" The sarcasm that hung on his tongue was rich. "Valerie, if you need a lawyer, you can get one before speaking to me. I'm on your side here. I want you to do what will protect you the best way possible."

No, I don't need a lawyer—yet. As long as no one interviewed Mother, they wouldn't be made aware that she knew about the trust. Chances were, Mother wouldn't even remember having told her about it.

Luke kept saying he was on her side. It was such bullshit. He was a cop. His badge made her guard go up breakneck fast. She didn't like that he had the power to overrule her. The power of the law. She wondered if he'd use it against her now.

Maybe he'll arrest me just to get back at me for breaking up with him.

Even on the phone, there was tension fizzing between them like a shaken pop bottle ready to explode. She knew he wanted an explanation from her about what had happened all those years ago.

"I'll talk to you, off the books. Listen, don't get any ideas about me. My marital problems are separate from my family ones."

"I need to talk to you today," he said.

Today. Valerie looked at the clock, and Isla would be home from school in a few more hours. "Luke, was Karl's arrest on the news today?"

"Yes, that's actually how I learned about it. It even made national news."

"Isla doesn't know about her father yet. I need to tell her first. I don't know how long that will take. Then I'll call you, and we'll figure something out."

"Okay, good luck. I'll talk to you later."

He hung up before she could say another word. Valerie slammed her hands down on the steering wheel. "Damn it."

This was not how this was supposed to go. Isla had enough surprises with her parents' separation, her grandfather's heart attack, her uncle's death. Finding out about Karl's crimes before Valerie had a chance to explain them would devastate her.

She looked up her ex's name on the internet, Karl Merrick.

Ten hits came up. The first one included a picture of Karl being hauled away in handcuffs. *Ugh. How humiliating.* She'd changed her name back to Fox, but everyone in town and at the school still knew her as Valerie Merrick. Strangely, she didn't feel anything else when looking at her ex-husband, hunched over and shielding his face from the camera. And that's when she really knew she could never forgive him.

The headlines confirmed what Luke had told her.

She'd known this day would come, but $1.2 million?

Karl!

Surely twelve-year-olds had far more important things to do when they snuck on their cell phones during the day than peruse the news.

Please, God, don't let her have seen the news yet.

Valerie didn't know how she was going to smooth this over now that Karl had stolen over $1 million. She'd planned on telling Isla that her dad would only be gone for a couple of years, maybe less with good behavior. It was better she hadn't divulged the details of Karl's crimes up until now, because Valerie wouldn't have had her facts straight.

It was bad enough he'd lied to Valerie, but he'd advocated for her to do the same to Isla.

Now *that* was criminal.

Valerie would never speak to him again.

He'd already left them with nothing.

Valerie had no intention of helping him pay back his mountain of debt or aiding in rekindling his relationship with his daughter. He'd have to fight that battle on his own.

She was in an awful position now, and she *hated* Karl for it. She was glad she'd busted open his head. He deserved it for how badly he'd hurt their family.

She was about to push her foot on the brake to start the car but hesitated.

What if someone fucked with my car too?

Her hands trembled on the steering wheel. *Dear God, is this what my life's become?*

This life she'd found herself in was everything she'd ever feared and everything she'd never wanted.

She'd been fooled by the man she was supposed to love, then left at his mercy because of all the mistakes he'd made—in no better position than her own mother had been in her entire life.

CHAPTER 15

MARIAN

She'd gotten rid of the cop last night, but she suspected he'd be back.

No matter. Marian had faced fiercer men than him. Like her own father. When she'd witnessed his violence over a nonpaying customer, an act her brother had condoned, she'd decided she didn't want to be a part of that family anymore. She'd turned her back on them and she and Hector had figured another way out. She'd do the same with the detective.

There was a part of her that'd enjoyed watching Kapinos squirm last evening when she'd mentioned Valerie's name, and especially after she'd said the words, "You don't remember me, sir. But I remember you."

His mouth had nipped at the air like a fish out of water.

Because that meant if Marian had been the one driving the car the night he and Valerie had broken up, she'd also witnessed Luke weeping for her not to leave him.

He hadn't understood what he'd done wrong. He'd wanted to make it better.

Back then, Marian had just been the one to serve Luke iced tea on a tray and ask him if he wanted finger sandwiches or chips and dip to snack on while he visited in the garden. Luke had sat there and fidgeted on the Parisian carved bench next to the lovely girl from the country club who was clearly out of his league. Watching the whole thing inspired bad poetry. Marian knew Luke wasn't good enough for Valerie, and that she would get over him the minute she arrived at college.

Following his moment of recognition last night, he'd said, "I'll circle back if I have any more questions." He'd looked the color of paste, his legs moving sluggishly.

Marian had turned him into a gelatinous mess.

She'd watched him stride away, wobble even a little, all the way to his SUV.

Today, Marian was walking to the memory center to make sure he hadn't stopped by to talk to Simone last evening.

She couldn't imagine he had. Marian had stirred awful memories for him. Poor lamb. He'd never know why Valerie had told him she never wanted to see him again.

It had been the only way.

Not even Valerie understood all the ins and outs of that breakup, only that it had to occur. The idea had been carefully planted in her mind, although she'd embraced it fully.

Marian had just been there to carry out her wishes. Valerie had wanted to become an independent woman with a career. At the time, she wasn't even sure she wanted children at all.

"You'll make up your mind after our trip."

"Why're you taking me here? I've seen where Luke's parents work."

Marian hadn't answered her, only maneuvered the Lincoln Town Car to the edge of Fox Chapel off Dorseyville Road. It was early morning, and she'd pulled into the back lot of the family restaurant, far away from the busyness of the opening workers.

Marian and Valerie watched as they put a giant hunk of lamb on a spit that would turn and cook all day. It was the key ingredient to their prize-winning gyros. "See that?" Marian pointed at the machine. "Is that what you want your future to look like? A sweating piece of meat?"

"That's ridiculous. I should've never agreed to let you take me here," Valerie had said indignantly. The thing about Valerie Fox was that she made her own decisions. She was there because she was having doubts about her relationship with Luke. She wouldn't admit that to Marian, though. Valerie had gotten a scholarship, and she was as career-oriented as she was practical. She'd make the right decision for her future here.

"You don't believe me? Luke will most likely take over the family business someday, the eldest son. You'll be a restaurant owner's wife. Do you know what that means?" Marian asked.

She'd shaken her brainy head, her dark-brown hair rustling around, doubt stamped all over her face.

"You'll be expected to come in on weekends, greet guests, take pride in your husband's business, maybe even work the floor yourself if he's short-staffed. Luke needs someone who wants to play that role," she'd explained.

Valerie looked down at her hands, practically hyperventilating, because she knew she couldn't be that person.

She'd already committed herself to Penn State University. She had plans.

Valerie had to understand what future she was deciding on if she stayed with that boy.

When Hector had moved Marian from Brooklyn to Pittsburgh, Marian had no idea what she was walking into. She'd only been seventeen years old, same age as Valerie. Hector's cousin had fixed them up with a "good" job. He worked nearby in a similar role. Marian had few choices back then. Valerie had the world.

The campaign to break up Valerie and Lucas Kapinos hadn't been Marian's idea, though.

Nor was it Simone's.

Simone hadn't paid the boy any mind when he was in her presence, clearly not friendly toward him, but she hadn't been outright rude either. He was Greek Orthodox, though, close enough to Catholic, she'd claimed, and she regarded him much the same.

The breakup had been Stefan's idea.

"Ultimately, it has to be Valerie's decision," he'd told Marian. "It's the only way we'll get her buy-in. She's too stubborn to do it just because we told her it's what's best. She needs to believe it for herself."

Stefan could be wise and make sharp observations about his children when he stepped away from his desk. He only seemed to do it when they were in peril, though. And he always sent others to grab them before they fell over their proverbial cliffs.

Simone had told Stefan not to meddle in their teenage daughter's relationship, even though she clearly hadn't cared for Luke.

And Stefan had begged Marian to do just that.

Simone hadn't been made aware of her daughter's entire situation. Only that she'd been having "relationship issues."

Marian had to choose between them—Simone and Stefan.

This happened occasionally, and she'd chosen Stefan in that instance, because his logic had made more sense to her. Marian wished she'd had a voice of reason to save her from her mistakes when she was that age. It'd been important to leave her neighborhood, but Hector had convinced her to make a clean break and not to contact her mother or brother afterward—a decision she'd come to regret.

Marian had also learned when to lean into Stefan and when to steer clear of him. He was a good decision maker with a careful hand. At that point in her tenure at the Fox residence, their relationship, Marian's, Simone's, and Stefan's, had formed an auspicious triad, and nothing seemed like it could touch them outside their walls on Old Mill Road.

Marian and Stefan knew that the last thing Valerie wanted was to be tied down to a man who worked impossible hours, one who left her to do all the housework and childrearing, totally dependent. The only reason Simone hadn't totally disagreed was because that was close to the description of her entire existence—but it wouldn't suit her headstrong daughter.

As detached as Stefan was, he'd wanted what was best for his children. He loved them from a distance, the way his father had. The fact that he'd cared enough to step in at all where Valerie and Luke were concerned told Marian that this was the right decision.

And after Valerie had made up her own mind and told Luke goodbye, it was Marian she sat with in the garden area where they sipped their tea. Quiet, pensive, smart, Valerie was perhaps the slyest fox of all. They'd solved one problem that evening. The rest would resolve itself—once the tea had kicked in, that is.

The detective had to have known if he was investigating this case that his involvement with Valerie Fox would be divulged. Marian had a plan for if he pushed things too far with Simone. He'd already visited Marian one too many times, and Eli had warned her not to say too much.

Why did I talk about the chickens?

If the detective tried to exhaust Simone into forfeiting information that was none of his damn business, Marian would call that other cop, Sharpe, and tell her everything—the whole sordid love story of Lucas Kapinos and Valerie Fox.

Well . . . not the whole truth . . . but her version.

Marian would make a claim that the detective was harassing Simone, a mentally compromised woman whose testimony was not in any way reliable, and then she'd ask that he be removed from the case.

Marian had checked the state laws after he'd left last night, and even though Luke and Valerie's courtship had been over twenty years ago, it could still be considered a conflict of interest, especially in a double-homicide investigation.

Her task for the day was to confirm Luke hadn't paid Simone a visit and to see if Valerie had been by to inform Simone of Christian's accident. If Valerie hadn't been, then the insurmountably painful task would become Marian's duty. She'd fretted all morning on how to deliver the news.

Eli had said the hospital was crawling with cops and that Christian's accident was being investigated as a murder. His inside tip at the firm told him the culprit was suspected to be a client of Fox Wealth Management.

After seeing Karl Merrick's arrest today, Marian couldn't help but believe the authorities would think it was somehow all tied together.

In Stefan's eyes, Karl had never been good enough for Valerie even though his family had hailed from Fox Chapel and were in good standing with the community. Marian and Stefan had worked as a team to get rid of Luke, but Stefan couldn't really say much about Karl.

Although it seemed like he'd wanted to.

It was as if Stefan was dissatisfied with Karl at a granular level that was never put into exact words. He'd said to Marian once, "I just don't think he's quite right for Valerie. He lacks wit." However, when Marian had asked, "In what way?" Stefan had come up empty.

Marian hadn't formed a negative opinion about Valerie's husband. She'd never formed a positive one either. He was quiet and often avoided conversation. He didn't golf, so he never played with Stefan, Christian, Glenda, and Valerie on the rare occasion Stefan took a day off.

There was an instance when Christian had made an offhanded remark about making clients on the golf course, and Karl had responded by saying that the nice thing about his architectural position was that he didn't have to attract clients. "I don't chase money. Money comes to me."

His comment had hit the other men in the family all wrong.

When Karl would stay behind at the house, he'd offer to watch all the children to get out of embarrassing himself. The children were more than he could handle, especially as the father of "Idle Isla." It's what Marian used to call her. She'd sit and color until you took her crayons away. Every nanny's dream.

However, Julian and Royce had given Karl a run for it. The children would always be watched at the Fox residence, where Marian was expected to cook for the golfers when they returned from their round on the greens. Karl would often say things to her like, "Our little secret," when he'd lost track of a kid or one fell down.

It'd irritated Marian to no end, and she understood why people didn't like Karl and how he could've committed the very crime she saw on the news today.

Because one thing was for certain—aside from his work, Karl Merrick was a lazy man.

And if he was as lazy with his investments as he was with everything else in his life, then that meant someone had told him he could make a quick dollar if he gave them a ton of money, and he'd believed them. And when it hadn't panned out, he'd sloppily tried to cover up his mistakes with more borrowed money. Only on his last attempt, it wasn't his own cash he was playing with anymore.

This Marian understood.

What she wanted to know was if any of this was connected with Stefan's and Christian's unfortunate predicaments.

Because that would mean that Valerie could be implicated. Or that she was implicated.

Rosalie waved to Marian as she walked through the door. She was on the phone and pointed to the common area where Simone sat most days.

Because of privacy concerns, Marian had the urge to take Simone for a walk outside. Marian used to love to stroll along the arbor line on the Foxes' property. It had never been so beautiful as when Hector was alive. The landscapers they'd hired to replace him weren't as good.

Nothing was as good after Hector died. She'd had to walk the world alone and raise a child all by herself.

"Mona? It's Mari." She crouched down beside her. "Would you like to go for a walk with me? Get some sunshine?"

"No, the kids will make too much noise. Jeremy was here. He talks too fast." Simone was looking all around, flustered.

"Jeremy? Was here?" He rarely visited.

"I just saw him."

"Did he tell you about Christian?"

"Who?" Simone asked. She was rubbing her thumbs over the knuckles of her forefingers. Marian had come to recognize this motion as a sign of distress.

This would not be a good day.

They would not go for a walk after all.

"Has anyone else been by to see you?" Marian tried.

"Who?" Simone asked again. She was rubbing harder now. Marian didn't want to agitate her further.

"Valerie?" Marian asked. Because that's who she'd really been wondering about. She hadn't expected the others would be sent as messenger, but perhaps Valerie was in over her head with Karl's arrest.

"More ice water, please, Nurse," Simone requested.

And Simone was . . . gone. Although Marian wasn't sure she'd ever been quite there today. "Okay, I'll get you some water, Simone."

Marian patted her hands, and Simone didn't flinch away this time. She didn't stop rubbing either. Someone had been there bothering her.

Marian rose from her seat and asked a worker to bring Simone water. She may have been out of it, but Marian knew she was likely really thirsty. She walked to the reception desk to speak to Rosalie. "Was anyone else here recently to speak to Marian?"

"Yes." Rosalie smiled. "A man."

"Do you have his name? She seems upset."

Rosalie held her finger up as she searched her notepad. "Jeremy Fox. Her son. I believe he may have told her about Christian's accident."

Marian frowned. Jeremy likely hadn't done it with much couth. Although Jeremy wasn't the one she was most concerned about.

"Has her daughter been by? Valerie?" Marian tried to peer over the counter at the sign-in sheet to get a gander. The only names on the list who'd recently visited were the ones Marian already knew—herself and Jeremy.

"She hasn't." Rosalie shook her head. "Must've sent her brother this week."

"Thanks, Rosalie." Marian walked away, doubtful. There were too many connections to Valerie Fox and the stirrings of unfortunate events lately.

Marian thought back to how punishing Valerie had been to Luke when he'd compromised her future. She'd destroyed him over things that were out of his control and without explanation. Valerie could be coldhearted when she was protecting her own interests.

What might she do to the next person who deceived her?

Or to the people who were behind beguiling her husband into a bad investment, consequently destroying her picture-perfect life?

After all, Valerie Fox loved order.

She was the only child who Marian rarely had to ask to clean her room. She liked things tidy, her clothes folded and organized, her desk immaculate. A great student. Marian hadn't needed to remind her to do her homework.

But in her need to have everything just right, Valerie had the ability to leave things that weren't serving her in a way that would give most people pause. She could kill off people in her life with vicious decisiveness, the same way another might swat a fly that'd been irritatingly circling them.

She'd barely mentioned Luke again after she'd broken up with him. It was as if she'd made an executive decision at work to fire him—*it had to be done*. It was all she'd offered her family. No one had disagreed.

How had Valerie evolved since then?

And how was Valerie making Karl pay for his infringements? Had she decided for some reason it was time for him to pay up, entangling herself in a bigger snare here?

Valerie's ears must've been burning, because Marian's phone chimed in her pocket, and it was her. The screen was shattered because she'd had a little mishap with it. Eli was due to stop by after work and pick it up to have it repaired for her. She couldn't have picked a better son if she'd tried.

Valerie: Mari, just checking in. Have you told my mother about Christian yet?? I haven't had a chance to come by.

Marian: I didn't, but the workers said Jeremy was here. He might have let her know. She seems upset today. That could be why.

Valerie: Jeremy?! Surprising . . .

Marian: That's what I thought. She's not coherent today, so I couldn't confirm.

Valerie: Can you please make sure she knows . . . and get her to the funeral? I've got a lot going on with Karl's arrest.

Marian: Certainly.

It's what they were still paying her to do, after all. Valerie was just being polite asking, and Marian was being equally polite by responding, but when it came down to it, none of the Foxes were nice people, and Marian was growing tired of appeasing them. Maybe she wouldn't have to for much longer.

CHAPTER 16

LUCINDA

The smell of garlic and onions sizzling in olive oil hit Lucinda as soon as the apartment door swung open. Her mouth watered in protest in spite of herself. Lucinda had a love-hate relationship with food. She was usually limited to meals that came free with the restaurant where she worked, which only included soup and salad before her shift.

She'd grown up with a private chef, but Lucinda had imagined her childhood nanny a witch of sorts, especially when she cooked. Marian would tinker back in the kitchen with the herbs she'd grow in their garden, mixing her ingredients together in the cast-iron and copper pots suspended above the island from the hooked thatch of barnwood. Everything Marian made was delicious, and Lucinda rarely complained, but she could feel Marian's watchful gaze on them as they ate and spoke.

Whenever she'd mention it to anyone else in the house—how Marian seemed to always be *listening*—it was thrown back at Lucinda. She was the one with the prophetic dreams and bizarre calls from nature. It wasn't Lucinda's fault that she'd noticed the murder of crows perched on the guesthouse the day before Marian's husband had died.

She'd told everyone about them before she even knew what a murder of crows was. Those birds had beckoned her with their beady black eyes, sitting in a hexagon formation around the metallic weather vane that spun on its axis above the guesthouse. When she'd pointed them out to the others, they'd laughed at her.

Until Hector turned up dead.

Then they'd all shifted their suspicion toward her as if it were her fault.

"Lucy mentioned the crows. Lucy, did you do something to Hector?" Valerie had asked, all gaspy.

Lucinda had been shocked, a little girl, only eight years old at the time. How could her sister accuse her of such a thing? Maybe if they'd listened to her warning, he'd still be alive.

She remained frozen in the doorway, marinating in the smell of Little Italy. Lucinda couldn't even remember the last time she'd gone grocery shopping, let alone been greeted with a homecooked meal.

"Hi, hon." Aja waved from the kitchen. She had on her large-framed glasses and the same baggy black T-shirt from the day before. It must be her *housecoat*.

"Hey." Lucinda waved back. It made her nervous having someone cook for her. Because of Marian, she associated the act with reconnaissance.

"I hope you like pasta." Aja was pushing around a wooden spoon in a stockpot.

"That smells amazing," Lucinda said.

Aja sighed. "Comfort food. As my mom would say."

Lucinda walked to the galley kitchen island. Her confliction for food matched her mixed feelings for this beautiful stranger who'd taken to preparing her meals. Aja appeared content with her makeup-free face, a light hum droning from her mouth as she stirred. She'd make a good wife someday. Just not to Lucinda. "Is your mom the one who taught you to cook?"

Aja's smile faded and then perked back up as if she were trying to conceal something. "She did. Before she died." She poked at the garlic a little harder, smashing at it with the wooden spoon.

Her dark eyes hardened, and for some reason, Lucinda was reminded of the murder of crows. "I'm sorry. Both my parents are pretty sick right now." Lucinda should go visit her mother if she was going to be there another day. She was running out of excuses not to.

"But you had your whole childhood with them." Aja's comment held spite, although Lucinda was sure she was just masking her own hurt.

"I did. Did you lose her when you were young?" Lucinda hoped this conversation didn't get much deeper. Her goal was to leave Aja with as little bad blood as possible, and here they were, bonding over spicy Italian and telling each other their darkest childhood traumas.

Aja forced a smile. "Yes, I was about ten. The therapist said that was a terrible age for it to happen, between a child and a young girl, right before puberty."

Lucinda cringed. "I'm very sorry." The way Aja's emotions vacillated from high highs to low lows so quickly scared her. Although, given Lucinda's mental state, she feared she was imagining it all. Aja was a sensitive person. Did she just wear her feelings with every fiber of her being, or was something wrong with her internal dial?

Aja continued to stir. "It's okay. It was just my father and me for a long time. He doesn't talk much. He's a lab rat. Introverted."

Uh-oh. That's why Aja was so clingy. Her mother had passed away when she was young, she had no siblings, and her father didn't speak to her. Lucinda had a bad feeling that her departure would be a rough one. "My mother was always more talkative than my father too. I'm sorry you lost her when you were just a girl. Was she sick?" Lucinda asked.

Aja turned her back to Lucinda and used the can opener to serrate the lid on the tomato paste. She spooned the paste into the stockpot, turned back around, filled the can with water, then harshly dumped it into the pot.

The splat and sizzle of the liquid made Lucinda jerk back.

"Of sorts." Aja's eyes flicked up. They'd turned opaque and marble-like again beneath her lenses. Lucinda swallowed. The spit got caught along with the burn of garlic singeing her skin. The scent was strong and clung to the back of her throat.

She coughed. "Sorry. I'm going to grab some water." Lucinda rose from the counter stool and poured herself a glass.

"You can make yourself useful and wash the lettuce while you're by the sink. The colander is right next to it."

"What's that?" Lucinda asked. *Oh . . . my . . . does she want me to cook with her in the kitchen?*

They'd morphed from dating to married in, like, seconds. The tiny, parchment-colored, randomly stained kitchen walls were closing in on her.

"Go on. Wash the lettuce. Help me out," Aja said.

"Okay." Aja had been serving her drinks just a few short days ago, and now Lucinda was rinsing her leafy greens. Lucinda ran the water over the lettuce inside the colander and let it drain as Aja did her thing at the stove.

"You have to pat the lettuce dry," Aja said, without turning back around to see that Lucinda hadn't already done this.

"Right." Lucinda unwound a couple of pieces of paper towel and patted the lettuce gingerly. It was all foreign, preparing vegetables for herself. For them.

"I guess you're wondering how she died?" Aja asked, her back still to Lucinda.

No, no, I really wasn't. I was thankful to change the subject to lettuce, and I don't even like lettuce.

"That's all right. You don't have to talk about it," Lucinda said.

"It's okay. It's been a long time." Aja's voice rattled. Clearly, it was like it had just happened yesterday. "She took her own life." Aja cracked the spaghetti in half.

And all Lucinda could picture was the snapping of a neck, possibly by a rope, or maybe after a bad fall down the stairs. Lucinda wrapped her arms around herself. Death was like a black cloud hovering above her, pacing her every move. "That's . . . heartbreaking."

Aja didn't break stride as she placed the spaghetti in a pot of boiling water.

"It was. My father had lost his job, and she thought he was planning on leaving us. Mom and he had fought nonstop. I think she couldn't stand the idea of being with him, but she couldn't take the thought of him leaving us, either, so she left him first. She left both of us."

Lucinda empathized with the notion of having parents who were at odds, one of them absent, if not physically, then mentally. What would Lucinda have done if she hadn't had at least one parent who was supportive? If she'd been left with her father, alone, who avoided speaking to her? Aja couldn't be quite right in the head after all she'd endured—no one would be.

"That's terrible. Things weren't perfect at home for me either. I had my mother, though," Lucinda said. *Until I lost her to an awful disease.*

"You're lucky." Aja sounded resentful. "You can cut the tomatoes and place them on top of the salad now."

"Right, I see them here." There were two lush Romas on the cutting board. Lucinda didn't mind being ordered to help as long as she was given exact instructions.

Their cadence was strained, though. Lucinda's eyes latched on to a stray leaf of lettuce clinging to the metal colander. She had a sudden fear that Aja was somehow going to make her pay for everything she'd been shorted on in her life, but she couldn't pinpoint why she felt that way exactly. Lucinda could sense things about people, and if this girl were an emotion, she'd be mercurial.

Mercurial. Mercury.

The knife sliced through the tomato. She froze at the thought.

The garlic was choking her again.

She was suffocated in this tiny space by the oniony aroma. She raised the clump of dried lettuce and placed it in the wooden salad bowl. Lucinda's hands shook as she finished chopping the tomatoes, and she really, *really* needed to get home before anything else bad happened. Before she was swallowed by the Death cloud and never heard from again.

"I might be flying home in a day or two. I don't think the restaurant will hold my job." This wasn't a lie. She'd told her manager she had to stay in town for a family emergency, but he wouldn't be able to cover her shifts much longer without replacing her.

Aja let out a harrumph. "This has to simmer, and I'll need the colander for the pasta. You can clear out of here." Aja waved her hand in the small space between them.

Lucinda slid from the galley-style kitchen to the counter side. "Did you hear me?"

Aja had a peeved look on her face. "I don't think you'll be leaving as soon as you think you are. Aren't restaurant jobs a dime a dozen in New York?"

Ouch. Talk about minimizing someone's career. She happened to like her job. "It's at one of the better restaurants in Midtown. People make stellar tips in New York. Much better than here. But why do you say that about me not leaving?"

"Did you happen to catch the news today?" Aja asked.

Oh no. Now what? "Did they publicize my family's recent drama?" she asked, leaving out the word *murder* for now, for fear her recent plight would be too much for Aja to handle. It was another reason she hadn't mentioned Christian's death. She was afraid Aja wouldn't want to be mixed up with all her crazy and would refuse to let her stay.

Aja never looked up from what she was doing. "Well, yeah. Your sister's husband was on there."

"Karl? Why? He's her ex, though . . ."

"He embezzled a ton of money," Aja said. A timer went off, and she stirred the spaghetti in the boiling water. Satisfied it was soft enough, she turned off the stove and lifted the stockpot. Her eyes met Lucinda's as she carried the steaming hot pot to the sink. Lucinda flinched.

But then Aja turned and drained it.

Lucinda swallowed the lump in her throat. "That's . . . surprising. It explains why my sister divorced him and then didn't talk much about it. Sucks for my niece." Lucinda had always thought her nieces and nephews were better off not knowing her. Isla had divorced parents now, one of whom was a convicted criminal, and Christian's kids were missing a dad. Maybe she'd been wrong.

"Did your sister tell you about him?" Aja asked.

"No, but we don't talk much. She'd just said I couldn't stay there because she had some trouble at home. Typically, Valerie's big dilemmas consist of a mother mishandling the funds at the bake sale for their private school or someone at work trying to railroad her with projects she didn't sign off on. That kind of stuff."

"I guess she wasn't embellishing this time." Aja wasn't looking at her as she spoke, concentrating on tossing the salad with a homemade oil-and-vinegar dressing. She was a methodical, efficient person. Someone would be lucky to have her one day. Lucinda just needed to eliminate herself from the running. And fast. It was like Aja wasn't hearing it when she told her she was leaving ASAP.

"I guess not. Was he arrested?" Lucinda asked.

Aja glanced up with a strange smile. "He was."

"That's too bad." Lucinda guzzled some more water, her throat stinging with fear. Her family was like a growing pariah of catastrophe, and she was anxious to escape their clutches. Valerie was having money problems—at the precise moment everyone in their family was dropping like flies. Valerie's situation was totally sus, one more coincidence that screamed of guilt, and it exonerated Lucinda of culpability—she hoped.

"It is? He's a criminal," Aja said.

Lucinda placed her glass down with a thud. "Yes. He committed a crime, and he should go to jail, but it's awful he had to lose his wife and child over a little bit of money. It's terrible when families are broken up."

Aja's smile slipped off her face again. "Yes. Yes, it is." She turned around to mix the sauce and noodles together and plate the food.

When Lucinda saw the steaming pile of capellini and marinara sauce, she was lost to its temptation. Lucinda was still uneasy of her new friend, though.

The horror of the last two days was overwhelming her, making her paranoid of people she shouldn't be. The fact that she hadn't told Aja her brother was dead yet was the telltale sign that Lucinda was experiencing some serious denial.

The first stage of grief.

She shouldn't be around anyone right now, let alone someone who was growing attached to her.

They ate in near silence, and Lucinda was relieved when Aja pulled some red wine (even though it was in a box) from the cabinet and poured her a glass. She could really use a drink. The tomatoes and garlic melted on her tongue, and Lucinda understood now why Aja had used the generous amount she had, because it'd cooked down to a perfect combination of spice and citrus.

Aja had bought a loaf of thick, crusty bread and had buttered a piece for each of them. Even though Lucinda was eager to leave, she had a damning feeling that this would be her existence a little while longer—living in this dirty apartment with her deranged new girlfriend, eating tons of food in their paper bag dresses made for lazing in the daytime and eating carb-laden meals at night.

Aja opened a window to let in a breeze, and they sat there and ate their food, staring at each other. "Did you go to school at Shadyside?" Aja asked.

Lucinda twirled the pasta onto her fork. She hated this topic. "I did for a while, and then my parents sent me to private school, middle of the state. How about you?"

Aja shook her head. "No. My parents couldn't afford private school. I was tortured in public school instead."

Lucinda dropped her fork, and it clanged loudly. "Oh." She didn't want to ask why, but she had a feeling she'd find out anyway.

"Were you bullied too? Is that why you had to move from one private school to the next?" Aja asked.

Lucinda cleared her throat. "No. I got into trouble at Shadyside. One of the teachers accused me of sexual misconduct."

Aja's hardened eyes met hers. "A male teacher?"

"Yes." She coughed. "We all experimented a bit in high school. No?" Lucinda asked.

"No," Aja said plainly.

Lucinda shrugged. She didn't need to apologize for her past or explain herself either. They weren't in a long-term committed relationship. Just because they'd slept together twice and had made dinner together once didn't mean Lucinda was going to divulge personal information about her past sexual partners. That was like a six-month-relationship-mark topic. Not six days. Or three days. Or however many dreadful hours and days had passed since she'd gotten there.

"The food is excellent," Lucinda said.

"I'm glad you like it." Aja's broad smile returned. Lucinda wasn't sure how much longer she could play house.

When they were finished eating, Aja cleared the table.

"Thank you. That's more than I've eaten in a month," Lucinda admitted.

"You're welcome. I have something for dessert," Aja revealed.

"Oh, I can't eat another thing," Lucinda said.

Aja walked over and placed her hands on Lucinda's shoulders. Lucinda's breath quickened, and she didn't know what Aja was going to do next, but then Aja began to rub her taut shoulders.

"Gosh, you're tight," she whispered in Lucinda's ear.

Lucinda let out a deep breath. "Lots of stress right now. Too many family members sick or hurt." *Or dead.*

"Let me help." Aja's lips were trailing her neck. Lucinda was reminded of how Aja had made her feel at the party. As if she'd really heard her. As if she could really see her and leap right through the windows of her soul and disappear inside her. Lucinda could feel it again—the danger. The desire. It was still there.

"I thought you said you had dessert," Lucinda said.

"I did. This is it. And you can have as much as you'd like."

CHAPTER 17

VALERIE

When Valerie pulled into her driveway, Glenda's SUV was parked out front. *Why isn't Glenda at the funeral home making arrangements for Christian?*

Valerie threw her car into park at the precise moment Glenda walked down the front steps with Isla's overnight bag.

Valerie rushed out of the car. "What're you doing?"

Glenda whipped around, surprised. "Valerie . . . Isla called me from school, frantic. She asked me to pick her up off the bus. She said her dad was arrested today and you knew about what he'd done and hadn't told her."

Valerie doubled over. There hadn't been a good time. And now she was too late. *Poor Isla.* "I was going to—"

"She doesn't want to stay here anymore." Glenda flexed her muscled shoulders. "What's going on, Valerie?"

The dread of her denial and procrastination was finally catching up. "I wasn't sure how things were going to shake out with Karl. I reacted poorly the day he told me what he'd done, but—"

"Yes, Isla told me you smashed a vase over his head."

Fuck. What else had Isla said?

"Listen, I need to talk to Isla first. She'll understand once—"

"No. I'm taking her to my house at her request."

Glenda sauntered down the driveway, and Valerie was left with her mouth hanging wide open. "Well, you have enough to deal with. The f-funeral—" Valerie sputtered.

"Yes, I do," Glenda seethed. "But my niece called me crying from school. And then my daughter called me crying from her bedroom. She's refused to leave since her father was charred to death in a car accident. And she also told me I needed to go get Isla!" Glenda's voice rose to a scream, and Valerie stepped backward. "Isla just kept saying, 'I can't believe she knew and didn't tell me.'"

But how does she know I knew?

Valerie had to explain this to Isla—herself. She had to make her understand. "You can't just take her," Valerie said breathlessly.

Glenda glared at her. "Get your shit together, Valerie. I told the cops to arrest Jeremy, by the way. I know about the bike accident when they were younger. I'm surprised you didn't say anything to the detectives," she said, ice in her voice.

Shit.

She played dumb. "Was that what happened? It's been years."

Glenda sucked on her bottom lip as if she didn't believe her. Valerie understood why. She was a terrible liar.

Glenda hadn't been shy about her disdain for Jeremy and Lucy. Valerie assumed Glenda merely tolerated her because she was part of their social circle and because their daughters were the same age. If the police had arrested Jeremy, Valerie would be furious at Luke for not telling her. Then again, he'd sounded disgruntled over the phone earlier. Maybe that was why.

Glenda bared her teeth. "I think they sent someone to talk to him at his work. I haven't heard of an arrest yet."

Valerie wavered at the thought of Jeremy being interrogated at work, the job he'd taken so much pride in. If an arrest had to be made, she'd hoped it would have at least been done with some dignity, at home, and not in front of his coworkers. But as she'd discovered today with Karl, there was no easy way to go down.

Glenda continued. "It's really no bother to take Isla. Emme's happy to have her. Besides, she's not going to stay *here*. At least not tonight."

Before Valerie could protest, the school bus pulled up.

The door opened, and Isla was red-faced and practically sobbing as she crept down the steps. She pushed up her glasses, shrugging her backpack farther on her shoulders. She ignored Valerie and ran over to her aunt.

"Isla, just give me a moment," Valerie insisted.

The bus hissed loudly as it pulled away, but it didn't stop Isla from screaming over the rumbling tires. "I don't want to talk to you!" She burrowed into her aunt's side, crying.

"We should talk about this, Isla. There's a lot about your father's case I need to explain." Especially now that she'd only just learned all the facts herself. But Isla was so boiling mad, she only shook her head at Valerie like she wanted her nowhere near her. *Will Isla ever forgive me for all of this?*

"You had your chance to tell me for six months," Isla fumed. "That's why you divorced him, right? Dad didn't want the divorce. He told me. Even after you beat him up!"

Glenda shot Valerie an unapologetic look. Isla had obviously figured out how long she'd known about Karl's criminal activity by the weeks that'd lapsed since Valerie had kicked him out.

Of course she had.

Isla was on honor roll, one smart cookie. Valerie just hadn't anticipated the news would break before she could unleash the truth to Isla herself.

"I'd give it a day or two." Glenda talked over Isla's shoulder. "I have plenty packed for her until then." She held up the bag. "She can borrow from Emme too."

Valerie threw her hands up in defeat. She'd been trying to tell Isla about her father for weeks. So much had happened in just the last few days. But none of that mattered to her angry daughter right now.

"Okay, but I'm calling tomorrow, and I want at least a conversation," Valerie demanded.

Isla leaned on the open back passenger door of Glenda's Volvo SUV. "Dad was having trouble, and you just left him. Just like that." Of all the reasons Isla could've been mad at Valerie, this one surprised her most. She'd thought Isla would be more upset about the fact that her father had committed a crime, not that Valerie had left him for it. She was speechless as her daughter slammed the door in her face. Perhaps Isla was making a statement, leaving her the same cold way Valerie had left her father.

Isla didn't understand.

I'm just trying to protect what's left of what we have.

Her sister-in-law didn't wave as she pulled out of the driveway. Valerie hadn't missed her accusatory tone when she'd asked why she hadn't mentioned Karl's legal issues to anyone.

It was because Valerie didn't want to be judged.

It was because her life was deconstructing.

If she were to use one of Karl's architectural terms, this stage of her life would be regarded as the demolition phase. She had to tear everything down and start over. Valerie knew they could rebuild their life, she and Isla, but she'd wanted total control on the steps they took to get there.

It's all she'd ever wanted—a firm grasp on her domestic life.

Valerie had decided early on that she would have a very different relationship than her parents. More than a "paper marriage." She had standards for her future other half, of course—career-focused, motivated, family-oriented—but loyalty and trust trumped those things. They were must-haves.

She'd have a small family, if one at all. And she'd do everything she could to keep order, meet everyone's needs, manage her own career. She didn't want to be financially bound to her husband.

Valerie had promised herself she'd always have monetary leverage of her own.

And then Karl did the unthinkable and took every penny they'd ever earned, solely and jointly, and practically gambled it all away.

Once Isla understood that deception, she'd realize why Valerie had to do what she did. It might take a while, but she had to believe they'd get there.

Valerie was the primary breadwinner now.

She'd taken a personal day today from her logistics job. Tomorrow she'd go back into the office, a normal environment. She'd fill orders, track shipments, hold meetings, send emails. She craved the monotony of it.

Valerie entered her house and locked the door behind her, but before she could decompress, the doorbell rang.

Valerie hoped it wasn't the press. She prayed they'd leave her alone. All she needed was a video camera shoved in her face with two ailing parents, her brother in a morgue, the other one possibly on the way to jail.

When she opened the door, she didn't find a video camera. She found Luke.

Luke.

That's right, he said he'd be over. She just wasn't ready to talk to him yet. She'd told him she would call him when she was ready for him. "Hey, Luke."

"Hi, how're you holding up?" he asked.

"I've been better." She pulled the door open wide, although she was a little miffed he hadn't called first to let her know he was coming. Her nerve endings were still on fire from her baby girl slamming a car door in her face.

"Did you talk to your daughter? Is she here?" Luke walked inside and took in the sharp lines of the house. Everyone did this when they entered, their eyes traveling to the eleven-foot ceilings, the open-concept design. Luke's gaze traveled the length of the refurbished timber beams that separated the foyer from the great room. "Nice place."

"Thank you. Karl designed it." She smiled tightly. "Isla's at her aunt's. Her cousin, Christian's daughter, asked her to come." That would be the lie she'd tell tonight. The truth was too painful.

Luke placed his hand on Valerie's shoulder. "I'm sorry, Val. I know I've said it already, but I don't know what else to say. It's a real tragedy. He was a hell of a guy."

She enjoyed the comfort of Luke's touch and had the urge to let the rest of her body collapse into his, if only to steal a hug, but she knew he was there on business.

"And what about my other brother? Is he still a free man?" she asked.

"We questioned him today. He's a bundle of nerves, that one."

"Should he be?" she asked.

"We don't have anything concrete on him yet. I'll let you know if that changes," Luke said. She doubted he actually would.

She sighed in relief and nodded toward the kitchen. "Beer? Wine? Liquor?"

"Beer is fine. Whatever you have."

Valerie was surprised he boozed this much on the job. She supposed his drinking habits had changed since their days of sneaking Mad Dog 20/20 into the Waterworks movie theater. And since he started this type of high-stress work.

Valerie sat across from him at the large square island, the top a wooden butcher block—Karl's idea. She wasn't much for design, but Karl had done a great job with the deep navy and gray accents of the kitchen. She'd never thought to question him much on his building materials, just like she'd never thought to ask him about what the hell he was doing with their money.

Valerie popped off the top of one of Karl's IPAs and handed it to Luke as she poured herself a glass of Pinot Grigio. Luke's Adam's apple bobbed as he took a sip. It was such a noticeable feature on his tall frame, and she'd remembered kissing the spot right beside it. The one near where his dark hair curled around his ear.

"I'll cut right to it. Have the Feds been by to seize anything?" Luke asked.

"Seize?" Her Pinot Grigio came right back up and dribbled down her chin. She grabbed a towel and dabbed at her mouth, embarrassed. "No federal seizures that I'm aware of."

"Have you used your bank cards with success today?" he asked earnestly.

"What the hell, Luke? Yes. I got gas earlier. My card worked. Why?"

"Karl was taken for a lot of money, Valerie. Money that shareholders and banks want back. They'll get it any way they can."

"That's why I divorced him. They can't take the little money I have," she insisted. She could barely contain the spitefulness in her voice just thinking about the fact that Karl could take more from her. *I'll kill him first.*

Luke eyed her sternly, not at all as the boy she once knew but as the man she'd never known, the one she wanted to.

"*They* can do anything they want to."

"How?" she asked, flummoxed.

"They can go after you for civil asset seizure and forfeiture," he said, drinking more of his beer. This conversation was apparently stressing him out. Valerie couldn't understand why he cared about her.

"My lawyer didn't say anything about that. What does that even mean?" she asked, because she thought she'd crossed all her t's and dotted all her i's where her personal legal interests were concerned.

"The Feds can put TROs, temporary restraining orders, on marital property, such as homes and assets, and when they do, it's hard to get your stuff back."

She dug her fist into the countertop, feeling as if the nails were going to pop out of the wood at any moment. Then she scratched at her arm with her fingernails, totally freaked out. "That has to be illegal."

He pulled her hand away so she'd stop mutilating her skin.

She looked down at her forearm, shamed. She just couldn't stand for things to be this out of order.

"Hey." Luke grabbed her arms until she focused on him. "It's wrong, but it happens every day. The government does what it wants to indicted felons. And their families."

"He hasn't been convicted yet. He's just been arrested today. Not sure they even have enough on him." She placed her chilled glass to the skin on her arm.

"They do, Val." The way her name sounded coming off his lips, gentle and carefree like the old days, pacified her.

This couldn't be happening. Karl couldn't take any more from her. "Ninety-five percent of federal indictments end in guilty pleas," he said. "Karl is going down."

She looked up at him, surprised, although she shouldn't be. Karl had lied about a lot. "Karl claimed he didn't leave a paper trail."

Luke bit the side of his cheek before draining his beer. "He also claimed he only stole $200,000."

She sighed. *True.*

Valerie didn't reply right away. It was hard to swallow her pride and admit she'd made a huge mistake both in trusting Karl and in marrying him. Luke sounded a little pompous, and she guessed a part of him was probably thinking, *You should've stuck with me.*

He must've sensed her discomfort. "I'm not trying to be rough on you here."

She rose from her counter stool and almost fell over at the sudden movement. He grabbed her arm. "Are you okay?" His breath was a wisp in her ear.

No, I'm not okay. My brother's dead, and my husband is in prison!

She wanted to cry, but somehow, Luke's touch and breath in her ear calmed her.

How easy it would be to fall back into the sound of his voice. She hadn't realized how much she'd missed it. She'd thought a lot about that quandary lately—should she have just stayed with Luke?

They'd been so young. There was too much he didn't know. And he wouldn't have wanted to stick around if she told him now. She'd kept a secret from him, and she didn't think he'd excuse her just because they were teenagers.

"I just can't deal. There's too much." She pulled away from him and snagged another beer from the fridge. "Here ya go."

"I'm here to help, Val," he said.

He kept repeating that phrase. She hadn't believed him before, but this time felt different. "You're in homicide. How do you know all the ins and outs of white-collar crime anyway?"

"I didn't wake up in homicide." He laughed.

"Right," she said. Luke had worked his way up to his esteemed position of detective. She had to continually remind herself that he was far removed from the unsure kid from O'Hara Township who'd stumbled onto her lawn with a handful of gerbera daisies. She still loved those flowers. Karl had brought home dozens of roses over the years. None was as satisfying as the boldly colored flowers Luke used to pluck from his garden for her, homegrown.

Karl's gifts were all purchased. Now she had to wonder with whose money. "It sounds like you did your homework here. What can I do?" she asked, taking in his sympathetic grin.

"Maybe I'm being insensitive bringing this up, with your brother . . ." He let the words hang in the air.

"No, I want to get a handle on it. And . . ." She laughed out loud so hard, she almost cried.

Luke glanced at her worriedly like she was cracking up.

"And what?"

She wiped at her eyes. "Believe me, Christian would want me to take care of my finances. I can hear him barking at me right now. *For God's sake, secure your assets, woman. You can't do anything about me—I'm dead.*"

He laughed with her for a moment—until she crumpled.

The tears tumbled along with a blubbering whimper.

"Oh, Val. Come here," he said, even though he walked over to her. She collapsed into his arms and wrapped them tightly around her. He swayed her back and forth, and she wiped her eyes on his shirt as they rocked in a silent dance.

"What do I have to do?" she asked.

"First things first, how long ago were the divorce papers signed? A lot of women wait because their husbands tell them it might be okay. Like yours did," he said, more gently this time.

How can you still care about me after how I left you?

She cleared her throat. "Six months."

Luke let out an exhale of relief. "Great. You might be in good shape."

"I initiated the divorce the day after he told me what he'd done. When he couldn't hide it anymore. I didn't report him myself because I didn't want to be complicit, but he was already being investigated by the Feds by then. My lawyer said it could only hurt me to turn him in myself." *An accomplice.*

He touched her shoulder. She watched his fingers meet her flesh. It wasn't just his voice she'd missed. It was his touch too. "You never knew about Karl's involvement, do you hear me? If they ask you, you didn't know. The divorce occurred because of marital issues, and you could mention his irresponsible spending if you have evidence, but that's it."

"Okay," she said. Their faces were close, like in the bar. Luke had just told her not to disclose damning information. He was an officer of the law telling her what to lie about and how exactly to do it in order to protect herself.

It was only in that moment that she truly believed—*he is here to help.*

She wanted to know why. How could he possibly care about his ex-girlfriend from twenty years ago this much to jeopardize his credibility at work? What if Valerie repeated what he'd said? She wondered how he could trust her when she'd inexplicably broken his heart.

He must've read the question mark smattered on her face. "I know you would've never gone along willingly with something like this. I've seen people get burned in these cases. Innocent spouses. I just didn't want you to be one of them."

"How do you know I'm innocent when you haven't talked to me in so long?"

Luke hadn't asked her about what he'd found out when he'd questioned Piedmont. And she sure as hell wasn't going to prod him for it.

He lightly rubbed the marks she'd left on her arms. "No one likes things in their place more than you do. Remember how I used to mess with your room on purpose? OCD queen."

"You were the worst." She smiled at the memory of how he used to take her carefully arranged throw pillows on her bed and toss them all over the floor. He'd move things around on her organized desk just to see if she'd notice. If she attempted to rearrange them, she'd be tackled to the ground and assaulted with the pillows.

She could still picture Luke back then, dressed in his baggy jeans and oversize Adidas hoodie, the smell of Cool Water cologne heavy on his neck, the thick gold chain he always wore sliding around on his beautiful tanned skin. The sweatshirt was black and white and too big for him, and she used to steal it after they'd make love and lounge around in it like a robe.

Almost a freshman in college, she knew her parents were never home, and Marian left her alone with Luke to tend to the younger ones. The memory of it all was as clear as flipping through a photo book.

"Strung tightly" was how Lucy sometimes referred to Valerie, and she knew it was true. Luke had a way of unwinding those strings. He unnerved her and relaxed her all at once.

He continued to softly stroke her arm. He was pulling on her strings right now, untightening them one by one. He used to do this when they'd dated, touch her lightly in places to mollify her. He'd feather her bare back with his fingertips, brush her hair. She needed his touch more than ever now. She didn't want the complication that came with it, though.

He was a mirror from decades ago that made her forget all her troubles of today. His reflection was pulling her in. His hand grazed her cheek.

But what about your wife?

She lifted her head off his chest. "Why aren't you wearing a wedding ring?" Valerie asked. She was no homewrecker.

"Because I'm not married. I'm divorced too," he said.

His fingers rubbed the underside of her wrist now, and she wondered if he could feel her pulse jump, if he could feel what he did to her.

"I'm sorry. What happened?" she asked. Not because she was being nosy but because she couldn't understand why anyone would want to leave him.

He frowned. "My ex-wife shouldn't have married a cop, that's what. I love my job. She hates it. On my off hours, I was one hundred percent committed to my family, but she couldn't handle all the disruptions when I was on duty. And the added worry of being a detective's wife"—he shook his head—"definitely wasn't for her."

"That's hard. Especially since you love what you do."

"When I was promoted to homicide . . ." He turned sideways, away from her. "Homicides almost always occur on weekends. After hours. Our lives were constantly interrupted. I'd never been so fulfilled at work, but I felt things coming apart at home." He drank some more. Valerie took his forearm in her own hand and started making swirls on it like he'd done with hers. He smiled.

"Anyway, I made a mistake in acting too late. I should've tried to transfer into a different department. I'd offered to do it. But by that time . . ." He bit the inside of his cheek again and looked away.

"What is it? I'm here to help." She echoed his words.

He smiled at her. It was a little too easy to be *them* again. It was like no time had passed at all. She'd realized, sadly, that she not only missed Luke, she missed the version of herself she was when she was with him too. He made her remember how playful she could be. Luke was so different from the people in and around her family. He'd alleviated the stress that came with being a Fox. When she'd been with him, he made her want to be carefree. Even when he'd worked in the restaurant business, it was to serve people. She knew he'd end up doing something to benefit the public, a true helper. And he'd turned into the best kind—a police officer. She knew not all officers were on the up-and-up, but Luke was, and she envied the hell out of him for that.

"She, uh, found a school guidance counselor who has all kinds of time to spend with her and our kids. Her new guy has nights, weekends, and summers off too. He's super sensitive to her emotional needs, being a counselor and all. Jackpot for her, right?" Luke polished off his beer, and now she understood why he drank so much.

"That's too bad," she said. "I'm sorry."

"Thanks. I held on to my job. I see my kids every other week. I have three." He nodded.

"You're blessed," she said. It was an annoying phrase she'd stolen from Glenda whenever someone said something that wasn't exactly positive but wasn't entirely negative either.

"Sometimes I don't know. Then there're moments like today that make me wonder if maybe I am." He touched her cheek, his hand finding the nape of her neck beneath her hair. She leaned into him. "Have you wondered why we're being pushed back together again? If maybe it means something else?" he asked.

Valerie's heart thrummed in her chest. "Yes. I've wondered it. I thought you were married, though, and it was just one more of God's cruel jokes being thrown at me," she said.

"I'm not a cruel joke, Val. I'm blessed, remember?" He dipped his head down toward hers and drew her closer. She shut her eyes and let his lips find hers. She threaded her fingers through the curls on the back of his head as he kissed her. Everything inside her hurt, but he made it feel better. In his arms, with those familiar lips pressed to hers, she was wanted and desired and—loved.

Luke abruptly pulled his lips away, leaving her wanting more. "We shouldn't do this. I'm the officer on your family's case. After the case, though. Okay?" He was breathing hard, and she could tell he was practicing a lot of restraint.

"Why did you kiss me, then?" she asked.

He squeezed his eyes shut. "I wasn't sure if I was reading your signals right. It's been hard being around you without knowing if you still feel something for me. Because I sure still feel something for you."

She grabbed Luke by the waist until he was flush with her body. "Don't leave me tonight," she said in his ear. "We can go back to reality tomorrow." She tugged at the back of his head until she was kissing him again.

He paused for only a moment before he reciprocated, more forcefully this time. She never stopped kissing him as she led him out of the kitchen.

If there was another time he tried to pull away after that, Valerie didn't know, because he was a man possessed, tearing her clothes from her body.

They made it as far as the couch before he picked her up, legs wrapped around him. She leaned into him and let his fingers unwind all her strings until she was putty in his hands. He laid her down and made her remember all the reasons she'd run so fast and far away from him.

Because he was one of the only people in the world who could make her come apart. One of the only ones who could drive her completely out of control.

CHAPTER 18

Marian

That evening, Marian walked back to the memory center. She'd decided to call Eli and tell him that the detective was sniffing around again.

"Don't worry about that. We just need to make sure you're protected, Mother. Don't talk to the detective if he comes back. And make sure Simone doesn't either," he said.

Eli, a contract lawyer, described his job as boring yet lucrative. But the final request he'd asked of Marian hadn't been dull at all. Marian already knew that the paperwork that'd been signed linked Simone's rights with her own. Stefan had thought Simone was just signing over her grantor rights to Fox Wealth Management, but Eli had her sign the charity papers too. The charity—a false shelter linked to a bank account in Marian's name. Marian had known something like this was added, had more or less requested it, but it all sounded different to her ears now.

Eli assured Marian that the children had been briefed and they knew a provision was added for her, but they just didn't understand how or what dollar amount was attached to it. All that mattered was that she was taken care of. Stefan had hired Eli's firm, and Eli had been the one to arrange for the men to show up at the memory center and have Simone sign the papers.

Her son had only been trying to protect her.

So selfless, her boy.

Eli explained to her that it wasn't unusual that his firm had received the assignment. He'd explained he had a little extra insight into the matter because he could view the documents at work, but what he'd asked of her now didn't feel right. He'd wanted her to try to reason with Simone and ask her not to mention the fact that they'd written Marian into the legal agreement.

Would Simone remember that Marian was included in the paperwork? She'd read it, but had Simone fully understood what she was signing? She'd had her senses about her back then, but legal documents had a way of blurring together, even when the most careful person studied them.

This was all necessary to protect Marian's interests, Eli had said.

He hadn't liked that her living situation had been arranged on the Foxes' good word alone and that it worried Marian. She couldn't blame him, really. Being a lawyer now, he wanted things in writing. He'd also convinced her it was merely what had been promised to her anyway. Only this time, it was legally binding.

Marian would see if she could get a little more from Simone tonight.

As they sat in the common area, most of the residents there stared emptily into the room. Simone's bright eyes seemed to be more lucid today, though.

"Do you remember the men coming here asking you to sign the papers, Simone?" She hated probing the fragile woman for details. Simone was in good spirits, though. And maybe, just maybe, Marian could get her to forget the only thing she seemed to remember.

Simone glanced out the window instead of answering her, even though it was dark outside.

There were days Simone recited events she'd attended in vivid detail. "Remember when B. E. Taylor sang 'Silent Night' at Heinz Hall for that Christmas concert? His voice . . . my God . . . and how the Christmas tree seemed to disappear into the chandelier and how the chandelier seemed to disappear into the plaster patching, the deco painting on the ceiling." Her eyes would bounce along with excitement to the story.

Simone had an eye for beauty. She would say things just like this, but when Marian would ask her about it the next day, the memory would be lost or altered.

A snippet of it might remain, like, *B. E. Taylor. Yes, I liked his Christmas album.* But the specifics of the historic building would be gone from the recount.

However, each and every time Marian had asked Simone about the men who'd arrived with the papers, she remembered exactly what they'd been there for.

Marian feared that Eli had relied on Simone's unreliable memory to ensure their anonymity. It wasn't illegal for Eli's firm to process the Foxes' paperwork, but she thought it could be considered a conflict of interest if it had Marian's fingerprint on it.

As Simone's health continued to deteriorate, it had niggled in the back of Marian's mind too.

What happens to me if Simone dies before Stefan? Or when they both go?

Up until the party, it was a given that Simone would eventually pass away first. If Eli had a say in the paperwork, Marian would likely get something to cover herself either way. But if the Fox children knew Eli had withheld financial information from them, they wouldn't like it. They'd have Eli's head—and his job.

Simone finally turned to Marian. "The men were here to get my signature to turn over the grantor rights to the Den money because I've lost my wits, dear." She'd repeated almost the exact sentence the other day when Marian had asked, only she added a new phrase.

"The Den? What's that?" Marian asked.

"The children's trust," Simone answered, as if Marian should know what she was talking about.

Marian feared Simone was falling off again. "The children don't have a trust. Remember? Stefan only wanted to pay for their college. I thought it was your rights to Fox Wealth."

Simone shook her head. "The company is one part. The children's trust, another."

Marian's mouth dropped open. Could it be true? Marian hadn't read the papers. Did a secret trust for the children exist? She feared that if one did, her son had just linked a false charity to it with her name marked as the recipient. Did he realize what he'd done? "Well, whatever you say. I'm just asking that you not repeat that. Not to anyone who isn't me." *Why is this the one thing you remember?*

"Who?" Simone asked.

"Any of them. Valerie, for instance. Has she been by? Had you mentioned anything to her about this?" Marian ground her teeth together.

Eli had gotten upset when she'd told him that Kapinos had asked to see Simone. "It's criminal to interview someone with Alzheimer's disease." Marian agreed.

"Valerie hasn't been by this week. I don't think," Simone said.

"What about Eli?" she added for good measure. Because she hadn't liked that her son had kept this from her. What other information had he withheld? He'd drawn up the papers. He had to have seen this trust.

"No. Haven't seen Eli in a while," she confirmed.

If Simone were questioned and her damaged brain recalled something that was entirely false, what then? Or if she got half the details right, that could cause confusion. What was most frightening was if the detective questioned Simone and she remembered the 100 percent truth—that Eli had written Marian into the legal documents without telling anyone else to more or less squander money from the trust and disguise it as a charity. Did Simone know about this?

Desperate, Marian needed to try harder. There was too much at stake here. Eli's career, her retirement—all the secrets of that house that if spilled could destroy everyone, especially Marian.

"Eli is a lawyer now, Simone. He's done well for himself. He never would've made it without your help. Now, let's not mention his name. Or your part in making legal changes that involve us. Okay? I've done everything over the years that you've asked of me." She pushed to make sure this plea nestled nice and tightly in Simone's scattered brain.

Simone's eyes focused on Marian in a way that disturbed her. "Did you, now? Did you tell yourself that it was for me? While it was happening?"

Breath that should've been long expelled burned in Marian's chest until she finally let it out. "What do you mean?"

Simone continued to stare right through her. "On Lucy's birthday, did you tell yourself that it was for me?" Marian felt naked under Simone's stone-cold glare, as if her knit shirt had just been lifted up for the world to see. She wrapped her arms around herself, pushing it back down, keeping herself covered up like she always had.

"You told me to," Marian whispered.

"Ha!" Simone laughed. It was a croaky, dry rasp of a giggle. "You wanted to, madam," Simone accused.

Marian gulped, terrified that the memory of Simone seeing her bare flesh hadn't gone with the others. If Simone's gray matter had limited space, she wished she'd leave that recollection out. Even in sickness, she wouldn't forget. "But you asked . . ."

"Yes, but who was it for, dear? Was it for you or me? Quit saying everything you did was for me. Because *that* was for you." Simone placed her head back on the chair and closed her eyes, signaling she was done for the day.

Broken as Simone was, she still had to make it known who was in charge here.

Marian's purpose was to receive requests from Simone, not the other way around.

Marian rose from her visitor's chair and strode nervously back to her apartment.

She quickly texted Eli: She still remembers.

Eli: Her memories are temporary. That one will be too.

Marian tensed. She was concerned Eli was being too optimistic regarding Simone. He was probably worried about his job. If something happened to it, it'd be all Marian's fault for opening her big mouth about her fears over Simone's health and her own place in this world. The last time she'd gotten ahead of herself, attempted to level herself with the Foxes, it'd nearly been her end.

She had done everything she could to protect her son's well-being back then, and she'd do the same thing now.

CHAPTER 19

LUCINDA

Hands grip her neck. Her body is pinned to the ground.

Cool morning grass laces through her fingers as she grasps at green straws. There's no leverage against the force that's holding her down. Her arms and legs won't cooperate with her mind.

She sweats against the sweet earth and chokes for breath, terror flooding her body.

Her eyes flutter, and she can see *them*.

The crows flap all around her. Six of them. The sound of their wings slices through her ears, loudly.

Her brother is there too.

A teenage Jeremy watches her from afar. He screams, "Stop. Stop." She doesn't know why.

She looks at her hands lying next to the tiny straws. She pulls at the earth for dear life, trying to get up, but her fingers are covered in blood.

Her head turns to find a fox staring back.

It crawls out of a nearby hole in the ground, startling as it is beautiful with its red coat and black stockings. It lies beside her in the grass and licks her bloody fingers, then bares its needlelike teeth, thick at the base, pointed and sharp at the bottom.

Wet spurts hit her face. She's paralyzed in place.

She peers up at a chicken as it dances in her front view. It's missing something—a head.

"I'm sorry," she rasps out through a broken windpipe. The fox growls at her, then dashes off in the chicken's direction.

The fox snatches the chicken by the neck and scampers away.

"Too many foxes in the henhouse." Jeremy screams. As hard as he tries to run, he can't reach her. An invisible wall is between them, and he's on the other side.

She's going to die there.

Childhood laughter echoes in her ear.

Jeremy falls to the ground.

Her vision comes and goes, pixilated, then dark—consciousness and total blackness. Jeremy screams.

His voice is razors in her ears.

She prays for it to be over. She begs to die.

And then she realizes the voice she hears screaming isn't Jeremy's. It's her own.

"Open your eyes, Lucy! My God!"

Someone turned on an electric fan, the voice close, like an echo through a seashell. *Aja.* Lucinda's eyes flicked open. Sensation flooded her body in a pins-and-needles rush. She could move now, but her blood was rushing like she'd just run a marathon.

What park did I just escape from? There was a park . . . for sure.

Aja's dark gaze met hers in the dim lighting. Aja was not in a park. Aja was on her bedroom floor, on the opposite side of the mattress.

Lucinda was no longer on the grass but in Aja's apartment.

"What're you doing?" Lucinda asked her. Lucinda sat up in bed, terrified. Her lips felt like sandpaper. They moved around like she had marbles inside. Her nerve endings felt stunned, scorched, like she'd brushed her body parts along a rug, now numb with abrasion.

"What was that, Lucy?" Aja asked, frightened.

Beads of sweat covered Lucinda's body in a slick coat. She shook head to toe. All she could do was touch her arms and legs and make sure they were still there.

The childhood rhyme ripped through her mind along with the giggle from her dream—*head, shoulders, knees and toes, knees and toes.*

Her digits were all there. "I'm not sure," she said.

"Oh my God. What is wrong with you?" Aja asked.

"I had a nightmare," Lucinda said. "Why're you down there?"

"You pushed me off the bed. Do you normally become violent when you sleep?"

Lucinda placed her hands on her collarbone. "No. Did you . . . Did you have your hands around my neck?" Her throat was sore. Not on the inside from screaming. The pain was on the outside, like her trachea had been pushed into her spine or crushed.

Aja scowled. "No. I was shaking you awake, and you tossed me off the bed. I could've hit my head."

It must've all been a dream. A freakish, terrifying dream trying to tell her something.

Lucinda peered at her sideways, still trying to normalize to the awake world. "I'm sorry. I've never sleepwalked before, but occasionally I do have night terrors."

She'd had them since she was a small child. Lucinda had never moved during them, though, only screamed. And she never had physical side effects afterward, like a sore throat. It was probably from screeching loudly. This had been a *bad* one.

"That was more than a nightmare," Aja protested.

Lucinda didn't disagree. "It was a warning. Sometimes my dreams do that. I have to leave. Now."

Aja gawked at her with fright.

Whether her heart had stopped in her sleep or her psyche was telling her to run before it did, the time had come to evacuate this situation.

"No. Look, you just scared me. You're going through a lot. I get it. It's coming out in your sleep." Aja morphed quickly back into her kind self. Lucinda's breath finally regulated, but her heart had started to flutter wildly again.

Entrapment. She felt caught in a trap with this woman. It's why her arms and legs had lost sensation. It was symbolism for how Aja made her feel. Paralyzed.

Something happened to Jeremy. She fanned her hands, front to back, making sure they really didn't have blood on them. *All clear.*

"I need to check on my brother," Lucinda said.

Aja turned toward the clock on the bedside table. "Why? It's three a.m."

"I don't care," she argued. She'd had a warning vision, and Jeremy was in it. She'd had a premonition before Christian crashed too. It'd happened hours before the actual event.

"Why can't it wait until tomorrow?" Aja asked.

Her hands quivered as she gathered her hair into a bun. "You don't understand. He was in my dream. And he was in trouble."

"What? It was just a dream, Lucy." Aja threw her dirty black T-shirt over her head.

Does she ever wash it?

Perhaps she had a drawer full of clean ones like Father once had. His were white. He'd wear them beneath his dress shirts. Lucinda would just tell herself that Aja put on a fresh one each day, especially after all the DNA they'd just exchanged beneath the sheets.

"Jeremy won't answer. He's a sound sleeper. I'm going there." Lucinda didn't care what hour it was. She had to get out of that apartment. And she needed to check on her brother. She threw on Aja's maxi dress again, no bra, and was on her feet, but Aja blocked the bedroom door.

"This is not a good idea." Aja's eyes hardened. The light cast an odd reflection, and Lucinda could see herself in them.

"I had a bad dream and Jeremy was in it. No one listened to me the last time I saw the crows and Hector ended up dead." Lucinda scrambled toward her.

Aja blocked her. "Who is Hector, Lucy? You're making no sense."

"I told you to call me Lucinda."

Aja sighed. "You're making no sense, Lu-cinda."

"I'm leaving. I need to check on my brother." Lucinda turned sideways, forming a pencil to slink by. Aja shifted quickly again, stopping her once more.

Aja pushed her back, catching Lucinda's shoulder on her cheek. "*Ouch.* It's not safe for you to leave at this hour. You're not thinking straight, and you need to calm down. Take a pause."

"I live in New York City. In terms of safety, three a.m. in Pittsburgh is like Times Square at noon. Get the hell out of my way." She shoved Aja with her hands this time and wiggled her way out.

Aja didn't follow her, thankfully, as she grabbed her backpack, jumped into her Birkenstocks, and beelined for the door.

"Whew," Lucinda said, once outside. She ordered an Uber. *I really need to find somewhere else to stay.*

Her black Ford Escape chariot arrived promptly, and she climbed inside. "Do you need me to take you to the hospital instead, miss?" he asked.

"What? Why?" Lucinda asked. She knew she looked rough, but his comment seemed extreme.

"Your neck." He pointed at his own neck.

She checked hers out in his rearview mirror and let out a squeak. Faint red finger marks circled her neck on both sides. Had she been choked? Was it a hickey?

Did Aja try to kill me in my sleep?

She gulped in a giant breath of air.

I'm just stressed. Stressed and losing my mind.

The alternative was that she'd choked herself, and she wasn't even sure that was physically possible. She tried to do it now, and it totally was.

The Uber driver was ogling her, waiting for an answer. She realized he was looking at a woman who had her hands around her own neck, and even though his early-morning pickups were probably bad ones, this one likely topped the charts. "You on drugs or something? Maybe you should get a different ride."

"No," she said, flustered. "If I were on drugs, I'd be in a much better mood, trust me. Please, just drive to the address on your service ticket."

He turned off his interior light, righted himself in the driver seat, and sped off.

She was thankful when he didn't utter another word as they made their way across the 10th Street Bridge toward the East End of the city. Squirrel Hill was one of those quasi-college towns, with its mix of eclectic restaurants, clothing boutiques, and independent shops that lined the streets. Jeremy had too much energy to live in a place without walkable venues, which was exactly where he'd met Daphne—at the local Indian restaurant. Lucinda had heard all about it when she'd called him on his birthday last year.

Daphne had been picking up a to-go order of *palak paneer*.

And he'd also been picking up an order of *palak paneer*.

They'd both remarked how it was odd that they'd had the same order, and Daphne had commented how she'd never met a man who liked the vegetarian dish.

And Jeremy had said something with cheesy endearment like, "It is strange we both love this unique dish, savored by only those with the best taste. It's not as if we're picking up *tikka masala*, like the rest of the carryout-ers. We should probably figure out what else we have in common."

Jeremy's pickup line had worked. They'd sat outside the restaurant in terribly uncomfortable metal chairs and eaten their takeout with disposable silverware. Lucinda smiled at the memory of their how-I-met-you story.

Women loved Jeremy's rough-around-the-edges, *I've screwed up in the past, but you can make me whole again* persona. Valerie claimed he attracted emotionally unavailable women and ladies with Daddy issues, but Daphne seemed like the real deal from what Lucinda had heard.

Jeremy's only problem was that he'd imagined himself to be cleverer than he actually was. Lucinda couldn't be the only person who could envision him studying the diagram for the mechanical specs of a Mercedes, fingering the screen, and saying, *I just have to cut here.*

It was also plausible Dashing Detective Luke would discover that Jeremy was in severe financial trouble and that he hadn't wanted Daphne to find out. Valerie wasn't the only reasonable suspect.

Just as long as they don't look at me!

Jeremy had been the one to find her the day she'd had the accident with the chicken. If her arm hadn't cramped up on the axe swing, she would've been able to chop that bird clean through.

Perhaps that was all the dream was, a distorted memory, a severe result of stress—or the unfortunate result of extreme asphyxiation.

The images from the nightmare were vivid and gruesome.

She wrapped her arms around herself, chilly. The memory of the way the blades of grass tickled her shoulders as the blood leaked from her body into the ground was hard to shake. The feeling would hang with her until she figured out what it meant.

When they reached Murray Avenue, the driver pulled up to Jeremy's Edwardian-style home. The all-red brickwork looked like dried blood from her nightmare. The thick wooden porch railings were stiff and uninviting. A single light scarcely lit the walk-up. She thanked the driver for putting up with her as she exited.

She could say she just needed somewhere to stay. It wasn't exactly a lie anymore.

Jeremy was actually who she'd intended to ask for shelter tomorrow, because there was no way she could remain in that apartment with Aja. And after hearing about Karl, she wanted to steer clear of Valerie.

Her sister was a woman possessed when someone upset her applecart. Lucinda couldn't imagine how she was coping with such a domestic upheaval.

Lucinda crept up the steps and rang the doorbell.

God, he's going to kill me.

Most days, Jeremy ran like a live wire that wouldn't stop—until he crashed. Then he went down and wouldn't wake up until the morning. Tonight was no exception. He wasn't answering.

She tried calling him, and his phone went straight to voice mail. It didn't even ring, which was a little odd. She didn't believe he'd allow it to go dead, especially with all his talk of the life-saving portable batteries.

Lucinda tried knocking. Waited. Nothing.

The only reason Lucinda knew where Jeremy hid his key was because he'd had the same chintzy key holder since college. It was a fake rock with his college alma mater—Pitt—with its vicious little panther painted on the front. She lifted up the rock, which was clearly plastic, and undid the slot on the bottom to find his spare.

She paused. *Should I do this?*

What if Daphne was there? She'd been intrigued to meet Daphne, but not like this.

Lucinda couldn't get it out of her head—the frantic look on Jeremy's face as he reached out to help her, frozen in place. It beckoned her forward. Or was it just a dream?

Her skin prickled at the thought.

She pushed the key in the lock and turned it. A cranking metal noise came next. Her fingers quickly found the light switch, and

Jeremy's foyer came into view with its parquet floors and sparkly chandelier she was sure came with the house.

In natural Jeremy order, his kicks were splayed all over the place, dress loafers mixed with Jordans and Yeezys. Not much for name-brand clothes, but he was a bit of a shoe whore. "Jeremy!" she called out.

She had no intention of posing as an intruder or being attacked like one.

Lucinda didn't think Jeremy owned a gun. Father wasn't a hunter, and they hadn't grown up with them.

"Jeremy," she called up the antiqued cherry stairs with the paisley runner. He had a charming house that might include a wife someday soon, if Father could ever pass away so he could afford a ring.

She imagined Daphne required a large nugget.

They were all waiting for the doctors to tell them there was nothing more they could do for their father. There was a lot at stake here. Jeremy knew it too. The first question he'd asked when the estate was disclosed—"how much?"

The upstairs was completely dark, but instead of climbing the steps, she paused. Lucinda's eyes were drawn to Jeremy's office off the kitchen. It was the only light that appeared to be on in the house, and the yellow shadow cast off the mahogany desk gave a sickly pale glow. There was a single piece of white computer paper on the polished floor.

Jeremy wasn't a tidy person, and she'd guessed he'd just had his cleaning crew in, because the hardwood gleamed with a waxy shine.

The paper resting on top of the hardwood floor bothered her.

It wasn't unlike her brother to leave garbage out and not throw it away, just like it wasn't out of character for him to drop something on the office floor and not pick it up.

She didn't know how he could stand it. Just like she couldn't comprehend how Aja could grind makeup into her rug and leave it unlaundered or how she could wear the same gross T-shirt all week.

Something about that damn piece of paper called to Lucinda, though, because from what she could tell through the white french doors, the rest of the office appeared immaculate—except for that single white square.

The books were lined up by color on the bookshelf, and Jeremy had never been much of a reader, but from what Lucinda could tell, he had a lot of nonfiction books. Jeremy was into self-help lit, constantly trying to better himself—or give the impression to others, like the ladies, that he was. A white book cover with bold black lettering, *The Power of Letting Go*, winked at Lucinda as she approached the office.

"I'm going in your office," she yelled, in case he had a camera or an Alexa or something else tracking her. She never discounted the possibility.

Lucinda pushed on the french doors. She immediately walked over to the paper and picked it up. There were just phone numbers on it and addresses, work stuff. She inspected the office and dropped that paper right back down on the floor. *"Oh my God."*

Jeremy was sitting at his desk, slumped over. It's why she hadn't seen him. He was hidden behind his computer monitor. Something rubbery was tied around his arm, a needle sticking from the crook near his elbow, his skin there bluish purple.

She wouldn't look at his face.

She could not look at his face. *"Fuck. Nooo."*

She couldn't feel for his pulse. But she had to feel for his pulse. He could still be alive.

Lucinda knelt on the floor and took her hand that was clamped over her open mouth and forced it behind the shag of Jeremy's hair, onto his neck, sticky and wet—where she detected a tiny titter of activity, a barely there pulse.

A smell like disinfectant and body odor hit her nostrils. She didn't have time to inspect more. She reached in her backpack for her cell phone and called 911.

Jeremy's skin was cold, and it made her think she was too late. She'd been delayed in getting here—*Aja*. She'd never forgive her if Jeremy didn't make it.

She'd seen the six crows.

No one would believe her, just like the first time with Hector.

As she collapsed on the ground next to her brother's seated, still body and waited for the ambulance, she cried until an officer arrived and picked her back up.

CHAPTER 20

VALERIE

After a night of unrest, Valerie crawled back to bed but was disturbed by the sound of a vibrating phone. She tussled beneath the sheets before she remembered who was lying next to her—and what year it was.

"Luke," she whispered. He'd been curled into her like a napping cat, and she'd lain there a minute longer and watched him, soaking in the moment because she knew it wouldn't last forever. His phone was going wild beside him.

She pushed on his shoulder, then reached around him to grab it.

A growl escaped his lips. She grinned.

It'd been nearly twenty years since she'd thought he was the one, then convinced herself to believe otherwise. She smiled at the memory of the moment that brought them together—when she'd snuck into the back of the six-seater golf cart to escape the wives of her father's clients who'd coerced Valerie into pairing up with them at the country club.

"Oh, is there not enough room up there?" he'd asked. "I can get another cart." She'd heard of people falling in love at first glance, but it was his voice that'd stopped her heart.

"No, there is," she said.

"Oh." He smiled and then looked away. His olive skin had caught a hint of pink on his cheeks.

"What's your name?" she asked.

"Lucas. Luke," he struggled.

"Well, hi, Lucas Luke. Odd name. I'd have words with your parents if I were you. I'm Valerie Fox."

He laughed. "No, it's Lucas Kapinos. Luke is what most people call me. Mrs. Pritchard almost had a cow when I told her my last name, though, so don't repeat it," he whispered. "And I know who *you* are," he said.

She fluttered her eyelashes. "Oh no, why did she flip?" Valerie whispered.

"I can't say right now," he whispered back, pointing behind them.

She giggled, a curiosity overtaking her. "It's funny we've been around each other all these years and haven't spoken."

"I was working," he said, as if she'd accused him of ignoring her.

"Valerie, you're up," she heard Mrs. Pritchard say.

She looked out of the cart to see where they were. "I have two requests of you, Luke."

He raised his eyebrows. "What's that?"

"One is that we hang out after you're done here today so I can hear the rest of your story of Lucas Luke." Because she wouldn't dare say his last name. "And two is that you grab my driver."

"Absolutely." He hopped out and snagged her club.

She met Luke afterward.

Luke's story of Mrs. Pritchard was hilarious. She'd ordered Greek food from his father's restaurant, which was simply named Kapinos, and claimed that the tahini sauce on her gyro must've been spoiled because it gave her such bad indigestion, she'd ended up in the ER. Apparently, Luke's father had given her a mouthful that the sauce was just fine, that not a single other customer had gotten sick, and that she'd just had a bad case of heartburn because she wasn't used to the food. Mrs. Pritchard told Luke that he was lucky, because if he weren't her caddy, she would've sued his family. Luke had hated her ever since, but he still held her clubs.

Mrs. Pritchard had also refused to call him Luke, because after referring to him as Lucas for a number of years, she claimed it was like renaming a child after they were born.

"Your child. The one you wanted to sue!" Luke shouted as he told the story. She loved watching his expressions and the way he talked with his hands while he told it.

Mr. Pritchard was a magnate in the metal-fastener segment, and Valerie thought him and his family to be about as interesting as a steel bolt too. Valerie was looking forward to attending a university with much less pretentious people. If she'd gone Ivy League, she would've been surrounded by more of the same.

She needed a change.

The dark-haired boy sitting next to her was a nice start. He wasn't like any of the other boys she'd been interested in before.

Valerie had made the first move back then, climbing into the back of the golf cart, asking him to meet her after work—kissing him. She was ready to break free of this place and these people.

She could barely be torn away from Luke all summer—holding hands, soaking wet on the Log Jammer at Kennywood, making out at Sandcastle pool parties, concerts at Star Lake amphitheater. All the different bands they'd watched at X-Fest. Luke saving her from her first and last mosh pit. Sitting in Luke's passenger seat on the congested two-lane road home, locking lips as they sobered up and waited for the cars to clear.

It was the best damn summer of her life.

Until the two pink lines showed up on a little white stick a few weeks after her period hadn't.

Marian found the test stick in the trash can when she was cleaning, and she knew it couldn't be Lucy's, too young. Mother had her tubes tied after Lucy was born at the insistence of Father.

It could only be Valerie's.

Marian had convinced Valerie what she already knew was true—Luke wasn't the boy for her, and whether she kept the baby or not, she had to break up with him. Luke hadn't enrolled in college anywhere and wasn't sure what he wanted to do. He was going to take a year off, work at his father's restaurant, and save some money. Marian convinced her that he would never leave that restaurant.

That people like him didn't.

That if he wasn't motivated to go to college right then, he never would be.

Marian had even offered to drive Valerie to an abortion clinic. When Valerie thought of the garden with its abundance of flowers and its thick concrete benches sometimes, she remembered the parties and the white tents that seemed to pirouette to the sky like whipped frosting when she danced beneath them. More often, it was that night sitting there with Marian, sipping their tea, deciding what she would do with her future that she thought about most.

Marian was supposed to drive Valerie to the clinic that weekend when her parents would be tied up at a benefit dinner, but from the moment Valerie had agreed with Marian that it was best to terminate the pregnancy, she doubted her ability to go through with it.

However, the pregnancy determined itself when the next day, Valerie woke up in bloody sheets.

She'd miscarried, and Marian did what she did best—cleaned up the mess. Valerie helped, eager to get rid of the evidence. Running away from Luke and toward something new seemed like the most logical decision at the time. But she wouldn't tell him now the real reason she'd ended things. It'd been better to spare him.

She was thankful nature had made the decision for her back then where the baby was concerned—a sign they weren't meant to be.

It wasn't their time.

But . . . is now our time?

"Luke." She nipped at his ear with her lips. "Your phone is ringing."

He shot up in bed. Valerie pushed back his dark curls pasted down on his forehead and handed him his cell.

He grabbed it from her, eyes barely open. "Detective Kapinos."

She watched him grab a pocket notebook and take down the information from the call—a case, possibly suspicious, in Squirrel Hill. He was wide awake now. His shoulders hiked in alarm as if the caller had just told him something awful. He covered the phone with his hand and side-eyed her, then said he'd be right there. Luke sprang from bed and threw on his jeans.

Valerie took it all in.

This was the life that his ex-wife had been bothered by—the late calls, the disruption to their nightly lives. Probably their daily ones, too, although Valerie assumed most murders occurred in the evening.

She understood it took a special kind of person to support Luke's call to duty.

She also thought she might just be that person. Valerie watched him in admiration as he quickly readied himself for work. He'd placed his gun on the nightstand when he'd unfastened it from his belt last evening. She'd been inexplicably turned on by the close proximity of the weapon to where they'd shed their clothes. She was sure he would've secured it better if they hadn't been so eager.

Perhaps, over time, if holidays and birthdays were constantly interrupted like this, she'd grow resentful of his work. As long as it didn't happen all the time, it seemed a fair compromise for someone who was honest. Especially after everything Karl had put her through.

It wasn't Karl's thieving that'd ended her marriage, Valerie had decided.

It was the lies.

Not only the ones Karl had told her leading up to his confession but the ones she'd learned after his arrest.

Luke's career made her want to do more with herself, something meaningful. Before Isla was born, she'd been a volunteer at an outreach program where they used horses as therapy animals for special-needs children. She'd like to get back to it, take Isla with her this time. Valerie was saddened her daughter had no interest in horses, but maybe she'd like the volunteer work. Luke spurred creativity in her and nurtured her altruistic side.

"Do you need to shower?" she asked.

"Um . . . no, that's okay." Luke refused to make eye contact with her.

"Are you having regrets?" she asked.

He stopped and sighed. "Not about this." He kissed her on the forehead, his lips hanging there a beat too long. And if he could apologize with his lips, he just had.

"What is it, then?" she asked.

"We should've waited until your family's case was closed," he said.

Ah . . . work again. His dedication to the badge was unwavering. She could see how this could cause a rift in a relationship, but only if she let it. "I know. We probably should've waited . . ."

"I have to go to this case, and then I'll call you." He still wouldn't look at her. She was nervous as to why, exactly. And if it had less to do with the case and more to do with her.

"Okay," she said.

He told her goodbye, and she heard the front door slam shut moments later, in such a hurry to leave her. Valerie knew he had to go to work, but after all they'd just shared, his abruptness left her icy, staring at the wall, naked and exposed. It made her wonder if her abandonment all those years ago would make it impossible for them to move forward now.

CHAPTER 21

MARIAN

For Marian, his life began with tiny fox pajamas, feet hemmed in, mittens on the sleeves so he couldn't scratch himself with his fine kit claws. Marian remembered Simone holding up the little outfit she'd bought during a run to Monroeville Mall to pick up some postpartum dresses. They'd purchased a baby gate, too, long before he could walk.

It seemed from the beginning there'd been extra measures to keep Christian Fox safe.

Stefan had been excited to have a boy. An excellent baby, Christian slept through the night after just eight weeks. He didn't cry much, mostly content to just be near anyone who would hold him.

Marian realized later that Christian's good behavior had ruined it for all the children who came next, because none of them was as easy as he was.

Especially Jeremy.

Jeremy would exhaust himself in his bouncy seat until he passed out, drooling on the plastic top. Sports seemed a reasonable solution to expend Jeremy's energy, but his stringy body couldn't hold weight, and his lack of coordination made him a below-average athlete. Christian played a couple of sports, football and baseball, and excelled at both.

That's where the yardstick of achievement had started with Stefan, and Jeremy had never measured up. How could he when Stefan would say things like, "Sit still and concentrate on something for a change," as if it were so simple. As if all Jeremy had to do was will himself to get an A and it would happen.

Yes . . . the pecking order had started at a young age.

And the only thing Marian could think of when she'd received the news that Christian Fox had died was that someone had finally figured out a way to peck the strongest one to death.

Eli said he'd be by at lunchtime to talk to her. And then tomorrow they'd attend Christian's funeral.

He had to understand the toll this would take on her. The Foxes were her children as much as they were Eli's brothers and sisters—the only dysfunctional family they'd ever known.

When Eli had asked about his *real* family, the one Marian had left in Brooklyn, she'd said that only her father and brother remained, and it was safer for Eli not to meet them. Marian's mother had died while birthing her. Household chores were thrust upon her shoulders at a very early age, while her first-generation Czech father built up his slum-lord reputation in the Greenpoint business district where they lived. Her brother was his predetermined successor. Marian's place was to keep house, a substitute for the woman she unintentionally displaced, it seemed.

When Marian and Hector fled, she knew her father would never forgive her. She was still needed at home. But her father had been a violent person. She could still feel the spray of blood on her cheek from when she witnessed him chop a man's fingers off over a few hundred dollars of missed rent money, and she feared his reaction if she tried to go back.

At the time, Marian had felt most useful cooking and cleaning. It pleased those around her. Hector's cousin had given them the lead for the job at the Fox residence. When she was introduced to the Foxes and their proud matriarch, it was a good fit.

Marian's father hadn't approved of Hector, from Bed-Stuy, a poorer neighborhood than theirs, and forbade her from seeing him. So they'd left, and she'd made peace with the fact that the line of communication with her family was now closed. Although, every time there'd been a school project that'd brought up the family tree, Eli would reopen that can of worms—"But what about our family, the ones in New York? Should we try to find them?"

She couldn't answer him, because she no longer knew those family members. Eli had stopped asking questions after a while. Marian back-filled his yearning for a real family with the makeshift one they'd made at the Foxes. Now she had to do the unthinkable and help bury one of his fill-in siblings, and it was all a little too much.

For them all, apparently.

Marian realized now why Jeremy had visited Simone at the memory center. He'd been stopping to say goodbye to his mother before he tried to take his own life.

She'd found out about Jeremy when a frantic Lucy had called Marian asking for a ride from the police station (not that it would be the first time). She'd said Valerie wouldn't answer her phone, but then a few minutes later, she texted Marian letting her know Valerie had picked up after all.

When Lucy had told her why she was at the station, Marian had dropped her saucer in the sink, shattering it. She was so glad Jeremy had been found in time, once again, but she wondered about his mental state right before his episode.

Maybe Jeremy hadn't mentioned Christian's death at all to Simone. Marian trembled as she walked down the tree-lined path to inform Simone of Christian's death. It had to be done before the funeral.

When she arrived, Simone was sitting in her normal spot in the community room. Rosalie waved her in. "It's not a good day, Marian."

Oh no. She hated to deliver such heart-wrenching news if Simone was *off.*

When Marian reached Simone, she was picking at the skin on her arm with such ferocity, it had begun to bleed. She was gouging herself, and Marian was afraid to agitate her further by pulling her hand away.

"Nurse!" she called in a panic. "Rosalie?" She glanced behind her.

Rosalie rushed over and took in Simone's raked skin. "I'll get someone."

Marian scowled at Rosalie for allowing this to continue for as long as it had. Although Rosalie wasn't to blame. She was just the receptionist. The attendant on staff shouldn't have left their resident to her own devices for such a long period of time.

A nurse came over with a medicine cart and began dressing Simone's wound. "I'm sorry this happened. She doesn't normally pick."

"Pick?" Marian asked.

"Yes, a lot of our dementia patients pick. We can't apply casts or bandages to many of them because they'll tear clear through them," she said as she pulled Simone's hand away and began to dress her forearm.

"Get away from me," Simone complained.

"She's only trying to help you," Marian said. "You have a cut."

"This is a good one," the nurse said.

Inches long, the injury was an awful mutilation. It was as if Simone had just kept digging at the same spot over and over again. The self-inflicted wound made her stomach turn.

We used to dress those wrists with Cartier bangles, my dear.

Simone had always taken pride in her looks. It was hard to watch her ravage herself now, total disregard for the skin she'd once slathered with the best lotions.

"Don't touch me," Simone barked.

Marian placed a gentle hand on her shoulder. "It's Mari. Stop hurting yourself, Mona."

The nurse finished up. "All set." She directed her attention to Marian. "Nerves and anxiety can cause picking. I'll put in for a psych evaluation." The nurse pushed her cart away, and that was that. Marian couldn't get Simone to focus on her face.

Marian should leave and come back tomorrow, but then Simone would have less time to process the death of her son before seeing him in a coffin. Maybe it was better to deliver the awful news while Simone was only partially coherent. That's what Marian would prefer if the situation were reversed. Her gut cinched up like chained links, one clinking into another, as she imagined the horror.

"Mona, it's Mari. I have some bad news," Marian said.

"I already know," she said. "A mother always does."

Marian sat down in front of her. Simone remained distracted. "What do you know?"

"Stefan filed a civil suit against that teacher, ruined his life. It's no surprise. I told him he shouldn't have. Too far," she said angrily.

Dear Lord, her mind had escaped to when Lucy was still in high school.

"Mona, it's not about Lucy."

"Well, of course it would affect everyone. What did he think? Lucy admitted to coming on to him. She's been expelled, he lost his job, which should be enough. Stefan doesn't need to drain every penny just because the man embarrassed him."

Marian's shoulders jutted up to her ears. She'd always had an issue with how they'd placed so much blame on Lucy. Sure, she was promiscuous, but she'd also been just sixteen at the time, underage.

"It was justly served. She was a student in his class." Marian went with this line of thinking, because sometimes she had to let Simone munch her way through the past before she had a chance of tasting the present.

"His life is over. His wife wrote me a letter begging me not to file the suit," Simone went on.

Marian looked at her wearily. She'd known nothing about a letter. She must've kept it from Marian, and it was goading Simone now for some reason.

"That was a long time ago, Simone. It's okay. Please don't scratch your arm."

"That woman's death is on my hands. It always has been," she said. "I couldn't stop Stefan. I did try," she told Marian.

"What woman's death?"

"The one you're talking about," she said. "Is that what you came here to tell me? She's died?"

Oh my. She's really confused now. "Not her, but someone did pass away, Simone. We're going to need to go to the funeral soon."

"I can't go to that woman's funeral. It'll be closed casket anyway. Never saw the point."

"It's not a woman, Simone." She grabbed for her hand now, already wishing this moment to end. "It's Christian. Christian has passed away." Tears crested Marian's eyes.

"Christian? Christian was just here," Simone said.

"I'm glad he got to visit you." She hadn't seen Christian's name on the visitor list.

Simone's gaze appeared miles away, but Marian saw the pain sweep in and knock her down. Simone's head hit the backrest of the chair, her arms going lax. "No, no. He'll be all right. He just gets himself wrapped up in his work."

Simone's arms twitched, and then she was asleep. A tear rolled down Marian's face. She wiped it from her cheek and then left the center.

Marian sat on her back patio, sipping tea, staring into open air. The Foxes' contract with her name embedded in it was at the heart of her worries.

She heard footsteps approach. She turned to find Eli. He handed her a list of the things she'd asked him to pick up at the store.

She smiled. "How did I get so lucky?"

Eli took her teacup, knelt down, and hugged her. "No problem. I'm sorry about Christian, Mom. I didn't know him as well as the others, but he was a good guy."

She smirked at him doubtfully. He was saying that for her comfort. Eli had gotten a dose of Christian when he'd returned home from college, and from what Marian could recall, it wasn't a good one.

"Are you going to become a landscape architect like your old man?" Christian had joked once, while simultaneously stealing the ball from Eli on the driveway basketball court. Marian knew boys busted chops, but Eli's father was dead, the comment degrading, and Eli had noticed.

"What do you think really happened?" she asked.

"I don't know. But you can't blame yourself for the terrible things they do." He must've sensed her distress. "Your service to them is over," he said definitively.

"But . . . everything that's happened . . ." She shook her head. Would this blow back on them?

"Is not your fault. You didn't poison Stefan Fox, and you didn't cause Christian's car to crash, and you didn't stick a needle in Jeremy's arm. You have to separate yourself from the Foxes now. You had nothing to do with this."

She hung her head. When she'd heard Jeremy had graduated to heroin, seven or so years ago, she knew that beast of a drug would eventually be the one to take him out.

"Mother, he's okay. Lucy found Jeremy in time. He's still out of it, though. He likely won't make the funeral."

"Understandable," she said.

"And as soon as he's well, the police are going to question him for the murder of Christian and the attempted murder of Stefan," Eli revealed.

"They found proof, then?" Marian asked.

"What more proof do they need? His own remorse drove him to overdose, an obvious suicide attempt by the amount found in his system." Eli announced each word as if he were preparing a case. Marian didn't like the frigid lilt of his voice. She suspected it was probably hard to separate work from real life when legal matters were concerned.

"Simone was really off today. She refused to acknowledge Christian's death."

"What did she say when you told her?" Eli was sitting at her side, dressed for work. She was sure he had to report straight back after meeting with her.

"She wasn't in a good place. She was in 2008, when Lucy slept with the teacher, rattling on about a lawsuit."

"What?" Eli asked.

She eyed him curiously. "Why does that upset you? She's had worse episodes than that."

"Why would she bring that up now?" he asked.

"Her mind has declined rapidly these last six months. It pulls memories like a short-circuited slot machine. I never know what I'm going to get," Marian explained.

He rose from his seated position on the small concrete outside area, righting the chair he'd slid askew. "That lawsuit was settled out of court years ago. Why would that come up when she pulled the slot lever this time?"

Marian grabbed her empty teacup, something to hold on to. She hadn't known about that lawsuit. So how did Eli? "Why is that lawsuit significant?"

"I went through all the Foxes' legal filings I could find with Piedmont when pulling the paperwork for their trust. I wanted to make sure I didn't miss anything. The lawsuit was among them. Not significant. Just strange because it's an old case," he said.

The trust? The trust *did* exist.

Eli sounded angry, and if Marian had to guess, he was lying to her for some reason. *If you've done something wrong to protect me, I'll understand.*

If anybody would, it was her.

"Okay. Well, it must've upset Simone long ago, because she scratched the skin right off her arm today. She's never done that before. I'm not sure what reminded her of it."

Eli glared at her. "Is she going to be evaluated?"

"Yes. They're doing a psych evaluation as soon as possible. Why?" she asked.

Eli flexed his palms on the back of the chair. "That's not good, Mother. She might tell them things we don't want her to. I don't want us mixed up with them. Jeremy is responsible for the murders, but the lawsuit makes me nervous, because they made that teacher pay dearly for what he'd done."

"I get that," Marian said.

Eli let go of his grip on the back of the chair, but none of his tension released with it. "No, you don't. The Foxes have money, and they take advantage of people like you and me who don't. And if Simone mentions the trust during her psych evaluation, they could come after us."

She understood the potential resentment Eli felt toward the Foxes in this case, but the teacher had done something terribly wrong, and they hadn't. At least not by their rules. It might've taken Marian sixty-two years, but she'd finally figured out how to play their game. She'd win *this time.*

CHAPTER 22

LUCINDA

They kept asking her the same questions over and over again. Different people with badges—male, female, regular cops, detectives, Valerie's ex-boyfriend's partner, Valerie's ex, who oddly smelled like her incense.

The flowery scent nearly gagged Lucinda. It'd been permeating Valerie's bedroom since 1993.

It made Lucinda wonder if Luke had been by to see Valerie first. It didn't seem possible considering the timeline of the evening. Maybe it was just his aftershave. In any case, mentally, she'd refer to Luke as Valerie's boyfriend now.

And then there was Jeremy's pale flesh, his searching eyes, his arms extended out to reach her. Her thoughts came and went in torrents—a completely normal one overridden by a volatile shake to her consciousness that her oldest brother was no longer a breathing human on this planet, and the other one was in the hospital in God knows what condition.

Gut-wrenching and unfair.

Lucinda had already thrown up once, the stress of it all too much.

If Jeremy didn't pull through, she could already feel the levity he brought to their family dissipating at an alarming rate. Jeremy was the other fuckup in the family, and now she was all alone to fend for herself.

"You're sure you arrived at Jeremy's unprompted?" Luke asked. "Forensics will be able to tell how long he'd been out before you called us, Lucy. You touched him. Your prints are on his neck. There's still time if you didn't get your story quite right."

"What're you saying?" She was exhausted, and she just wanted to go home. Then Lucinda remembered she had no home. In one weekend trip, she'd lost everything—her career prospects, her apartment, her job (confirmed from her manager's text this morning), her brother(s). She needed some help. "Is my sister on her way?" she asked. "I called her, but there was no answer." Lucinda had run fresh out of family and had resorted to calling Marian, but then Luke assured her he'd get ahold of Valerie. Suspicious. Why would she pick up for Luke and not her?

With no other choice, Lucinda would beg Valerie to stay with her until at least the funeral.

"I called her," Luke said. "She's on her way. But can you answer my questions?"

"H-he was almost gone. And blue and gray, his skin." She sucked in deep breaths at the memory of the horror show she'd discovered—her brother hunched over and barely breathing. It was an image that would haunt her for the rest of her life.

"The Uber receipt you submitted to evidence from your phone said that you were dropped off at 3:42 a.m."

"That's correct." She didn't know why she had to keep rehashing the events of the night. She'd been at the police station for hours. Luke had given her a ride. If this were a game where they were trying to get her to flub up and confess to something, they were wasting their time.

Luke leafed through his papers again. "We're going to interview the person you were staying with and verify times. Aja B—"

"Yeah, she's crazy too," Lucinda interrupted. "She may have tried to choke me in my sleep."

"That's what you said in your initial police report." Luke didn't sound like he believed her, and she couldn't blame him. The finger marks around her neck had vanished, no bruises to be found. "Are you prone to nightmares, Lucy?"

"Sometimes."

"Is it possible you dreamed that someone was choking you? Because you could file a complaint against her if you're sure it really happened. We take domestic violence very seriously in our precinct."

Lucinda shook her head. "No, I can't be sure, which is why I don't want to file a complaint." Detective Sharpe had already asked her that. Lucinda realized that admitting she couldn't remember the details of the evening damaged her credibility.

"Okay," he said. "If you change your mind, let me know."

"Why're you asking me all these questions? Jeremy was smacked out. He OD'd."

"You say the dream is what made you drive to check on him, although the phone records you submitted indicate that you hadn't tried to call him first. If you were worried, wouldn't that have been your first step? Call or text?" Luke's dark eyes exuded gentleness, and Lucy could see how he'd be able to coax confessions from guilty parties, trick them into believing they could trust him. But she was no fool, and she would offer him nothing more. Her brother had been in trouble, and she'd done what she needed to do to save him, but would Jeremy regret it now that he'd likely spend the rest of his life in jail?

"I see your point, but I decided to go straight to his house. The dream was a clear warning." How long had she waited once she'd woken up to order the Uber? How many minutes had Aja cost her before she was finally able to leave that apartment and check on her brother? The doctors had said she'd reached him in time. He'd still been breathing— no brain damage.

She hadn't checked on his condition for herself today to know how he was doing. She wished she could crawl inside Jeremy's brain and ask him what he'd seen.

"Why not a simple phone call to make sure he was all right?" Luke wouldn't give up on this line of questioning. It might be out of character for a normal person to take off in the middle of the night based on a strong hunch, but she wasn't your average girl.

"I got into a fight with Aja. She didn't want me to check on him at that hour, and then I felt trapped. Threatened, really, after I thought she'd put her hands on me. I fled the apartment and decided to grab an Uber."

"And what happened when you got there?"

"Jeremy's a sound sleeper. I knew he wouldn't answer. And I had a horrible feeling . . ." And she still did. Her stomach rumbled, her head hurt, and she thought if she could just rewind to last week, start over again, and opt out of the charity event, everything would be different; her father would be okay, her brother would still be alive. Jeremy would be on the right side of the law.

"You called Jeremy when you arrived outside of his house. The phone record showed that as soon as the Uber dropped you off, you called him. Why then?"

Hello, repetition, Luke's old friend. "Because I had second thoughts about waking him up. But I just knew something was wrong, so I keyed in."

"I see. When you called his phone, it went straight to voice mail, you said. When we found Jeremy's phone, it'd been turned off. Kind of strange for a guy who works for a cell provider, don't you think?"

Lucinda shrugged. "I thought so too."

"What's stranger is that his alarm clock was set on his phone. He doesn't have a smart watch. If his cell was turned off, he'd never be able to hear it ring the next morning. We checked with his work, and he was due to report today at eight o'clock. Wouldn't that be bizarre to have his phone turned off if it was his sole alarm? There didn't appear to be another one in the house."

"Well, I sure as hell didn't turn it off. Which is evident by the fact that I called it before I even went inside."

"Lucy, was your brother suicidal?" Luke asked.

She threw her head back in surprise. The question felt too large for her to answer. Plus, she hadn't been around much the last few years to even know. "Not that I'm aware. He enjoyed his life. He seemed content. In a committed relationship. He was going to propose."

Luke looked down at his papers again. "To . . . a Daphne Abrams?"

"That's correct. I never met her."

"I'm going to see her later today. What did you know about his involvement with her?"

"Not a lot. Look, I don't live here." She threw up her hands. Luke remained silent, waiting for an answer. "Their relationship was serious. He was talking about buying her a ring."

Valerie rushed in at that moment, escorted by Detective Sharpe, who shot Luke a wary glance as if to say, *Found your girlfriend.*

Valerie's eyes were puffy and red, and her shoulders quaked as she hugged Lucinda. But if Lucinda had to guess by the way her gaze drifted over to the detective, it was his arms she wanted to be wrapped inside. Luke remained in place, behind his desk. Lucinda wished her sister would just leap over the desk and find her *happy* already. At least one of them deserved to be.

"I'm sorry about Jeremy, Val," he said, as if he were talking to a stranger. "It looks like he's going to be all right, though. Stable condition," Luke confirmed.

She didn't say anything back, only glared at him, because they both knew it wasn't Jeremy's physical condition she was most concerned about. Jeremy had more or less turned himself in as the murderer by sticking that needle in his own arm. "Can you give my sister and me a minute?" Valerie asked.

"I can't leave you in my office unattended, but I'm about done with Lucy for now if you want to take her. I assume you'll be staying in town for Christian's funeral in case we have any more questions?" Luke asked her.

"Yes," Lucinda answered hesitantly. "Let's go, Val," she said, because she was more than ready. "Hey, can I stay with you, please? I cannot stay with Aja again." Lucinda made a terrified face. "And I've got nowhere to go."

Valerie gaped at her. "Yeah, sure, but first, I have questions. How did you know to go to Jeremy's? I'm confused by this whole thing. And he was . . . just drugged out?" She sounded out of breath and irrational. Lucinda didn't recognize this version of Valerie.

"I—I had a dream," Lucinda stammered, trying not to sound like Martin Luther King Jr.

"No, stop," Valerie complained. "You said you had a dream about Christian too. What led you to Jeremy's house, Lucy?" Valerie asked. "Did he text you or something?"

Lucinda remained sitting there, unable to react. "No, Val. It was a dream. We'll go home . . . and talk . . . ," Lucinda tried.

Valerie shook her head furiously, trying to remain composed and failing. Everything she'd tried to hold together—her imperfect marriage, their messed-up family—had been ripped open for the world to see. It was probably demoralizing for her, but Lucinda wasn't the villain here.

"What did you do to him?" Valerie accused.

Lucinda's mouth hung open in disbelief. "Nothing!"

"Valerie, let me escort you to your car," Luke said.

Valerie shifted her attention to Luke. "Why didn't you tell me about Jeremy? You found him hours before you called me."

"I'll explain later. I'll call you, okay? I just can't . . ." He sounded congested. "Here."

"I need to know why you didn't tell me the minute you found out," Valerie insisted.

Luke sucked in his cheeks like he was about to blow his top. "You know I had to investigate it first."

"It's all the things you couldn't tell her . . . ," Valerie said, as if she'd just made a startling realization. "Your divorce. That's why she left." Valerie placed her hands on her hips.

Luke's dark eyes blew back, and he stood from his desk. "Out of line, Val," Luke said. "Let's go!" He was shuffling them out the door now.

Whoa. Lucinda was mildly entertained by all this. One thing she knew for sure—there was definitely unfinished business brewing between these two. Until Luke had just pissed Valerie off somehow. Neither one may get their resolution now.

Her strong sister was an emotional mess. It was definitely a role change, one Lucinda wasn't equipped to handle. "Can you drive?" Valerie flung the keys at her.

Lucinda caught them by the key ring. "Sure." Val had never let her drive her Beamer before.

Luke walked them as far as his office door and closed it behind them after they exited. Lucinda couldn't decide who was madder, Valerie or Luke. And why, exactly.

"Okay, listen, I need to buzz by Aja's apartment and grab my things. There's not much there, and she should be at school now. Then I need to rest, and I promise I'll talk more after that."

They climbed into Valerie's cherry-red 5 Series and sped away. Valerie leaned her head on the window and mumbled, "Was he breathing at all when you got there? The last time, they were able to give him that drug."

"Narcan?" Lucinda asked. "Yeah, they gave it to him. What last time?"

"His last overdose, it took three sprays to bring him back," Valerie said.

"It was only one this time," she said shakily. Lucinda had seen one too many *creatives* in the theater district use drugs for extra inspiration, followed by the angels of death who would arrive in their ambulance, rushing in with their trusty miracle nasal spray to save them.

"How was he? Could he talk at all?"

Lucinda shook her head. "He was passed out and cool to the touch."

Valerie placed her hand over her mouth. Black streaks of mascara accentuated her crow's feet.

Lucinda knew how quickly the sick could sneak up. She'd internalized a lot of what Valerie was externalizing now, hours ago. "Do you need me to pull over?"

"No," Valerie said.

"We shouldn't have ridden him so hard at the hospital," Valerie said.

"They would've caught him eventually," Lucinda said.

"What was your dream of? What is wrong with you? Why do you have them?" Valerie barked out each question like she was mad at her for finding Jeremy, but at least she was acknowledging her dreams were real this time.

"Six crows. Like Hector. I was dying, near our property. Not Jeremy. I might've been in the park, though. Near the bridge. Jeremy was there screaming at me, 'No, no.' And the headless chicken was there, mocking me. You know the chicken . . ."

"Ugh." Valerie put her hand up for Lucy to stop, then sat up in her seat. She gripped her head and straightened it as if forcing herself to look ahead. "How can you be calm? Our brother is dead. The other in bad shape," she wailed.

"I know. I process differently." Lucinda's eyes were getting droopy. "And I'm so fucking tired. Wait until the tidal wave of exhaustion hits you once the tears subside."

"Do I need to drive? Can you not manage this?" Valerie asked.

"I'm fine. Quit being rude. I'm hurting too. I'm the one who found him."

At that, Valerie clamped her mouth shut and leaned on the window again like a distraught Labrador. Lucinda parked outside of Aja's and placed the parking brake on. "If I don't come out in a few minutes, either call someone or come in and get me . . . with a weapon."

"Jesus H," Valerie said. "Next time you're thinking of coming home, don't."

"Fine by me." She slammed the door, and just like when Lucinda had portended Hector's death, Valerie automatically blamed her somehow for Jeremy's demise. It was frustrating and unfair.

When Lucinda opened the apartment door, she was relieved no one was there. The smell of ripe fruit hit her in the face. Aja had a single crappy wall air conditioner that rattled when it was turned on. It blew only tepid air half the time. Lucinda could hear the plastic bang of the clunky machine.

Lucinda found the culprit of the stench. An overripe banana produced a stinky sauna. She threw it in the trash.

Her exodus from this place couldn't come a minute sooner.

Lucinda gathered her belongings in a plastic bag and hurried back downstairs. Her sister was asleep in the passenger seat.

When she opened the door, Valerie awoke with a start.

"What is it, Val?"

"I fell asleep and forgot Christian was dead. Then I woke up and remembered."

"Oh." She patted her sister's cheek. She was freaking out. "I don't know why this is happening to us."

Lucinda started the car and sped off. "And I'm not blind. Something is going on between you and Luke. I think Sharpe knows too. But don't be surprised if he never speaks to you again after the way you talked to him today. That was harsh, bringing up his divorce."

"I know," Valerie admitted.

Well, well. "We always try to gouge the ones we love the most for some reason. That's how I know you have a thing for him. You rarely lose your cool."

Valerie shut her eyes tightly. "Is that what you did to Jeremy? Christian? Father? Lose your cool?"

Shit. Not this again. "Stop this. Valerie, even if I wanted them dead, this wouldn't be the way for me. Jeremy, on the other hand . . . clearly he targeted Father and Christian and couldn't handle the guilt. Although your boyfriend seemed to be questioning me like he thought otherwise."

"That's because Jeremy's overdose is marked suspicious. Luke got a call earlier, but I didn't know it was about Jeremy. He wrote it in his notes," Valerie revealed.

Lucinda's hands gripped the leather steering wheel. "When? What notes? He didn't mention that to me. Did he tell you that over the phone?"

"No, I found out when he was lying in my bed this morning and writing down the details for the case."

Lucinda almost drove off the road. "I knew it."

CHAPTER 23

VALERIE

Pictures of Christian were spread around the funeral parlor like a kaleidoscope of pain. They were short bursts of her brother's energy that'd burned out too soon. He was grinning in each photo, a powerful glint in his eye.

It was hard to keep Christian down. A snapshot of him holding a football threw Valerie off guard. One of his high school friends must've brought it in. He really had been an achiever.

Christian had called them "kids."

Even though it had annoyed her, he was the one they came to when they had a real family issue, and now he was gone. It was completely altering, a tear to the fabric of her being, a rip in her infrastructure. Now Valerie was left wallowing in a black suit, wondering what else she could've done differently.

She'd been wrapped up in her own problems—Karl, Isla . . . Luke. Valerie bit back tears at the decisions she'd made, her lip the enemy. She shredded it beneath her front teeth. She deserved to hurt.

Under pressure, Jeremy often cracked. He'd been fraught even before the cops had asked to speak to him. Not to mention, she and Lucy had just made things worse by getting in his face and accusing him of cutting Christian's brake lines without giving him a chance to explain. He must've felt ambushed.

Valerie pulled her suit jacket tighter, the regret tearing her internal fissure larger. Her shoulders shook. Guilt poured from her and leaked all over the floor. She was sure the people filtering through the door could see it. It was one thing for Lucy to call Jeremy a murderer, but Valerie knew her opinion carried more weight.

Lucy surprised her when she tapped on her leg with the spiky end of her stiletto. "She's a knockout."

"What? Who?" Valerie asked.

They were positioned next to the closed coffin in a receiving line of two. Glenda was seated with her children and Isla.

Valerie's eyes were drawn to the door. A tall, thin woman in a long black dress was being held up on either side by equally willowy people. The woman didn't make eye contact with Valerie as she was escorted inside.

"Daphne?" Valerie whispered.

"I think so," Lucy said. "Looks like her profile picture online."

"She's gorgeous," Valerie said in amazement.

"I know," Lucy practically shouted in equal surprise.

Valerie elbowed her. "Shh . . ." Although she wanted to scream. Valerie hadn't expected Daphne to attend. After all, her boyfriend was the suspected killer. What did that make Daphne?

Valerie focused her attention back on the children. Isla had graced her with the courtesy of a hug when Glenda had brought her to the service. She now sat listlessly with her aunt and cousins in the front row. All of them appeared washed out and horrified. She was sure Glenda had told them Uncle Jeremy had gotten high and killed Christian. She was looking for a silver lining in all of this, but there really wasn't one.

Marian, Mother, and Eli walked in next. Valerie had arranged to have Marian bring her so she could prepare her speech. Valerie's emotions were all over the place.

"My heart breaks for you girls," Marian said as she approached, tears in her eyes. Mother appeared lost, and Valerie knew immediately by looking at her that she was. She wouldn't remember today at all. Valerie wondered if Marian had asked the nurses to medicate her for the funeral.

"Thank you," Valerie said. "Hi, Eli."

Eli nodded at Valerie. He'd forever be the boy positioned just behind his mother. He was all grown up now, and Valerie appraised him as if she were looking at him for the first time in his three-piece suit.

Valerie wiped the tears from her eyes and hugged the woman who'd looked after them their entire childhood. Valerie embraced her mother, too, but she didn't seem to acknowledge it. "Hello, Mother. Christian has passed away," Valerie whispered in her ear.

She nodded and smiled. "He'll be back," she said. "He likes to hide."

Valerie inhaled unsteadily. She couldn't decide if it was better that Mother couldn't feel the soul-wrenching pain of losing her child or if it was worse that she'd never properly mourn because she wouldn't be able to remember it.

"Marian," Lucy said, but she didn't attempt a hug. Lucy's relationship with Marian was even more delicate than Valerie's. Lucy saw Marian as the woman who'd constantly gotten her in trouble, but as her nanny, Marian had only been doing her job. "Eli," Lucy said with equal regard.

"Lucy, I'm terribly sorry. Christian was a great guy," Eli remarked, his tone clipped. Lucy had borderline tortured Eli when they were kids. Valerie thought she'd just liked having someone younger than her to pick on, but it was possible they genuinely hated each other.

"Thanks, E," she said.

"My condolences," Eli said. Valerie noted how his diction was polished and formal. He'd come a long way from the quiet boy who'd hung around their property, trying to stay out of everyone's way, but he seemed to still be doing it. They quickly moved down the line to find a seat.

Glenda had scheduled only a single viewing at the funeral home. It was all any of them could handle. Lucy had informed Valerie that if she did not return home by the end of the week, she would in fact die.

Not in the figurative sense, either, and as much as Valerie had wanted to dismiss Lucy's dramatic declaration, she was fearful of her sister. Lucy's prophetic visions had become beyond freakishly accurate, and if Valerie were being honest with herself, she was eager for her little sister to skip town and take her shadowy premonitions with her.

The minister entered. It was almost time for the eulogy. Glenda had requested they give one here, since there would be only a handful of people at the burial tomorrow.

Lucy said she was only a writer, not a speaker.

Glenda had told her she "just *couldn't*."

With Jeremy in the hospital, that left Valerie. Glenda would only let someone from the family speak.

Valerie thought she knew Christian, but keeping it together while she spoke about him, and trying to be compassionate and witty while doing so, was a whole different matter. She had her speech on notecards, which she'd planned to recite word for word, her mind a mound of mush. Lucy pinched her shoulder. *"Val."*

"Shh . . . I'm looking at what I have to read."

"Luke is here," Lucy said.

Valerie gripped the cards, and they folded inside her hands until they were tiny, creased papers.

"I wanted to give you a warning," Lucy whispered.

Valerie peered up to find Luke's dark figure shadowing the doorway, looking sharp in gray slacks, a dress shirt, and a navy blazer. His expression was conflicted as he made his way to the front of the funeral home with the last of the stragglers. He hadn't called her yesterday like he said he would.

Valerie wondered if it was standard practice for a police officer to attend the funeral of the family he was investigating or if he were just there for her. She suspected the latter.

Luke approached her first and opened his mouth as if to speak. Then their eyes locked, and he was speechless. The swarm of people, the dull gray walls, the bad frankincense smell all faded away for just a moment, and it was just the two of them.

He shut his mouth and opened his arms. Valerie tried not to fall into him as she soaked in his embrace. She could hear his heart thumping in his chest. He pulled her away. She knew how this looked. "I'm so sorry this happened," Luke said.

He'd chosen his words carefully, but she didn't think he was referencing Christian. He was talking about Jeremy.

If Valerie had to pick two people responsible for Jeremy's overdose, it was herself and Luke, and he likely knew that. Luke had just been doing his job interrogating him, but he and Sharpe had rattled Jeremy good.

What had they said to him? Would she ever know? And why hadn't Luke called her the exact moment he'd discovered what had happened to Jeremy?

"Me too," she uttered, because she wasn't sure what else to say.

"I'll talk to you later, Val. Lucy, my condolences."

She smiled at him ruefully. "Thank you, Detective. I'm staying at Valerie's tonight. Will you be over later?"

Gah. Valerie could murder *her*.

Luke's eyes blew open. "No, I'm afraid not."

He turned and walked to the rear of the room. If he'd tried to sit any farther away from Valerie, he'd be in the embalming chamber in the basement.

"I *hate* you," Valerie whisper-screamed to Lucy. "I didn't need that right now." It was almost time for Valerie to address their guests.

"He yelled at you at the station. He deserved it," Lucy remarked.

I deserve it too.

"But he showed up tonight," Valerie said. It did mean something. She wasn't sure what, exactly. It still bothered her that Jeremy's incident was marked suspicious. *Why?* She'd never gotten to ask Luke.

The Protestant minister announced he would be saying a few words.

Valerie's obsessive-compulsive ticker was on overdrive. She had a speech to give and a brother to bury and an ex-boyfriend to question.

As the minister moved from the podium and announced Valerie, she walked to the front of the room, pressing her elbows into her sides, holding herself together. Valerie stood before the crowd, a full house.

"What can I say about my big brother, Christian Fox? An accomplished businessman, he helped my father build an empire managing a portfolio worth a billion dollars. I give a dollar amount because I know my brother would like that."

The crowd let out a low laugh. Christian wasn't Father, though. He was better than him. And everyone should know that.

"His dedication to his family was unwavering. A devoted husband and father, he could often be seen on the sidelines at events for his three children, who will sadly miss him."

Valerie wiped a tear as she heard the emotions erupt from her niece and nephews in the front row.

"Out of the four of us, he was by far the most successful. One of the most amazing things about Christian was his resilience to get it right. He was all about the particulars, and everything he did was with the greatest of care. Determined. Steadfast. Those are all words to describe Christian Fox. The world has lost a great leader today.

"We're all incredibly saddened that Christian was taken from us before he could accomplish all his other dreams and see his children reach theirs. All we have are the wonderful memories and, of course, all the wild shenanigans he pulled. So as you go about the rest of your evening and your day tomorrow, try to think of something Christian did to make you laugh and smile. It's what he would've wanted."

The crowd clapped, and Valerie had done her job. She could almost hear Christian whisper the words, *Great job; that was certainly passable*, as she stepped down and the services concluded. But she had a feeling this was far from over.

On her way out, the stunning mystery woman in the black dress approached Valerie.

"Daphne Abrams." She stuck out her hand, forceful yet jittery at the same time.

Valerie shook it. "Hello, Daphne. Sorry to meet you like this. How's Jeremy?"

"He's holding up. Stable condition. But he hasn't woken yet. Do they have any leads on who did that to him?" Her face was stern.

Valerie withdrew her hand and placed it back at her side. "I'm sorry?"

Daphne stared down at her through thick lashes. She was quite tall. "Jeremy's head was practically bashed in. The doctors said they were more concerned with the potential effects of the head wound than the overdose."

"What?" The hole that'd started in her interior had officially ruptured, her insides pouring out, viscous and all over the floor.

"You didn't know? They didn't . . ." Daphne turned her head, as if she were searching for someone. "Maybe I shouldn't be talking to you." She began to walk away.

"Wait . . ."

Valerie tried to go after her, but the two people Daphne had walked in with were yanking her away and glancing over their shoulders with disdain at Valerie. She could only assume they were Daphne's parents.

Valerie placed her hands at her sides, protecting herself. She spotted Lucy exiting and used her sister's shoulder to hold herself up. "Why didn't you tell me?"

"Val, what's wrong?" Lucy asked.

"Lucy," she whispered.

Lucy's robin's-egg-blue eyes grew larger. "What?"

"Daphne said Jeremy's head was bashed in." Valerie remembered Luke's phone call and the word *suspicious*.

"It was?" Lucy asked, bewildered. Valerie had given Lucy a black dress to wear, and her body seemed to swim around in it as she twisted uncomfortably in place, trying to piece together the information Valerie had just told her. She'd been there. How could Lucy not know he'd had his head cracked open? Wasn't there blood? *What did she see?*

Valerie's arm hairs stood on end at the thought.

Was she turning a blind eye to their brother's attempted murder in real life to make fiction?

"If Jeremy's head were injured, I didn't see it. He was slouched over his desk. It was dark. I felt for a pulse and called the cops and never looked back." If Lucy were lying, she could be a pathological killer, too, because she was convincing. Her flesh was so white, it was almost translucent, her teeth chattering. She was clearly unnerved, her mouth clanking together uncontrollably.

Valerie couldn't stomach this. She was frozen, unable to react.

How could Luke have not told her about Jeremy's head wound? This was the kind of complication he must've been talking about when he'd said they couldn't start a relationship until her family's case was closed.

"Stop glaring at me. I didn't know he was hurt. I just saw the needle," Lucy panicked.

It was time to leave, but Valerie didn't think she could let Lucy stay with her now. She knew more than she was letting on. But Lucy would convince her she didn't. Just like with the teacher and those damn chat sessions. She'd make up some bizarre moral reason for why she'd done it and try to convince Valerie she was right. Psychopath.

She had to ask Luke what the hell was going on, but when she searched the crowd for him, he was nowhere to be found. Neither was Marian, Mother, or Eli.

"Did they leave without saying goodbye? Mother and Mari?" Valerie asked Lucy.

"Your mother was tired," Glenda said, appearing out of nowhere. "The kids are in my car. I'll drop Isla off with her belongings in a bit."

"Thank you. This is all so awful for the kids. Please let me know what I can do to help. I could—"

"Cut the shit, Valerie," Glenda griped.

Valerie's mouth fell open, stunned. "Excuse me?"

Glenda's athletic hands landed on either side of Valerie's shoulders. Lucy was elbowed out of the way. *"Ouch."*

"I guess you got what you wanted. Piedmont called me this morning. According to that new trust drafted, you're now the sole owner of Fox Wealth Management," Glenda said.

"What're you talking about?" Valerie's face flushed with heat.

"Please don't play innocent. After all I did for you, taking Isla, convincing her you were only trying to protect her after you assaulted her father," Glenda said.

"Assault?" Lucy tried to interject. Glenda boxed her out again.

"I had no idea about any of this, Glenda," Valerie said frantically. Although she realized how it looked. She could barely get the words out. "Really . . . I've been so busy . . ."

"Plotting and scheming."

She tried to breathe. Her head spun. "No." She wished Luke were there to grab on to, but he'd left. She'd been too hard on him at the police station, but now it seemed she might have a chance to see him again—in handcuffs. *Oh God, this looks bad.*

"In the event that Stefan and Christian should pass first, in order to keep the business in the family, it goes to the next eldest sibling. You're up. And his clients want a statement. Tomorrow. People have already started pulling out of the investment firm. Your best bet is to sell, but all that money isn't going to help you in jail. I know you did this. All of it." Glenda's breath was hot in her face. "And I'm going to prove it."

Lucy popped her head into their intimate little space. "Now, that's completely insane, Glenda."

"Shut up, Lucy! The cops know you didn't show up at Jeremy's by accident either. You're in on it too. Big sis gonna cut you in once you get everyone else out of the way?"

"Glenda, I would never . . . ever . . ." Valerie was stunned stupid. Her mouth wouldn't cooperate with her thoughts. *Unbelievable. Who's trying to railroad me?*

"Save it for your attorney." Glenda pushed them aside. The world moved out the door with her.

Valerie realized she was the prime suspect now.

That's why Luke had been short with her.

But he knew the truth.

After all, she'd been with him the night of Jeremy's attempted murder.

She realized he could tell no one or he'd lose his job.

Now what? Was he really on her side?

Guess she'd find out.

CHAPTER 24

MARIAN

Simone hadn't shown signs of clarity for even a moment tonight. *Defense mechanism?* If that were the case, Marian could hardly blame her. If she could've had an out-of-body experience, found a way to mentally transport from that funeral, she might've done it too.

Poor Christian. Poor Glenda and Royce and Julian and Emerson.

Eli hadn't said much about Christian's death, only, "A true loss."

He had fretted over Simone's declining health the whole way in the car. "She has no idea who I even am." Marian explained there were many days, just recently, when Simone had acted like this.

Marian still had a hard time with the fact that they'd accused Jeremy of murder. Then again, she really hadn't spoken to him much since he'd left the house. It's how it'd worked with all the Fox children. They were in her care for eighteen years, and then one day they weren't, and Marian was just supposed to wake up, put one foot in front of the other, and let them go.

With the windows open in her apartment, the insects chirped outside as she sat now with her hot cup of tea, feet up, remembering the day Jeremy had moved out. He'd stopped to talk to her before he'd left for the University of Pittsburgh. She'd been cleaning in the kitchen. "Best of luck, Jeremy. You'll do great."

"We both know I probably won't." He'd grabbed an apple and took a bite, that mischievous grin on his face. It'd been present since he was a toddler.

"Listen here, I always told your parents there were programs that could help you with your schoolwork. Your father never wanted to hear about it. You're a grown man now. You can make your own decisions. If you need the help, get it. I believe in you."

"Thanks, Mari." He hugged her. "I'll do my best."

"It's all you can do. And, Jeremy . . . make good choices."

"Right." He'd given her a wicked smile before Stefan had called him from the driveway. It was time to go. College drop-off day was something Stefan had actually attended. It was his proud moment to deliver on his promise, the only thing he had to offer his children in exchange for the time he never spent with them.

"Jeremy?" she called to him one more time.

"Yeah, Mari."

"Remember . . . make good choices."

"Always." He winked at her and strode away. Even though Lucy was the reckless one, it was Jeremy Marian had always worried about. Lucy was smart and cunning, but her messes were intentional. Jeremy left a path of destruction wherever he went whether he wanted to or not. He was accident-prone, and some of Marian's most fraught days were at the country club swimming pool.

Her eyes would constantly survey the pool. *Where's Jeremy?*

She was afraid he'd get himself stuck beneath an inner tube, take a dare from another kid to hold his breath, with his eyes closed, while swimming backward. You just never knew with him. Marian had always worried he'd turn himself upside down in the pool of life and not be able to flip back over, drowning—and that was exactly what'd happened here. At least someone had jumped in and saved him in time.

Marian's phone rang. It was Valerie. The only time Marian caught up with her was at the memory center. "Yes, dear," Marian answered.

"Hi, you left without saying goodbye." Valerie sounded irritated. Marian didn't think it was a requirement that she announce their parting. After all, Simone was Marian's responsibility, not Valerie's, as she should be.

"Your mother was tired." Simone really wasn't, but Marian had been. It was exhausting trying to get Simone to pay attention to what was happening, yet secretly hoping she'd never poke her head above the surface of reality.

"Jeremy's skull was smashed in," Valerie said breathlessly. "His girlfriend told me. The cops didn't."

Marian's own scalp prickled with nerves and uncertainty. "Oh my. Are you sure she had her facts straight?"

"Mari . . ." Valerie's voice trailed off and broke.

"What is it, dear?"

"Lucy found Jeremy. Do you think Lucy could've done this?"

Marian's gut instinct was *yes*. But what a question. And how to answer it? She wanted to say neither *yes* nor *no*, but her lips fumbled over a solid *maybe*. "I don't know. Remember when Lucy tried acting? Before she was a writer. How she used to method act? Get really into her roles. Perhaps reality and fantasy have crossed." She stiffened in her chair, fear settling into her bones.

Valerie breathed into the phone. "But this doesn't sound like one of Lucy's plays. I'm asking because she's at my house. The police didn't tell me about Jeremy's wound. I think they suspect me, which is ridiculous, or Lucy, and they're afraid I'll tip her off if they say anything to me. She's staying *here*," Valerie said in a hushed voice. "I'm not sure if I should let her. Isla is here."

Valerie didn't need to say any more. If Lucy were somehow involved in Christian's death, Valerie wouldn't want her anywhere near her daughter. "You need to find out if the girlfriend's claim was true."

"How?" she asked.

"Well, call the detectives and ask. You have a right to know," Marian said. She wasn't used to Valerie asking her for guidance. After her miscarriage in high school, Valerie hadn't spoken much to Marian. Their relationship had changed. It might've been because they shared an awful secret, but Marian thought Valerie blamed her for it all somehow. She couldn't have had reason to, though.

"You know it's Luke. My old boyfriend. Working the case?" she said.

"Yes." Marian cleared her throat. "He's been by to visit. I had to remind him who I was."

"I guess he didn't end up working at the restaurant after all," Valerie said.

And there it was—what she blamed Marian for. "Just because you're going through a divorce doesn't mean you have to trade one mistake for another, dear."

"Ha! Interesting for you to talk about mistakes."

This was why Eli had cautioned her not to speak to the Foxes.

"You're going through a lot, Valerie, but my advice for you is to find out what happened to your brother. If he was murdered, kick Lucy out until they rule *her* out. And watch your back. It wouldn't be the first time Lucy has intentionally caused harm."

There was silence on the other end. "No, it wouldn't be, would it?"

Valerie hung up, and Marian was left in a tizzy. She called Eli to get his take on what had happened to Jeremy. His phone went straight to voice mail. He'd given her Giselle's number, but Marian had only met her son's fiancée a couple of times and had never called her.

What does he really know that he hasn't told me?

There was no way she could sleep tonight if she didn't find out.

It was awful to still have such an attachment to these children. They never thanked her for all the time she'd spent shuttling them around and patching them up. They likely thought she'd only been doing what their parents were paying her to do. Although, never in her job description had Marian signed on to nurse heartbreaks or police raging hormones.

When Marian had caught Jeremy with Christian's ex-girlfriend, that had been a messy one. It'd seemed they'd wanted to be found naked in the hot tub—in clear view of the path leading from the main gate—right after Christian's football game.

Marian dialed Giselle's number, and she picked up on the second ring, sounding sleepy. "Giselle, it's Marian, Eli's mother. Is he there?"

"No, he's supposed to be with you, at the funeral," she said.

"That's been over for hours."

"Oh . . . Have you tried calling him? Maybe he's still hanging out with his family. At the wake?"

"Hmm. No, I don't think so."

"I know he's been trying to connect with them more lately. All of them," Giselle said.

What kind of cheery picture had Eli painted for Giselle about his upbringing? Certainly, not an accurate one. "His phone isn't ringing. And the burial isn't until tomorrow."

"Well, I don't know where he is. And I'm sorry I couldn't make it there tonight. I have a horrible head cold. I didn't want to spread it. I'm glad I got to meet everyone at the charity event. Hard to believe one of the people I met isn't even here anymore," Giselle lamented. "Maybe Eli's brother's death was a lot on him, and he went for a drink."

Marian almost laughed out loud. *His brother?* Did Giselle not realize Christian was over fifteen years older than Eli? They'd hardly played backyard football together. "Right. Well, can you please text me when he comes home? Ask him to call me?"

"Absolutely."

Marian hung up and sat completely still, holding her breath for a moment, staring into the cool night air. Valerie talked of mistakes Marian had made. Did she somehow know about her greatest mistake of all? Simone hadn't forgotten.

Had she told Valerie somewhere along the line? And what did it mean for all of them now?

Simone had encouraged Marian to read in her off hours. With four of Simone's children to watch plus her own, Marian rarely had the time to finish a book. Although she'd come to love poetry and books of quotes—quick spurts of inspiration or romance.

She was also interested in anatomy, her secret aspiration to become a nurse.

When the children were ill, one of Marian's favorite things to do was try to diagnose their condition before they saw a doctor.

"That's green phlegm. Infection. It'll require antibiotics."

The Foxes had books on nearly every subject. Marian loved their library. The bookshelves were thick and deep, the color of coffee. The sliding ladder was made for climbing to the tallest shelves. The boys spent far more hours in there hanging from it than climbing it to find a book. Even so, Marian found that the copper-clad windows and the long, flowing curtains shielded the sun and brought peace.

The library was where Hector could find Marian in the summertime, when work was done and school was out and there were no sporting activities to attend. It was amazing how many hours she'd spent at that house and how quickly and forcibly she'd been kicked out.

When she'd left, she'd taken a few books with her without asking, ones she knew no one would miss. One was a book of quotations by European authors.

She searched for the box now, and when Marian found the book she was looking for inside, a faded green one with a broken cover, she flipped through the pages, all the way to the back—W, Woolf—for the line her battered heart yearned for now.

"I can only note that the past is beautiful because one never realizes an emotion at the time. It expands later, and thus we don't have complete emotions about the present, only about the past."

How true this was of her time at the Foxes'.

And how true this was of her time spent with Stefan, alone.

Marian remembered the day everything had changed.

Simone had been ranting about her time in Paris. Her father had been French, and Simone had spent her summers in Sceaux, a town near Paris. She was going on about how Americans were unrealistic and petulant in their quests for monogamous relationships. She'd just gotten back from the Field Club. She rarely accompanied Stefan there because that's where the Catholics hung out.

"Catholics with their repressed notions of marriage and celibacy." Simone would never say it to their faces, of course, but she much preferred the company of the Protestants at the country club.

The story she'd told Marian next was important for what drove her beliefs and helped Marian understand Simone's position on the topic.

Simone had followed her own father to one of Paris's infamous sex clubs.

She called it the first—Les Chandelles.

It was a tale that'd never left Marian: "Sex and chandeliers" is how Simone had described the venue. Dark labyrinths and corridors upholstered like an upscale boudoir, purples and pinks in plush fabric in one room, another in regal reds and burgundies, all illuminated by sparkly ceiling fixtures, dazzling as they showed off every soft spot in the room to sit—or screw.

Marian couldn't imagine such a place, having grown up in a small ethnic corner of Brooklyn, not the streets lined with lavish brownstones that most of the Foxes' friends were familiar with. Marian had listened to Simone as they sipped their drinks as if she was the most entertaining person on the planet, because to Marian, she was.

Simone's father must've liked to entertain too.

"The French have it right. That is what real adult relationships are like. Not chaining men down, forcing them to fight their most basic needs, causing unfulfillment and dullness in the marriage."

For as much as Simone talked, Marian noted she never sought relationships outside of her own marriage. Although she'd described the women at these clubs with idolization, she'd never likened herself to one of them. Marian found it contradictory, but she'd never uttered a word about it.

Stefan had overheard their conversation and had plenty to say about it—none good.

"Hold your tongue. Quit talking like trash. God forbid our daughters overhear you!"

"Oh, bull. I won't raise daughters who're taught to choke down their sexuality to fit better into a Puritan society."

Marian didn't think Stefan really cared about the impression Simone's words left on Valerie and Lucy. What she thought he was angry about was Simone's blatant disregard for the sanctity of their own marriage. Marian believed he'd felt shorted and that he hadn't gotten everything that came with a wife, including adoration.

Stefan wasn't French; he was German. He'd grown up differently, in a traditional household, and Marian thought it crushed his ego that Simone didn't mind that he had other women.

Simone had explained to Marian that the only reason Stefan still wanted her was because she wouldn't surrender herself to him completely. And *that*, she claimed, was the key to a lasting marriage.

Marian never bought it. She placated her employer into believing that she had, though.

It was maddening, really, watching Simone and Stefan tiptoe around each other, pretending they didn't care what the other one did.

But when Marian had gotten right in the middle of the two, that's when things got heated.

"Just sleep with her already, Stefan. You might as well have licked your lips, the way you undressed her with your eyes when she'd leaned over to clean the bookcase like you were going to take her right there."

Marian froze in place by the bookcase. Stefan stopped working at his desk and pushed away from his computer. "What did you just say to me?"

The lashes Simone and Stefan threw at each other were often misguided. That day in late October was no exception. Simone had been upset about Stefan's inability to attend Valerie's horse show because of an acquisition at work, even though Simone had circled the date on his calendar as a "must-do" months ago.

Simone hadn't mandated that Stefan attend many events, and she was livid with him for missing this one. Valerie had brought home the blue ribbon.

It wasn't unusual for Stefan to sneak glances at Marian as she worked. Petite but curvy, when she leaned over, Marian sometimes revealed more than she'd intended to. Marian had assumed it was just his nature and that she was no different from the other women he ogled, but Simone had apparently noticed too.

"I have eyes. I see. Get it out of your system. Both of you," Simone ordered.

Embarrassed and angry at Simone for using her as a pawn in her marital war, Marian gathered her cleaning supplies to leave the room. Simone had already stalked away.

"Mari?" Stefan called to her.

She'd turned around, and Stefan was leering at her, desire in his eyes. It wasn't the first time he had, but even Stefan knew *she* was off-limits—an employee, the kids' nanny, and his wife's only confidante, if not friend.

"I'm sorry about that, Stefan. I don't know why she said that." Marian quickly scanned the house to make sure Hector and the children hadn't heard the argument, but she and Stefan were all alone.

"Just let me know when you'd like to redeem her offer." He smiled, a rare occurrence, and he looked charming when he did, and she hated that she thought so.

"You know I can't do that." She blushed.

"You can. It's just a matter of if you will. Will you, Mari?" His teeth gleamed white and sharp.

"I have work to do." She scurried off and tried to push the whole encounter away—until Stefan approached her one day when the kids were at school, Simone at the farmers market, Hector working in the yard.

There were other people who worked in that house, but Marian knew she was special. Or she had mistakenly thought she was.

Under their spell, she was the only one who was allowed to have drinks with the missus.

And she was the only one who was permitted to sleep with the mister.

Her own husband hadn't shown real interest in years by that point. Simone had practically begged her to do it, but there was more to it than that. Marian longed to be appreciated for a greater purpose than to serve someone a hot plate. To instead be served and desired. It didn't need to be Stefan, but he had wanted her. At the time, it'd been enough of a reason—that, and the feeling of power it gave her.

She'd expected Stefan to be rough, but he wasn't. His sheets were satin, much nicer than hers, his lips just as soft. She wrapped herself in his warmth, his large body. Stefan was a great lover, a pleaser, and she understood a little more after she'd slept with him why he had no regard for his wife.

He had so much to offer her, but Simone wouldn't receive him.

It was like the Virginia Woolf quote. Marian's emotions weren't fully realized at the time either. She was under his influence, the intoxicating trance of Stefan Fox that had lured many women before her.

After the first time, there was a second. And their polygamous rela-tionship became her normal, something no one on the outside would understand. Her own marriage fell completely by the wayside as her home life became *their* home life. Her family. *Her* kids. And it was fine and something no one questioned.

Her involvement with Stefan must remain hidden now.

It was something no one could find out about.

It didn't last long.

All Marian knew was that when the first snowfall hit, she and Stefan had begun sleeping together at least once a week. At Christmastime, she remembered driving through Hartwood Acres with the whole fam-ily, a 629-acre park, once the estate of a sixteenth-century-style Tudor mansion.

That winter, she rode in the back seat to view the three-and-a-half-mile celebration of Christmas lights displayed for Project Bundle Up, a charity drive to supply needy children with winter gear. The whole family oohed and aahed, and Stefan had smiled at Marian in the rear-view mirror as Lucy sat on her lap, pointing.

Lights twinkled, casting sprays of neon color across the Fox chil-dren's cheeks. They were like fireworks in the night, the beautiful reflec-tion of *her* family.

Marian had been disillusioned into believing that this reality might last.

Or a slightly different, better version of it. Stefan had begun whispering ridiculous things in her ear, about how he thought maybe Marian and he should be together. How she understood him better than Simone had.

Marian knew she shouldn't have believed it. But the problem was she had. She knew the conversations Stefan and she had about the children were different and more impactful than the ones he had with Simone. And Marian knew the affection she showed Stefan was greater too. She was betraying her friend, but Simone's permission made the accountability for her actions muddled.

Marian believed she was different.

Special to them.

Special to him. She'd always known this.

But by the time the snow melted off the ground, their relationship had faded to nothing too.

It was the only time Simone had put a stop to one of Stefan's affairs.

On the way to pick up the cake for Lucy's birthday, Simone had forgotten her purse in the primary bedroom. She'd run back upstairs to retrieve it, and there they were—she and Stefan—naked beneath her bedsheets. Marian thought Simone already knew something had happened between them. Stefan had been discreet with Marian like the others. Simone had commented once that a man known to cheat on his wife might cheat his clients out of money, too, so she didn't worry about Stefan flaunting his behavior. It was bad for business if he was caught in public.

Only this time, his tryst had occurred in Simone's home. In her bed. Stefan had never disrespected her there before.

Simone had simply cleared her throat and grabbed her quilted white Chanel bag. The only thing that made Marian certain she was unnerved was the fact that she'd knocked her sleeping pills off the dresser in the process. Marian froze and couldn't look Simone in the face.

"Mademoiselle, ça suffira." Miss, that'll be enough. Simone knew she couldn't translate French, but Marian understood everything she needed to in Simone's inflection.

She'd looked the meaning up later to confirm the interpretation.

It was the end—of many things, including every freedom Marian had ever had until that point. It was the midnineties, and she couldn't be done yet. Their job placement there had gone so well. She had another good thirteen years or so left with Lucy.

Marian had never clarified with Simone how long she'd known, but it'd been longer than that day. Their strong triad had lost a spoke, Marian the straggling third, hanging on by her years of servitude alone.

Simone gave her the most impossible jobs as punishment.

She hadn't told Hector about the affair, for which Marian was grateful. But Simone made her suffer in different ways.

Scrubbing the toilets with a fine brush.

The ice cubes had to be cracked in half on a daily basis.

Simone drank a lot more in those days too.

But the martinis Marian poured were never strong enough. Never cold enough either.

Simone had complained endlessly of Marian's inefficiencies—for months.

And when Simone had finally stopped her tyrant behavior, Marian had just assumed that'd meant justice had been aptly served. They'd never had a discussion about it.

But she'd been wrong.

When she'd approached Stefan and asked why Simone had taken it terribly, he'd said, "Don't you see? That was a test. And we both failed. Simone might've made the offer, but she'd wanted us to say no. And if we'd said yes, she hadn't wanted us to carry on. She just wanted us to get it over with already."

The last words he'd ever said to her before she moved out of that house had leveled her completely. "I may have been with other women, but you're the only one she never forgave me for."

It was terrible because there were days Marian hadn't forgiven herself either. This was one of them.

CHAPTER 25

LUCINDA

Frank Lloyd Wright's transformer arm—the guest room—was suspended from the rest of the house in an L-shape wing. Lucinda stared at it, wondering if she could actually sleep soundly on that ledge tonight. She was nervy after their silent car ride home. Valerie hadn't spoken to her. It was as if she were chewing on something that was too hard to swallow. Did she fear being arrested like Glenda had insinuated? More important, was there cause for those worries?

"I think we're both exhausted. Should I just turn in?" Lucinda asked.

She peered up. The gray outcropping looked dark and ominous and totally messed with her feng shui.

Valerie turned to Lucinda, her face a blank slate. "Look, Isla is here after being at her aunt's for a few days, and I just don't think I can have you here too . . . given everything we've just learned."

"What? You told me I could stay," Lucinda said, exasperated.

"That was before I found out about Jeremy. And the company." Valerie clenched her fists.

Jeremy? She thinks I hurt Jeremy.

Lucinda fought to get the words out. "Wh-what do you think I'm going to do, Val, murder Isla in her sleep?" Her garbage bag was hanging over her shoulder. She hoped her sister would reconsider throwing her out.

Valerie pointed to the door. "That's not funny. You can't stay here."

"I did not try to murder Jeremy," Lucy said.

"You were at his apartment the night he almost died and left out the fact his head was smashed in," Valerie quipped.

"It was dark; his hair was hanging over his face. And it's not like I was trying to take a closer look. I was in shock, Val."

"He had a significant head wound," Valerie said. "How could you not notice?"

"Did your boyfriend tell you that?" Lucinda shifted the weight of her large bag. The spike of her high heel poked through and dug into her rib. She held her phone in her hand because she had nowhere to shove it at the moment.

"He won't answer my calls. Thanks to you. Detective Sharpe is the one who told me." Valerie's gaze destroyed her with that same bitterness she used to freeze everyone else out. "I have to protect Isla, and I don't trust you. Jeremy did not just suffer an overdose," Valerie insisted.

She keeps saying that! But how does she know?

"Because today you decided you're a crime scene investigator?" Lucinda asked. She wished she could remember the condition of his body better, but it'd been dark in that room, the little Tiffany lamp her only light source. Her hands had been wet—with blood—and she'd washed them, but she'd been so wound up, Lucinda hadn't remembered that detail immediately after. She was protective of that information now.

Valerie tensed, her face pinching into something ugly. "Somebody is trying to murder our entire family. And frame other people for it."

Lucinda shook her garbage bag, frustrated and scared. "Which is why we should stay together. Look, I can help protect Isla. You've kept her in a bubble all this time. Shit is getting real." Lucinda's teeth involuntarily chattered together again.

"What's that supposed to mean?" Valerie asked.

Lucinda hadn't been able to shake the chill from her body since she'd discovered Jeremy unconscious. She understood it was a side effect of trauma. The anxiety from finding her brother half-dead peaked and troughed throughout the day, and she thought if she could just leave this place, the horrible feelings would stay here and free her somehow.

Can I really make it one more night?

"What's the real reason you only had one kid, Valerie? Is it so you could control her every move? So she wouldn't have the upper hand of conspiring with a sibling to outsmart you?"

Valerie shook her head in disbelief, absolutely livid.

Was she thinking of all the ways Christian and Jeremy had formed alliances to best her? Sibling rivalry was normal, but the boys had taken it to the *n*th degree the year after Valerie had beaten Christian in the charity competition. Christian and Jeremy had conspired, raising the money themselves, but it hadn't been about the wounded veterans—it'd been about dominating Valerie.

"You named her Isla, for God's sake. It literally means island."

Valerie seethed. "That is not why I named her that."

"Valerie's little island. Under your sole dictatorship. Look how that worked out for you. You're all alone now, that's for sure." Lucinda couldn't help herself. Valerie had probably driven Karl to steal. Chained up in this ergonomically perfect house that he'd designed just for her, an open concept where she could watch his every move. He'd likely been dying to keep a secret from her—any secret. Right was right, and wrong was wrong with her, no gray areas for Valerie. Lucinda envisioned a similar scenario when Valerie had found out about Karl.

Lucinda's phone buzzed.

Valerie was fake laughing now. "Nice monologue! Are you still talking to that waitress?" Valerie pointed at Lucinda's phone. There were lit-up messages on the screen from Aja.

"No." Lucinda hadn't gotten a chance to describe her experience at Aja's apartment. She sure didn't feel like confiding in Valerie about it now. Lucinda tossed her phone in her bag.

"*Really?* Because she's blowing up your phone, and you're a damn liar trying to take us all down. You've been planning something since the minute you got here."

"Me? You're the chief suspect. The one who just inherited Father's company! It should make conjugal visits a lot easier if you and Karl can share a cell."

"*Get out.* You can wear my dress again tomorrow for the burial, and then you can drop it off here before you fly back to New York. Sleep on the street for all I care." She pushed Lucinda by her shoulder. "Be at Pine Creek Cemetery by ten. Don't be late." Valerie slammed the door in her face.

Shit. Where does she expect me to go?

Lucinda faltered on the steps made to replicate aquatic waves, the edging on the stone uneven. Valerie's phone charger dangled from the top of the garbage bag, banging the exterior in an annoying slap as she made her way to the driveway. Lucinda was surprised Valerie hadn't tried to confiscate the charger from her before she left. Maybe she should just turn around, ring her sister's doorbell, and wrap her phone charger around her neck until she stopped breathing.

She really couldn't take it anymore. No one would give her a break. She was probably going to jail anyway, might as well add one more felony to the list. Then if Jeremy didn't recover, and Valerie was gone, she'd inherit the company. Not that she had any desire to run it, but she sure could sell it for a whole bunch of money.

Valerie would try to run the company or find someone else to. The family legacy meant something to her. She was as much of a problem as Christian had been, wanting to contest that damn trust.

And *someone* had to make sure that wouldn't happen.

Lucinda shivered, looking over her shoulder down the dark driveway. She wouldn't be surprised to see her sister's Beamer roaring down to finish her off at this point.

As she walked carefully, she saw the missed text messages from Aja. She'd heard the pings during Christian's service but hadn't looked at them on the car ride back to Valerie's because she had no intention of speaking to Aja again.

Aja (4 hours ago): I just heard about Christian and Jeremy from the cop. I feel terrible. If I would've known, I would have stopped by the viewing.

Aja (3 hours ago): You should've told me you were psychic. I was scared. I'm sorry for how I treated you. Please forgive me.

Aja (2 hours ago): You don't have to respond. I don't deserve it. I just want to let you know that I'm thinking about you. And if you want to reach out, I'm one phone call away.

Lucinda exhaled into the night air. She clamped her mouth shut, willing her teeth to stop their incessant movement. She quickly looked over her shoulder, holding her breath. She thought she saw a figure, but it was just the shadow cast by the streetlamp.

I can't control my thoughts. I can't control my body.

She was spiraling here. What she really needed was a drink or a joint or something to chill her the fuck out so she could make it through tonight and tomorrow.

Aja would supply her with at least alcohol if she went over there.

The texts sounded like an invitation. This abusive relationship could continue for one more evening, she decided, just until the funeral.

In Aja's defense, Lucinda admitted her clairvoyant behavior was disturbing.

She rubbed the side of her neck.

Who had hurt her? The blood on her hands in her brother's kitchen dashed through her mind like a camera flash.

No, no, no. You didn't do anything. It's them. They're the enemy.

This place was driving her insane, turning her into somebody she wasn't.

One more day. She just had to make it one more day.

Lucinda thumbed the Uber app before pressing the button that would deliver her to Aja's. It was a dangerous move. Aja might've apologized for overreacting, but she hadn't said a word about playing defensive linebacker when Lucinda had tried to leave the previous evening.

Thinking ahead, she sent her bestie in New York a text:

If I don't return tomorrow evening, assume I'm dead.

She saw bubbles immediately populate her screen.

Aster: WTF???

Lucinda didn't respond.

Was this a suicide mission? This entire trip kind of felt like one, but what choice did she have now? No one would forgive her if she didn't attend Christian's burial. Hell, she wouldn't forgive herself.

A black Honda Accord pulled up, window down, mustached driver. "Ace?" Lucinda asked.

"The one and only," he replied.

She giggled despite herself at the lame joke he probably told a zillion times a day. "Heading to the South Side 'n' that?" he asked.

"Correct." She climbed in, wrinkling her nose at his Pittsburgh-ese dialect.

He pulled away, and Lucinda dozed off. When she woke up, she saw Aja's neon Kia Soul parked on the cliff beside her duplex. Lucinda wearily dragged her bag of belongings out of the car as Ace eyed her with pity.

"Thanks." She waved. Legit luggage had never been a necessity before. She had little use for it with no money to travel and nowhere to store it in the tiny places she rented. Lucinda trudged up the steps and knocked on Aja's door. She was surprised to hear shouting on the other side.

A man's voice reverberated through the thin walls.

Aja opened the door, her hair a messy ponytail on top of her head, her glasses smudged and positioned crookedly on her face. She was wearing her standard black T-shirt and what appeared to be men's boxer shorts. "Lucinda, what're you doing here?" she asked. Aja scooted into the hallway, her foot wedged in the door.

"I got your text messages." Lucinda tried to sound pleased. "Look, I'm sorry for racing out of here too. And for how I acted." She hoped she sounded genuine. "I took the texts as an open invitation. Is this a bad time?"

"I said to *call* anytime." She closed the door behind her now. "Not come over. And yes, my dad is in there. He works in the lab at one of the hospitals, and he was pushing for a clinical trial on stem-cell transplantation to be conducted at a neighboring hospital. One he was going to work on. It didn't get approved. Funding." Aja shook her head.

"That stinks," Lucinda said, but she still didn't understand why it mattered. Couldn't she crash after he left?

Lucinda could hear the man complaining through the door. "Aja, who is that?"

"A friend," she yelled back.

"Why is he being aggressive?" Lucinda asked.

Aja shuffled a bit. "He isn't. He's just upset. He hasn't been able to get the type of work he's wanted for a long time. This was supposed to be his big break. Like your *Love Is Love*," Aja said in a singsong voice, but Lucinda thought she might've been mocking her and immediately regretted telling Aja about her play last night as they'd fallen asleep next to each other.

At least Lucinda had a dream.

If she wasn't homeless, Lucinda might've asked Aja what her big life aspiration was—becoming J.Lo's makeup girl? Instead, she opted for vying for Aja's sympathy. "Valerie kicked me out."

"Why?" Aja asked. She was still speaking in a hushed tone.

"Why don't you want your dad to know you're talking to me out here?"

Aja teetered around some more like she had to use the bathroom. "He doesn't know about me, okay? He's still waiting for grandchildren someday. I'm his only kid, and I'm not *out* yet. And this isn't the right time for that conversation. He already had one dream crushed today."

Lucinda narrowed her eyes, uncertain. "You just told him you were talking to a friend. I can play that part." Because that's all she really was. If even that.

"It's not a good time. I'm sorry you got kicked out, but you can't stay here."

"Aja, hurry up out there," he said from behind the door. Aja jumped.

Lucinda didn't like the way he was talking to her. "Are you sure you're okay? We can run away from his testosterone-filled rage together if you'd like." She stroked the side of Aja's cheek. It was hard not to. She had such nice skin. Aja probably owned all the best moisturizers. Lucinda's attraction to Aja went far beyond her skin-care regimen, though. Aja was the only one who'd shown her the least bit of kindness here, real interest—from the way she'd noticed how lonely Lucinda had appeared in her family photos to how Aja had wanted to be the one to keep Lucinda company when her family hadn't.

"I'm fine. But you have to go. I'll call you tomorrow. *Sorry.*" She crept back inside her apartment and closed the door, the second person to shut one in her face that evening. It was demoralizing.

In New York, if you showed up at a friend's place with a garbage bag of clothes, they let you in. It's what you did. She missed her tribe.

Lucinda wrapped her arms around herself and bounded back down the steps. She heard the man yelling on the other side. "This wasn't what we agreed to. I was promised my trial."

"He tried. They decided not to fund it, Dad. You can't blame anyone."

Lucinda shrugged, thinking of Fritz and her theater project. She'd assumed Aja had been lying to her about that man in her apartment being her father, but it seemed now as though she was telling the truth. The man's voice sounded much older, familiar even. His tone was what was disturbing, though, as if he were blaming Aja for his work disappointments.

Would he make her pay for them, too, somehow?

It was an eerie thought but also the first one that'd entered Lucinda's mind after overhearing his belligerent voice.

Surely Aja would've let her intervene if that were the case. Lucinda knew she was far from the expert on father-daughter relationships, but that one wasn't healthy.

Mental illness may have been to blame for Aja's mother's death. Could it be on both sides? If that were the case, Aja had likely inherited it. Lucinda had seen glimpses of Aja's violent temper here and there. Maybe it was good she couldn't stay there tonight, but where to go now?

Glenda had already told her, "Don't even think about it." She still presumed Lucinda was conspiring with Valerie to take over Fox Wealth Management.

Jeremy's house was a crime scene.

Valerie was a disappointing no.

Lucinda didn't believe in coincidences, and Valerie had just been handed a company worth millions, days after her husband was carted away for embezzlement. The optics were horrible. Valerie was all about the visuals. She played nice with Christian and Glenda at the country club, but Lucy knew she held spite for them. Now, it appeared to be all in an effort to get close enough to Christian to pick him off so she could preserve her wealth after her husband had destroyed theirs. It seemed so calculated . . . so . . . Valerie.

Lucinda's shoulders quivered with the chill of the night air again. She needed shelter and food and alcohol.

She couldn't afford a hotel.

There was only one other place she could possibly stay—the Fox guesthouse.

Lucinda knew how to get onto the property, and she'd just lie and tell Marv she'd gotten permission to stay there for the funeral. If he gave her a problem, she'd wrestle that little shit to the ground.

The small barnwood guesthouse on Old Mill Road was located off the garden area. Both the main house and the guesthouse appeared to be unlit and unoccupied as Lucinda made her way inside the smaller one.

She flipped on the light, and it was exactly as she remembered. One plaid couch was positioned in the middle of the room on hand-scraped hardwood floors. It separated the kitchen from the open living room. Off to the right was a single bedroom where Marian used to sleep. Lucinda could see it through the cracked door. The awful floral bedspread was still on the bed. The short spiral staircase led to the upstairs loft, overlooking the main sitting area.

It was hard for Lucinda to turn her head in that direction without thinking of Eli. That was his room. It still felt like it belonged to him, not that she'd exactly respected his space. No one had respected hers, that was for sure.

The nostalgia of being back there pummeled her, seeing as how three members of her family weren't around anymore—Father, Mother, Christian—and Jeremy, hurt.

Jeremy beaten to a bloody pulp, more like.

She collapsed on the couch, finally safe and sheltered. She still couldn't get over how angry Valerie had been with her for not remembering the minutiae of Jeremy's incident. Lucinda had decided her brief memory lapse was due to PTSD after discovering her brother smacked out and barely alive.

Did Valerie really think I could've hurt him?

Lucinda's hands had touched something wet when she'd felt for Jeremy's pulse.

She recalled it once more, clearer this time, washing her hands before the police had arrived, the red rivulets flowing down the sink until the water was clear and the basin was stainless steel again.

Jeremy had been bleeding, and she'd just washed him down the drain.

Her mental state had been compromised, and she hadn't remembered doing it. When she'd hacked the chicken, Marian said she'd helped bathe her because there'd been so much blood, but Lucinda hadn't remembered that, only the metallic tang in the air, so pungent, Marian had bleached the tub afterward. The therapists her parents had made her see had tried to get her to recall it, but she couldn't remember the physical remnants of the blood, only the smell.

Lucinda recalled the same coppery tang at Jeremy's, but it was only a sensory memory, not a visual one.

What else had she not remembered where Jeremy was concerned? She'd smelled cleaning supplies and body odor, but she couldn't remember the rest.

The fingers in her dream closing around her neck was one thing.

The details of Jeremy's body were another.

Her alibi for earlier that night was provided when Aja was interviewed, and that had kept Lucinda out of jail, she was sure. Jeremy had also been dosed for hours by the time she'd gotten there. Valerie should've been thankful she was able to save him in time. Instead, she'd acted as if the whole thing was her fault. Valerie went into full shutdown mode.

Lucinda wished she could shut down right now.

Jeremy's cold, discolored flesh. His fleeting breath. She couldn't forget it, though she wanted to. She wished she could speak to him, but he hadn't been conscious last time she'd checked in at the hospital. Her heart pounded in her chest as the exposed barnwood walls closed in around her. Constricted and trapped in a place she'd been forced out of, one she'd never felt comfortable in to begin with.

The quietness of the house was deadening.

She was jonesing for something to take the edge off. Her brothers and sister sometimes hid weed in a loose floorboard under the bed in this house. It was anonymously gifted during her older siblings' college days.

The last person who'd stayed there was to leave some drugs for the next person. A family pass down of sorts. They'd coined it "The Giving Tree" after Jeremy had compared it to that awful book by Shel Silverstein about the boy who kept taking from his favorite childhood tree until all that was left was a stump.

It was supposed to be a tale about the careful balance between gratitude and greed, but it'd only made Lucy depressed. Jeremy had joked and said that if he had nothing else to offer, he'd leave them pot.

She walked into the room and pushed the bed to the side, then kneeled on the floor. Her sweaty hands fretted with the board. Her breath was ragged. Exhausted but too keyed up to sleep, she used her fingernail because she didn't feel like grabbing a butter knife.

Lucy couldn't calm down.

She'd need to raid her father's liquor cabinet in the main house if her search under the floorboard proved unfruitful. Remembering she'd had her brother's blood on her hands was wigging her out.

She picked at the wood until it wiggled loose.

No one believed her that she was innocent. The cops may have let her go for lack of evidence, but that didn't mean she was completely in the clear.

It appeared someone was picking them off one by one, and Valerie thought now was a good time to split up. It was like a bad horror movie. Not to mention Valerie's bloodcurdling stare as she slammed the door.

Any human being who was that cold could commit murder. According to Glenda, Valerie had also assaulted her ex-husband . . . somehow . . . and Valerie had conveniently not mentioned it to her.

Valerie had always defended her in the past, but she was showing her true colors now. The most important person in Valerie's life was clearly Valerie. *It's me against them, just like it's always been.*

They'd had all that time with those sealed manila envelopes, and Valerie was a quick study. She could've leafed through the papers and seen an opportunity to snag the company. After what Karl had done to her, who knows how far she'd go. She'd always been resentful that Father hadn't shown her the same interest as Christian where her career was concerned.

Maybe her jealousy had turned into blind ambition. Perhaps Mother had made Valerie aware of the trust, and she'd played none the wiser in Piedmont's office. Valerie would do anything to protect her little girl, financially and otherwise.

Finally, Lucinda pulled up the board. She did a quick sweep with her fingers, and the contents were empty. *"Damn."* The Giving Tree had truly been depleted.

The limbs of her family tree had been falling off, one by one.

She started breathing hard again. She thought she might have a panic attack.

Alcohol would do. Just a shot. Her father was a fan of whiskey, especially since bourbon had become all the rage. Father wouldn't be left behind on that hot moneyed trend.

Lucinda changed into her sweats and scurried over to the house. The garden was lit by spotlights. The shiny gazing ball was at the center of the garden, held in place by a scepter-like stand. It was an object of magic in Lucinda's youth, its image tarnished over the years, just like everyone else's in their family. The gazing ball distorted the reflection of her face, stretched out and terrified.

She wondered where Marvin was.

Maybe they'd fired him because Father didn't need an attendant anymore. It sounded like something that would be in his marching orders.

Within thirty days of my unconscious state, relieve the help of their responsibilities . . .

With all the children out of the house and her mother gone, Lucinda knew they'd dropped the cleaning service down to every two weeks. Marvin was the only live-in resident other than her father, but as Lucinda made her way to the rear of the house, no one appeared to be inside.

The hidden key was where it'd always been, and when Lucinda entered her childhood home, she was greeted by darkness.

A spider crawled up her spine, the chill of this big, old house nipping at her heels. She shivered and flipped on the kitchen light. "Hello?"

No one home, it appeared.

Marvin's quarters were in the downstairs bedroom off the kitchen, and the door was open, but he wasn't inside.

The same haunting feeling welled inside her chest as when she'd broken into her brother's house. What would she find here? Another dead body? "Get me out of this town," she whispered to the walls.

She made her way to her father's office, where he kept an apt supply of alcohol in a cabinet behind his desk. Lucinda turned on the light with fright, remembering Jeremy's body hovering over his own desk. Her teeth chattered again.

The images won't leave me.

She'd need therapy to get over it. Even she knew that wouldn't stop the visions once they made their way into her subconscious. There were days she still saw Hector's eyes rolled in the back of his head. She'd run in right behind Jeremy when he'd screamed for help.

She'd had therapy before.

The therapists didn't believe in her dreams. "Just your mind's way of working things out." No, that wasn't true. She'd given up trying to explain the importance of her visions to people.

Like her sister.

And Fritz.

She quickly made her way over to the cabinet and grabbed a bottle of Weller and a shot glass. She loosened the cap and took a whiff. "There she is." It was the good stuff. Not like Father could make use of it right now anyway. She poured the amber liquid into the glass.

Down the hatch. "Ah." It burned so good as it slid down her throat.

She sat at her father's desk. His black leather chair was worn at the base of the seat from all the time he'd spent working there.

Father wouldn't like her sitting in it.

Lucinda wondered if he would ever wake up. If he would ever sit in this seat again. Last she'd checked, his condition hadn't changed.

She honestly didn't care. Nothing would be any different if he regained consciousness. He wouldn't have a sudden come-to-Jesus moment and decide that he loved her.

Her fingers shook as she poured herself another shot. One wouldn't do.

Not tonight.

She dribbled a little bit of the alcohol on the papers on his desk.

"Shit."

Marvin would smell it when he entered the room, and he'd know someone had been in the office. It would prompt him to check the cameras, find her, arrest her. She found some tissues and mopped up the small mess, but some had dripped into the file cabinet.

"Damn it. Clumsy." Lucinda grabbed more tissues and opened the file cabinet to dab at what she could. It was still going to smell like a distillery in there. *Paper files? Really, Father?* Such an old-timer. She wondered how his business thrived if he couldn't embrace the digital age. As she was about to close the cabinet, she saw it.

A file labeled *The Den*. It cauterized her eyes, forced her to pay attention.

Lucinda wouldn't call herself a psychic, because she couldn't control her auspicious visions or channel them to perform magic at will. They came when they wanted to.

Moments of warning sliced through the night sometimes like wind rustling through the leaves. She never mentioned them to her friends, only murmured things like, *Let's try the next crosswalk; the light here is burned out*, or something of the like when she sensed danger.

There were also times when she was led places with intention, and she didn't realize it until she'd gotten there. Like the movie in Astoria Park where Fritz Zimmerman just happened to be in attendance with his partner, Lance. Lucinda had heard just that week that Fritz had moved up the chain as theater director at his production company, and she'd just finished her second pass of the script for *Love Is Love*.

As she strode across the crowded venue to meet him, she also knew the universe hadn't placed her in that park at that precise moment for a movie, a rom-com she didn't even like, by accident.

Just like she knew her sister and Aja hadn't turned her away by chance either.

Her movie mind kicked into gear again.

Act 2:
Daughter of wealth management mogul finds hidden file in cabinet revealing secrets about the family trust.

Oh my. This was it, wasn't it? The big reveal. Every nerve ending in her body was urging her ahead. *Open. Hurry. Move. Read. Faster.*

Lucinda picked up the file, whiskey burning in her belly. The cap was still off. She wasn't done with the bourbon yet. She flipped the file open and saw the proposed changes on what must've been an original version of the Den in a whole lot of red. Her mother was crossed out of nearly every line except for ones linking to her care at the memory center.

Lucinda's teeth knocked together, her body frigid.

Is this what death feels like?

Her throat constricted. And that's when she saw it.

The page that listed the changes to the dependents. There was a lot of legal language she didn't understand, but there'd been a change made that in the event that one of the siblings died, the others shall split their share.

Give it to my children in equal shares. In the event any of my children shall predecease me, said deceased child's share shall be distributed equally among my then-living children.

It was initialed by both Father and Mother.

In April.

It was only May.

Mr. Piedmont had read that disclaimer to them as if the provision had always been there, a jumbled bunch of legalities spouted off to them for full disclosure. But that's not what he was doing at all.

The reason he'd had them all gather there was because he'd needed their verbal understanding on all the changes that'd been made.

And that was one of them.

They hadn't read along with Piedmont. He'd just handed off the documents, envelopes sealed. Why didn't he want them to see the changes? Was it so they wouldn't fully understand the harshness with which their mother had been removed from the trust, line after line, or something more sinister?

Lucinda snapped photos of all the papers with her phone, not sure what to make of them. Did it all jibe with what she'd gathered in Piedmont's office?

She pulled out her phone to send them to the detectives, but she heard a noise in the house. It was subtle, like a creaking on the stairs.

Her hand froze on the file. She tried not to breathe.

This old house did moan.

It'd been awfully hard to sneak in and out of when she was a teenager. She was trying to figure out how to right now.

Lucinda froze in place, bottle of whiskey clenched in her hand. She should dial 911, but she was breaking and entering herself.

Another floorboard made a distinct sound. Movement. Footsteps. Dear God, she wasn't alone.

"Don't come any farther—I have a gun," she announced.

A dark silhouette slithered through the doorway. There was something in their hand, and it gleamed sharp and shiny. She held her breath, wishing it were an illusion, but the shadow moved toward her.

She shrieked. The shadow's full form became apparent in the grim light . . . *but why?*

Mr. Brennan?

"What're *you* doing here?"

He didn't answer her, his face changing from solemn to angry. Fury rose in his brown-black eyes, all the pain she'd caused him and his family brimming to the surface.

He raised something above his head—*a hammer!*

A ripple of fear flooded her body as she bolted past the desk and threw the whiskey bottle at him. She aimed to squeeze out of the side of the office.

Try to shimmy sideways—make a pencil—squeeze through like I almost did at Aja's.

As the bottle crashed to the floor, his arm swung out to grasp on to her, and once it did, she couldn't wrench it loose.

She tried to punch through.

Brennan, dressed all in black, grabbed her by the leg, yanking her hard so she lost her balance. She went down awkwardly, her shoulder and head smacking the hardwood. He was much bigger than her, and she tried to kick, but he was pulling her back toward him, effortlessly.

"Stop!" she screamed.

Shards of glass and amber liquid were spread all around her as she flailed, trying desperately to break free, kicking wildly.

Lucinda screamed as loudly as she could. She fought, but the force against her was too strong.

Hands clenched her neck and squeezed, and unlike her dream, she knew they weren't her own.

She choked and struggled. Fought for breath.

This was it. She'd known it all along.

She wasn't dreaming at all.

This time she really was dying.

CHAPTER 26

VALERIE

"I'm off the case, Val. I had to disclose what happened between us. Sharpe suspected as much, but she wanted to bring you in after the news broke about Fox Wealth. And the trust. I told her you had an alibi the night of Jeremy's overdose. With me. I could've lost my badge." Luke was hovering in her doorway, and she had doubts about letting him inside.

Isla had only half forgiven her, and Valerie didn't feel right about having Luke there imposing on their delicate mother-daughter time.

"I'm glad you didn't lose your job." She'd been working on the email to Father's clients when Luke rang the doorbell. She had job stresses of her own.

"Valerie, the timing of you acquiring your father's company looks very suspicious."

"And if you find an inkling of evidence that I had a thing to do with any of this, please entertain me with that information. Because you were a little light on the particulars surrounding Jeremy's case," she said.

"Listen, I couldn't tell you all the details about Jeremy's case until we ruled out attempted homicide. You have to understand, these are the sensitivities of my job, and your sister was a suspect."

Valerie glared at him. "My sister should *still* be a suspect. It's why I kicked her out. And if you closed the file on Jeremy's case already, you're not as good at your job as you think you are."

Luke made praying hands, pleading. "Can I come in? I'll tell you anything you want to know."

"Too little, too late. I almost had a nervous breakdown in that funeral home. I had to learn from my brother's girlfriend, whom I've never even met, that Jeremy had been discovered with a broken skull. That should've come from you, Luke."

"I thought Lucy might've told you. If you would've asked, I could have disclosed the information. But you didn't."

Now he was blaming her. "What the hell is that supposed to mean?"

"Protocol. They wanted to keep his other injuries unknown until we could examine the case further."

"Your protocol is bullshit. You should've told me."

"You have to understand the position I was in," he said angrily. "I've done a lot to try to help you."

She thought of all the advice he'd given her to protect her finances. She huffed, then waved him inside. "My daughter is here. She's in her room. If she comes down, please don't mention anything of a graphic nature."

"You have my word."

He walked inside and sat down at her clean butcher-block countertop. Everything was different from the last time he'd sat there. Their whole requited-love vibe—gone, replaced by distrust. "Beer?" she asked.

Luke held his hands up. He'd always been a hand talker. "Yeah, fine."

Valerie grabbed one from the fridge and then sat down opposite from him on her counter stool. She slid the bottle to him. "You think Jeremy busted his own forehead in while he was overdosing?"

Luke popped off the top of the bottle. "There was no bashing, Valerie. There was a nice-size contusion. Could he have gotten it before he stuck that needle in his arm? Possibly. But the drugs he injected were laced with fentanyl. Forensics determined he likely had a seizure and smacked his head off his desk during it."

She shook her head. "That's not right."

"What do you mean? The report is the report," Luke reasoned.

Luke's hands slid on top of hers. They were gentle, comforting, but she couldn't accept them right now. She pulled away. "Is there any evidence that Jeremy committed the other crimes? Father and Christian?"

Luke bit his lip and sighed. "No, but Jeremy was working at his computer when he overdosed. We found a printout tracing the different cell signals that were at the hospital when your brother's car was tampered with."

"So?" she asked.

"So Jeremy knew he'd screwed up. Twice. He was trying to peg his mistakes on someone else. Using his work connections to find their locations in and around the hospital. Possibly a place that would associate them with the crime. But everyone's phone Jeremy had traced checked out. You, Lucy, and Christian had all been by to see your dad, but you were all exactly where you said you'd been."

Valerie remembered how Jeremy had traced Lucy's cell signal to find her at Aja's and how he said he could've gotten fired for it. She also remembered how Jeremy had said he could trace anyone's phone who used TeleCom as a provider.

Her brother was no dummy, extremely resourceful when he was interested in a topic, useless when he wasn't. He had been onto something here. And someone had snuffed him out before he could follow his own lead. "Where were the phone records when you got there? On his computer?"

He looked down. "No, on the floor in his office. Your sister picked them up."

"Can I see them? The papers?"

He turned his head away from her and rubbed the stubble of his beard. "Val, you know I can't let you see evidence. Besides, we already investigated it." He was looking at something on his phone. "Oh, and there were some international calls we already checked out. Jeremy had been looking into buying a diamond direct from a broker."

"Cut and clarity." She put her hand over her mouth.

"Excuse me?" Luke asked.

"Africa. He'd been talking about diamonds, not drugs," Valerie said, furious with herself for assuming as much.

Jeremy had been brokering a blood diamond from Africa. *Cut* and *clarity* were terms used for engagement stones. She'd never gotten into the semantics with her own engagement ring. She remembered Glenda rattling on about hers, though, because Glenda's diamond was very large—and very clear.

"Well, there you go." Luke sounded proud of himself. "We've checked his call log. It's clean."

"Interesting it's clean if he's to be a murderer." Valerie's record was clean too. If phone records were the guilt predictor here, she should be free and clear as well. She was confident she would be—soon.

Luke took a swig of beer. "He's our prime suspect. We're questioning him as soon as he's physically able."

The terror returned, the same feeling she'd had in the funeral parlor when Daphne had leveled her by revealing the condition of Jeremy's body. "That can't be right. Jeremy had found something on his computer. Why would he shoot dirty drugs into his vein? He might've done it because he hadn't found anything. But what if he had found something? And someone else hadn't liked it. So they tried to kill him. If his call log is clean, show it to me."

Luke reluctantly logged on to his phone. "I don't usually have these things in my camera reel, but it was odd that this page was found on the floor near his body. Much of the time, evidence is found in the last place you look. Occasionally, cases involving drug users will have it right out in the open because the victim was in an altered state when they left it behind."

Luke handed her his phone.

She took a screenshot and sent it to herself. "Thank you."

"Please don't tell anybody I let you see this. The captain gave me mercy because of our history. He won't do it twice."

"I'm not looking to get you fired, Luke." She had the urge to brush his dark hair out of his face, but touching him led to trouble. And they'd had enough of that this week to last a lifetime.

"You could've fooled me when I showed up and you told me what a crappy job I was doing investigating your family's case."

"I just think you're wrong about Jeremy." Her brother had found something in his search. She was sure of it.

"Not likely, Val." His dark eyes met hers with certainty. "Unless there's something you're not telling *me*. I know about the trust and the disclaimer about the company going to the next eldest sibling. I've interviewed Attorney Piedmont. As you're aware, the press have released the fact that you've inherited the company."

She sighed. "But I didn't know I inherited the company until Glenda told me at the funeral. And I was with you the night Jeremy OD'd. What more do you want?"

"You've had the paperwork disclosing this for days."

"Luke, do you think I've had time to sit around and read legal documents? For Christ's sake. Half my family has gone down. The only thing I thought was in that paperwork was the trust. Piedmont made no mention of the company going to the next eldest sibling in our meeting, and I sure as hell wasn't reading between the lines to find it."

"Piedmont said he disclosed everything."

"Not that." She placed her hands on her hips.

"You see how this doesn't look great. If you're torn up over Jeremy because you know someone else is responsible, you can tell me," Luke said.

"I don't know any more than what I've told you." She was going to send a mass press release to all of Father's clients tomorrow informing them that their investments were safe and the junior advisers at the company would be looking over their finances until further notice. It was both a relief and a tremendous burden that this windfall had been bestowed upon her.

She'd discovered that the entire portfolio, worth about $1 billion, would likely sell for just under $10 million. It solved all her financial problems but had increased her social and legal ones by tenfold.

Although clients were pulling out of Fox Wealth left and right.

She was interested in the work her father did, but she didn't have enough time to learn the ropes before taking it over. Selling it off to the highest bidder didn't feel right either. She'd keep it in the family and have one of the junior wealth managers run it until she could hire someone else.

"And the timing around Karl . . ." He leaned away from her.

She stood her ground. "I know the timing is interesting. But it's not related."

"You know what I think? Jeremy saw the opportunity to make all his troubles go away by offing the two men who'd made him feel like a lesser species his whole life. Family toxicity can build over time. Most of my homicides that aren't gang-related are hate-related. Cases just like this but without the millions of dollars. You sprinkle that much money into the mix—"

"Jeremy isn't a killer, Luke!"

"You're right, Val." He sipped on his drink.

She looked at him, dumbfounded.

"He tried to be a killer and failed with your father. Then he succeeded with Christian and couldn't live with it, so he tried to kill himself. Because he knew we were onto him."

Valerie ran her fingernails down her forearms, scraping at her tender skin.

"Don't do that." He pulled her hand away.

She shook him off. "Don't tell me what to do."

"You only do that when you're really upset."

She pressed her fingers to her temples. "Quit acting like you still know me. You don't. The other night was a mistake."

"It sure didn't feel like a mistake. You're pushing me away. Again. You don't like people knowing the real you." His eyes locked with hers again, and she didn't argue the point. "And once this is all figured out, I'm coming back for you, Val. Maybe months from now." He made a motion pointing between the two of them. "Because this didn't happen by accident. And it's not over. I'm not losing you twice." Luke spoke with confidence, and Valerie didn't know where it came from.

"I'm not sure about anything right now." It was the best she had to offer him. She couldn't feel anything properly, her emotions stunted after all that'd transpired. "Are you closing the case, then? On Father and Christian?"

"For now. They're pulling security on your father tonight."

Her eyes blazed open. "But . . . how can they be sure?"

"Our budget for private security is limited. The captain believes the culprit was Jeremy. With the threat gone . . ." He shrugged.

Luke's lovely face was illumed by the square lights that hung from her kitchen bulkhead. His wife hadn't been able to forgive him for putting his job first. And as caring as Luke was, Valerie didn't think she could either. "I don't believe it. I'm going to continue to investigate without you if you won't help me."

He grimaced, almost amused. "Investigate what, exactly? You're not allowed at the crime scene."

She pushed away from the counter. "I'm not sure."

He got up from his stool. "Well, let me know if you get any hot leads."

She walked him to the door. "It's too bad you don't believe me."

"Think about what I said."

She closed the door behind him, unable to think about anything else.

She pulled up the picture she'd taken of Jeremy's computer research. It was the last thing he'd looked at before he'd been attacked. Jeremy had been tracking everyone who'd been at the hospital to see Father because that's where Christian's car had been compromised.

Strangely, Jeremy had traced his own phone. Valerie could only imagine that it was to help prove his innocence. He'd tracked himself at home, at work, a couple of places in Squirrel Hill, a deli and a coffee shop, and one unknown residence, which Valerie assumed was Daphne's.

That didn't really prove much. He could've gotten the tools to mess with Christian's car another time, stashed them in another location close by.

Jeremy had been after someone else here.

As Valerie examined the time stamp of each trace, she couldn't find anything amiss. She wondered if the police department had even bothered to check his computer. To see what else he'd searched in his browser history. Or if his employer had any thoughts on the matter. Had Luke interviewed his direct reports and employees to find out if Jeremy had displayed odd behavior consistent with drug use? Valerie had to go into work the day after the funeral. Her grouchy, younger, childless understudy had thrown her hands up to their supervisor today in her absence. Then again, she'd just inherited a company worth millions.

If something in Jeremy's records did point in her direction, she'd have the money now to lawyer up and make it go away. The thing that unnerved her was Daphne's insistence that Jeremy had been attacked. Would Daphne let it lie if justice wasn't served? She'd seemed pretty fired up at the funeral.

If Valerie could verify that Jeremy had purchased the drugs himself, maybe Daphne would quiet down. It would also put Valerie's mind at ease if she could get ahold of his phone records. Then she could pinpoint who Jeremy had been talking to at the hospital and what he'd been intending to buy.

She didn't think Luke would give her Jeremy's cell phone records. In fact, she knew he wouldn't.

Maybe she could break into his phone records herself, though.

Jeremy was a mess when it came to adulting, specifically organization and bill pay. The basics were a struggle. He often used the same usernames and passwords for everything so he didn't forget them.

Valerie logged on to TeleCom's site, and her own automatic bill pay showed up. She didn't think it could be that simple, but she switched her username to Jeremy's email address, the same one he'd had forever. FoxyJer24@hotmail.com.

She giggled at the name. Always the jokester.

His password used to be OldMill591#. It was the house number and name of their street, an easy one to remember. Valerie was both surprised and not surprised when she was able to access her brother's online records.

She quickly printed out this month's log of calls. Why would Jeremy shoot up right before he was about to propose? It didn't make sense. He'd been looking for the killer hours before he died.

What had he found in his search?

Valerie was mad at herself for telling the cops and other people that she'd overheard him buying drugs. She hadn't. She'd misunderstood, jumped to the worst conclusion.

It was up to her to prove he wasn't a drug user now, save his reputation. It was the least she could do.

No one else cared. Lucy was out of here after the burial tomorrow.

Glenda was convinced Valerie was a cold-blooded murderer and thief. With all the damning information stacked up against her, Valerie understood why. She had to figure this out for both her brothers and herself. Luke was "on her side," but if the killer decided to plant any more evidence to pin these crimes on her, all bets were off. It was only a matter of time.

Valerie continued to scan the phone numbers on the record log, focusing on the ones on the same day as Jeremy's death. Who had threatened him? There was one incoming call that'd been recorded multiple times that evening. She assumed it was Daphne's.

The calls had come a few minutes apart. They were later in the evening, after midnight, and they were only minutes long. If it were Daphne, Valerie couldn't understand the brevity.

Had Jeremy been having service issues and dropped the call?

Was it a lovers' quarrel?

Luke's words came back in a flash—"Most of my homicides that aren't gang-related are hate-related."

Valerie was disappointed if Luke hadn't bothered to examine Jeremy's phone records before labeling his case an OD. She also couldn't help but think part of that was her fault.

The repetitious phone number was burning a hole in her brain right now.

Valerie could call and just pretend she was checking up on Daphne. It didn't seem totally illogical.

Oh, and hey, did you speak to my brother late the night he almost died? What was your conversation about?

She dialed the number, but to her surprise, a contact lit up in her phone.

It wasn't Daphne's number—it was Marian's.

CHAPTER 27

MARIAN

"Calm down, Valerie." Marian shouldn't have answered Valerie's call. She knew the second one meant trouble. For so long, her job had been to serve the Foxes. It was a hard habit to break.

Valerie screamed in her ear the same way she had when she was a neurotic teenager.

"No, I didn't call Jeremy the night of his overdose. No, I have no idea why the call log says I did. I'm sure there's a—"

Valerie carried on about calling the police.

Marian had to rein in this situation. "Can you just calm down? I'm sure there's a reasonable explanation. You really need to rest. Clear your head." Her voice remained calm like it always had when she'd coached a Fox child, but inside, Marian was a mess. She had to check dates, but she may have had her phone serviced the night of Jeremy's accident.

It'd been taken to one of Jeremy's branches.

More chatter from Valerie. More ridiculous accusations. Marian trembled again at the word *police*. "Valerie, Jeremy had a drug problem. He'd had one for a long time. I know it's hard to deal with, but that's the culprit here."

Valerie sputtered to a screeching halt of tears. Then she got snippy with Marian, stating that her father's clients were expecting a statement and she was in charge of Fox Wealth now.

Well . . . excuse me.

She went on to blabber that Christian was gone and she'd inherited his share of the trust and the company. And to please call her when she figured everything out.

"Will do. Promise me you won't call the police just yet," Marian prompted.

"Yes, Mari," Valerie agreed.

"Thank you." Marian hung up, clutching her phone in her hand. She'd been waiting for her son to call her back. She couldn't remember a time when he'd taken this long to respond to her, especially when she'd implied it was urgent.

She'd texted him as well, which should've told him it was just that—urgent.

Marian couldn't settle her thoughts.

It was bad news that Valerie had scoped out Jeremy's phone records and had found her number on them.

The teacup resting on her lap jangled as her legs bounced around beneath the afghan that she'd tossed on to quell the chill of death all around her. She thought she knew what Eli's nonresponse had been about now. Especially after Valerie's call.

Marian had ignored the warnings, because she didn't want to believe it was true. She'd raised Eli right, that she knew, but she shouldn't have discounted his abilities—he was part her. But he was part his father too. Something had rubbed her the wrong way when she'd spoken to Giselle. She'd said Eli had been "trying to connect with them more lately. All of them."

Trying to connect with whom? All of them, as in all of the Foxes?

Is Eli turning on me? After all I've done for him?

She set her teacup down and looked outside at the dark sky, terrified.

Foxes hunted at night, after all.

The moon was peeking through her window. Evening had settled in without her permission.

Where is Eli?

They'd jointly agreed to have Simone sign the papers securing her future. Was Eli regretful of that decision now? Was he in hot water at his firm because of what they'd done, and he wasn't telling her? The pile of things he hadn't told her was turning into a mountain.

She remembered a Nietzsche quote from her little book she'd stolen from the Foxes' library. "People don't want to hear the truth because they don't want their illusions destroyed."

It was very true. Hers had held up for a long time.

She and Eli didn't have any secrets between them.

Eli had practically grown up in a flower bed, laughing and playing among the well-tended begonias and zinnias and peonies. He was too soft to commit murder.

Marian knew she'd have to be the one to end this madness once and for all.

She packed her supplies in an old tote bag. Marian dressed in scrubs she'd acquired from the memory center. They'd asked her to place them over her clothes one day when Simone had been vomiting and Marian's presence had been requested. Marian hadn't protested one bit. The memory center had never asked for the scrubs back, so she'd held on to them.

She never knew when she might need to pose as a health-care worker.

Like tonight.

She hated driving, especially in the dark. Saint Margaret's was only seven miles away, and she could creep up the back stairwell of that old hospital, but the ICU might be a tough one to breach with doors most likely securely fastened.

But she had to try.

It was about Eli now. It always had been. She couldn't let all her efforts, all her suffering, be for naught. She understood how hard rage was to control when it took over. How one's arms and legs were not their own under the wrong circumstances, a body possessed by the evils of its wrongdoers. Marian had been there before, and here she was again.

She also realized that all of this wouldn't be over until Stefan was dead.

Once he passed away, there could be no more *shares*. The Den would go into effect, and there'd be no more subdividing of inheritances among the siblings. And . . . her secret could remain hidden. She knew her son best. He'd likely drafted the contract so that when Stefan took his last breath, the trust would be set in stone.

But she was doing this for Stefan too.

Stefan as an invalid was a disastrous thing.

He hadn't woken up yet, and Marian had observed how these things had turned out for her other friends who'd been unfortunate victims of stroke. If Stefan did regain consciousness, he likely wouldn't have full range of some of his body parts, and if he did, his mind wouldn't be sharp enough to remember how to use them.

Stefan's condition was severe.

Marian had been checking on him here and there for a reason, but it wasn't because she was hoping he would improve. She'd sent Eli to the hospital personally to verify that Stefan's health was as bad as everyone had said it was. There was only so much information she could acquire over the phone, and she hadn't wanted to visit Stefan herself or ask the Fox children about him.

His health status had remained critical. At best, if he woke up, he'd likely be condemned to a life in a wheelchair. One where one side of his face would droop, and a nurse would be employed to feed him his soup.

This existence, for a man who'd once had her drive his suit to Bloomfield to commission a custom Italian tailor when his regular seamstress had been on vacation, would not do.

He'd had monthly massages and had commented once that it was good for his complexion because it increased blood flow.

Marian knew Stefan, and he'd prefer death to a life of impairment.

His kids probably realized it, too, but they couldn't pull the plug. The three-month mark was the earliest acceptable time to do so. That's what her online research had told her anyway.

Marian had been content to let that time lapse. Allow nature to take its course.

She was a mostly patient person, and she'd told herself that before the seasons had officially changed and the leaves had turned from green to red to a crunchy, dried brown, the bare branches of the trees reaching out like withered, bony fingers to greet the incoming snow, Stefan Fox would be dead.

And her position at Longwood would be secure.

And then Eli could stop worrying about her.

But now she was the one worried about him.

As tricky as Eli might've thought himself to be, he could never be as clever as a fully vetted Fox. They'd get him. *Over my dead body.*

She'd end this.

Right here. Right now. Tonight.

She parked her car in the far corner of the lot, near the two medical buildings that were positioned to the left of the main hospital. She was sure the open parking lot didn't have cameras anywhere nearby. She parked far away from all the light poles in the event that there was a surveillance device hidden there.

Marian had gotten good at dodging cameras.

First when she'd fled New York and then within the walls of the Fox residence.

Marian had made sure no one saw when she'd minced the papaya leaves and mixed them with thyme and sage, her special tea for Valerie to drink when she was plagued with the Greek boy's baby. It'd worked back home when she'd had to travel to the other side of Brooklyn to buy the special ingredients for the women who couldn't afford to go to the clinic. Stefan had asked Marian to get rid of the baby, to save Valerie's future. Valerie had said she'd go the clinic, but Marian feared she'd back out.

Marian had believed offering her the tea was the right decision.

Another place there also weren't any cameras was the Foxes' guesthouse.

When Hector had discovered her affair with Stefan from a note he'd written her, one that'd simply said, "You've given me everything she couldn't and more," hidden in a book of poetry, Hector had made the mistake of striking Marian.

He'd made that mistake only once.

And his demands that'd followed, well, those had been life altering. "You will leave and go back to your father, and you will never come back. You're a disgrace."

Oh my God, the panic she still remembered when he'd said those words. She hadn't spoken to her father or brother in decades.

She couldn't go back. And she had nowhere else to go.

It was either Hector or her, the way Marian saw it. He'd threatened to make it public knowledge to the children that she'd seduced Stefan. They would surely revolt against her, and she'd be out on the street.

Having Simone in the know was one thing, but the kids would lose it if they found out. She hadn't amassed enough wealth to leave the Foxes, and Hector had blown through what little savings they had.

She'd expressed to Hector her dreams of someday becoming a nurse, a natural extension of what she already did, spending all her hours caring for others. Hector had only laughed at her aspirations.

"We have jobs here to do. We are paid well, and how will you get into a university without a high school diploma?" He'd treated her more like a colleague than a wife. Their relationship had been mostly absent of affection. Couldn't he see why she'd sought out another man's?

It didn't mean she didn't sometimes study on her own, though.

After Hector had fired his hand across her cheek, Marian ran from the guesthouse and holed up in the Foxes' library, looking for a way to stay.

A way to get rid of Hector.

Determined to preserve her place there, she researched natural remedies to incapacitate her husband. She had to buy more time.

Whatever love she'd held for him had turned to vengeance. Her hands and limbs and mind were no longer her own, and she wasn't responsible for what evil they did. All that mattered was protecting her unborn child from a controlling, abusive father—one like she'd had.

Marian had only the items in the household to use against Hector.

She needed to move quickly, before he outed her.

She had a few things at her disposal. There were the sleeping pills Simone sometimes used. If she could get Hector unconscious, it was possible she could slip him something to put him down. Stefan had been working late that night, and Simone was still busy running kids.

Marian had stayed home with Lucy, and she was sleeping already. Marian soundlessly bounded up the steps to snag some pills from Simone's nightstand.

Then she'd snuck into the guesthouse. Hector's after-work beer was sitting on the end table, a welcome opportunity. While he was in the bathroom, Marian crushed the pill and slipped it into his drink. Marian watched as he chugged it down and passed out.

Which was perfect, because then she could creep back in to inject him with the windshield-wiper fluid.

The methanol poisoning occurred next.

It sometimes mimicked brain aneurysms, which was what they'd deemed the cause of death for Hector. His death certificate had solidified her position—in that house and on the Fox's payroll. She'd been saddened to lose Hector, the only remnant of her old life. But he didn't love her by that point. She was a fixture to him, someone to lie next to at night. And when he'd turned violent, it had lit her blood up hot and angry. She'd had to protect herself, and killing him seemed the only way.

After Eli was born, all her priorities had shifted, and she was officially stuck under the Foxes' golden thumb, whether she wanted to be there or not.

She'd studied for hours in that library.

One had to pick their poison carefully. There must be precision when striking to kill.

And of all the lessons she'd taught Eli, how to be a killer wasn't among them.

Marian placed her hair in a surgical cap to hide her identity. She kept her head down when she entered the hospital so the cameras couldn't identify her. Once she figured out the floor for the ICU, she took the back stairs. Her walking legs were in great shape for climbing. Once on the fourth floor, she paused at the locked door.

She hovered there, pretending to fiddle with her tote bag as a med tech brushed by her.

"It's a zoo in there," he said.

"Ain't that the truth," she replied, head still buried in her bag so he couldn't see her face, but not so much that she couldn't grab the door before it shut behind him. He raced down the steps. Young people were always in such a hurry.

She crept inside. Now she had to find out which bed was Stefan's without asking the nurses. If she went to the nurses' station, they'd immediately know she didn't work there. She walked by each room, monitors beeping, oxygen machines whooshing.

She grabbed a medical cart sitting idle in the hallway to give herself purpose.

As she reached the end of the hall, she saw Stefan. Marian stopped pushing the cart and observed him through the window, a moment of stark conflict. He'd been such an influential force in her life. Provider, employer—lover. Monster, dictator—banisher.

She had to remind herself he was none of those things to her now. Stefan was the man standing between her and Eli's freedom. He was also the man who'd impregnated her, never acknowledged their son, and then kicked Marian out of the house the moment Simone didn't need her anymore. The fury those realizations brought with them urged her on. *You deserve this.*

His wandering eyes couldn't rove over her anymore.

And his sharp mouth couldn't reprimand her.

And his soft hands couldn't touch her.

He'd been reduced to a listless, wrinkled old man, held together with tubes and a machine that pumped oxygen into his lungs for him. Marian's chest rose and fell with his, horror cresting and falling with each exhale. She could practically hear him whimper in her ear, *Do it for me, Mari. Put me to sleep for good.*

He'd want this.

If his spirit could hover above her and watch what he'd become, he'd give her his consent to end his life. She knew him better than most.

Marian pushed the cart into his room, making sure to keep her head down. She looked like every other small-statured nurse in blue scrubs. Her surgical cap set her apart, but no one had questioned it. Surgical caps in hospitals blended in like baseball caps at ball fields.

She pulled her needle from her bag and drew up as much air as she could.

Marian hovered over Stefan's arm. His fleshy white skin jarred her. Countless women had been wrapped in those arms, although none who'd truly loved him back—at least not the way he'd desired. For having been mostly concerned with being powerful, in the end, he'd been rendered powerless.

A fat green vein egged Marian on.

I can't go on like this, Mari. Do it. His voice echoed in her ear. She'd want someone to do this for her if the situation were reversed.

It's what's good for Stefan, and it's what's good for Eli.

With no more hesitation, she stuck the needle into his vein and pushed the plunger all the way down. She had exactly five minutes before the air embolism would take effect, giving the appearance of yet another stroke—one that would kill him this time.

CHAPTER 28

LUCINDA

Pain wraps its ugly hands around her voice box. She can barely make a sound.

"Stop," she tries. The words won't come.

She's being yanked along a wooded path like an unloved rag doll. The tiny stones in the packed earth embed in her wounds. The protected ferns along the trail, once good for riding horses, graze her broken body. The property leading away from the house is flanked in green and silver, shimmering in the night sky. She's lost in the veil of trees—the memory of hoofbeats.

Lost . . . She has to stay awake. Alive.

The moon is a bouncing white orb. She can barely see it.

Her eye, the one that isn't swollen shut, catches sight of a rickety wooden bridge.

There won't be anyone there this time of night to save her.

She's dropped along the creek bed, wet dew seeping into her scalp. It muddies the water with hints of red. It drips down her face and into her mouth.

She imagines the sun creeping through the trees.

By the time morning falls over the Allegheny Valley . . . she will be dead.

Her hand twitches as she tries to raise it.

Pain sears her limb, her arm flopping back to the ground.

Soon, she'll pass out.

Or drown.

Choking on her own blood.

"You never could keep yourself out of places you didn't belong. The football players' locker room. The principal's office. The teachers' lounge," Brennan says.

She can't respond, only moan in pain as he drags her by the feet. She tries to whisper, "Why?"

"And you couldn't stay out of Daddy's office either. We have an app connected to the cameras in your dad's house. We could see you on camera rooting through the files," Brennan says.

The cameras. Father always kept one in the office, pointed at his work.

"Why're you doin' this?" She tries hard to get it out, her voice crackly. The pain is visceral, a scalpel to her brain.

"What did you say?" He yanks her hair. It pulls on the gash in her scalp, and she wails, the feeling of her flesh pulling away from bone inhumane. *Kill me.*

"Why?" she tries to say again. She can barely make out the sharp features of his face, his pert nose, full lips, dark hair.

Lucinda is fading in and out of consciousness, the pain so agonizing, she can barely breathe. Her blood is leaking faster now, and she doesn't know if she'll make it to wherever he's taking her. She almost hopes she doesn't. Fearful of her punishment. Begging to be out of pain.

He drops her on the ground again. Splinters of fragmented spikes ricochet through her body. Tiny, jagged edges sear through her head as her body makes contact with the dirt. She can barely keep her eyes open. *Dying.*

Then she sees he's not alone.

CHAPTER 29

VALERIE

Isla had agreed to watch a movie. It seemed she was just as exhausted as Valerie. Isla curled into her lap, popcorn between them. She used to do this when she was younger, fold her little legs up and wedge herself between Valerie and Karl. Even though there was plenty of room on the sofa now, she still preferred to sit as close to Valerie as possible. She wondered if Isla missed the bookend on the other side.

"Do you want to talk about your dad?"

"Not tonight," she muttered sleepily.

Thank goodness. Valerie didn't have the energy either. "Tomorrow night, then."

"Fine," Isla agreed.

The day after tomorrow, Valerie would return to work, and Isla would go back to school with a swim practice in the evening, and they'd try to return to some kind of normal. Watching movies with her daughter was a good first step, but Valerie couldn't concentrate on a romantic comedy while she was waiting for Marian to give her an explanation as to why her cell number showed up on Jeremy's phone records the night he was attacked.

Could it have something to do with Father? It wasn't like Valerie could call Luke or anyone else from the police to investigate, because—case closed. He had his mind made up.

She was on her own.

Isla's giggles kept Valerie's eyelids from fluttering shut.

The movie continued, and Valerie tried to pay attention to Kate Hudson playing a journalist, hopping around on one heel, a welcome escape, but a noise outside like screeching tires made her body go rigid.

Then the crashing of glass upstairs put her right on her feet.

Immediately, the fire alarm went off. Valerie smelled smoke.

"Go outside!" she yelled at Isla. "Call 911. Fire."

Isla, petrified, threw off her blanket and started to run outside with her cell phone in her hand. "What about you?"

"Just go!" Valerie had already sprung from the couch and grabbed the extinguisher from beneath the kitchen sink. She ran upstairs and reached the source quickly. Isla's bedroom was engulfed in flames. Remnants of busted glass were on the floor. Something had been tossed into the house through Isla's open bedroom window.

Her daughter could've been in there. *Dear God.*

Valerie pointed the red canister at the fire and pushed down on the extinguisher. White foam spouted from the black hose to conquer the flames, but the orange licks of fervor were spreading too rapidly.

Not our house. It's all Isla has left of her old life.

Valerie kept trying to fight the flames, but they were moving unbelievably fast, up and down the walls in radiating waves. Once she put out one spot, it was overcome by another. A chemical smell, not gasoline but something pungent and overpowering, mixed with the smoke.

"*Mom.* Mom, out here!" Isla yelled, terrified. Crying. "The fire truck is here."

Valerie could smell plastic melting and choked on it, the air swirling from gray to black, her eyes stinging with the assault of the fire and kerosene smell.

It was no use.

Valerie coughed harder and relented down the steps and out the front door, where Isla received her in her arms. The firefighters went to work as an ambulance driver stuck Valerie on a stretcher and immediately applied an oxygen mask to her face. Isla sat there with her, sobbing.

Valerie was lying there for a while in disbelief before Luke showed up. He gave Valerie a quick shoulder hug and then ran inside. She couldn't understand why this was happening, but she had a feeling her new ownership of Fox Wealth had something to do with it. She remembered something her father had said about people in positions of public wealth. "If you have something worthwhile, it's only a matter of time before someone tries to steal it. Protect your money and pick worthy partners." He'd commented that picking the wrong spouse could be detrimental to their very existence.

"Always get a prenup, girls. I don't care how much you love him."

Karl—mistake.

Lucy couldn't possibly be diabolical enough to torch Isla's room. She wouldn't endanger her own niece, *right?* Then she remembered the suspicious text messages from Aja, whom she'd claimed she wasn't speaking to. Lucy had lied right to her face about that. *Why?*

Valerie coughed, her lungs protesting. She was light-headed, too, but she was sure the crash of adrenaline she was experiencing had more to do with the narrow miss on her daughter's life than the smoke she'd just inhaled.

Luke returned with evidence in a bag. He brought it over to her. It was pieces of glass, black and charred.

She ripped her oxygen mask off and sat up.

"How are you?" he asked.

Forget the niceties. Valerie pointed at the bag. "What is that, Luke?"

"This was definitely arson. A flaming bottle, Molotov cocktail–style, thrown through the window. The fire is out, but there's a lot of damage."

Isla edged farther away from them, unable to look at the thing that'd tried to burn her alive.

Valerie gripped onto the end of the gurney, her vision faltering. Luke's expression of consternation faded, zooming out, then growing near again. She was going to pass out. He was saying something, but it was barely audible.

Tinnitus had set in.

Once the bells stopped ringing, maybe she could focus.

"Val, do you have any idea who did this?" Luke asked.

Sharpe addressed her partner. "You're not even working this case, Kapinos. Let me ask the questions. Go home."

But Luke didn't leave. He ignored his partner.

"Tighten security at the hospital around Jeremy. Find Lucy. I think someone's trying to take me out to get closer to Fox Wealth," she said.

Luke's Adam's apple bobbed noticeably as he swallowed. "Okay." He radioed something into his handheld dispatch that she couldn't decipher.

Valerie struggled to breathe, even though she'd just inhaled plenty of oxygen. "You still think he OD'd, Luke?"

"I don't know." Luke focused his attention skyward, at the stars that'd populated the night like tiny fireflies, the smog from the fire and clouds moving past them like a gauzy blanket. Valerie's head hurt, and nothing was clear.

"I also discovered Marian Vega's number on Jeremy's cell records the night you found him unconscious. Late evening," she said.

Luke pressed his lips together tightly, and maybe he was realizing his blunder of closing Jeremy's case too soon. "Are you going to do something? They went after Isla, Luke. That was her bedroom on fire."

He turned toward her, startled. "Was it the only open window in the house?" he asked.

"Maybe." She couldn't think of any others that were open, but it still felt like a targeted attack.

"Don't poke around in his records anymore, okay?" Luke ordered.

Sharpe pointed her finger at Luke. "You can't poke around anymore either. You. Are. Off. This. Case."

"I know." He made praying hands with her like he'd tried with Valerie earlier, and he should just give up on that gesture. Sharpe widened her eyes at him, completely irate.

"I don't want you to get into trouble," Valerie said.

Sharpe strolled away, relaying code words into her walkie-talkie. Something came back through that caught Valerie's ear. "459A at 591 Old Mill Road."

Luke met her terrified eyes. "That's my father's house. What's a 459A, Luke?" Valerie asked, panic settling back into her chest.

"Burglar alarm," he said.

"Marvin should be there," she said.

"I'm going to check it out. Will you be okay? You can't stay here overnight. I could have you stay—"

"My aunt Glenda is coming to get us," Isla interrupted. "I already called her. Can I get any of my stuff out of the house, Mom?"

Valerie shot an imploring look at Luke as if to say, *Is there any of her stuff left?*

He frowned, understanding what Valerie was asking him with just her eyes. And these were the moments between them that made her want to believe in him even when she didn't want to. Maybe if he'd taken her pleas seriously, none of this would've happened.

"No, I'm sorry, Isla."

Her daughter stalked away down the driveway to wait for her aunt. Valerie knew Isla still hadn't forgiven her completely for Karl, and this certainly didn't help. *Does Isla blame me for the fire too?*

"Go check on the house, and call me, please," Valerie said.

"Right. I'll be in touch." Luke scurried off.

"Off duty!" Sharpe yelled at his back.

Luke stuck his hand up in disregard. Valerie clenched her fists. She sure hoped he didn't get fired because of her, but she was also running out of family members who weren't seriously hurt or injured.

Plus, Luke had fallen short the first time. He owed her.

She shivered as the paramedics put a blanket over her torso. Glenda arrived shortly after and consoled Isla in a way Valerie wasn't capable of at the moment. Her lungs hurt when she took in air, and her body shook even though she tried to will it to stop.

Sharpe appeared later with a grim look on her face. Had the other officers beaten Luke to the house? What had they found?

"I'm sorry this has been such a hard evening for you, Ms. Fox, but the hospital just called, and your father has passed away tonight. Another stroke. This time, they couldn't stabilize him."

"No." She lay back, unable to hold herself up any longer.

I never got to say goodbye.

In the hours since Christian had passed, every minute was met with new challenges that had stopped her from concentrating on her father's health. Now it was too late.

Another funeral?

She didn't have it in her. There should be a limit to the number of family members one could bury in a single week.

"Ms. Fox. Shall I have the hospital take you in?" Sharpe asked.

"No." She shot back up.

"She did experience smoke inhalation," the paramedic said.

"It was minimal. I refuse to go to the hospital." She knew they couldn't take her if she said that. Valerie hopped off the cot.

Glenda rolled down her window, looking haggard. She must've been exhausted after all she'd been through too. Valerie didn't want to overburden her again.

"Can I get in, Glenda? Clearly, you can see Isla and I are victims here too," she said. Glenda had better have an apology ready and waiting.

She only nodded at Valerie.

Valerie quickly took Isla's hand and climbed into the rear of the vehicle. It was safe in there. Large and composed of extruded metal with Glenda's strong, knowing arms maneuvering it. Valerie's thoughts were still shaky.

Sharpe leaned on the vehicle by the open rear passenger window. "I'm sorry for your loss. We'll be in touch about the house." She tapped the SUV and walked back to her cruiser. As hard as Sharpe rode Luke, Valerie was convinced she was a good cop just trying to do her job.

"I'm so sorry, Isla, but your grandfather has passed away." Valerie said it all in one breath. There was no other way to deliver all this awful information anymore. It just kept coming and coming, and no one knew why it had started or when it would end.

"Oh no," Isla said. She fell on her mother's lap, hugging her. "I'm sorry, Mom." Her embrace was clearly more for Valerie's comfort than her own. Isla was tearless. Or maybe she was just all cried out.

Glenda turned to her in the back seat. "I'm so sorry, Val. I knew he wasn't doing well. It's probably for the best."

"Yes, it probably is," Valerie said, although death never seemed *best*. There wasn't much anyone else could say or do at that point.

A sensation like fingers treading up her neck made her hold her breath. Whoever had thrown that firebomb through her daughter's window had been watching her closely. They'd known she was home—researching.

Someone was trying to take her out. They'd tried to burn her to death! She couldn't die and leave Isla all alone. With Karl in prison, Valerie was all Isla had left.

Valerie's phone rang. It was Luke. "Hello."

"Did you know Lucy was staying at the house? We found her things here. In the guesthouse."

Valerie shut her eyes. Lucy must've been really desperate if she'd gone home. She hated that place. "I didn't know where she went. I just told her she couldn't stay with me."

"Val, there's a sign of a struggle in the main house. In the office. Alcohol spilled on the floor. A broken bottle of whiskey." He paused.

"What else, Luke?" Because she knew there was more.

"Blood," he said.

"Shit."

"Did your sister know there was an alarm on the window to the office? Someone threw the whiskey bottle that way, and it's what tripped it."

"Yes, that was set up a long time ago. The office has Father's sensitive files."

"Would everyone who ever lived in the house know that?" he asked. She knew why he was asking.

"Yes. Have you found Eli?"

"Not yet. Would anyone else have any idea of where your sister might be?"

"Maybe Aja, the waitress. Or her best friend in New York, Aster. I have a number for Aster, and I only know where Aja lives, no contact," Valerie said fretfully. What had she done turning her sister out?

"I have the waitress's number. Share the contact info for the friend. And please, *please* stay put," he said. Luke thought Lucy was in trouble too. *Oh my God, I'll never forgive myself if something happens to her.*

"Okay," she said, but she had an awful feeling as she hung up the phone. *Whose blood is it?*

Valerie sent Aster's contact to Luke.

"Is Aunt Lucy in trouble, Mom?" Isla asked. Glenda's eyes were frightened silver dollars in the rearview mirror, the reflection from the headlights on the road making her appear demonic.

Valerie quickly replied, "No, honey. It's fine."

"I heard the cop, Mom! Lucy had a dream the night Jeremy died. I overheard her saying it at the funeral home. Her dream took her there. To his place. She was the one who died in her dream."

Valerie's throat closed. Her sister had said that if she stayed in that town, she'd be next. It'd all sounded so Lucy. Flaky. Perhaps not. Everything else she'd predicted had come to fruition.

"That's right," she whispered.

"Mom, where did she say she was at when she died? In the dream?" Isla asked.

"Either the house or the park," she said breathlessly.

Valerie had shared Aster's contact with Luke. She also decided to text Aster herself. She wanted any reassurance her sister was still alive.

Valerie: Aster, it's Lucy's sister. We can't find her. Have you heard from her?

Aster: I just talked to a cop. She texted me last night that if she didn't return tomorrow evening, to assume she's dead!

"Oh my God. Pull over the car," Valerie demanded.

She could see the entrance to Old Squaw Trail Park in the distance. If someone had taken Lucy, and they'd already kidnapped her from the house, she was in that park being murdered right now.

And Valerie didn't have time for a leisurely walk or jog to get there.

"What is it?" Glenda asked. "Are you going to be sick?"

"No." Valerie grabbed a golf club from Glenda's bag in the trunk. She needed a weapon.

"What're you doing?" Glenda asked.

"Drive me to the park," Valerie said.

"No, not at this hour. You've taken in too much smoke, Val. You're not thinking clearly."

Isla's dark eyes lit up. "That's where Aunt Lucy is, isn't it? The park?"

Valerie looked between the two of them, frantic. She needed to get to her sister. And she wasn't going to be able to convince her stubborn-ass sister-in-law to drive her there. She couldn't endanger Isla either.

"Forget it. Call the cops if you think she's there!" Glenda griped.

Valerie called Luke—straight to voice mail. "Damn it. No answer."

Valerie's fingers twitched on the pitching wedge. She could feel her sister nearby. They were still pulled over on the side of the road as Glenda tried to merge back into traffic. Valerie could open the door, hop out, and try to find Lucy.

She thought she knew right where she might be. Valerie stuck her head out of the window. They were still close to her neighborhood, even closer to the park.

A horse stable was just over the hill. Valerie was familiar with that property too. It was the Pritchard estate. They knew her well. She just needed to borrow one of their horses.

"Stay here, Isla." Valerie leaped from the car and broke into a dead sprint for the stable.

CHAPTER 30

MARIAN

Marian had changed at the gas station before returning to her apartment. She'd already received word from Valerie via text that Stefan had passed away from an additional stroke.

She smiled as she pulled into her spot, satisfied that she still had the ability to pass off murders for naturally occurring ailments. Toxic herbs for a miscarriage, window-washer fluid for an aneurysm, air embolism for a stroke.

It was a talent, really.

After Eli was born, there was no time to go to nursing school, but at least she hadn't spent all those hours in the library studying medical books for nothing.

She'd shot Eli a quick text notifying him that Stefan had passed away and to please call her. He must've realized what her message had really meant.

It's finally over.

Christian was gone, and the others were so eager to get their hands on the money, they'd never pick apart that trust now. Marian would get her money, and Eli wouldn't get into trouble for adding the charity to the trust because nobody would audit it to discover what he'd slipped in there.

They'd bested the Foxes. She and Eli had nothing to worry about anymore.

Except for Marian's unexpected visitor.

Detective Kapinos was standing on her front porch when she exited her vehicle.

Marian sucked in a deep breath. "Officer, you scared me, standing in the dark. You could give an older woman a fright that way."

"Apologies. Where were you tonight, Marian?"

"Just out and about." She shrugged. *What's this about?*

"At this hour?" Kapinos looked at his watch. "It's funny. I went down to the memory center, and Rosalie said you rarely drive at night, if ever."

The memory center? He talked to Simone.

The pulse in her throat throbbed. He wasn't there to talk about Eli. He was there to talk to her. "That's true. But I couldn't sit here after the funeral. I went to one of Christian's favorite childhood spots and sat there."

"Where's that?" the detective asked. And she knew that question would be next. She had to make something up, something close to the hospital in case they had her on cameras.

"Oh, it's silly. Just the Waterworks movie theater. I'd thought about seeing a show by myself, but I just ended up sitting in the parking lot instead. I used to drive the kids there."

Kapinos eyed her strangely. "Odd that the movie theater is right beside the hospital. Where Stefan passed away tonight."

The detective was better than she'd thought. She should've mixed a special tea to take him out long ago when she'd had the chance.

Marian chirped, "I heard about Stefan. Very unfortunate. But I'm weary, Officer. If that message was all you had to deliver . . ."

"It's not. Can I search your car, Marian?"

"Well, what for?"

"I have reason to believe your son might've been involved in the death of Christian Fox and the suspicious circumstances surrounding Jeremy Fox's overdose. I want to search your car for evidence."

Oh dear . . .

"That's absurd."

"Valerie said you called Jeremy the night he overdosed. Jeremy was discovered with a massive head wound. Why would you have called him that night, Marian?" Kapinos asked.

"Who knows. You can't trust Valerie. You know that. Or maybe you don't." Marian wouldn't bring up Eli's name. She still wasn't sure if he was trying to cross her.

"What do you mean?" he asked.

"Did she tell you about the baby? Back then. That's why she let you go—didn't you know?" Marian asked.

His mouth fell open, and she thought she had him. But then his voice went soft. "Well, that was a long time ago."

Damn it. "My phone was being serviced. At one of TeleCom's satellite offices, mind you. They had it overnight. The same night Jeremy had his little accident."

"Are you sure about that?" Kapinos asked.

She looked away. "What do you mean?"

"Your son took your phone to be fixed, no? A broken screen."

She felt the gooseflesh erupt from her pores. He'd returned it to her with the list of other things she'd asked him to grab at the store. "That's right."

"That type of repair doesn't require overnight service."

"He got there right before it closed. He said they didn't have time to fix it."

"He lied to you. We have a receipt from TeleCom showing your screen was replaced in less than an hour. Eli held on to your phone."

Oh no. How could he be so stupid? "Valerie's just trying to condemn Eli so her brother isn't remembered as the addict and killer everyone knows he is," she tried. Marian cared for Jeremy, but she'd easily trade her own son for him. Eli was going to make something of himself. Jeremy had been set up to fail from the beginning, and his addiction issues would only make his demise more imminent.

"Then you won't mind my checking your car?" he asked.

She pulled at her open cardigan. It'd only make him more suspicious if she refused. She handed over the keys. "Sure."

Marian could see Luke's phone blowing up, but he was ignoring it. He opened her car doors, and she looked around for a shovel to club him over the head with, but none materialized. She wasn't at the Fox residence any longer. She was depleted of her arsenal of garden tools and herbal supplements. Marian looked around helplessly.

The pop of her trunk made her palms sweat. "Just junk back there," she assured.

Why didn't I throw it all away? I wasn't expecting him so soon . . .

He riffled through some boxes before he went to the one place she feared—the storage compartment in the trunk that housed her spare tire and other things. There he found her bagged-up scrubs, a surgical cap, and a hairnet that most certainly contained a hair or two with her DNA in it. "Want to tell me what this is?" he asked, holding up the plastic bag.

"I have no idea. My car is used. I never had one when I lived at the Foxes'. Must be from the last owner. Probably a nurse." She shrugged. Marian leveled her shallow breathing, although she was screaming inside. *He's found me out.*

"I don't think so. I pulled up the video surveillance from the hospital tonight, Stefan's floor, and you're on it. Wearing this."

He grabbed his handcuffs and spouted something into his walkie-talkie. He was bluffing. She'd had her head down the whole time. They had nothing on her. Except for all the damning things he'd pulled from her trunk. *No, this can't be the end.* "Why would I want to hurt Stefan?"

"To fulfill your son's wishes. Of whatever he had written into the Den."

She rasped, "What're you talking about?"

He walked closer to her. "You see, Marian, I went to visit Simone before I came here. I know you didn't want me to. And when I asked Simone if Eli had been by to visit, she told me he had. She said he'd asked her to sign some papers for the family trust to turn the money over to you all in the form of a sheltered charity. I understand now why Christian, the one who tried to contest it, was targeted. I still can't figure out why you tried to take out Jeremy and Valerie. In either case, you killed Stefan to secure your hold on that money. And now I'm arresting you for it."

"Let me explain."

"Save it. Please turn around and put your hands behind your back, Marian. You're under arrest for the murder of . . ."

CHAPTER 31

LUCINDA

When Mr. Brennan speaks, Lucinda thinks she might be dreaming.

When people die, they reflect on their past. She can't see the light, but she's back in her junior year of high school, and he's teaching the periodic table.

"I lost everything because of you. My job. My teaching certificate. My ability to work with children ever again. My daughter. My wife. She killed herself because of you."

"Wha—?" Lucinda is blacking out now, but as her teacher speaks of his wife, she thinks she understands a little better now. Suicide reminds her of the conversation she had with Aja, and can it really be true? "Aja?" she croaks. "Is your daughter?" She slurs out the words.

"Never was the brightest student in class. Just the most trouble. That's right. Aja was able to lace your father's champagne glass without a hitch. Too bad she couldn't have done yours too. Got a little too attached studying you over the years. Obsessed, more like. Now we have to kill you because you saw those documents. Who knew the old man kept paper copies? Didn't trust anyone but himself with his affairs. It's not a hiccup we anticipated," Brennan says.

Aja is Mr. Brennan's daughter? Lucy's mind aches, but she remembers the name—AJ. He had a child, and he must have called her by a nickname.

Lucinda sees it now in her distorted head. The resemblance. She was immediately drawn to Aja, her dark curly hair, large brown eyes, attentive smile. Lucinda's attraction to her was instant, overly familiar. Now she understands why. Aja looks just like her father.

The voice . . . She heard his voice from her duplex hallway. His teacher voice.

She still doesn't understand what Mr. Brennan has to do with anything. She wants to say more. All she can whisper is, "Why?"

There is the rustling of paper. A package exchanged. And Mr. Brennan is gone.

There's another man there, and she knows that one too.

Eli . . . *Why?*

"You can go now," Eli says.

Eli has paid Mr. Brennan to do this to her?

"Why, you ask?" Eli says, his voice spiteful. She fights to remain conscious. "Because you take and take and take what you want from people, Lucy, and you never stop to think about the ramifications of your actions. Mr. Brennan is a client of mine. I was working on a project for him at the hospital that didn't pan out. I'd promised him a cut of my portion of the Den as long as he helped me attain it. He was a handy person to have in the toxicology lab," he sneers.

"No," she mumbles.

"Good thing I had Brennan watching you on the app. He saw you taking pictures of your dad's files. The electronic copies are safe with Piedmont, but your father's paper file was a problem for us. Once we realized it existed, I was able to install the camera after a visit to the house, but I didn't have time to snag the documents with Marv watching me. Marv was fired by Piedmont just this morning, and he had until tomorrow to clear out. Lucky for you, he left a day early. Well, not really."

"Why?" she manages again and then putters completely out. Those are all the words she has left for this world.

"Why me?" He kicks her in the ribs, and she wheezes in agony. "You always treated me like the boy who was merely around to shine your shoes. And the way you slipped off your clothes in front of me on purpose, you little nymph. Gross, actually, considering your lecherous father couldn't keep his hands off other women. My mother included. Too bad I wasn't treated like the other Fox children, though."

What? Other children? *It can't be true.*

Then she remembers the provision in the Den.

The new provision. And it all makes sense.

"Stefan decided to take your mother out of the decision-making process. Christian thought the rider in the trust about the siblings had always been there. I couldn't let him dig any deeper, contest it, and find out it was new."

It can't be true . . .

"He'd have discovered the changes making me a rightful heir. He would have contested that too. Your father didn't know about me, and he would've cut me out. Robbed me of my inheritance. We had to sneak that wording in there very carefully. Christian would've found it, though."

Christian's accident. Eli was at the hospital to check on Father.

"And your other foolish brother saw suspicious activity on my phone record and actually called my mother about it. He didn't think anything of it when I pulled up to his house and asked to speak to him in person. Too bad he survived the dose of heroin I'd given him. Seems he'd been lying about using, because that should've put him down for good."

Jeremy. That's why he was trying to save me in the dream.

311

It's the last thought she had before her lights went out—at least she saved Jeremy first, but who's going to save him second? And who will save her?

Who will save all of them?

Like a sick dream, Valerie could vaguely see a man careening out of the forest on foot as she rode in on the Pritchards' horse, River, indicated by the Hollywood star chalkboard on his stall door.

Her first inclination was to turn River around, chase the man—the murderer? Whoever he was. She didn't recognize him. Who was this madman terrorizing their family? She was about to change direction, but then she saw another man, and she knew that one.

Eli was standing near the creek, hovering near a female—*Lucy*.

Eli! It hadn't been Marian who'd made the calls.

Eli had borrowed his mother's phone to call Jeremy. Shock invaded her body. Eli had seen Jeremy as a threat to his mother after that, so . . . he'd attempted to take Jeremy out?

Eli . . . the little butler.

Eli . . . the murderer. Valerie dry heaved.

He was standing over a body. *A body.*

Is Lucy dead? Am I too late?

"Eli, step away from her!" Valerie was on higher ground than Eli. She'd chosen a Morgan in her rush, the thoroughbred in the Pritchards' stable much too large and untamable. And she'd only had time to grab a halter from the barn to throw over the horse's muzzle and some lead ropes, but no bridle or saddle and no stirrups to hold her in place.

Eli knew horses too.

He could easily pull her off, but Valerie couldn't see any weapons near him to finish the job once he did. She'd take her chances.

"What're you doing here, Val? This didn't need to concern you. I thought you'd be tending to your house," Eli said.

"What did you do to her?" Valerie fumed with anger and fear. Lucy was badly injured, only a couple of feet away, coiled into a ball, bleeding and unmoving. "Lucy?" Valerie screamed. No response.

Valerie coughed because yelling hurt, and holding her breath stung her freshly blackened lungs even more. *"Lucy? Answer me."*

Eli laughed, and Valerie's hands tightened on the golf club, her body filling with rage like the night Karl had set her off. Golf clubs were much more damaging than vases. She couldn't see anything around Eli that he'd used to cause this severe damage to her sister, but she was looking for hidden devices that he might've stashed around him. It was confounding that the little boy who'd grown up on their property was picking them off. *Traitor. Mother would be aghast at what you've become.*

Where's your weapon, you little wimp?

She was planning her attack because this was fucking war.

Valerie could see that Lucy's scalp was pulled away from the bone. She stifled the rising bile in her belly.

What had he hacked her with?

I'm going to hack him.

"Step away from her!" Valerie shouted again. "The police are on the way. You should run."

"What, and risk fighting you with that golf club?" Eli laughed again, hateful and sadistic. He was measured, too sure of himself. "No way. I can't wait to wrestle it from you. That way, I can get a two-for-one deal here. This actually works out better. If none of you are left, I'll get Fox Wealth Management."

Valerie's body filled with fire, hate coursing through her veins. River whinnied. The horse knew she was tense. If Lucy were a spirit guide and Isla was one with the water, then Valerie was the damn horse whisperer.

She patted River in a way that conveyed it was time to get to work. Then she gave him a light kick. "Ya!"

She galloped toward Eli, charging him like an armed polo player. He put his hands up in defense, but she was faster. "Leave my family alone!"

When Valerie set her sights on a target—she didn't miss.

He tried to duck, but when Valerie swung the pitching wedge as hard as she could, it made contact with Eli's forehead. The metal club-head connected with Eli's skull in a hard thump. Valerie yanked the lead rope to make a quick turn and urged the horse back around, coming at Eli again.

She had to make sure he went *down*.

Eli yelped when she cracked him again. He dropped over onto the ground.

Valerie wanted to keep bashing him the way he'd done to Jeremy.

She still didn't understand *why*.

Instead, she dismounted the horse. "Good boy." Valerie knelt beside Lucy, assessing the damage. Eli was knocked out cold.

Lucy was in horrible shape.

Her hair was soaked in blood, and she wasn't conscious. Valerie lowered her ear to Lucy's mouth, and she could detect a ragged breath. Valerie remembered she used to do this when Lucy was a baby. There were bassinets all over the house so Mother could be near her. It was Valerie's job to protect Lucy now.

Valerie called Luke, shivering with adrenaline from the pure violence of what'd just occurred. She told him what'd happened, and he informed her that the police were already on their way. Glenda had called the station.

And then she heard a man's voice behind her. "Put your hands up."

Valerie turned slightly, dropped the golf club, and exhaled.

It was Luke.

CHAPTER 32

VALERIE

Six Months Later

Seated in the front row of Cherry Lane, Greenwich Village's oldest off-Broadway theater, Valerie stared in awe at the setting switch for the third act of *Love Is Love*. It was a modernized kitchen, sleek gray faux-wood cabinets, a cramped Manhattan apartment with all the fixings, including a bougie plum silk bed, two women seated on the edge, their relationship hanging in the balance.

She's sorry, Violet. Stay.

Aster's part as Violet had been breathtaking so far. Valerie tensed as they neared the end.

Thea: Stay, Violet. People make mistakes.

Violet: It has nothing to do with mistakes, Thea. It's who you are.

Luke gripped Valerie's hand, because they'd both made their fair share of mistakes, that was for sure. She was still surprised when Luke had shown up at her door months after he'd arrested Marian, Eli, Charlie

Brennan, Aja—and Attorney Piedmont. But she shouldn't have been. It was exactly what he said he would do, and Luke was a man of his word.

Violet: What do you mean? Knowing you has been my greatest pleasure. Was it because of *him*?

Thea: It's not because of him. It could've been anybody, really, and I'd feel the same. It's because I wasn't enough. And I never will be. You're not meant to be with just me. I have to let you go. So you can be free to be who you are.

Tears stung Valerie's eyes. The play mirrored her recent learnings. After you unintentionally hurt people, you had to let them go. If they came back, so be it. If not, they must be set free. She'd told Luke she couldn't be with him—twice—but now he was right where he was supposed to be, by her side. It was finally *their time*.

Luke had apologized for not looking harder into Jeremy's case. A mistake that had resulted in a fire at her house and almost her sister's death.

And Valerie had apologized for not telling Luke about the baby all those years ago.

Marian was being charged with three murders—Hector's, Stefan's, and Valerie's unborn child.

Once she was arrested, Marian told all.

The burden of lies she'd been carrying had been punishing, too, apparently.

Luke had reasoned that Valerie had never really gotten to make a decision in the matter of the baby. They'd never know what she would've done. Either way, they'd both decided they'd been victims of her murderous meddling nanny.

In the end, he was able to forgive her. And she was able to forgive him.

Valerie just wished she could say the same for the characters in the play. She'd hoped they could somehow find a way to be together. She'd sat through the first two acts in exquisite awe, the storyline and presentation both a work of perfection. Lucy was able to tell her story and explain herself through her play better than she ever could in real life. Valerie had developed a deeper understanding of her sister just by watching it.

When the scene closed, the theater faded to black, and Valerie laid her head on Luke's shoulder. Isla sat to her left, wiping her eyes. It'd gotten to her too.

Valerie could see the bright sparkle of Daphne's ring as she raised her hand to pat her face dry. Jeremy had given Valerie a thumbs-up regarding the play. Daphne was a good influence in Jeremy's life, making him go to rehab once more. Good thing he'd made it out of the hospital. Charlie Brennan's next strike would've been making sure Jeremy never left, per Eli's order.

Glenda and her children sat next to Isla. Mother was at Glenda's side in the exit row seated in a wheelchair. There was one empty seat on the end of the row, beside Glenda. It had a sign on it that read, RESERVED FOR CHRISTIAN FOX.

Christian, in trying to impress their father, had lost out on so much. Valerie decided to picture him enjoying being there with them if he'd lived, instead. He might've had a chance to reset too.

A bouquet of roses sat in Jeremy's lap. He'd realized Lucy had saved his life. She'd been admitted to Harmar Rehabilitation for months to treat her brain injury and had fully recovered with Valerie's help. The day they'd wheeled Lucy out, Valerie had taken Polaroids, something she used to do when they were younger. Jeremy stuck his tongue out in every single photo. Valerie asked the two of them to keep the pictures somewhere nearby, and whenever they were feeling demonic toward each other, to look at them—and remember they were family.

Valerie was tired of talking to lawyers by the time Father's estate was finally settled.

Corbin Piedmont had been the biggest fraud of all. He'd done the most for his promised piece of the Den. At Brennan's advice, Piedmont had been the one to eat lunch nearly every day at the Field Club with Father, promising he'd lose weight on the swordfish diet and that the fish oil would improve his complexion while lowering his cholesterol. Piedmont also knew Father's recent medication changes, a subject that'd casually been brought up during their lunches, and information that'd been used against him in the end. A car expert, Piedmont provided guidance to Charlie Brennan on how to cut brake lines, and he'd slipped out of the hospital once he'd received the order from Eli to puncture them. All in exchange for a large payout when it was all said and done, but Valerie knew it was about more than that.

Piedmont had been smitten with their mother. He'd made off-handed remarks that she was the one who'd gotten away. Piedmont hadn't found love again and had no children. He likely blamed Stefan for that.

Piedmont had known for months that Eli was their half brother.

Valerie still had a hard time with that one.

Valerie wasn't shocked that Father and Marian had an affair.

Eli had been. According to his testimony, he'd fooled himself into believing that his mother couldn't have possibly slept with Stefan willingly. He claimed that she'd been forced or felt threatened into doing so.

It was his motivation for all of this.

That and getting his grubby little hands on their inheritance.

Eli had received a genetic test from his fiancée—his now-ex, Giselle—and lost his mind when he matched with a distant cousin of Stefan Fox. Eli had wanted to know where he'd come from. A plea he'd made to Marian many times and one his fiancée had turned into a reality for him—changing all their lives forever.

Funny, when Valerie examined all the evidence during the trial to put Eli away, she'd discovered their family really wasn't from the same lineage as the Fox family who'd settled the land in the Allegheny Valley all those years ago. Fox Chapel wasn't named after their family line after all.

It had been a tale their father had made up to sound more regal, or perhaps one he'd just wanted to believe. To Lucy's delight, she discovered they had ties to the historic Fox sisters out of New York, responsible for the first-ever occult séance. Lucy finally had the validation she'd been looking for all her life, on- and offstage. After the violence that had ensued over the trust, Valerie wondered if Father had kept it a secret from his children to protect them. He hadn't wanted to raise lazy children, but he certainly hadn't wanted others to take advantage of their wealth either.

It was just like Father—to protect them from afar.

To care for them the best way he knew how.

There'd been so much poison.

Between Brennan, a licensed chemist, and Marian, a lifetime studier of poisons, it was amazing any of them had survived.

The excessive buildup of mercury in Father's system was a toxic combination with the thallium laced in his cup by Aja, a deadly cocktail that only a chemist like her father, Mr. Brennan, would know. Charlie Brennan confessed he felt he was owed something from the Foxes after a lifetime working in basement laboratories and losing his wife over Lucy Fox.

Aja had been a co-conspirator but had developed feelings for her victim. She'd claimed her father had promised Lucy would never be harmed. The suicide of her mother had prompted Aja's preoccupation with Lucy Fox. When Aja's childhood psychiatric files had been unsealed, it'd been discovered that she had a doll she used to grip by the throat when she was stressed. It was a rag doll with long blonde hair that Aja had refused to part with after she'd left the hospital where she'd spent the year following her mother's death.

That doll was named Lucy.

The criminal psychologists determined that Aja had regarded Lucy much the same as that doll. Lucy Fox had become an object of fascination that Aja had simultaneously wanted to throttle and love. Aja had admitted to strangling Lucy at her apartment and tampering with Stefan's drink at the charity event. She was placed in a psychiatric facility for further evaluation following her arrest.

After the packed theater rippled in applause and Lucy took her bow, she strode down the steps in a little black dress to greet them. She appeared nervous and beautiful, her wavy hair covering the small scar on her forehead.

"Bravo!" Valerie shouted. Luke whistled by her side. Lucy shot them a megawatt smile.

Jeremy was the first one to stand.

"Well, what did you think?" Valerie heard Lucy ask him.

He handed her the roses. "I thought it was absolutely brilliant."

Lucy's blue eyes were rich with pride and love.

She really had hit her stride as a playwright. It had just taken a little while.

As for Fox Wealth Management, Valerie was taking it one step at a time.

With Valerie's freshly appointed VP of Sales, Jeremy Fox, and creative consultant, Lucy Fox, there was new management in town. It wasn't just a company anymore. For the first time, it really did feel like a family, and they wouldn't let anyone with harmful intentions inside their tight-knit Den.

ACKNOWLEDGMENTS

I really hope you enjoyed *The Den*. If this is your first time reading one of my books, thanks for giving me a look. If you're wondering which of my novels to try next, I would recommend either *Sweet Water*, my other Pittsburgh-based domestic suspense novel, or *Into the Sound*.

The Den was born in a fiction workshop in my MFA class at Lindenwood University. The rest of the book was written mostly on the sidelines of the football field during my daughter's summer cheer practice.

Thank you to my agent, Ella Marie Shupe, and to everyone at Thomas & Mercer for making this book possible, with a special shout-out to Liz Pearsons, Sarah Shaw, and my stellar developmental editor, Tiffany Yates Martin, for going one extra round of edits to make this one just right.

I would also like to thank my family and fellow writer friends who were early readers on this book: Savina Cupps, Virginia DiAlesandro, Nancy Hammer, Carolyn Menke, Kim Pierson, Vickie Reinard, Janice Sniezek, and an extra-special thank-you to my beret-wearing, talented beta reader, Lori Jones, whose notes really shaped this novel.

Thank you to the longtime residents of East Pittsburgh, Kathie Shoop and April Dunmyre, for your research help, and to my Mindful Writers retreat group for giving me the time, peace, and space to hit my final deadline.

A special thanks to Annamaria Carrington, my good friend and horse expert, and her horse, River, who inspired the only hero in this story without a muddy past. To Holly Puett, an extraordinary piano teacher who helped me hit all the right musical notes with this one. To Rob Singer and Tim Sechler, for their input on the financial and family law aspects of this book. You took the time out of your busy day to help me with my creative venture and I truly appreciate it.

And of course, to my supportive husband, Justin, and my kids, Jackson and Charlotte, you're the ones who give me the courage to keep dreaming—thank you.

ABOUT THE AUTHOR

Photo © 2019 Lisa Schmidt, Moments Kept Photography

Cara Reinard is an author of women's fiction and novels of domestic suspense, including *Into the Sound* and *Sweet Water*. She has been employed in the pharmaceutical industry for eighteen years, and while Cara loves science, writing is her passion. She currently lives in the Pittsburgh area with her husband, two children, and Bernese mountain dogs. For more information, visit www.carareinard.com.